Alison Roberts i [illegible] y
enough to be livi [illegible] so
lucky enough to w [illegible]
Romance line. A p [illegible] life,
she is now a quali [illegible] travel
and dance, drink c [illegible] and spend time with her
daughter and her friends.

Marion Lennox has written over one hundred romance novels and is published in over one hundred countries and thirty languages. Her international awards include the prestigious RITA® award (twice!) and the *RT Book Reviews* Career Achievement Award for 'a body of work which makes us laugh and teaches us about love'. Marion adores her family, her kayak, her dog, and lying on the beach with a book someone else has written. Heaven!

Also by Alison Roberts

Stolen Nights with the Single Dad
A Surgeon with a Secret
A Pup to Rescue Their Hearts
Christmas Miracle at the Castle

The Vet's Unexpected Family
is Alison Roberts' 100th book!

Also by Marion Lennox

Pregnant Midwife on His Doorstep
Mistletoe Kiss with the Heart Doctor
Falling for His Island Nurse
Healing Her Brooding Island Hero

Discover more at millsandboon.co.uk.

THE VET'S UNEXPECTED FAMILY

ALISON ROBERTS

A RESCUE DOG TO HEAL THEM

MARION LENNOX

MILLS & BOON

First Published in Great Britain 2022
by Mills & Boon, an imprint of HarperCollins*Publishers* Ltd,
1 London Bridge Street, London, SE1 9GF

www.harpercollins.co.uk

HarperCollins*Publishers*
1st Floor, Watermarque Building,
Ringsend Road, Dublin 4, Ireland

ISBN: 978-0-263-30116-8

02/22

MIX
Paper from
responsible sources
FSC® C007454

This book is produced from independently certified FSC™ paper
to ensure responsible forest management.
For more information visit www.harpercollins.co.uk/green.

Printed and Bound in Spain using 100% Renewable Electricity
at CPI Black Print, Barcelona

THE VET'S UNEXPECTED FAMILY

ALISON ROBERTS

MILLS & BOON

To each and every one of my readers, because you make it possible for me to keep doing what I love.

And to Megan, my wonderful editor, who continues to inspire me to write the very best stories I can.

Thank you all so much. xxx

CHAPTER ONE

Uh-oh...

About to walk into the waiting area of Coogee Beach Animal Hospital and summon her first patient for the afternoon clinic, Hazel Davidson stopped in her tracks. She took a step backwards, in fact, which put her behind the half-open door.

How had she forgotten it was Wednesday? One of the days when she had to be careful that she didn't end up being caught on camera by the television crew who had a weekly episode of *Call the Vet* to pre-record? Or rather, it *had* been *Call the Vet* in Series One. Now, halfway through Series Three it was more like *Call Dr Finn, Australia's Favourite Celebrity Vet—Not to Mention the Country's Most Eligible Bachelor.* And maybe that was why she'd forgotten to keep her head down today. Lately, there hadn't been as much filming happening in this veterinary clinic because the female fan base that gathered outside was starting to become a problem.

Maybe Hazel could catch the new receptionist's attention and get her to find the sixteen-week-old puppy waiting for its final health check and vaccination and bring it into the consulting room? That way, Hazel could stay completely below the radar, which was what she'd managed to do ever since that unfortunate appearance she'd been persuaded to make in Series One.

'I need you, Hazel,' Finn had said, and who could ignore a plea like that when it came with a smile that had always made her melt? *'It'll be fun,'* he'd said. But it hadn't ended up being fun at all, had it?

Kylie, the young receptionist, was watching Finn get some makeup brushed onto his face and then some hair-spray on that floppy, sun-streaked hair, with the kind of dreamy expression that he probably inspired in all his biggest fans. It wasn't the first time that Hazel felt grateful her childhood had taught her the self-defence mechanism of hiding that kind of personal reaction—she would have looked like that herself in the early days of being around Dr Finn. Whatever… Kylie wasn't about to notice Hazel hovering behind the door.

She knew she should just go out there and find her patient herself. Except that one of the two cameramen had his camera secured on his shoulder and looked as though he could be filming already, even though Finn was deep in conversation with the person who seemed to be in charge, while he was getting the attention of the makeup artist, and there were three or four other people busy setting up equipment. She couldn't see an adorable puppy being cuddled anywhere, either, unless it was inside that solid, plastic pet carrier tucked in beside the wall display of dog toys and treats. The temptation to go back to her consulting room in the hope the television crew might have vanished by the time she came back was strong enough to really annoy her.

'Oh, for heaven's sake,' Hazel muttered. 'This is ridiculous.'

Lifting her chin, she pushed the door fully open and stepped into the waiting area, only to find that nobody even noticed her entrance. They were all turning in the opposite direction, at exactly the same time, as the automatic glass doors were sliding open and they could all hear someone calling for help.

'Oh, *no…*' Hazel pressed her fingers against her lips as she saw what they were watching. 'No, no, no…'

Someone was coming into the reception area at speed, holding what appeared to be a dog in their arms. A middle-aged woman, who was clearly distressed, her clothes streaked with blood.

'Please…can someone help? It just ran out in front of me…' The woman was sobbing. 'There was nothing I could do…'

Hazel was already halfway across the large room, oblivious to the fact that there were now two cameras trained on her. She reached the woman and took the dog as gently as possible from her arms, but it yelped in agony and Hazel could already see that its hind leg was deformed enough to be badly broken.

'This way…' Finn was guiding her towards his consulting room with a hand on her shoulder. The television crew scattered to create a clear path but, even as Hazel rushed past, she could feel their excitement. This was the kind of drama that couldn't be faked. It would have viewers on the edge of their seats and push their ratings sky high.

To his credit, however, Finn seemed just as disinterested as Hazel about who was watching. Their focus was entirely on a little black dog who'd just been hit by a car. A dog who was clearly shocked, whimpering in severe pain and breathing too fast as they laid him on the table as carefully as they could.

Hazel unhooked her stethoscope from around her neck but took a moment to lay her hand on the dog's head. He was mostly spaniel, by the look of those ears and the feel of his silky hair and he was no youngster, judging by that white muzzle.

'It's okay, pupper,' she said softly. 'We'll look after you...'

'No collar...' Finn noted. 'And he looks a bit under nourished. Could be a stray.' He ran his hands gently over the body of the dog, looking for the source of the bleeding as well as any obvious internal injuries. 'No life-threatening haemorrhage. Or not externally, anyway. There's a couple of lacerations that will need cleaning and suturing. Abdomen seems okay.'

'He's tachycardic.' Hazel held her stethoscope with one hand on the side of the dog's chest, where the beat was most prominent. She had the fingers of her other hand on the femoral artery. 'Pulse is weak. I'd say his blood pressure's too low.'

'I'll get an IV in.' Finn nodded. 'And put some fluids up.'

'I'll get some pain relief drawn up. We should get some oxygen on, as well.' Hazel looped her stethoscope back around her neck. 'We could do with another set of hands in here. Where's Anna?'

'I'm here.'

Hazel looked up to see their senior vet nurse, Anna, squeeze past a cameraman and a sound technician who was holding a fluffy microphone on a pole but she pushed aside the unwelcome realisation that she was being filmed. She was still too concerned for this dog's welfare to allow any distractions.

Finn picked up some clippers and Anna moved in without being asked to hold the dog's front leg still as a long patch was shaved to make it easy to find a vein.

Hazel opened drawers and swiftly found the IV supplies that Finn needed, putting them on the table beside him. A disinfectant wipe, cannula and plug, tape and bandage. Turning back to open the drug cabinet, she paused to unhook some tubing from the side of the anaesthetic trolley and turned on the oxygen cylinder. She put the end of the tube on the table near the dog's face.

'Flow-by oxygen at six litres a minute,' she told Finn, who nodded his approval. 'Anna, can you keep the tube as close to his nose as you can while you're holding him?'

Finn slid the needle into a vein, inserted the cannula smoothly, capped it and unclipped the tourniquet in the space of seconds.

'Sorry, doggo,' he said. 'You'll feel better soon, I promise.'

Hazel had drawn up an opioid analgesic ready to inject by the time Finn had secured the IV firmly in place with tape and then a bandage on top. It seemed like it had been far too long but in reality it had only been a few minutes before they could all breathe a tentative sigh of relief. The injured dog was visibly relaxing as his pain level dropped, closing his eyes as the panting slowed so that he looked almost as if he was peacefully asleep. Now they could get on with the real business of stabilising their patient and potentially going ahead with emergency surgery to save its leg, if not its life.

Finn was drawing a blood sample from the IV line. He handed the syringe to Hazel. 'Can you run a CBC and electrolytes, please?' he asked. 'And do a catalyst chem seventeen. I want to know what the liver and kidney function is and whether it's safe to go ahead with anaesthesia if it's indicated. Which is very likely, going by that obvious fracture in his hind leg. That could well need some complex surgery.'

'Sure.'

But Hazel couldn't help a tiny head shake as she turned away to take the sample to the small room next to the X-ray suite that housed their state-of-the-art analysis technology that provided an in-house laboratory. While Hazel's reluctance to appear on the popular television show meant that they very rarely worked on the same patients these days, he knew that she knew exactly what blood tests were called for in an emergency situation like this and what the results could tell them. This was his television-speak, wasn't it? Demonstrating his expertise at the same time as explaining things for an audience that had no medical background?

'I could do that,' Anna said. 'And then make sure Theatre's good to go?'

Hazel shook her head. 'I've got a full clinic,' she said. 'The waiting room will be getting backed up.'

'No…' Finn glanced up swiftly from assessing the nasty leg fracture. 'Don't go. I need you, Hazel.'

There was no charmingly persuasive smile to go with the plea this time but a direct glance like that from those dark eyes still never failed to melt something in that hidden space.

'Orthopaedic stuff like this is as much up your alley as mine,' he added. 'And I know just how talented you are.'

Anna was nodding her head to back him up. 'I've sorted the clinic,' she said, taking the blood sample from Hazel's hands. 'Nigel finished his surgery and he's taken your afternoon list. I could see that Finn needed you. And, even if people are waiting a bit longer, they understand when an emergency like this comes in.' She was halfway out the door, now, and Hazel had lost any opportunity to escape.

Part of her didn't want to, anyway. The dog's eyes were open again, although it was still lying calmly on the table and it was watching her with big, brown spaniel eyes. Finn might have tugged at her heartstrings by saying he needed her but this dog was telling her that his need was far more genuine. Desperate, even. And it felt like he was trusting her to stay close. She'd promised to look after him, hadn't she?

Hazel might have learned, over the last few years, to brush off any visceral response she still had to Finn's charisma but there was no way she could resist this dog. Her hand was already reaching out to stroke its ears again.

'We need X-rays,' Finn said. 'But I'm thinking that it could be a mission to save this leg, especially in an old fellow like this. Can you top up his pain relief and then I'll carry him next door so we can see exactly what we're dealing with?'

Hazel's thoughts were racing as she drew up some more medication. She had to stay now. To fight in this old dog's corner. What if it really was a stray and there was no one to pay what could end up being an exorbitant bill for medical treatment and rehab? What if the surgery was going to present such a challenge that would make it far easier to simply amputate the leg? Or, worst case scenario, would someone suggest that euthanasia was the sensible option?

Hazel closed her eyes as she drew in a slow breath, suddenly grateful that this emergency was being filmed. She didn't actually give a damn what people might say about her this time. She could ask the hard questions and make it impossible for easy decisions to be made too quickly. She could not only help to save this dog's life, she might get an opportunity to tell a lot of people about the passion in her life that had led to her becoming a vet in the first place and what she did in her time away from work. She could tell them about the Two Tails animal refuge up in the Blue Mountains and—who knew?—it might even lead to some badly needed financial support for the niche refuge run by Hazel's best friend, Kiara. The place that she headed for whenever she could, to do whatever she could to help.

Dealing with any fallout from a nationwide television appearance would be a small price to pay for being able to do something potentially more significant than simply turning up to help clean out dog runs or work alongside Kiara in her small veterinary practice.

Wouldn't it?

This was *great*.

Like the old days, when Hazel had first come to work at the Coogee Beach Animal Hospital. The days before *Call the Vet* became such a huge part of Finn's life, when almost every waking hour—and a few when he really should have been asleep—had been spent at the veterinary clinic he'd poured his heart and soul into building up after he'd come back home to Sydney.

He'd recognised the same passion in Hazel when he'd chosen her for the new position of a permanent veterinary surgeon at the hospital and it had been the best decision he'd ever made. Her glowing references hadn't been exaggerated and they'd quickly formed a partnership in the operating theatre that was second to none. Finn hadn't realised quite how much he'd missed working with her, though, until they were deep into the intricate work of repairing the fracture on this emergency case that had come through the doors of the clinic this afternoon. He'd almost forgotten how clever her fingers were, how she could make thoughtful, balanced, major decisions in what seemed like the blink of an eye and… how much she *cared.*

He was watching her now, as she painstakingly picked out every tiny piece of shattered bone from the opening she had carefully created to expose this dog's serious leg fracture. Finn was happy to be Hazel's assistant as she tackled the delicate task of exposing and then repairing a complex fracture. Not only was he enjoying watching her skilled work, he knew that being this focused on the task at hand would make her forget she was being filmed.

Finn was very aware of what else the show's creative director would want, however, which was why this programme had become so astonishingly popular. He spoke quietly to the camera crew positioned on the other side of the clinic's main operating theatre to include the people who would, no doubt, be watching this procedure with fascination.

'So this is what we call a comminuted fracture,' he explained. 'Which means that the bone is broken in more than two places. Hazel's removing tiny shards of bone that could create problems for this dog down the track and then she'll decide the best method for stabilising the fracture so it can heal.' He adjusted the overhead light a fraction to put the brightest point above the hole in the sterile drapes covering their patient. He really wanted to draw Hazel into talking about what she was doing. If she enjoyed this, maybe she would consider being on the show on a regular basis.

'What are you thinking, Hazel?' he asked. 'Pins and cerclage wire? External fixation? Or plates and screws?'

'Plates and screws.' Hazel didn't look up from her work. 'We've got enough bone length both distal and proximal to the fracture to allow for the minimum three screws in each fragment. It's going to be the most stable solution.'

Finn smiled at the cameras. He knew the smile wouldn't be seen beneath his mask but it made a difference to the tone of his voice. It could make the audience feel as if they were sharing privileged information.

'As vets, we have what's called the "fifty/fifty" rule,' he said. 'You have to have at least fifty per cent of the ends of fractured bones in contact with each other and that fifty per cent reduction is the absolute minimum for bone healing to be possible. It has to be stable, too. Something like a splint or an external cast is the least stable method to reduce a fracture. Internal fixation using things like plates and screws is the most stable. Plus, it's the best choice for restoring length to a bone where there are lost pieces like the ones Hazel's removing.'

He paused, knowing that the camera would be zooming in on the stainless-steel kidney dish that Hazel was dropping the small bone fragments into. He was still doing too much talking, wasn't he? He needed to come up with a way of getting Hazel really engaged and hopefully wipe out the bad memories of the aftermath of appearing on the show for the first and only time.

Even now, well over a year later, it could make Finn cringe. Not that he'd been present when that unpleasant woman and her daughter had brought their Persian cat in for an appointment but he'd heard all about how unhappy they'd been when Hazel had arrived to welcome them. He'd read about it, in fact, when it got splashed over social media.

'Nah...' The woman had made sure everyone in the crowded waiting area could hear her. *'Like we said when*

we rang up, we want to see the TV vet. That's why we've come right across the city.'

'Dr Davidson is one of the TV vets,' the receptionist had told them. *'She was on the show only last week.'*

'It's the guy we came to see. The good-looking one.'

The daughter had been even more blunt than her mother. *'That's right. We don't want the fat vet.'*

So Hazel was curvy? So what? As if that made a difference to her amazing skills and an awesome personality? Finn considered Hazel to be one of his closest friends and he'd been mortified on her behalf.

'It's the camera,' he'd told her. *'Everyone knows it adds a heap of weight. Good grief... I'm sure I look like the Hulk sometimes.'*

But Hazel had refused to talk about it. And now she was simply doing her job and not talking at all if she could help it. She might be doing an amazing job but even if viewers could recognise that, Finn wanted more. He wanted people to respect her. To like her—as much as he did.

'So…did you catch up on that guy who came into reception while we were doing the X-rays on this leg? The one who works at the Brazilian barbecue restaurant?'

Hazel shook her head. 'Have we got a two-point-five-millimetre drill bit on the trolley?'

'It's right here. Hiding beside the lag screws.'

'Thanks.'

'This guy heard about the accident and came in to talk to Kylie. He reckons he's been feeding this dog meat scraps for a week or so now. He's been trying to get close enough to catch it and take it to a refuge ever since but, while it'll take a bit of food, it always runs away if he tries to touch him.'

'Really?' This time, Hazel looked up. 'I forgot to

ask when I got busy scrubbing in but did Anna check for a microchip, too?'

'There isn't one. We decided to go ahead with the surgery, though. As you know, we've got a fund to cover the occasional emergency like this.'

He could hear the way Hazel snatched in a quick breath. 'I know who can help after we discharge him. I've got a friend I've known for years—since vet school—and she runs the most amazing refuge centre up in the Blue Mountains.'

'Oh? Can they cater for a dog that's going to need intensive rehab? An old dog? Judging by his teeth and eyes and all that grey hair, this one could be well over twelve years old. Maybe fourteen or fifteen.'

'It can cater for any animal in an emergency but it specialises in rescuing cases exactly like this. Dogs or cats who are too old for most people to consider rehoming because they might not live that much longer and they often have expensive health care needs. The kind that vets get asked to put down all the time because their owners have died or gone into care themselves and there's nobody else to take on their pet.'

Finn was nodding. He'd had to face requests like that himself in the past and he'd hated it. It hadn't happened recently, though. Was that because he was more involved in his television work than the day-to-day work of a busy veterinary clinic or had Hazel been quietly rescuing these animals without him knowing about it?

He'd known how much she cared about her patients but his admiration for how much she cared for animals in general had just gone up several notches.

'And old dogs are *so* special,' she added, with a catch in her voice. 'I grew up with a dog who lived to be eighteen and he was…' Hazel hesitated and then seemed to change her mind about whatever she'd been planning to reveal. 'He was the reason I decided to become a vet,' she added. 'How could anyone even think of putting them down for the sake of convenience, or worse—dumping them when they can't possibly understand what they've done wrong because they *haven't* done anything wrong?'

Wow… Hazel had really come alive. She looked and sounded animated and her eyes were sparkling. The beeping of the heart monitor in the background made for a dramatic pause as she stopped speaking. Finn found himself wanting to know what it was that Hazel had decided not to say but he guessed that asking a question that touched personal ground could be the quickest way to make her back off again and he didn't want that to happen.

The conversation wasn't distracting her from the meticulous work she was doing, keeping the slippery stainless-steel plate she had already shaped to fit the bone in place as she drilled holes to take the screws that would secure it and Finn was experienced enough with this television stuff to know when he was onto a good thing. He could sense how clearly her passion would come across and how fast it would draw people in. Listening to this, the last thing anyone would think of would be to tag her with a derogatory physical descriptor like 'fat'. No…it would be words like 'passionate' and 'kind' and a 'totally awesome human' that would spring to mind. Maybe Hazel would get some feedback that would make her feel as good about herself as she had always deserved to feel. Finn was smiling beneath his mask again.

'Tell me about this refuge.'

'It's called Two Tails.' It sounded like Hazel was

smiling as well. 'We came up with the name together. Because, you know—you can be as happy as a dog with two tails?'

'It's a great name.'

'It's two tales, as well. As in stories? Because they have a sad story that brings them into the refuge and a happy story in the end, or that's what we do our best to achieve, anyway.'

'We…?'

'I help out whenever I can. That's why I drive a dodgy old van instead of a proper car.'

'It's hardly a dodgy old van. It's a vintage Morris Minor delivery van.' He gave one of his trademark grins directly to camera, as if he were talking confidentially to someone who was watching the programme. 'Bright red. Very cute.'

Hazel snorted. 'Whatever. What matters is that I can fit a couple of crates in the back and I don't care if I have to cross the city to pick up a dog or cat from a vet clinic or refuge after work or if the phone goes in the middle of the night because there's an animal in distress somewhere. Not that I can do everything. We got a call about a donkey who has to be urgently rehomed because it hasn't had its feet trimmed in so long it can't walk but I couldn't have fitted her in the van and, anyway, there isn't paddock space at the refuge.'

Finn made a sympathetic sound but didn't want to interrupt. He'd never heard Hazel so eager to talk about something that was part of her private life.

'I totally love the refuge,' she added. 'And I have the greatest admiration for what Kiara does. Some of the stories are heartbreaking but she does her absolute best every single time. Even now, when it's getting so much harder.'

'In what way is it getting harder?'

'Oh, you know…' Hazel had put the last screw in and was examining the bone and surrounding tissue before starting to close up the wound. 'Financial stuff. It's never cheap looking after animals, especially if they've got underlying health issues and, sadly, some of them come back or even end up staying at the refuge for the rest of their lives.' She looked up from her work to let her gaze rest on that sleeping face with the grey muzzle. 'I would hate that to happen to this old boy. I'd take him myself, in a heartbeat, if I could but I live in a basement bedsit with too many stairs. If he does end up at Two Tails, though, I'll be there every day.'

Finn made a mental note to talk to the show's producer. They could put the details for Two Tails up as a subtitle or at the end of this episode, directing people to where they could make a donation, perhaps. Not that it would be on screen for a while, yet, but it could help in the long run. He'd tell Hazel about the plan later. If nothing else, it would ensure that she wouldn't back out of letting herself appear on screen and Finn wanted this episode to go to air. He had a good feeling about contributing to a rescue case like this and for one of his colleagues to be passionately directing public attention to the welfare of a section of the pet population that many people probably hadn't considered an issue.

He also had a good feeling about how successful this surgery would be. He leaned closer to look at the result as Hazel irrigated the wound and swabbed it dry.

'You've done an amazing job plating that,' he told Hazel. 'I can't even see the fracture lines.'

'We just need to close up and splint this leg and then deal with the other lacerations. I'd like to get him out of anaesthesia as soon as we can.'

Finn reached for some sutures. 'He needs a name. We can't just put "Old Dog" on his crate, can we?'

'Ben.' Hazel's suggestion was so quick, Finn knew it was significant.

'Was that the name of your dog?' he asked quietly. 'The one you grew up with?'

Hazel didn't look up. 'Yeah…he was black, too.' Her tone was dismissive enough to signal that this topic of conversation was terminated. 'Now…let's get this periosteum wrapped back over the bone.'

It was well over an hour later when Ben the old, black dog was finally tucked up amongst soft blankets in the hospital ward, under the care of an expert vet night nurse who was being briefed by Anna. The television crew was packing up their gear, the waiting room had emptied of patients and their owners, Kylie the receptionist was getting ready to head home and Hazel had changed out of her scrubs and into street clothes.

'I'm just going to grab something to eat and I'll be back,' she told Finn. 'I'm going to stay and keep an eye on Ben for a while.'

Finn nodded. He was with the show's producer and they were both peering at the monitor attached to one of the huge cameras.

'That's a great shot, Jude,' he said. 'I should do a voice over to explain what's happening but I'd hate to cut anything Hazel's saying about the refuge. That's gold, isn't it?'

'I like it,' the producer agreed. 'Might be worth thinking about following up with a visit out there. It's a cute name, isn't it? Two Tails?'

It didn't matter that Hazel had missed lunch. Any urgent need to find something to eat had just evaporated.

This was exciting. It might even be a turning point for the refuge. She turned back well before the automatic doors were triggered to open, searching for the right words that might encourage the idea of Finn and the crew visiting the refuge, when something stopped her saying anything at all.

A sound that was so completely unexpected in a waiting area that was empty of any patients, it was shocking. It was a demanding kind of sound, like the yowl of a hungry Siamese cat. Hazel wasn't the only person bewildered by the noise.

'What on earth was that?' Finn asked. 'There's no one there.'

Hazel was looking in the direction the sound had come from, over by the display of toys and treats for dogs and cats. Oddly, there was a pet carrier on the floor, which didn't match the kind that the clinic had for sale and Hazel realised she'd seen that carrier before—when the area had been crowded with people waiting for the afternoon clinic to start. Just before the chaos of the emergency had kicked off.

'Someone must have forgotten their pet,' Hazel said. 'It wouldn't be the first time. They'll get home and panic when the carrier's not in the back of the car.'

Shaking her head, she walked over to the carrier and crouched down to peer through the wire door on the front. Or rather, try to peer past a small sheet of paper that had been taped to the door. She read the words on the paper but they made no sense. So she opened the door and stared inside, as the cry came again. Louder this time.

'Oh, my God…' she breathed. 'It's a *baby*…'

'No way…' Finn was staring across the waiting area. 'It can't be…'

'It *is*. There's a note, here, too.'

Hazel could see the cameraman and the show producer exchanging a meaningful glance as she peeled the paper from the wire door. The camera got swung back into position on the man's shoulder. There was more drama happening at the Coogee Beach Animal Hospital and they didn't want to miss a moment of it.

'What does the note say?'

Hazel hesitated. Finn might not want to make this public. The way his long strides were eating up the space between them, there was no time to keep this completely private but at least she could show him the note rather than reading it aloud. She could also watch the colour drain out of his face as he read it.

To Dr Finn

You look after animals all the time on your show.
So you can look after this kid.
She's yours.

CHAPTER TWO

The huff of sound that came from Finn was beyond incredulous.

'She's mine? Someone's trying to give me a *kid*? What is this—some kind of joke?' He swung round to face a camera pointing directly at him. 'It is, isn't it? A prank? Is it someone's birthday or have I missed a milestone for the show or something?'

'I don't think they're trying to give you someone else's child,' Hazel said quietly. 'I think this note suggests that she's already yours.' The muscles in her face felt oddly tense. 'That maybe you're the father?'

Nobody else was saying anything, except for the baby who let out its loudest wail yet. Anna had walked into the waiting area as Hazel was speaking but was now frozen to the spot. Kylie was staring at him with her mouth open. Jude, the show's producer, had raised her eyebrows so high they'd vanished under her short fringe. The guy with the camera on his shoulder looked as if he could be smirking.

'What…?' Finn was looking even more gobsmacked than he had when he'd finished reading the note. 'You can't possibly believe this could be *true*…?'

His head was turning and Hazel knew he was about to catch her gaze. That he would be quite sure she would back him up a hundred per cent—the way she always did. And she wanted to be there for him. To hold his gaze and let him know that she'd always be there for him but, instead, for some reason, she found herself ducking her head the nanosecond before he could make eye contact and reaching into the pet carrier to carefully extract the baby.

Goodness knew how she had stayed asleep for so long but this infant definitely needed attention now. Her bottom felt distinctly damp through its towelling stretch suit so Hazel pulled a fuzzy blanket, printed with yellow ducks, out as well, to wrap around the damp patch. She got to her feet with the small bundle firmly clutched against her chest and, by some miracle, the human contact made the baby happy enough to stop crying. She was looking up at Hazel with wide open dark eyes as she looked down and, oh, boy…this wasn't a squeeze on her heart in response to the most adorable baby she'd ever seen, it was more like a squeeze on her ovaries that was so fierce it really hurt.

She'd always adored animals, dogs in particular—and Ben most of all and for ever—because of the unconditional and unlimited love they offered so willingly but oh, my…there was an unfamiliar yearning deep inside her belly right now that suggested a baby could fill an even bigger gap in your life. *Her* life, anyway.

'Oh…you're *gorgeous*…' Hazel had to touch the longest, darkest hair she'd ever seen on a baby. It was also the softest. 'I've never seen a baby with actual curls like this. And look at those eyelashes…'

Anna had recovered the ability to move and she was by Hazel's side in a heartbeat, also ready to coo over the baby.

'It must be a girl. Nobody would put a boy in a pink, unicorn onesie would they?'

'It is a girl,' Hazel told her. 'The note referred to her as "she".'

Finn made an exasperated sound. He screwed up the note and threw it away. He glared at the cameraman. 'You can stop filming right now, mate. This isn't funny. For heaven's sake, everyone knows I've been in a relationship with Shannon Summers for at least a *year*.'

Hazel bit her lip. Surely everyone also knew it was an on-again, off-again kind of arrangement? She couldn't be the only one to think there was something phoney about his relationship with such a popular social media star that hooking up had made them Australia's most talked about IT couple? Everyone would, no doubt, suspect there were limitless women waiting in the wings for the celebrity TV vet to be ready to take another break or move on and many of them would be tall, super-skinny blondes like Shannon.

Like all the women he'd dated over the first year or so when Hazel came to work here, for that matter. The kind of women that had let her know instantly there was no point even thinking about ever being invited to step out of a 'friend and/or colleague' zone for Finn, even if his charm often seemed to border on flirting with those meaningful glances and *that* smile. Hazel knew that was just part of his charisma and it was like water off a duck's back for her now.

'Maybe we should call the police,' Jude suggested. 'Abandoning a baby has got to be against the law. It's certainly headline news, that's for sure.' Her gaze slid sideways towards her cameraman.

'Uh, uh...' Finn had seen the look. 'This is not getting anywhere near a news broadcast. Whoever's done this must be after the publicity for some reason. It's the sort of thing that happens to celebrities all the time.'

'I'm not sure about that,' Hazel murmured. 'Paternity claims, maybe, but actually leaving your baby where the father is going to be forced to take care of it? Not so much…'

'I'm *not* the father.' Finn had such a haunted look in his eyes that Hazel knew he was telling the truth.

'You could get a DNA test done,' Jude suggested. 'I've got a friend who works in a lab that does them. I believe it's possible to get an urgent result through in forty-eight hours or so. Want me to give them a call?'

'And have you filming it?' Finn shook his head. 'I'll pass on that one, thanks. There's no point doing it anyway. The chance of me being this baby's father is about the same as a snowball's chance in hell. You may as well all go home.'

'I wonder if there's anything else in here.' Anna crouched to examine the carrier. 'Yeah, look…there's a bottle and some formula at the back. And a few nappies.'

'She needs one of those.' Hazel nodded. 'I'll change her if you want to make up a bottle.'

'Okay.' But Anna was frowning as she looked up. 'What else did the note say, apart from her being a girl?'

Hazel glanced at Finn who was still looking anguished. She looked at Jude and her crew who were looking very reluctant to leave this new drama unfolding in front of them. Kylie helpfully dived for the screwed-up ball of paper and unfolded it to hand to Anna.

'Wait,' Hazel ordered. 'Let me see that?' Both she and Finn had only seen the note scrawled in dark ink on one side of the paper. Now she could see there was something written on the other side.

'Elena Ferrari,' she read aloud as the baby started crying again. 'Date of birth twenty-ninth of August… so that makes the baby…'

'About six weeks old,' Anna supplied. 'And obviously hungry… I'm going to make up that bottle.' She reached into the carrier to take the items she needed.

'Ferrari…?' Finn was frowning. '*Elena* Ferrari?'

'Maybe someone knows what sort of car you drive.' The suggestion came from the crew's sound technician.

'He drives a Porsche,' the cameraman said. 'Black. Late model. Better than a Ferrari if you ask me.'

'It's an odd name.' Jude sounded thoughtful. 'Italian, but not that common in Australia, I wouldn't have thought.'

Hazel was watching Finn. And she couldn't help herself—she wanted to get involved. To try and help, somehow. Good grief, the urge to touch him was astonishingly strong. Not just the touch of a friend, either. She wanted to wrap her arms around Finn and hold him tightly. Luckily, the urge was easy to dismiss thanks to the baby she was holding.

'Do you recognise the name?' she asked.

'I had a friend at high school,' he said slowly. And *her* name was Elena Ferrari.' He rubbed the back of his neck. 'Weird coincidence, huh?'

'Was she a close friend?' Hazel couldn't agree with his assumption. 'A *girl*friend?'

She could see the answer to that query in the way Finn's face softened, even before his single, slow affirmatory nod. The misty look that had darkened his eyes to a real, deep sea kind of blue made her think that Elena must have been someone rather special. A first love, perhaps?

Lucky girl…

But that odd frisson of something like envy was fading rapidly because there was a part of Hazel's brain that was doing a bit of rapid calculation, having decided that there was more to this than coincidence. James Finlay was thirty-six years old. He would have been about seventeen towards the end of high school. If the mother of this baby was also that young, then…

Then…

'Oh, my God, Finn,' Hazel whispered. 'This doesn't have to be your daughter to be yours, does it? Has it occurred to you that this could be your *grand*daughter?'

Okay.

That did it.

Finn hadn't got to where he was in life without being able to take charge of a tricky situation and get himself out of trouble. Not that he'd ever expected to find himself in a pickle quite like this, of course, but the absurdity of even the idea that he could have a grandchild made it imperative that this got nipped in the bud. *Now.*

'Anna, can you please make up some formula for the baby? Kylie… I know you're heading home but could you please do a supermarket run first and get a few supplies that we might need in the next hour or so?' He offered her the most persuasive smile he could summon and it seemed to work.

'Like what?'

'Another pack of nappies, more formula. Anything else that looks useful in the baby aisle.' He handed her a card from his wallet. 'Use the practice account.' He shifted his gaze as the automatic doors opened for Kylie to exit. 'The rest of you can go home, thanks. I'll be getting in touch with the police or Social Services or whoever deals with this kind of thing and we'll have it sorted in no time. Oh…and, Jude? I might get the name of that friend of yours, after all. The one who works with DNA testing? Just in case.'

Hazel was walking towards him and, to his horror, Finn got the distinct impression that she might be planning to hand over the baby. Did she think he'd included her in the people he had just told to go home?

'You can't go home, Hazel.' He spoke firmly so that his message was completely clear but the way her eyebrows shot up made her look astonished. Appalled, even?

'I need you,' he added. He tried that smile again—the one that had worked so well on Kylie—but it seemed to have lost its magic. 'Please?' He simply mouthed the plea but he held her gaze and tried to add whatever else it might take because he really *did* need her.

I know I sound like I'm in control, but I'm not... I'm a bit lost, to be honest...and, out of all my friends, you're the one I trust the most...

Maybe Hazel was a bit telepathic. Or maybe she was just confirming what he already knew—that she was the nicest person in the world.

'I'm just going into the consulting room,' she said, calmly. She held up the nappy in her hand. 'I need a flat surface and some wipes.'

Finn stayed in the waiting area, grateful for the empty space while he took several deep breaths and tried to decide who he needed to call first. The police? His agent? His solicitor? Or Shannon—to warn her that something was developing that she might not want to use to update her status? Kylie came back before he'd made that decision with what looked like a pack of nappies big enough to last a month under one arm and a bag of more supplies in her other hand.

'I have to go now,' she said. 'I don't want to miss my bus.'

She left as Anna came back with a bottle of warm formula at the same time as Hazel returned with the baby who didn't appear to appreciate having clean pants. It was howling the roof down. Anna handed Finn the bottle of milk.

'I need to get back into the ward and check on our post-op cases. Including your Ben.'

'Oh…'

Hazel was biting her lip. She clearly wanted to go and see the old dog, too, but that would mean that Finn would be left with the baby. He didn't give her a chance to move first. He handed her the bottle.

'Come and sit down,' he said. 'You'll be much more comfortable.'

'I'll look after Ben,' Anna promised. 'He'll probably just sleep for the rest of the night, anyway.'

'But…'

'The police will need to talk to you,' Finn added. 'You're the one who found the kid, after all. You might be able to remember something else?'

Hazel sank down on one of the padded benches. The pet carrier that had been the cause of this new crisis was still nearby. Empty now, with its wire door hanging open. A bomb that had already been detonated.

'It might have fingerprints on it,' he said hopefully. 'We can find the mother.'

'Mmm…' Hazel sounded dubious but she was focused on getting the baby to accept the teat of the bottle. She adjusted her hold and made soothing sounds but it took another attempt or two before the red-faced, miserable infant latched on and then started furiously sucking. It looked like it was glaring up at Hazel.

'Poor thing,' Hazel murmured. 'You were starving, weren't you, Ellie?'

Finn almost winced at the shortened form of a name that echoed in his memory banks. No…he wasn't going to think about the Ellie he remembered. About the way his life had been so devastatingly derailed.

'What did you mean,' he demanded, 'by "mmm"? You don't think the mother's going to be found?'

'That wasn't what I was thinking about. But I'm sure she'll be found if she wants to be found.'

'What's that supposed to mean?'

'She might be really young and having trouble coping. She might need a bit of time. This could be a cry for help—maybe to the only family member she, or possibly *he*, can approach.'

'I'm *not* a family member.' But it was beginning to feel like he could well be clutching at a straw, here.

'Think about it, Finn,' Hazel said. 'A baby gets left for you to find. A baby who has the same name as a girl you were in a relationship with, what…seventeen, eighteen years ago? Can you be absolutely sure the first Elena Ferrari that you knew didn't get pregnant?'

'I wouldn't know.' The words came out curtly. Good grief…he'd thought he'd left that hurt behind nearly two decades ago. 'She left school before I did. I never heard from her again.'

'Mmm…'

Hazel was making that infuriating sound again—as if he was being a bit dense, not joining the dots. And, okay…being a pregnant, unmarried teenager could be the reason she'd left school so abruptly, especially with an already less than ideal home situation but…

But the enormity of considering that this could be true—that he'd simply skipped fatherhood to become a *grandfather*?

No. No, no, no…

Baby Ellie had certainly been hungry. As her little tummy filled she was sinking into Hazel's arms, feeling both limper and heavier. Her eyelids were getting heavier as well, and she was having trouble keeping them open. Hazel had bottle fed orphaned kittens or puppies and even a kangaroo joey or two in her time but, somehow, she'd got to be thirty-two years old and had never fed a human baby. If it was like this with a bottle, it was mindboggling to imagine that it could be even more intense to be breastfeeding. She could feel emotions stirring that were big enough to become overwhelming and Hazel was blinking them away when she became aware of something else.

Finn was watching her.

Really watching her. Not just observing her, as he'd been doing when he was watching her operate on Ben's fractured leg. Or the way he'd look when he was teasing her, if they were out in a crowd having 'after work' drinks or celebrating something, by giving her those appreciative glances as they clinked glasses as a toast or laughed at someone's joke. Hazel knew, when she looked up, that she wouldn't see a persuasively raised eyebrow or lopsided smile on his face and it was in that moment she suddenly realised that a lot of James Finlay's life was a disguise. Some form of protection?

For different reasons, no doubt, Finn was grappling with some overwhelming emotions himself, wasn't he?

And there was a connection here, between them. Because he was watching her holding this baby and it felt like he was seeing her—really *seeing* her, as a person and not a colleague or a friend or inside any other people box he might have a label on—for possibly the first time ever.

'What if it's true?' His words were no more than a whisper. 'It would destroy my image. My career, probably. My life, possibly.'

'You never know,' Hazel said. 'It could turn out to be the best thing that's ever happened to you.'

Finn gave one of those incredulous huffs again. 'What am I going to do? Shall I call Social Services? Do you think they have an emergency refuge for babies like we do for dogs or kangaroos or whatever?'

Hazel could feel her hold on baby Ellie tighten just a fraction. 'What if it is true?' She tried to keep her tone casual. 'Don't you think that abandoning your grandchild to an emergency foster home might be worse for your image?' Then she frowned. 'Have you not called someone already?'

Finn shook his head. He looked beyond miserable. 'I can't think what the best thing to do is. How I'm going to keep the media from getting hold of this. It's already out there, isn't it? Jude might be looking out for me, but there's plenty of other people in that crew who'll have friends in the industry who'd love a scoop like this.'

Okay… The emotions Hazel could feel surfacing now weren't anything like the ones that could have brought tears to her eyes. She was feeling rather fiercely protective of this baby she was holding. She was also feeling more than a little disappointed in how superficial Finn was making himself sound. So what if the life and persona he'd built were some form of protection? This was…well, it was unacceptable, that was what it was.

'No wonder you and Shannon Summers are so perfect for each other,' she found herself saying aloud. 'You both believe that what other people think—preferably the millions of people who follow you on social media—is way more important than anything else, don't you?'

Finn blinked at her. He'd been expecting support, not an attack. And this was not the time to be letting stuff out that had probably been building for a very long time—ever since Hazel had realised she might have fallen in love with Finn—but it felt like a pin had been pulled from a grenade and there was no stopping it now.

'You're superficial,' she snapped. 'Both of you. You skate through life on your good looks and wealth and… you're fake. It's all fake. All that celebrity and social media crap. This…' Hazel looked down at the baby who had fallen deeply asleep now, the teat of the bottle loose in her mouth. 'This is real. *This* is what matters.'

She stood up, pressing the bundle of baby against Finn's chest, knowing that he would instinctively bring his arms up to protect it.

'Meet Ellie,' she finished. 'You might not believe this, but I think showing you care about a baby who's very likely to be your granddaughter will do a lot of good for your image. And your career. And, most of all, for your life.'

She turned her back on him, intending to walk away to go and see how Ben the black dog was doing but she suddenly needed to get a lot further away from Finn than that. Completely away from this clinic, in fact, which made her swerve towards the automatic doors. The nurse on duty in their post-op ward would be taking excellent care of Ben and she could text Hazel at any time if she had concerns. And Anna was right—with the painkillers Ben was receiving along with the IV fluids, he was more than likely to be comfortably asleep all night.

She couldn't go home though. How awful would it be to sit in that lonely little apartment in the wake of what was turning into the worst day of her life, what with the horror of seeing Ben being rushed into the clinic like that, finding Ellie and stirring such strong feelings about motherhood that she hadn't been aware she had and…and seeing Finn with the filter that was a mix of physical attraction and a much deeper level of affection well and truly peeled off? She'd been suppressing a one-sided attraction ever since the first day she'd met this man so was this the first occasion that she was seeing the *real* James Finlay? Someone who was so focused on his celebrity status and popularity that he was totally missing even some compassion for a helpless baby who'd been abandoned?

There was only one place she could go that might turn her day around.

Two Tails.

And the sooner she was there, with her own reality of true friendship and doing some good in a world that all too often lacked compassion these days, the better.

CHAPTER THREE

THE BLUE MOUNTAINS covered thousands of square miles of rugged country west of Sydney, Australia and they had earned their name because, from a distance, the eucalyptus and gum trees that blanketed the area created a haze with a distinctly blue tinge. A popular tourist destination, the mountains were known for forests and sandstone cliffs, canyons and waterfalls, underground caves, hundreds of miles of walking tracks and a rich, indigenous history and culture to explore.

Even as preoccupied as she was with the emotional overload she was escaping, Hazel couldn't miss the spectacular haze of the mountains this evening, accentuated by the sun beginning to set behind them and she could feel some of her stress already evaporating as she drew in a long slow breath and then let it out in a sigh. She would feel even better when she took the turn off to the small town of Birralong that was isolated enough to have never become part of the Blue Mountain tourist trail, despite being only an hour or so from central Sydney.

She was longing to be there—sitting on the shady wide veranda of the tumbledown old house her best friend Kiara had inherited from her grandmother on the outskirts of Birralong, with its rambling garden and forest surroundings—because Hazel knew it would be the perfect place to unpick one of the worst days she could remember in a very long time. Not that she could have a glass of wine tonight, because she intended to get back to work later and check on Ben, but maybe she and Kiara could even find something kind of funny about her car crash of an afternoon. Dr Finn's fall from stardom because his love life had finally caught up with him, perhaps?

No. Hazel might be seeing her boss in a disappointing new light but she'd never take pleasure in bad things happening to anyone, let alone someone she cared about as much as she cared about Finn. Her sigh this time wasn't one of relief. It was more like satisfaction that she wasn't doing the wrong thing trekking right out of the city when it hadn't been planned for today. It certainly wasn't going to make her day any worse to be with a person who was so special in her life and in a place that had captured her heart to the point of feeling like a real home years ago now.

Not that she would ever be able to afford to live out here. It was enough of a struggle for Kiara to make ends meet despite having been lucky enough to have been gifted a property. The rambling garden around Kiara's cottage, with just enough land cleared in the forest to provide space for the refuge and her small veterinary clinic, had to be worth a fortune with it being within such easy commuting distance from Sydney.

It was priceless as far as Hazel was concerned, anyway, and she couldn't wait to get there. She could already feel her mood lifting as she slowed her speed to drive through central Birralong but then she saw something on the side of the road near a bus stop. Something that made her hit the brakes hard on her beloved van, Morrie.

It was a dog.

Lying so still it could be dead but, even if it *was* dead, she couldn't leave it here. Her heart heavy, Hazel opened the back of her van. She had warm blankets in here, along with the crates. There was a powerful torch for an emergency at night, a shovel and crowbar in case of entrapment and thick gloves that could offer protection from a frightened or aggressive animal. She put the gloves on and took a blanket.

'What's happened?' A man had crossed the street and was approaching as Hazel crouched on the road and covered the dog's body with the blanket. 'Did it get hit by a car?'

Two dogs hit by cars in the space of one afternoon would be much less of a coincidence than, say…a baby that just happened to have been given the same name as an old girlfriend, but Hazel was shaking her head.

'I don't think so. There's no obvious sign of external injury. It may have been abandoned because it was sick and someone couldn't afford to take it to a vet.'

'Unbelievable. At least it's not dead. I can see it's breathing.'

Hazel blinked. But the man was right. The blanket over the dog was moving. She pulled it back and the man sucked in his breath.

'Crikey…look at the way his bones are sticking out.'

'Mmm.' Hazel had no words to find. She was looking at one of the worst cases of animal abuse she'd ever seen. A skeletal, black and white female dog, possibly a border collie but it was hard to tell with that matted hair and those infected sores. But she *was* breathing and her eyes were half open.

'There's a vet not far away,' the Birralong resident told her. 'At the refuge up the road.'

'I know. That's actually where I'm heading.' And it wouldn't be the first time that a sick or injured animal had been left close enough to the refuge to be easily found.

'Oh...that's good, then.' The man hesitated for only a moment. 'I can help you put it in your van, if you like.'

Hazel simply nodded. She was starting to feel a bit numb, to be honest. This was the last thing she needed to deal with right now.

The man waited until she'd closed Morrie's back door, ready to transport her blanket-wrapped patient. 'Doesn't look good, does it?'

'No. But thanks for your help.'

'I've heard she's good—the vet up at the refuge. She should be able to help.'

'I hope so.' Hazel got into her driver's seat. She wasn't sure anyone would be able to help this poor dog but at least she and Kiara could give her a more comfortable place to die than on the side of a road.

It was just as well it wasn't far to Two Tails because Hazel had tears rolling down her face by the time she parked the van and gently carried the dog towards the front yard of the house, knowing that it was unlikely that Kiara would be in the clinic building this late in the day.

'Kiara?' Her voice sounded as strangled as she was feeling inside. 'Kiara? Where are you?'

'In the pens. Hang on, I'm coming...'

'I found her on the side of the road near the bus stop in Birralong,' Hazel told her friend as soon as she appeared. 'She's...oh, Kiara...this is just awful...'

Kiara crouched beside her, taking in every horrible

detail that Hazel had already seen but it was still like seeing it all over again through her eyes and…it was too much. She had to turn away as she blinked back tears. Looking back, she saw Kiara cradling the dog's head in her hands as she looked at it the same way she had looked at Ben only hours ago. It was enough to break her heart all over again but someone had to be practical, even though she hated that it had to be her.

'Can we even do anything to help her?' Hazel asked quietly. 'It might be kinder to…' She couldn't bring herself to say the words and she had tears flowing again. 'On top of everything else that's happened today… I don't think I can bear it.'

Kiara flashed her a glance that let Hazel know she wanted to hear about what else had happened today, but not yet. They had something far more urgent to deal with.

'She's only young,' Kiara said. 'Maybe…'

'Oh, Kiara…look at her. She's been so abused that, even if we did manage to save her life, how scarred is she going to be? Physically and emotionally? Then there's the cost. Who's going to pay? We both know that sometimes the kindest thing to do is…is to let them go. We can make sure she's not in any pain.'

'We're going to do more than that.' Kiara hadn't looked away from the dog. 'Let's get her into the surgery.' Finally, she looked up, meeting Hazel's gaze square on. 'I know it doesn't make sense and we can't afford to take on a case like this but, dammit, Hazel, we set up Two Tails for a reason. If I'm going to end up bankrupt, then I'll go down doing what I do to the end.'

Maybe fighting talk was exactly what Hazel needed to hear. A reminder that when the going got tough was when the tough got going. Kiara was tough. And Hazel knew she was tough as well, deep down. She'd got back up after repeated knocks over the years, hadn't she? To be fighting on the same side as someone else, with the same goal and the encouragement and support they could give each other to succeed, was a gift that had come late in life for Hazel.

Meeting Kiara at vet school had given her the kind of friendship she'd only dreamed of having throughout her childhood and adolescence. The kind of friendship that was based on the things that mattered in life, like who you really were and not what you looked like. Things like love and loyalty and compassion. The kind of friendship that could give you the strength to tackle challenges even if they looked impossible.

They could do this.

What followed was a far more intense and difficult session treating a dog than this afternoon's efforts had been. Even giving enough sedation to allow them to work on the collie was precarious due to how close to death she was.

Because Kiara and Hazel were very used to working together and knew exactly what they were doing, they could distract themselves from unpleasant tasks, like removing matted hair and cleaning nasty lesions, by talking about other things, even if they were also disheartening.

'Have you any idea how you might cover costs?' Hazel asked at one point.

'Why bother?' Kiara shook her head. 'What's another debt among so many? Two Tails is doomed to close anyway.'

'What? No...'

'I got a quote to repair the termite damage and it's...

well, it's impossible. Even if I mortgaged the property to find the money, I wouldn't be able to meet the repayments.'

'You can't close.' The thought was horrible. 'What if you charged more?'

'How? By taking in more dogs and selling them to the highest bidder? That's not how we do things.'

'Publicity, then? I took part in an episode of *Call the Vet* that was being filmed today and I talked about Two Tails. The show's producer is interested in coming out here and doing an episode and, with a bit of luck, it could lead to donations.'

'Wait a minute…' Kiara seemed to be ignoring a potential solution to the money problems. 'I thought you swore over your dead body that you'd never appear in that programme again?'

'I did. But there was a hit and run outside the clinic.' Hazel shrugged. 'I guess it comes with the territory but this one got to me. A gorgeous, old black spaniel who's apparently a stray.' Hazel looked away from Kiara's gaze. 'He needed surgery to plate a tibial fracture. Finn thought he must be about fourteen or fifteen years old. He also needed a name, so I called him Ben.'

'Ben? Wasn't that your first ever dog?'

'Yeah.'

'So we're both suckers for dogs.'

'I guess we are.'

They worked in silence for a minute. Kiara knew about Ben. How her old dog's company had been the only friendship Hazel could count on as she got bullied viciously throughout her school years and how it had given her the ambition to become a vet. How devastating it had been to lose him even though he'd lived to such a grand old age.

Kiara had also guessed long ago that Hazel had feelings for Finn that didn't mesh with simply being a friend or colleague.

'Well, then…' It was a slightly hesitant push. 'Was that what made it a bad day for you? Having to work with Finn? Or did Ben not make it?'

Hazel shook her head. 'Ben's doing well as far as I know. I'll go and check on him when I'm done here.' She hesitated for a heartbeat. 'It's Finn who's not doing so well. A baby got left in the waiting room with a note that said it was his.'

'No…' Kiara was thoroughly distracted as she continued working. 'Tell me…'

So Hazel told her all about finding baby Ellie. And all about how disappointed she'd been in Finn's reaction.

'To be fair,' Kiara mused, 'it would be a bit of a shock to find out that you're a grandfather when you are out there as—what was it? Australia's most eligible bachelor?'

'Doesn't excuse him being so shallow.'

'His girlfriend won't be happy. Isn't she the one who makes her living by kneeling on beaches with her hands behind her head and then getting the photos touched up to provide unachievable body goals for other women?'

Hazel had to laugh. 'Yep. She's an influencer.' She straightened up to ease the ache in her back from bending over for so long. 'I'm just going to get a glass of water.'

She checked her phone that was lying on the bench beside the sink. She'd missed hearing the alert for a text message, which gave her a beat of panic that Ben's condition had deteriorated but the message wasn't from the night nurse at the hospital. It wasn't from Anna, either. It was from Finn.

Where are you? The message said. *Can you please call me?*

Hazel was not ready to communicate with Finn again yet. She could still hear the echo of her own voice, telling him he was fake and that celebrity status and money were more important to him than something that really mattered. Instead of responding to the message, she pulled on a fresh pair of gloves to continue the work on the collie. They were getting close enough to see the end point of this first attempt to rescue her and, while shaving more and more of the matted hair away wasn't doing anything to make the dog look more attractive, it still felt positive. Hazel just wished that Kiara would start looking a bit happier.

'The world's gone a bit mad,' she told Hazel. 'People have enough stress to deal with these days without people like influencers making it worse.'

'Who did you have in mind?'

'I had my own share of drama today, too. With a man who's got major issues of his own and, on top of that, he's now got responsibility for a little girl—his niece—who's traumatised after her mother took her own life. His sister came to see me the other day and asked if I'd provide a dog for them. She seemed to think a dog would solve all their problems and she offered me pretty much enough money to sort out the termites if I could organise it.'

'Really?' Hazel paused before turning on the clippers again. 'That sounds too good to be true.'

'The amount she offered me was ridiculous,' Kiara finished. 'And I don't even have a dog suitable for a child.'

'How about this one?' Hazel suggested.

Kiara had also paused. She was staring at her. 'Are you out of your mind?'

'Maybe. But it sounds as if there are two wounded souls that need help. Why not make it three?'

'Hazel, that's ridiculous.'

'You'll need to find a home for her, even if you are bankrupt,' Hazel pointed out. 'Especially if you're bankrupt. You know, I've sort of fallen for her, too. Why not give her to someone who can pay?'

'Maybe I could call her Bunji.' Kiara sounded thoughtful. 'It means a mate. A friend.'

Hazel nodded. It had to be an indigenous word. Kiara's gorgeous colouring—along with her own name—was due to her grandmother being indigenous so she knew a lot more about the language than Hazel did.

But Kiara was looking doubtful now. 'Who am I kidding? How could I give such a dog to a ten-year-old?'

'Give her to the uncle. He sounds like he needs a friend, as much if not more than his niece. And hey, if he falls for Bunji, he might even be prepared to backpay for her treatment. How's that for a thought?'

'They really don't want a dog. Besides, I'd have to stay there. A week at least, he stipulated, and who's going to take care of this place? I can't ask you to take more time off. I can't afford to pay anyone. The whole thing's impossible.'

Hazel frowned, trying to think up a solution. And then her phone beeped and almost immediately beeped again.

'Two messages? I'd better see what that's about,' she said, stripping off her gloves. 'I'm worried about Ben.'

The first text wasn't a message about Ben this time, either. It was another text from Finn and this one made Hazel catch her breath.

I'm sorry. You're right. About everything. This *is* real and I can't do it by myself.

Oh... *Finn*... The emotional exhaustion of today's events was making it too hard to protect herself by not getting too close. And then she opened the message that had come in straight after and staying angry with him or even deeply disappointed suddenly became a lot harder.

I really need you, Hazel.

'I need to go,' she told Kiara.

'Ben?'

'I...no. I'm sure he's okay but I would like to see for myself. And you'll want the results on those blood samples as soon as possible.' Hazel was going to arrange to have the samples analysed at work.

Kiara nodded. 'No worries. We've done all we can for the moment. I'll finish up and get her settled. Thanks so much for your help.'

'Think about what I said before. About giving Bunji to that uncle. Maybe it's true that people—and dogs—come into our lives for a reason.'

And babies?

Hazel sent a message back to Finn as she went out to her van.

Out at Two Tails but on my way back. See you soon.

CHAPTER FOUR

WAITING FOR MORE than an hour for Hazel to get back and then across the city was winding the knot of tension in Finn's gut so tight the pain was becoming intense but, in comparison to everything else exploding in his life right now, it was insignificant.

When Hazel didn't pick up when he called her, Finn's heart sank to new levels, but she called back within a minute or two.

'I had to pull over,' she said. 'A nineteen-seventies Morris Minor doesn't run to Bluetooth.'

'When you get to my apartment block, park around the back by the rubbish bins. There's a fire escape door and you can get in with a code. I'll text it to you. You'll have to come up the stairs rather than take the lift.' His huff of laughter was ironic. 'Sorry about that. Who would have thought that living in a penthouse would have its disadvantages?'

'What's with all the cloak and dagger stuff?'

'Someone leaked at least part of this story to the media. Probably that cameraman who thought the whole drama was so amusing. They might not know everything but they know that something's going on and they've set up camp in front of the building. They caught Shannon when she was arriving but, luckily, she could tell the truth when she told them she had no idea what they were talking about.'

'Shannon's there?' There was an odd note in Hazel's voice. Was she about to change her mind about coming because he had someone with him?

'Not for long,' he told her grimly. 'Apparently she doesn't "do" babies.'

There was a heartbeat's silence on the other end of the line. He thought he could hear Hazel take in a quick breath. 'So you've taken Ellie home? How *is* she?'

Finn walked across the vast living area of his penthouse apartment. To one side, he could see Shannon on the balcony, with its stunning, panoramic view of the Coogee coastline. She was currently pouting at the phone in her hand, probably adjusting its position to capture the lights of the cityscape behind her. The sliding doors were firmly shut to keep the smoke from her cigarette outside. Finn spared her no more than a weary glance. Ahead of him, tucked up inside a nest of cushions on the couch, was the baby. It felt like she hadn't stopped crying since he'd brought her home after the visit from the police and a representative for Social Services. He knew that Hazel would be able to hear the sound of the miserable infant clearly now.

'Oh…' The sympathetic sound in his ear gave Finn a very odd sensation—surely it couldn't be tears forming? He hadn't cried since…well, since Ellie. The first Ellie, that was. There was a note in that low sound that gave him hope that Hazel wasn't mad at him any more, even if she did think he was a complete failure as a human being. That she might understand that it wasn't just the baby who was feeling unbearably miserable. That he could possibly depend on her to be on his side and, in this moment, it was the best feeling he could hope for.

'I need to pick her up,' was all he said. 'She might be hungry again. I'll text you that code in a minute.'

Shannon came inside as he was juggling the baby in the crook of one arm and reading the instructions on the back of the can of milk formula. She stood there, looking impossibly gorgeous in her skin-tight, sequinned black evening dress with a thigh high split and deep neckline that left virtually nothing to the imagination.

Looking…fake?

Looking absolutely furious, that was for sure.

'I can't believe you're doing this to me, Finn. You knew how important it was to be seen at this fundraiser this evening. There are potential sponsors for me there that could make or break my career.'

'I've said I'm sorry. I didn't exactly plan for this to happen.' Finn carefully measured a scoop of the creamy powder into the bottle that already contained cooled boiled water. When did being so popular on social media become a 'career' exactly? When the number of people who followed you got past half a million? Would there be a degree in social media at university one of these years, to give it the status of a *real* career?

'If we hurried, we could still get there in time. Surely you know someone who could look after it for a while? Or take it away?'

It? Even if he hadn't exactly dismissed the baby as no more than an unwanted object himself, he'd acted as if it was, hadn't he? A problem to get sorted. Something to hide so that nobody else found out. He looked down at the small bundle he was holding. She was still crying, but it was a whimper rather than a howl and that felt like a win. He screwed the top onto the bottle and shook it to dissolve the formula.

He could see why anybody would think his girlfriend's lifestyle was fake but *he* had a real career as a very successful veterinary surgeon. Just because he'd added an extra dimension to that career by becoming unexpectedly well known on television didn't mean he was fake. And why did it matter so much what Hazel thought, anyway?

Because, deep down, he was ashamed of how he'd felt when he'd considered the possibility that he was this baby's grandfather? He'd seen a reflection of himself in Shannon's reaction.

A grandfather? As in a whole generation removed? Do you know how old that makes you look? How utterly un*sexy that is?*

Oh, yeah…he knew. But maybe he was getting used to it. Like the way he was getting over the shock of the weight and warmth of holding his baby in his arms after Hazel had shoved Ellie into them, hours and hours ago now. He would have thought that it wouldn't be much different from holding a big puppy, like a fluffy Old English sheepdog, perhaps, but, oddly, nothing in his career had really prepared him for how this felt.

It was more than simply holding a child this young. It was the idea that he might have a connection with another person that came with expectations. Responsibilities. The potential for heartache…

Things that he wasn't anywhere near ready to even think of including in his life. He was a bachelor and that suited him perfectly. A bachelor with a successful career, the kind of wealth that meant he was safe from ever having to worry about not being able to pay his bills and…okay…it wasn't exactly unpleasant to be so popular with women.

'Why don't you go alone?' he said to Shannon. 'You

can go out the fire escape and you won't need to talk to anybody.'

'Why should I have to sneak around? *I* haven't done anything wrong.'

'It might save you a bit of temporary embarrassment.'

'What will embarrass me is to attend a function without my boyfriend. A function that he was the one who was invited to. We're supposed to be a couple. How can I go on my own?'

'You'd be fine. You don't need to be on my arm to attract attention, you know.'

'Don't flatter yourself,' Shannon snapped. 'When we're out in public, it's my arm *you're* on, not the other way round. How many followers do *you* have?'

The chime of his doorbell suggested that he had at least one and Finn was only too happy to check the camera and see that it was Hazel. He had to step back not only to allow Hazel to enter his apartment but for Shannon to have room to leave because that was what she appeared to be doing as she marched into the foyer with her clutch purse under her arm. She paused when she noticed Hazel, however.

'You work with Finn, don't you? Have you come to babysit, then?' She was glancing at her watch as she spoke. Working out if there was still enough time for Finn to get changed into a tuxedo and make an appearance at the fundraiser? As her man bag?

'No.' It was Finn who answered before Hazel could even blink. 'Of course she hasn't. Hazel's here to help me for a bit, that's all.'

Shannon flicked that extraordinary mane of blonde hair that brushed her buttocks as she looked over her shoulder at Finn.

'Call me.' The ice in her voice was not a warm invitation. 'When you've got rid of it.'

The look she gave the baby in Finn's arms was a death glare. And maybe, a few hours ago, Finn might have been relieved if he could have walked away from this problem with no more than a look of such extreme distaste but Shannon's attitude was suddenly making him feel…what, protective?

He was feeling something, anyway. The numbness of feeling like a stunned mullet with this serve that life had thrown at him from left field was wearing off. Finn suspected that the death glare had been successful, though. Not that it was the baby who would suffer, he'd make sure of that, but it definitely felt as if his relationship with Shannon might well have just had a death blow delivered.

Not that he had the slightest inclination to waste any more emotional energy on the woman who had, if truth were told, been an annoyingly high-maintenance girlfriend.

Fake, a small voice whispered in the back of his head. *Like you...*

Oh, dear…

The fury Shannon Summers left in her wake was palpable. Had Hazel caught the finale of a much bigger row? Maybe that was why Finn looked so incredibly wrecked. His collar was unbuttoned and his sleeves loosely rolled up. He had a five o'clock shadow that was almost designer stubble and his hair was standing on end, as if he'd combed it with his fingers many times.

And, heaven help her, but he'd never looked more attractive. On any level that Hazel could think of and both her body and heart were automatically responding. She wanted to smooth his ruffled hair. Offer him comfort and reassurance that everything was going to be okay. And, yeah…there was a ridiculously strong desire to drift close enough to try and find out whether kissing him would make the world and its problems vanish, at least for a little while.

The desire was not only ridiculous because Finn's girlfriend had only just walked out of the door and she knew how horrified Finn would be if she hit on him, it was totally inappropriate given that the man was holding a whimpering infant on one arm as he led Hazel into the living area of his apartment, trying unsuccessfully to get Ellie to accept the bottle of milk at the same time.

'It might work better if you sit down,' Hazel suggested.

To his credit, Finn didn't ask her to take the baby. He did sit down and he tried again, by slotting the teat into a tiny mouth that was wide open in mid-howl. Some milk dribbled in but got spluttered out and the intensity of the howling increased. Hazel managed to resist the urge to step in and help—until Finn looked up and she could swear she saw tears in his eyes.

'I'm hopeless at this,' he said.

Hazel was quite sure she could actually *feel* her heart melting as a liquid warmth spread through her body. Nothing on earth could have stopped her trying to help. Trying to do whatever it took to make Finn at least a little happier.

She sat on the sofa beside him and took the baby into her own arms. For a moment, she just held the infant against her heart and jiggled her, bending her head to murmur a bit of soothing baby talk and finally planting a kiss on those astonishingly soft curls. She touched Ellie's cheek with the teat of the bottle and then, as the baby opened her mouth and turned her head sideways, it felt as if it was her choice to accept the milk and it wasn't being forced on her.

The moment that the howling changed to sucking noises, Finn dropped his head back against the couch and let out a loud sigh.

'Thank you,' was all he said.

They sat there in silence for a minute. And then another. And it seemed as if an out-of-control world was also pausing to let out a bit of a sigh. Hazel was sinking into the feeling of holding this baby in her arms. She was also very aware that Finn was sitting right beside her. She could almost feel the warmth of his thigh so close to her own. If she moved, just a fraction, they would be touching…

Hastily, she broke the silence to shut down that thought. 'So…tell me what's been happening. I gather Shannon's not very impressed with developments?'

Finn's hand gesture dismissed his beautiful girlfriend as totally irrelevant and Hazel couldn't help a frisson of relief. He deserved a real relationship—with a real person—not something that was as staged as food photography for a recipe book.

'I talked to the police. And someone from Social Services. We agreed that the important thing was to keep the baby safe and that, if there is a family connection, the mother might be more likely to approach me than official channels and also that it could be easier to put Elena into foster care than take her out again immediately so they were prepared to let me look after her.'

'Wow…' Hazel was impressed that Finn had even considered it as an option. 'That was brave.'

Finn had covered his eyes with his hand and was rubbing his temples with his thumb and middle finger.

'It's only for a day or two. Maybe three. I also got hold of the guy who knows about the DNA testing and he came and took swabs from me and Elena. I've paid a considerable amount for an urgent service, which can be through in forty-eight to seventy-two hours if I'm lucky. It might be a lot less time than that if whoever left the baby comes back for her.'

Hazel's gaze drifted to the bags on his kitchen counter in this open plan living area. 'I know I was out of town for a good few hours, but how on earth did you manage to fit shopping in? You've even got a car seat there. Did Anna help?'

'No. It was the woman from Social Services—Margaret. She's been really helpful. Anna did call, though. She wanted me to know that your spaniel is doing really well. He woke up, had a drink of water and even wagged his tail. She topped up his analgesia and he should sleep through the rest of the night now. There's no need for you to go in.'

'Okay… I guess I can stay here and help you, then.'

When Finn shook his head, it felt like a rejection. But then he took a deep breath. 'I can't stay here,' he told her. 'Not with the media camped outside. The mother of this baby—or possibly the father, as you suggested—would be just as unlikely to go near them as turn up at a police station. They could well be scared of getting into trouble. I'm not about to give any press statements, either—not until I know what I'm actually dealing with and I won't know that until the DNA results come through.'

'What will you do when you know?'

'If Elena's no relation to me, we'll go public and try and find her mother.'

'And if she is?'

Finn met her gaze with a direct look that was unlike any Hazel had ever seen before. It looked, oddly, as if he'd just grown up a whole lot more.

'If she is my grandchild, then I'll step up and do the right thing.'

Oh… Hazel couldn't tell him how proud she was of this new attitude. There was relief to be found as well because she hadn't been that blinded by how she felt about Finn. He *was* a good person, beneath the celebrity exterior. Someone it wasn't stupid to be more than a bit in love with.

'That's where you come in,' Finn said.

She couldn't meet his gaze in case he saw even a flash of what had just gone through her head. 'Oh…?'

'I'm going to go out to my weekend place. The house I've got up in the Blue Mountains and I'll lie low there with the baby until we know which direction this is going to go in. I'm hoping we can sneak out the back and use your van and that way we'll escape any attention from the paparazzi camped out the front.'

Hazel had heard about the property Finn had purchased some time ago. There'd been pictures of it in a magazine article and she knew it was only a little further into the mountainous region than Two Tails. It was quite a long way to go to offer what would be a taxi service for a man and a baby, mind you, but Hazel found herself nodding slowly. This was a way she could offer some real help—to someone she cared about far more than was probably wise.

'I'm also hoping that you'll stay there with me,' Finn added. 'At least for just one night?'

Just one night…

It sounded like the title of a romantic movie or a book.

Just One Night
A fantasy starring James Finlay from
Call the Vet
Also starring newcomer Hazel Davidson
Oh…and a cute baby

'I know you've just done that round trip but I can drive out there.' Finn sounded hopeful. 'And it would be much more sensible to stay the night than driving back again, wouldn't it? I gave my housekeeper a call a while back and she's made sure there are beds made up and food in the fridge.'

Hazel found herself smiling wryly. She'd already known better than to buy into any fantasy but that tiny moment in time had been rather delicious. Finn interpreted her smile rather differently.

'You'll do it?' There was more than hope in Finn's tone now. It sounded almost like excitement. 'Oh, man… I can't tell you how grateful I am.' Finn leaned sideways and planted a kiss on her cheek. 'I love you, Hazel. You're the best friend anyone could have.'

The friend zone. It was better than no zone at all, wasn't it? It was a bit of a warning bell that a platonic kiss on the cheek could send spirals of sensation all the way to the tips of Hazel's toes but how could she possibly let Finn down? He needed her and she couldn't deny that it felt good. Something had changed between them since this drama had begun unfolding. Hazel had felt like he was seeing her properly for the first time. She was also seeing something new in Finn. A maturity that she hadn't noticed before. And that moment when she'd seen what looked like tears in his eyes as he admitted how out of his depth he was? Well…that kind of felt like a glimpse of the man behind the image that James Finlay presented to the world. Possibly to himself as well?

Whatever. Something was changing. Something important.

Hazel was holding a now soundly sleeping baby. She got to her feet and put Ellie carefully back into a nest that had been made with cushions at one end of the sofa and tucked the fuzzy duck blanket around her. Then she straightened her back and smiled at Finn. Properly, this time.

'Let's get this show on the road, then, shall we?'

CHAPTER FIVE

In the first soft light of dawn, Hazel opened the French doors in the bedroom she'd used in James Finlay's country house and stepped out…into a fairy tale. Well, she'd actually stepped out onto a veranda, but it was a supersized version of the one she loved at Kiara's cottage and the difference wasn't just in how enormous it was. Or the generous scattering of gorgeous wicker couches and chairs with soft cushions that were begging to have someone curl up in them and chill. They were just part of a much bigger picture. Another dimension, almost.

The wrought iron lace on the outside edge of the roof provided an anchor for a wisteria vine that must have been growing for decades to have become so luxuriant. White racemes of fragrant flowers that had to measure half a metre created a curtain through which Hazel could catch glimpses of neatly clipped box hedges in a formal rose garden, a pond, fenced paddocks that looked like lawns and tall, tall gum trees that marked the edge of untouched bushland.

The scent of the flowers was intoxicating. So was the sound of birdsong including the laughter of a kookaburra, as the Blue Mountain wildlife woke up, until it was drowned out by the screech of cockatoos. Hazel couldn't see the yellow crest on their heads, but the flash of white wings was spectacular and she followed their flight until they settled on the branches of one of the massive gum trees, making it look like large, pale flowers had suddenly bloomed.

'Sleep well?'

Hazel jumped, her head turning swiftly to the figure who'd walked around the next corner of a veranda that could well be wrapped right around this enormous, colonial house. She hadn't taken much in by the time she and Finn had finally arrived here at nearly two a.m. after their dramatic, secret escape from his apartment that had been like being photoshopped into a spy movie.

'I went out like a light,' she confessed. 'I'm sorry I didn't help you get Ellie to bed.'

'Bed? What's that?' Finn's smile was crooked and he looked even more rumpled and unkempt than he had when Hazel had seen him yesterday evening after responding to his plea for help. 'I did put her in the cot. I even started to get ready for bed myself but…it didn't quite work out.'

'Mmm…' Hazel was taking in the rest of Finn's appearance now. He had bare feet beneath his jeans and a shirt that was completely unbuttoned. The only part of his chest that wasn't revealed was the bit that was covered by a bundle of blanket wrapped baby lying on one arm. A baby that was making hiccupping sounds, which could either be the end or beginning of a much louder session of misery.

The shadow of beard on Finn's face was even darker in this early light and there were deep lines at the corners of his eyes, as if it was hard work to be keeping them open. Hazel felt guilty that she'd had a few hours of deep sleep in the most comfortable bed ever. She also felt a rather powerful blend of pity and pride for Finn, who was facing up to what had to be an overwhelming challenge—one that he could have easily sidestepped by handing Ellie over to Social Services and an experienced, emergency foster family.

'Let me take her,' she offered, reaching out for the baby. 'You might feel better after a shower?'

'She might kick off again if I move her and this is the quietest she's been in more than an hour. Coffee is what I need. If you could bring me a large mug—black, no sugar—I would be eternally in your debt. Oh…and Beanie here will be needing another bottle, I expect.'

'Beanie?'

'It's that hair. It looks like a hat. Have you ever seen a baby with so much hair?'

'She could give a labradoodle puppy a run for its money in the cute stakes, that's for sure.' Hazel resisted the urge to touch the baby, who was still making squeaking noises. 'Coffee it is. I'll be back in no time.'

Hazel was smiling but she was also backing away, relieved to have a mission that meant she could duck into her bedroom on the way. How had she not registered that she was wearing her pyjamas? Soft, silky harem style pants and a clingy singlet top that did nothing to disguise her top half. It had, in fact, not done enough to actually cover her top half with that gap of a couple of inches between its hem and the elastic of the pants. She hadn't brushed her hair, either, so she had a tangle of mousy frizz brushing her bare shoulders and it hadn't occurred to her to even splash water on her face before greeting the day, let alone try and improve her appearance with a kiss of any makeup.

It all added up to the horrific thought that she might as well have been naked. Not that Finn had seemed taken aback in any way, fortunately, but he was too shell-shocked and exhausted to notice and, besides, he'd never seen her as potentially physically attractive anyway, had he? Hazel threw on the same clothes she'd been wearing since she'd changed out of her scrubs yesterday, dragged a comb through her hair and was securing it into a messy bun as she went off to look for the kitchen she vaguely remembered Finn pointing out when they'd arrived here in the early hours of this morning.

'Make yourself at home,' he'd said. 'What's mine is yours.'

And wouldn't that be a dream come true? Hazel thought. Her bedsit apartment could have slotted into any one of these wide hallways with their high ceilings, let alone the huge rooms leading off them. Polished wooden floors had beautiful rugs and there were so many windows there was already enough light to know that the house would be flooded with sunshine later in the day. The kitchen had a flagged, stone floor and a French country theme that could have—and probably had—been photographed for some 'home and living' magazine.

A huge, double-door fridge was well stocked with food and a walk-in pantry looked like a miniature supermarket. Hazel had no clue how to drive what looked like a commercial coffee maker, but she found a plunger jug and a tin of what smelled like freshly roasted and ground beans. She put some wholegrain bread in a toaster and then tackled a mess on the bench that was a clear sign that Finn had been making up baby formula under stress in the last few hours. She had no idea what he might like on his toast, so she went with what had long been comfort food for herself.

The way Finn's face lit up when he saw the plate

piled with toast and its covering of melted butter and a generous amount of crunchy peanut butter gave Hazel a surprising jolt of pleasure. She put the tray down on a table beside the chair he was sitting on.

'I thought you might need some sustenance.'

Finn was carefully lifting a mug of coffee, keeping it well away from the baby. He closed his eyes as he took a sip and then another. When he opened them, he was looking directly at Hazel, his gaze so warm, she could feel the heat.

'Perfect,' he murmured. 'Thank you.'

'You're welcome.' Hazel picked up her own mug and shifted her gaze before she could start reading something that wasn't there in the warmth of that look. 'Oh… Are those kangaroos in that paddock?'

Finn spoke around a mouthful of toast. 'Yep. I often see them at this time of day.' He swallowed his mouthful. 'Not often enough, to be honest. Every time I do get out here I wonder why I don't do it every weekend. Or live out here and commute. I love this place.'

'It's gorgeous,' Hazel agreed. She helped herself to a piece of the toast. 'What do you use the paddocks for? Do you have horses?'

Finn shook his head. 'I have a couple who manage the place for me who have a farm nearby. Sandra does the housework and shopping and so on. Her husband looks after the grounds. He mows the paddocks with his tractor to keep them tidy.' His eyes drifted shut, not to savour the taste of anything this time—it looked as if he simply couldn't keep them open any longer.

'Why don't you go and get a few hours' sleep?' Hazel suggested. 'I'm not rostered on for the morning clinic and I'm only in Theatre for a few routine desexing surgeries early this afternoon so I can look after Ellie for a bit. Give her some breakfast and a bath, perhaps. I guess you'll be wanting to come in with me in the van to pick up your car?'

But Finn shook his head. 'I don't want to go near my apartment building. I really don't want this getting splashed all over the media. Which means I'll probably have to stay away from work, too, even if it's where Beanie's mother might go to make contact. I'll give Nigel and Anna a call later and sort out cover.' He was watching Hazel as he spoke. 'I could organise cover for you, too…'

She raised an eyebrow. 'Why? I'll be back in the city in plenty of time to go home and get changed and still be early enough for any pre-operative checks before surgery.'

Finn was holding her gaze over the sleeping baby. 'I thought I might be able to persuade you to hang around for a day or two.'

'What for?' Hazel mentally stomped on an errant flash of hope that Finn genuinely wanted more time with her simply because he liked being with her by deliberately frowning. 'Oh, I get it. You want me to look after Ellie for you. You need a babysitter?' She broke the eye contact, reaching for a piece of toast even though eating something was the last thing she really wanted to do. 'Reality's a bit of a shocker, isn't it?'

The reminder of yesterday's accusation that he was fake wasn't fair.

Thanks to how exhausted he currently was, it was actually rather hurtful. He was doing his best here and he'd made a point of not disturbing Hazel's sleep in the last few hours as he tried, and failed, to get the baby to settle.

He just wanted her company. Was that so weird? He wanted to be with someone who could share the trauma of the current crisis in his life. Someone he felt comfortable enough to be around when he looked like hell and was only half dressed. When they were in their pyjamas and there wasn't even a hint of any underlying sexual agenda—although, to be completely honest, it had been a rather pleasant surprise to see more of Hazel than he ever had before. More importantly, she was someone who somehow knew that peanut butter toast was his favourite guilty pleasure. And Hazel had never been overly impressed with his fame or fortune, either. He knew she didn't follow him on any social media platform and she certainly had no connection to any of the groups he mixed with in his fast-moving, A-list social life.

And the clincher? He now realised that Hazel could see right through him despite his oh, so carefully constructed persona. She was quite probably the only person who could recognise what was still there deep inside and, while it was just as much of a shock as having a baby land on his doorstep, a part of Finn couldn't deny that it might be a good thing that someone had the guts to call him out on how he was living his life. Did he *want* someone to see him for who he really was? Or had been, anyway?

No. That part of his life had been left behind long ago.

Until now, anyway. Until a baby named after the girl who'd pretty much saved his life turned up. Finn shook his head to dismiss that flash of thought and the action prompted him to speak with absolute sincerity.

'No way. I would never ask you to babysit. I'm taking total responsibility for Beanie. It's just that… I don't know, it's going to be a lonely couple of days out here by myself and… I kind of like the idea of spending some time with you. Away from work. We've never really done that, have we?'

Her gaze grazed his. Just long enough for him to register the same feeling he'd got when she'd reacted to his suggestion that she hung around for a day or two. He hadn't been able to interpret her expression but whatever it was, it had morphed into suspicion with that frown. This time, she looked away before he had any hope of gauging her reaction but it might not have made any difference, he decided. Women were experts in hiding what was going on in their heads, weren't they?

'I just thought you might like a change of scene. How long is it since you had a few days off?'

'A while,' Hazel admitted.

'What did you do with them?' Finn was genuinely interested. 'Where did you go?'

Hazel smiled. 'Not far. I was helping Kiara build some new pens out at the refuge.'

Ah…the refuge. Hazel's passion. Finn was having a lightbulb moment and it centred around the dog she'd named after a treasured pet in her childhood.

'You know how you said you'd rescue Ben if you didn't live in a bedsit?'

Hazel really looked startled by this turn in the conversation. Wary, even. 'Yeah? So…?'

'Bring him here,' Finn suggested. 'You could look after him here until he's sorted.'

Hazel was staring at him as if he was talking nonsense. 'Ben's hardly going to be sorted in a couple of days. I'll have to take him to Two Tails even if it's not ideal. Kiara has way more than she needs to deal with at the moment.' Her sigh was heartfelt. 'And I'm responsible for a rather big part of that after what happened yesterday.'

'What happened?' Finn could feel himself frowning. How could Kiara have been affected by the dramatic events that had unfolded in his own life yesterday?

'I was on my way to see her after...' Hazel looked away. 'After I left work.'

That hesitation was telling. What she meant was, after she'd walked out having discovered how disappointing a person Finn was.

'I found an abandoned dog on the side of the road. A really horribly abused dog. I took it to Two Tails because there wasn't anything else I *could* do and now Kiara has got a dog on her hands that's going to take all the time and energy she's got and all the money she *hasn't* got for weeks and weeks.'

'So it would be a lot better if you could look after Ben.'

Hazel shrugged. 'As I said, a couple of days wouldn't make much of a difference.'

'You *could* stay here for as long as you like,' Ben said. 'I hardly ever get the chance to come out here and it's a shame that a place this beautiful doesn't get used.' This was the first time Finn was feeling guilty about it, however. Was that because he could suddenly see it as Hazel might see it? As an advertisement of wealth and privilege that was no more than a staged background for part of a perfect life?

Hazel wasn't saying anything. She was staring straight ahead of her even though there was nothing much to see through the dangly flowers other than his empty paddocks.

'So...you'd let me live here with Ben until he was

well enough to rehome? In return for keeping you company and helping out with Ellie?'

Finn nodded.

'We could cover each other if there was something urgent to do in the city. You could do your surgery this afternoon and then come back out, with Ben. And whatever else you need to get settled here. I could go in if… if there was something important to do.' He caught the look Hazel gave him. 'I'm not talking about media stuff. I meant talking to the police or a solicitor or something. I still have no idea what I'm going to do if those DNA results come back positive.'

'Mmm.'

There was a thoughtful silence that hung in the air between them. Hazel looked away and then back to hold his gaze. 'Those empty paddocks…' she murmured. 'In particular, that one with the stable block…'

Finn blinked. 'Yes…?'

'You remember that donkey I told you about? The one with the feet that are so bad it can't walk? Could it come too—if another place hasn't been found yet? For as long as I'm here with Ben?'

She was clearly bargaining but Finn was prepared to do whatever it took, within reason, to persuade her to stay. It wasn't as if she was asking for something for herself—she was obviously going to base her decision on how many other creatures she could help. How many people would do that?

Nobody could accuse Hazel Davidson of being fake. What you saw was what you got. A warm, compassionate, genuine human being who was also intelligent and a highly skilled professional. It felt like something was melting a little, deep inside Finn's chest. She was special, that was what Hazel was. Funny, but he'd never noticed before that her eyes matched her name. A golden, hazel brown with shiny flecks in them that matched the glints in her hair the sun was just beginning to catch as it rose high enough to see over the gum trees. She had a cute nose, as well, come to think of it, and lips that looked…really soft. Kissable, even…? Good grief… that startling thought needed to be pushed away as fast as possible.

'I think that can be arranged,' he heard himself say, relieved at how calm he sounded, given what he'd just been thinking about. 'When I've had a shower, I'll ring Sandra. They keep horses and I know they've got a float. I could probably arrange for them to go and collect the donkey. They'll know a good, local farrier, too, who could start treating its feet.'

The bundle in his arms was starting to feel very damp. It was also starting to squirm and he could see a small face getting rather red as the energy was gathered to communicate the need for a clean nappy. Or breakfast. Or maybe just a change of carer. It felt like pressure, anyway, and it was enough to trigger an alarm bell—maybe one that had already started ringing when he'd had the astonishing notion of Hazel Davidson being kissable.

'As long as I don't end up having to look after them,' he added as a warning. 'I have a rule about dependants. Like pets or kids or wives. I don't do them. Not on a long-term basis. Not on any basis, really…'

And yet here he was, with a baby in his arms and hoping, rather a lot, that he was about to get a woman as a companion twenty-four-seven for the immediate future, along with an injured dog and a lame donkey. Was he out of his mind?

But Hazel was smiling at him and, for some reason, Finn was feeling a lot better than he might have expected.

'Wives? Plural?' Her smile widened. 'I'm learning quite a lot about you, Dr Finn.'

'So you're going to stick around?' He thought that smile was already giving him the answer he wanted but he needed reassurance. 'You might learn even more of my secrets.'

'How could I resist?' Hazel stood up and came to take the baby from his arms. 'Now, go and have that shower. And take a nap. We'll sort everything out if the offer's still there when you're not totally sleep deprived.'

Finn smiled back at her.

He wasn't going to change his mind. Having Hazel around to share the roller coaster he had a feeling this crisis could well become was nothing short of a lifeline.

When Hazel took the small, heart-shaped silver frame from her bedside table and put it with the items she considered essential for at least the next week or so, it felt as if she were leaving her bedsit apartment behind for ever because she was taking her most precious possession with her—the photo of her first dog called Ben.

When she gently settled her second dog called Ben into the back of her van and began the return journey to Finn's beautiful property in the Blue Mountains, it felt like…

Oh, help…it felt as if she were going home.

She wasn't. She needed to remember that this was temporary. She might be going to be living a fantasy for as long as it took Ben to recover from his surgery and for his broken bones to heal but she'd better not get too used to it. At some point, she would have to find a new home for Ben and return to her bedsit and her fulltime job at Coogee Beach Animal Hospital. She would also need to find a new home for that donkey, as well. What on earth had she been thinking making a new rescue animal part of the deal?

Finn had run a staff meeting via video link when Hazel had gone in to work at lunchtime. The staff all knew about yesterday's drama of the baby being abandoned and Finn's popularity was evident in their willingness to do whatever they could to help. Everybody was put on alert for any potential contact from anyone associated with the baby, with instructions to be non-judgmental and quick to offer any assistance asked for. Both Hazel's and Finn's workloads were picked up by others until further notice, with plans to review strategies once the results of the DNA tests made the situation clearer.

'It just goes to show,' Hazel said when she phoned Kiara on her way out of the city, 'that it wouldn't be that hard for me to get some time off for personal reasons. Not immediately, maybe, what with this baby crisis, but sometime soon—so if you change your mind about taking that job offer with the uncle I'd be able to look after Two Tails.'

'I won't be changing my mind,' Kiara said. 'I don't even like the guy and I don't have a suitable dog, anyway. Bunji's not going to be fit to rehome for a very long time. If ever.'

'How is she today?'

'It's still touch and go. I can't even think about anything else.'

'Did someone call you to get the details about that donkey?'

'Yes.' She could hear a wry smile in Kiara's tone. 'How on earth did you persuade Finn to let you do that?'

'I thought Ben and I would need some company. We could be there for quite a while. He'll have to have his activity restricted for the next eight to ten weeks. I imagine the baby business will be sorted within the next few days and then Finn will be back in his penthouse at the beach. You should see his house, Kiara. It's one of those amazing colonial mansions. Actually, you *could* see his house. It's not that far from Birralong. Fifteen minutes' drive at the most.'

'I'm not going anywhere if I can help it. Not until I know that Bunji's going to make it. How's Ben doing?'

'I'm happy with how it's going. He's still groggy after the anaesthetic and we had to carry him outside to toilet but…he's a lovely old boy. I think he recognised me when I went in to collect him. Or maybe he just loves everybody.'

'I doubt that, after the way he's been treated. He must trust you. Hey, I need to go and look after Bunji. Good luck with getting Ben settled. Call me if I can help.'

Finn was only too happy to help Hazel get Ben settled in. He helped her unbandage the dog's leg to check his surgical wound and then redress it, offered the leftover poached chicken from his lunch for Ben's first meal, carried the little dog outside himself to do his business and then found a way to barricade the door to a laundry area to give the dog a safe, confined space to sleep.

It felt good to be able to help with Ben. It put them on a more even footing and he didn't feel guilty about asking for Hazel's help with the baby because that help went on for many hours before the baby was finally asleep in the bassinette that Finn had had delivered today, along with many other items from a Sydney baby shop. It felt good to be making toasted sandwiches and choosing one of the better wines from his extensive cellar to have a very late dinner ready for Hazel after she'd unpacked the last of the things she'd brought from her apartment to make her stay here more comfortable.

Oddly, though, Hazel didn't look too happy at the offering he'd arranged on one of the wrought iron tables on the veranda. He'd even remembered to turn on the fairy lights that were wound through the wisteria vine on the fretwork and, even if he did say so himself, he thought he'd set up an irresistibly attractive corner. A scene with the kind of romance that most women loved.

'You don't drink red wine? I can find something white? Or champagne? Or don't you like cheese toasties?'

Hazel laughed. 'Are you kidding? Who doesn't love cheese toasties? I was just surprised, that's all.'

'Okay…' Finn picked up a glass of wine and sat down. 'I get it. Sorry—I'm just not much of a cook and Ben ate the last of the chicken Sandra made for my lunch.'

'Oh, I didn't mean I expected you to cook.' Hazel put the baby monitor down on the table and picked up one of the sandwiches, a handful of serviettes and the other glass of wine. She gave Finn an apologetic glance as she sank down onto the feather-stuffed cushions on the other end of the couch. 'I was just surprised because bread was totally forbidden the last time a man made my dinner and…oh, wow…this is *so* crispy. Did you fry these rather than toast them?'

'Yes. There's bacon in there as well.' But Finn was frowning. 'You're not gluten intolerant or something, are you?'

'Not at all. It was just the latest diet I was supposed

to be on. Wasn't my idea.' Hazel smiled at Finn and then took a bite of the sandwich. 'Mmm…this is delicious.'

Finn said nothing but he was thinking fast. Who on earth would have been trying to force Hazel to follow a diet she didn't want? More than one diet, even, if going without bread was part of the 'latest' one. A boyfriend, perhaps? Come to think of it, he'd met Hazel's partner a long time ago, at some work function and…he hadn't liked him much at all.

'What was his name?' he said aloud. 'That tall, skinny guy you were living with when you first came to work with me?'

'Michael.' Hazel reached for her wine glass. 'But I didn't say it was him that wouldn't let me eat bread, did I?'

'*Was* it?'

Hazel shrugged, not meeting his gaze. 'He's long gone. It really doesn't matter now.'

But Finn had the feeling that it did. He was suddenly glad that he hadn't made her a plate of salad for dinner. He was also feeling mortified on Hazel's behalf that someone she had been in a relationship with had been trying to change her in such a blatant manner. How could it not make you feel like you weren't good enough the way you were?

He didn't know Hazel well enough to try and offer some kind of reassurance, though, so he simply smiled as she took another bite of her sandwich.

'Good?'

'Mmm.'

They sat there in companionable silence after that, until Hazel had eaten all she wanted and was stifling a huge yawn.

'Go to bed,' Finn said. 'I'll take the monitor and get up if Beanie starts crying.'

Hazel shook her head. 'I'm happy to get up. That way, I can check on Ben, too.'

They both stood up at the same time. They both reached for the monitor handset at the same time. They both pulled away as their hands touched but then they both smiled at each other.

'You can have it tonight,' Finn conceded. 'I'll have it tomorrow night. After that, we might not need to fight over it.'

Weird that it felt like getting this crisis sorted and baby Elena back to where she belonged might happen too soon. He felt like he was just getting to know Hazel a lot better. And he liked it. He liked it a lot.

Finn's smile faded. He was standing very close to Hazel and she was still smiling at him. Without thinking he reached up and touched her cheek with the back of his forefinger.

'It's a good thing that Michael is long gone,' he said. 'The guy was a complete jerk.'

There was something in Hazel's gaze that he'd never seen before despite it looking like something that could have been there for ever. Something…lost? It made him want to take her into his arms and hug her. Instead, he just held her gaze.

'Don't let anyone think you're not beautiful just the way you are,' he added softly. 'Because it's not true.'

It felt like time had stopped. Or maybe Hazel had just frozen, shocked by what he was saying. She didn't believe him, did she? But what else could he say that might convince her?

Maybe he didn't need to say anything. The idea of showing her was a lightbulb moment, like tempting her to stay here by offering a place for Ben to recuperate. Only this flash of inspiration wasn't purely intellectual. It was more of a physical thing.

Because...because Hazel really was beautiful and... and he really did want to kiss her.

Just gently. Good grief, he wasn't trying to seduce her or anything. He just wanted her to know that he meant what he'd said. And that she deserved something a hell of a lot better than someone who didn't think she was perfect just the way she was.

And...maybe it was his imagination but it looked as though Hazel *wanted* him to kiss her. She certainly wasn't ducking for cover as his mouth drifted slowly closer to her own. And then his lips brushed hers and it was Finn who felt like he needed to duck for cover because there was a strange sensation that came with that barely-there kiss. A tingle that felt like static electricity or something. A strangeness that was disturbing, anyway.

So Finn backed away fast. He put on his most charming smile, as if that kiss was nothing out of the ordinary for two friends, and turned away to pick up the tray on the table.

'Call me,' he said. 'If you need any help in the night. With Beanie *or* Ben.'

CHAPTER SIX

FINN HAD BEEN gone for many hours. All afternoon and now the evening was ticking on. He'd had urgent meetings that needed to happen face to face. The police apparently had some information for him. Jude and executives from his television show's channel wanted a word and senior staff at the animal hospital were also asking for his attention.

There'd been so much going on out here in the mountains that Hazel had been too busy to wonder what information the police had discovered or why Finn hadn't made contact to say he would be so late back. And she'd been far too busy to let her mind keep drifting back to what had kept her awake for rather too much of the night. Not that she was feeling tired from the lack of sleep, however. If anything, there was a curious source of energy to be found in thinking about it.

A kind of buzz that could be turned on repeatedly. Every time Hazel touched a fingertip to her lips, in fact. Just ever so lightly. With exactly the same pressure that Finn's lips had touched her own last night. Not that it had meant anything, of course. He'd probably been intending to kiss her on the cheek, like he had when he'd told her that he loved her, as a friend whose help he appreciated, and he'd just missed his mark. And, even if it had been deliberate, it certainly hadn't registered as a passionate kind of kiss but…

But it was delicious to remember it.

And it was just as well she was so busy she couldn't spend any time letting her heart try and convince her head that there was any significance to it at all.

Finn's housekeeper, Sandra, had been here for most of the day to help with caring for Ellie, which was just as well, because her husband had arrived this afternoon with the neglected donkey in their float and the farrier had arrived not long after that to tackle the sadly overdue footcare that had taken several hours to complete.

They'd all left a while ago now, but Hazel had needed to feed and bathe baby Ellie and get her settled, she'd given Kiara a quick phone call to share an update on the newly rescued donkey and now she was rummaging in the pantry to find treats, like carrots and apples, that she could mix into the mash she planned to make from feed pellets that had been delivered along with the straw she'd used to line the stable. Sandra had left meat and vegetables roasting in the oven for when Finn finally came back and it would be nice to set a table out on the veranda perhaps, where they could share the meal.

So, there was still plenty to think about and there was no excuse to keep remembering that kiss when Hazel carried the bucket of mash out to the stables in one hand, with the baby monitor handset in the other. Seeing her beloved red van coming down the driveway and knowing that Finn was behind the wheel *was* an excuse to let her brain wander back to that touch of his lips on hers but, even before the vehicle came to a halt, Hazel found herself thinking about something very different.

Something that wasn't delicious at all.

She'd thought Finn had looked wrecked that night

she'd gone to his apartment, with his shadowed jaw and finger rumpled hair. She'd seen him look so vulnerable when he'd confessed how hopeless he felt trying to look after a baby. And, just yesterday morning, he'd been so obviously exhausted it seemed to have stripped yet another layer from what she was used to seeing in Finn but what Hazel was looking at now, as he climbed out of the van, was a combination of all of those impressions. This was a person who was possibly completely shattered. A person she would always be there for even if he was never aware of how deeply she cared about him.

'Oh, my God, Finn…' Hazel's grip on the bucket loosened. 'What's happened?'

His eyes looked so dark in a face that was too pale.

'The DNA results are back. There's no doubt that I'm related closely enough to Elena to be her grandfather.' Finn was pushing his hair back from his forehead yet again. 'They call it the "grandparentage index value".' He gave an ironic huff of sound. 'I've always revelled in getting a high score in any tests I've done but, this time… I'm still trying to get my head around it.'

Hazel nodded. 'Of course you are.' She tightened her grip on the handle of the bucket she hadn't quite dropped. 'Come with me for a minute. I've got something to do in the stables.'

Finn's nod was almost absent-minded as he followed her. 'You need some help? Did the donkey arrive, then?'

'Yes. I've got a bit of a treat for her supper before being left for the first night somewhere new and scary. It's been a big day.'

'Is she okay? Did the farrier come?'

'Yes. And yes. The farrier was amazing. The poor thing could barely walk off the float but he's managed to create almost normal looking hooves. He even had a portable X-ray machine to check the position of the pedal bones before he started. The feet are still too sore to move much at the moment, so I've got her shut in the stable on deep straw, but she'll be able to get out into the paddock in the next few days.'

Hazel kept talking as she led the way to the stables, hoping to give Finn a moment's distraction from his crisis. A moment of calm before a new storm, perhaps, and there was no better place to find calmness than in the company of a donkey.

Sure enough, Finn walked through the straw and began stroking the small grey donkey and scratching her neck just below an enormous ear. The donkey leaned against him and rubbed her head up and down to encourage the petting to continue. Hazel could almost feel some of his stress evaporating, which was exactly what she'd been hoping would happen. This was the first gift she'd been able to think of offering Finn but it felt like she was getting just as much pleasure from its acceptance. Especially when Finn smiled at her like that.

'Friendly little guy, isn't he?'

'He's a girl,' Hazel reminded him. 'Probably around five or six years old and it's possible she's never had her feet properly trimmed. Her elderly owner loved her but had no idea how to look after a donkey and now she's been taken into a rest home and the RSPCA got called in to help with various pets.'

'Has she got a name?'

'Isabella.' Hazel moved closer with the bucket and the donkey lowered its head to sniff the contents. Finn was still smiling as he watched the curious donkey swing her ears forwards but then it faded rapidly.

'The DNA results were just one part of the worst day

I think I've ever had,' he told Hazel. 'I had a journalist hounding me for my comment on Shannon being seen out with another man. Some celebrity chef. It seems like she's backdating the end of our relationship to a point that means she was never involved with a grandfather.'

'She said that?' Hazel was appalled. 'She's spread your private business on social media?'

'No. The official wording is that we've both moved on in an amicable separation but it's only a matter of time until the news is out there. I'm going to have to make some major changes in my life.'

For a long moment, Finn stood there silently, still stroking the donkey, and then he let his breath out in a long sigh. 'What was it that you wanted me to help with? Isabella doesn't seem unwell. She's scoffing whatever's in that bucket.'

'She's fine. I've already given her some more painkillers for her feet. She won't need anything more until morning.'

'Oh…' Finn was frowning. 'I thought that's why you asked me to come out here. To help with the donkey.'

'No…' Hazel's smile was gentle. 'I thought some donkey time might help *you*.'

She was holding Finn's gaze as she spoke so she could see the moment he understood not only why she'd brought him out to the stable but that she'd wanted to help because she genuinely cared about him. About who he really was, not the competent colleague or TV star or even the unexpected grandparent, but the person who was hidden beneath all those layers. The person he'd been right from when he was a small boy and the things in his life that had shaped him into the man he was today.

A man who was still looking shattered.

'Your amazing Sandra made dinner that's keeping warm in the oven. I'm guessing you haven't eaten much today?'

Finn shook his head. 'I haven't been remotely hungry. I haven't told you what the rest of the afternoon threw at me. What the police have found out. About my…about Ellie's mother…'

It was the first time he'd called the baby 'Ellie', Hazel realised. And had he been about to call the baby's mother his daughter? No wonder he was rubbing at his forehead now, as if it might help with shellshocked thoughts that were bouncing around in his head.

'I'm willing to bet you'll feel hungry as soon as you get a whiff of that roast beef and crispy potatoes,' she assured Finn. 'There's even a jug of real gravy that didn't come out of a packet.'

Did he realise that she was offering another pause? A reprieve from having to juggle the onslaught of more than one huge life change that had been thrown at him in the space of a single afternoon? Hazel was more than happy to listen to whatever he wanted to tell her and offer whatever comfort she could, but she was also happy to simply be with him because she knew that it was always better not to be alone when life seemed too difficult. Ben the first had taught her that lesson.

And maybe Finn had also learned that lesson a long time ago because he draped his arm over Hazel's shoulders as they walked back to the house. A casual gesture of friendship, perhaps, but she knew the memory of this touch would get filed in the same special place as last night's kiss. Along with his words.

'Asking you to stay was probably the best idea I've ever had, Hazel. And, you know what…?'

'What?'

She looked up in time to catch the beginning of a smile that grew wide enough to suggest that Finn was gladly accepting the offer of some time out.

'I'm *starving*,' he said.

There was a formal dining room in the house with a gorgeous antique table big enough to seat at least twelve people that had been included in the furnishings when he'd purchased this property, but it didn't occur to Finn to suggest using it tonight. Sitting on antique, spindle-back chairs to eat at the old work table in the kitchen was not just the easiest thing to do—it felt...right. As if he and Hazel did this all the time because it was comfortable and familiar.

Because it was home.

There were interruptions to the casual meal, with Ben needing help to go outside and Ellie needing to be fed and changed and settled into her bassinette, but it didn't matter that the food got a bit too cool or that there was a long gap between the main course and the wonderful, gooey chocolate pudding that Sandra had made. They shared what needed to be done because that felt just as natural as eating in the kitchen. They were a team, weren't they?

And amazingly—given what Hazel had said about how superficial his lifestyle was and that he himself was fake—it seemed that she cared about him. She wasn't here simply because he'd bribed her by offering a place for Ben to recuperate and an opportunity to rescue a neglected donkey.

She really cared, didn't she? Putting two and two together and realising that Hazel had deliberately taken him out to the stables when he'd arrived home in such a state because she knew that being with, and touching, a gentle animal like Isabella could make him feel better had given Finn a weird sort of melting sensation deep in his gut. When was the last time someone had cared enough not only to wonder how he was really feeling but to try and make things better for him?

Probably not since Ellie.

Because he'd never allowed anyone to see how he was really feeling?

It wasn't as though he'd consciously taken down any barriers for Hazel, though. They simply…weren't there… Because he'd known all along that Hazel was the friend he could trust the most, which was why he'd been so desperate for her help with this crisis? Why he still needed her to be close?

It was getting really late by the time Finn poured the last of the bottle of wine they'd shared with their dinner into their glasses.

'We should probably go to bed,' Hazel said. And then she caught Finn's gaze and, to his astonishment, her cheeks flooded with colour as she ducked her head. 'Oh… I didn't mean… I just meant it was late…'

Her reaction was charming, but it was also poignant. Had people in her past, like that jerk Michael, made her doubt how attractive she was to the point that she might think a first move on her part might be unwelcome? Not that Finn had the head space for anything more than a flash of remembering the unexpected attraction he'd felt for Hazel himself because he was still thinking about the way she had revealed how much she cared about him and how that had opened a space where so many other memories had been locked away.

'I need to tell you about Ellie,' he said quietly. 'And about what the police found out.'

He could feel how still Hazel became. How intently she was already listening.

But where to begin? Finn closed his eyes, letting his breath out in a sigh, as he failed to find a logical starting point and then he heard Hazel's soft words.

'You loved her.'

'I reckon she saved my life.' Finn opened his eyes. 'We were in the same class at high school when we were fifteen and we were the kids that everyone felt sorry for. Elena, because her father was known for being vicious and me…well, I was the kid no one had ever wanted, or not for very long, anyway. I started at that school after I'd been moved on to yet another foster home and it was only a matter of time until I got into enough trouble to get sent somewhere else—like juvenile detention, maybe. Ellie caught me one day trying to set fire to the school shed and she told me how stupid I was. That, if I wanted to get anywhere in life, I'd better learn to stay out of trouble.'

He let his eyes drift shut again because these were memories that, even after all this time, still hurt.

'I get it,' Hazel said. 'Not that I did stuff to get into trouble, but it was too hard to hide from what the other kids dished out.'

Finn's eyes snapped open. 'You got bullied?'

'I was the fat kid.' Hazel shrugged. 'Easy target.' She gave her head a tiny shake as if she was done talking about it. 'I wish I'd had someone in my corner like you did.'

Finn almost told her that he wished *he'd* been that someone in her corner. How crazy was that? Instead of saying anything, however, he touched her hand in a simple gesture of connection. She understood the despair of feeling unwanted and that connection meant he didn't need barriers with this woman.

'We had two years together,' he told her. 'And we pushed each other to do well at school because we were both going to conquer the world as soon as we were old enough to escape. We were the best of friends and then we fell in love and then…and then she just disappeared. Her father told me she'd been offered a job in Sydney and what was the point of girls finishing high school anyway and her mother…well, she wouldn't even speak to me. And… I never knew why she'd gone without even saying goodbye. Until now… I think her mother must have arranged it and warned her never to come back because her father would have killed her if he'd known that…that…'

'That she was pregnant…' Hazel finished for him.

Finn nodded. 'The police found a record of Beanie's birth. Isolated outback town. No father mentioned but the mother's name was Jamie Ferrari.'

Hazel's breath caught. '*Jamie?* Ellie named her baby after you?'

The prickle at the back of Finn's eyes couldn't be simply blinked away. Not when Hazel was thinking exactly what he'd thought.

'She loved you, too,' she whispered. 'And it was precious to her that she had your baby. Did she have to give her up for adoption?'

Finn shook his head. 'She still had Jamie with her when she died ten years ago and she was a single mother with no known family so Jamie went into foster care because she was only eight.' He had to swallow hard. 'Talk about history repeating itself.'

The tears that had been forming got big enough to escape his eyes and somehow, Finn wasn't the least bit surprised to see that Hazel was also crying. And it was as natural as anything else that evening that they both leaned close enough to put their arms around each other and stayed in that hug for the longest time.

'You were so right,' he said, finally pulling back so that he could see her face. 'About me being shallow.'

He could feel Hazel taking a quick breath to say something but he didn't let her.

'When Ellie vanished,' he continued quickly, 'I was devastated. And then I was angry. And then I made up my mind that nobody was ever going to do anything like that to me again. I was going to work my butt off and make enough money because that meant the security to do whatever I wanted and that I was going to become *somebody*. Somebody important enough to be special.'

To be loved, he almost added. But he didn't say it aloud because it was too personal. A longing that had been buried deep in his heart for so long it was too hard to share. And he'd got lost somewhere along the way, anyway, so that money and fame and everything that Hazel quite rightly deemed less important in life had taken over. But it seemed that he didn't have to say it aloud in any case, because he could see what looked like complete understanding in Hazel's eyes.

'You are somebody special,' she said. 'And, because you're so well known, your daughter knew where to find you. And I think Jamie will come back because you have something very important in common.'

'What? That we're related? I've never met her. I didn't even know she existed.'

'You both knew Ellie. *Your* Ellie. And you both loved her. You had a baby with her. And Jamie named *her* baby after her. And…' Hazel reached up to brush a tear from Finn's cheek. 'And I couldn't have been more wrong. You're not shallow, Finn. You know exactly what matters most in life—I think you've just been scared of trusting it.'

She got to her feet and held out her hand. 'It's been quite a day, hasn't it? We both need some sleep before Beanie wakes up again.'

Finn took hold of Hazel's hand as he got up. He found he didn't want to let it go when they reached his bedroom door.

'Stay with me?' he asked quietly. 'Please?'

Oh, help… Did she think he was asking for sex? He wasn't. He just wanted to be close enough to feel her warmth and hear her breathing. They could both sleep with their clothes on, but he *needed* to be near her right now. He'd never get to sleep by himself and he didn't want to lie awake for the rest of the night.

'Just…just for company?' he added. 'You're right—it's been quite a day…'

He couldn't read her expression exactly, but it was something soft. A bit like the way she'd looked when she'd suggested he went to the stables with her. That look of caring.

Of a kind of love that was the opposite of anything shallow. Or fake.

Hazel wasn't letting go of his hand, either. Until they both kicked off their shoes and lay down and Finn pulled the duvet over them as Hazel curled up in his arms. He'd never been this close to someone this soft, he realised, as he let his head rest on her shoulder—exhaustion already pulling him towards the blessed oblivion of sleep. Or someone so warm—in every sense of the word. Was this so different because it might be the first time he'd ever invited a woman into his bed for something other than sex? How odd was it that this actually felt more intimate?

More...*real*.

It felt...

Well...it felt like home...

Hazel stayed very, very still in Finn's arms. And she tried, very, very hard, not to fall asleep because she didn't want to miss a second of feeling like this—as if she was the one person that Finn had trusted to tell his story to. The one person he needed to be with him so that he could feel safe enough to sleep. She listened to his breathing as it grew quieter and slower and she could feel the thump of his heartbeat slowing as well as he slid into unconsciousness.

Was he dreaming about Ellie? His first—and his only—true love? Hazel could only begin to imagine how bewildered and heartbroken he must have been when she simply vanished from his life and, when she couldn't fight sleep any longer, she dreamed of a youth who'd pinned his hopes on being able to buy safety, and even love, if only he had enough money and status and her own heart had to be breaking as she slept because she could feel the dampness of tears on the pillow when she opened her eyes at some point before dawn.

She wasn't the only one awake. Hazel had turned in her sleep and she was facing Finn now, instead of having him pressed against her back. His face was only a few inches from her own so the eye contact felt as intimate as a kiss. The intensity of it made Hazel catch her breath, which was when she realised that her breasts were pushed firmly against Finn's chest and... oh, help...her leg was hooked over his and it didn't matter that they were both still dressed because she could feel that Finn was becoming aroused—probably because of the way she was draped all over him—and, oh, man… Hazel needed to find a reason to slip from this bed before Finn found an excuse to move away himself. It would be really great, she thought, if baby Ellie would start crying, like right *now*…

But there was no sound other than the quiet sigh of their breathing. Finn had his arm across the pillow over her head and, just as Hazel had decided she could say she'd better go and check on Ben and/or Isabella, he moved his hand to stroke her hair and any coherent thought evaporated before it could become speech. And then Finn cupped the side of her head and came closer and Hazel was expecting another gentle brush of his lips on hers, a friendly sort of insignificant kiss that could easily morph into an exit strategy, but as soon as she felt his touch it was very obvious that this kiss was going to be nothing at all like the one they'd shared on the veranda the other night.

This…was as real as a kiss could get.

As powerful as a taste of distilled desire and, with the first glide of Finn's tongue against her own, she could feel an edge that was almost dangerous—something wild that had yet to be unleashed. And maybe it shouldn't be unleashed, because it might be only on her side of this physical equation and…

And Finn was looking at her again and it felt as if he was seeing her for the first time ever and he was looking…astonished…

'Where on earth did you learn to kiss like that?' His voice was almost a growl.

'Like what…? It was just a kiss…'

'Are you *kidding*? That's *just* a kiss for you?'

'I'm a bit rusty. It's been a while.' Hazel could feel

her lips curling into a smile because she could hear more than amazement in his tone. She could hear desire. His as well as her own. She could feel it, too. A tension that was building rapidly into something that could very well explode.

'Hazel…'

'Mmm?'

Finn blinked very slowly. 'This might sound weird because I know we've only ever been friends but…but I really want to make love to you.'

Hazel's mouth suddenly felt too dry to make it easy to say anything.

'You can say "no",' Finn added softly. 'It's probably the last thing you'd want, right?'

'Are you *kidding*?'

That tension, on Hazel's side, had already started a countdown to the point where all control would be forfeited. She could only hope that baby Ellie would choose this night to sleep as long as possible after the dawning of a new day. She was the one who was closing that gap between herself and Finn this time and her words were no more than the ghost of a whisper.

'It's the *only* thing I want…'

CHAPTER SEVEN

'SHE'S SMILING AT ME.'

'No way...she's never smiled at *me*.'

'Well, she smiled at me. Look...she's doing it again...'

Hazel put the still sizzling pan of bacon, eggs and mushrooms onto the metal trivet on the kitchen table with a clatter, moving swiftly to peer over Finn's shoulder, leaning close enough for his hair to tickle her ear and for every cell in her body to respond to that feather-light contact with a delicious combination of both desire and blissful satisfaction.

The way those same cells had responded, only an hour or two ago, to every touch given and received in Finn's bed this morning when they'd made love for the first time.

When Hazel's world had changed for ever.

She had to close her eyes for a heartbeat now and simply take a breath. Nothing could ever be the same, could it? Maybe...okay, probably, this new level of her relationship with Finn wasn't going to last. Maybe, for Finn, it was nothing more than a physical connection and maybe she'd never find anyone else that she could feel this way about but something in Hazel had changed for ever.

Because she knew what it felt like to love—and be loved—like that.

And it was adding a whole new, amazing layer to what was currently happening in this kitchen. It had been Finn who'd given his granddaughter her breakfast bottle as Hazel was cooking and he'd remembered to burp her against his shoulder when she was finished. Hazel had been laughing at how proud Finn was of Ellie's ability to burp so loudly but then he'd made the announcement and…

And now it was a moment that was…huge.

Almost seven-week-old Elena Ferrari was smiling and smiling, looking overjoyed at this newfound talent, and her grandfather was smiling back at her and making the sort of nonsense sounds that even the most intelligent adults used to communicate with babies they had totally fallen in love with. And then he looked up to make sure Hazel was sharing the moment and she could see by the way he was blinking back a tear or two that he was just as aware as she was of how huge this was. Maybe he was even feeling some of the lingering magic of their lovemaking adding its own layer to this new bond between them.

Hazel had to blink back the mistiness in her own eyes as her heart overflowed with its own joy in this moment. It was very close to being overwhelming, in fact, because there was nothing she would want to change about her life in this tiny pocket of time. Why would she? She had everything anyone could possibly want. For an odd nanosecond Hazel could imagine looking down on this scene from a long, long way away. She would see a gorgeous house in a beautiful part of the world, a kitchen that was made for family meals and laughter with the aroma of delicious food filling the room, a dog who was lying on the floor nearby—his tail gently thumping the mat—a baby who was smiling for the first time that they knew of and a man who had just become her lover. A man who was a very different person from the man who'd been so shocked that his celebrity lifestyle was about to implode.

But this was the *real* James Finlay right here. The man who had bonded with the daughter of the daughter of his own that he'd never known existed and this tiny baby had broken a barrier around his heart. That was the most important thing that had happened since baby Ellie had landed in their lives but in its wake, by some miracle, Hazel had been allowed into that inner space where she could properly meet the man she had fallen totally in love with. He'd shared things she was quite sure that nobody else knew about and, while they might have been unwanted by their peer group for different reasons as they'd grown up, there was a connection there that Hazel had never found before.

Maybe she'd always been able to see a glimpse of that man and that was why she'd had that instant crush on her employer that she'd had to try and quell ever since she'd started work at the Coogee Beach Animal Hospital. It had made no sense to be so attracted to someone like *Call the Vet* star Dr Finn who would only ever have someone like Shannon Summers as a partner but she'd never been able to make those feelings go away completely and now she knew why.

Her love for Finn was also very real.

The kind that could last a lifetime.

And there was no hiding from that any longer. Not that she was about to scare Finn by telling him how she felt. Not when they were such new lovers and every moment together, especially in bed, had an edge of new-born, miraculous fragility that was too precious to risk damaging in any way. She held his gaze a heartbeat longer, though, the way lovers were allowed to do, so that she could feel the joy of *his* joy.

And to feel a perfection that could never last more than a moment because something would change any second now. Maybe Ellie would stop smiling or Ben would stop wagging his tail or Finn would simply look away or…yep…the toaster popping was enough. But it didn't matter because Hazel knew there would be another moment before too long and it would be just as good—maybe even better.

'There's our toast. Would you like butter or avocado on it?'

'Avo, please.' Finn was smiling down at Ellie again. 'Nom-nom-nom. Avo and bacon and eggs. The breakfast of kings, that's what it is, Beanie. Who knew that our Hazel was such a brilliant cook?'

Our Hazel.

She liked that. She liked it so much it was almost another one of those moments all by itself.

Finn had always known that life had turning points that you could look back on and realise that everything had changed. For ever.

Like that day when he'd been on the verge of deciding that life simply wasn't worth living and maybe he was going to do something about that after he'd torched the school shed and Ellie had appeared from nowhere and torn strips off him for being so dumb and…it had felt as if someone actually cared whether or not he was breathing.

Or the day he'd faced television cameras for the first time as both his life and career took a new direction and he'd loved it because it made him feel important and he suspected it was going to make him a lot richer and they were both the things that mattered the most, weren't they?

Finding Beanie in the pet carrier in the waiting room was the latest turning point and one that was most definitely going to change everything for the rest of his life. He had a family member for the first time ever and she was totally dependent on him.

But was that dramatic moment really the latest turning point?

What about that night he'd made love to Hazel Davidson for the first time?

His gaze slid sideways to where Hazel was sitting in the passenger seat of her van. Finn was driving, because he was enjoying the novelty of using manual gears after only driving automatic cars for so long. The transmission of this vintage vehicle couldn't be considered smooth, of course, but the muscle memory of using the clutch and shifting the gear stick had been easy to tap into and…it was *fun*.

So was making love to Hazel.

The way their friendship had expanded to include this kind of intimacy would have been unthinkable even a couple of weeks ago and yet it seemed like it had always been meant to happen. The way Ellie had been meant to find him that day at school and change his life for ever? No…sleeping with Hazel wasn't that much of a turning point. It couldn't be, because trusting another person to that extent—even someone like Hazel—was a mistake he was never going to make again. Did he need to make sure that Hazel understood? So that she wouldn't get hurt by hoping for something that was never going to happen?

This was about friendship, that was all. And about the unexpected bonus of such great sex…

As if she'd read his thoughts, Hazel ducked her head as if she was a little embarrassed, but she was smiling as she turned to look into the back of the van where Ben was lying in a crate.

'Is he okay?' Finn asked. 'He's not getting too bumped around, is he?'

'He seems happy enough.' But Finn could hear the anxious note in Hazel's voice.

'I think he's doing well,' he said reassuringly. 'The incision's healing beautifully and he's not needing painkillers any longer. It's only a matter of time before he starts trying to put some weight on that leg.'

'So you don't think I need to X-ray him? Will I be wasting clinic time and resources?'

'Not at all.' Finn threw her a smile. 'I think it's exactly what you should do to give you peace of mind about his recovery.'

Plus, it meant that he had the pleasure of Hazel's company for a trip into the city for appointments and Sandra had been only too happy to step in to babysit Beanie.

The reminder of why Hazel was coming with him and that he'd shamelessly used Ben to persuade Hazel to stay with him so he wasn't entirely alone in dealing with a life crisis made him change his mind about that latest potential turning point in his life because it eased his concern that his control of this surprising new level of friendship might be at risk. Hazel knew him well enough to know that it wasn't going to continue for ever, didn't she? Wasn't that partly why she'd accused him of being like Shannon? Being superficial? She knew that Finn didn't *do* relationships like that—or not with women, anyway. Or pets, for that matter, but Ben the dog and Isabella the donkey were also only temporary additions to his lifestyle—a kind of package deal that came with Hazel.

He'd certainly never expected to have a close relationship with a child, either, but he didn't have any choice about that now and, with more than a week of it under his belt, he was starting to get used to it. There were moments he was actually happy it had happened, in fact—like the other morning when Beanie had smiled at him and it had melted his heart. Finn found himself smiling as he remembered that moment, shifting down a gear at the same time to take a sharp curve in the road more slowly.

Making love to Hazel had also been surprisingly memorable, mind you, and not simply because the desire to do so had seemed to come from nowhere with such unexpected strength to it. Or that Hazel had seemed to want the physical connection as much as he did. No…the real revelation had come later. Could it really be that he had totally forgotten what *real* breasts felt like? Everything about Hazel's body was soft and delicious and, best of all, she was the most generous lover in her response and initiation of everything they'd played with on several occasions now. He'd never felt so appreciated in bed.

Loved, even?

No…he wasn't about to go down that track. That was the route to losing perspective. Control, even.

He was confident that he and Hazel were on the same page, here, although a conversation to confirm that, before too long, would probably be a good idea. They were friends who, thanks to Ben needing a place to recuperate, were sharing what was a kind of temporary, forced isolation from the world and normal life, apart from taking turns to go into the city for work commitments or, like today, travelling in together because they both had things they needed to do.

Hazel was going to run a morning surgery session and X-ray Ben's leg and he had an appointment with Jude and TV station executives involved with *Call the Vet* to discuss upcoming shooting schedules, a consultation for a specialist orthopaedic opinion on a dog and an appointment with Social Services early this afternoon. Thinking of those appointments made it easy to forget about a conversation with Hazel that really wasn't a priority. They were clearly both quite happy with what was happening and maybe talking about it could change things.

Finn didn't want to change anything. Not yet, anyway. And, if it wasn't broken, it didn't need fixing, did it?

'I think I might go and collect my own car after my meeting this afternoon,' he told Hazel. 'Surely the paparazzi will have given up staking out my apartment building by now.' He smiled at her again. 'Not that I'm not enjoying driving this relic, but it would be rather nice to reclaim a bit of normality.'

It was only someone like Dr Finn, TV star, who would consider driving something like the latest and most expensive model from Porsche to be normal but Hazel could understand why he was looking forward to driving a vehicle he loved. She found herself wondering what other parts of his life he might be desperate to reclaim. Living in that sleek penthouse apartment with its stunning sea views? Repairing his relationship with Shannon Summers yet again?

Hazel swallowed hard as she pushed that thought away. Deep down, she knew perfectly well that this fantasy she was living wasn't going to last for ever but… she could dream for a bit, couldn't she? Hope was such a seductive emotion and it had been a very long time since she'd felt it was close enough to touch.

Hearing her phone ring was a welcome reprieve from any seed of doubt that was trying to implant itself in her mind although seeing the name on the screen created a new worry. Kiara wouldn't ring at this time of day unless something was wrong.

'Hey…what's up? It's not Bunji, is it?'

'No…she's okay. Not that I've had time to do much with her yet. I'm on my own and there's too much to do. Anyway, I've had a call from the police. They're at a residence in Glenbrook. Elderly person's been found dead and there's a cat…'

Hazel turned to Finn a few moments later. 'Did you notice where that last motorway exit was for?'

'Warrimoo.'

Kiara had heard his response. 'So you're already heading into the city?'

'Into Coogee…' Hazel bit her lip. 'I guess it's not that far to take a detour to Glenbrook.' She turned back to Finn. 'Would we have time to rescue a cat? Owner's been found dead and the police want the cat taken care of. The local vet put them on to Two Tails but Kiara can't leave the refuge right now. Her specialty's rehoming dogs, anyway, but no one else seems available to pick this cat up so if I can go she'll take it.'

'Sure.' Finn glanced at his watch. 'I've got plenty of time before my first appointment.'

Hazel ended the call, having scribbled down address

details, and then she used her phone to find out how far it was to the exit they would need to take.

'Kiara can never say no, even if she doesn't have the time or space. But it sounds like this cat needs a vet, anyway. The police officer at the scene says it won't let anyone near it and it's making funny noises.'

It was a bizarre scene they arrived at a short time later. There were police cars and a hearse parked outside the house and neighbours gathered on the footpath to watch the events that had disrupted their ordinary, suburban normality this morning. The arrival of a small, bright red, vintage van only added to their interest.

'Oh, my God…' Hazel heard someone say. 'Isn't that Dr Finn? From…you know… *Call the Vet*?'

'He'll be here to rescue Mittens,' someone else said. 'Look, he's got a carrier box. And that's just the sort of thing he does, isn't it?'

Well…not quite, Hazel thought, but it seemed he was branching out today. They went into the house to find the funeral home people preparing to remove the body from the house.

'You can't really complain,' a police officer was saying. 'To die in your sleep when you're ninety-four is not a bad way to go, is it?' She turned as Finn and Hazel came in. 'Are you from the animal rescue place?'

'Yes.'

'Cat's over there. Hiding beside the chest of drawers in the bedroom.'

Hazel peered into the dark space between the chest of drawers and the wall and made soothing sounds, reaching in to stroke the cat, but it hissed at her and shrank further back, making odd chirruping noises.

'I'll find my torch. Maybe it's injured.'

Finn knelt down and looked into the space. 'Hey…'

he murmured. 'What's going on, puss? Things are a bit weird around here this morning, aren't they?'

The cat wasn't hissing. Finn kept up his reassuring conversation as he carefully reached into the gap and the sound Hazel heard from the cat sounded like a relieved miaow. One that might even morph into purring?

'She likes you.'

'She's a nice cat,' Finn said. 'A Birman, I think. She's very fluffy and she's got little white socks.'

'Possibly why she's got the original name of "Mittens".' Hazel was smiling as she handed him her phone with the torch app activated. 'Poor thing. She must be really scared at what's happening. Let's get her into the carrier. It'll be a nice, safe space.'

'Um…' Finn was staring into the now well illuminated gap. 'Maybe not just yet.'

'Why not?' Hazel leaned in to see what he was seeing. She had to press her head against his shoulder to get a good view. 'Oh…'

'Mmm… That's a kitten born in the last five minutes, I'd say.'

The tiny creature was stretching miniature legs and had its mouth opening in silent mews. It was an unusual colour with big black spots on a mainly white body.

'So *cute*,' Hazel whispered.

'I don't think she's finished yet,' Finn whispered back. He caught her gaze. 'I think we'd better put our midwife hats on. Looks like she's having contractions.'

'Have you got time? What about that appointment with the TV people?'

'I can let them know I'll be late.' One corner of his mouth lifted in a lopsided smile. 'I think babies are becoming my thing.'

Oh…it wasn't just this baby animal that was impossibly adorable, was it? How could you not love a man who was prepared to dismiss everything in favour of bringing helpless kittens safely into the world?

It was nearly an hour later that Finn picked up each of four tiny kittens to place them, with their mother, in the carrier, which Hazel had made cosy with a hand-knitted rug from a chair in the living room of the house.

'I'm sure she would want her cat to have something that smells familiar with her,' Hazel said. 'She looks like a much-loved pet. I'd better let Kiara know there's more than just the cat that will need rehoming.'

'She'll need watching for the next few days to make sure she's coping with the kittens.' Finn had one of the newborns in the palm of his hand. 'Didn't you say your friend is a bit too busy at the moment?' He held the kitten up, closing his eyes as he very gently touched noses with it. Then he opened his eyes and smiled at Hazel. 'Maybe we should take them all home with us.'

Hazel smiled back. She knew it was a misty smile that was probably inappropriate for a friendship that might include benefits but hadn't earned the status of a significant relationship by any means, but she couldn't stop herself. 'Because babies are your thing now?'

'Temporarily, anyway,' Finn agreed. 'Might as well go with the flow.'

The 'flow' was moving more swiftly than Finn had realised. And the direction of the current was changing unexpectedly as well. Maybe it had had something to do with delivering those kittens that morning. Or possibly, it was due to the fast-paced atmosphere of the meeting he had with the television station executives later that day where ideas were being thrown around about how they could use Finn's popularity to take the show in new directions. Perhaps Dr Finn could go travelling to do stories on unusual animals in different countries? Or, as Jude suggested, he could get involved in rescues that could be with domestic or wild animals. Someone else said that they were fielding requests for him to make guest appearances on both cooking and quiz shows. Finn was wondering, for the first time, if branching out from being the star of a reality veterinary show was really the direction he wanted his career to go in.

Another unexpected swirl in the current of that flow appeared when he got Hazel to drive him to his apartment building when she was ready to head home, with Ben back in his crate and a glowing report card on his healing fracture and Mittens with her kittens in the carrier beside him. He would take his own car to the meeting with Social Services and then follow her out of the city.

'Stop here,' he directed, a little way from his building. He shook his head only a short time after Hazel had parked discreetly. 'See that guy? The one in the leather jacket, leaning on his car?'

'Yes…oh…that's a camera bag on his roof, isn't it?'

'Yeah…and even if I sneak in through the back and get into the basement garage, I'll still have to drive out onto the street right there, by the front entrance and my car's a bit too easy to recognise. He'd be on my tail instantly and the last thing we want is someone following us out of town.'

'Mmm…'

'Keep going,' Finn told her. 'There's a car dealership a block or two away.'

'You're going to rent something?'

'I might *buy* something.' As the words emerged, they felt like the right thing to be saying. 'A Porsche isn't exactly the kind of car you want to be strapping a baby seat into, is it? I'm thinking it might be time to look at, oh, I don't know…an SUV, maybe?'

It wasn't that Finn was really expecting to be adopting his grandchild and bringing her up but he fully intended to be a significant part of her life and he could keep two cars, couldn't he? An SUV for times with Beanie and the Porsche for his own playtime. He glanced at his watch.

'We've got thirty minutes. If I pick one, they might even be able to have it ready for me by the time the meeting's finished.' He grinned at Hazel. 'Come with me?'

'What, to pick the colour of your car or be the taxi to your meeting?'

'Well, I'd certainly welcome your opinion on colour but…' Finn's smile faded. 'But I think you should come to the meeting with me, anyway.'

'What? With the people from Social Services? Why?'

'Because you're just as involved in Beanie's care as I am so you should know what's going on and I'm sure Margaret would love to meet you.'

Of course she would. Who wouldn't love Hazel? And who wouldn't approve of the combination of Hazel and Finn caring for a vulnerable baby? If he'd ever thought of settling down and having a family of his own, then someone like Hazel would be exactly who he'd choose as a partner.

No…not someone like Hazel.

Just… Hazel.

Good grief…where had that thought come from? When only hours ago he'd reassured himself that he was completely in control of what was going on between them and that they were both on the same page? Finn felt like he'd been ambushed by something he'd been avoiding his whole adult life. Hazel would probably be as alarmed as he was by the idea so he owed it to her to dismiss it once and for all. Finn cleared his throat.

'Margaret's great,' he added quickly. 'She's passionate about the kids and babies that she's involved with and she's probably in her sixties, I guess, so she's seen it all before.' Hunching down in the passenger seat as they drove past the photographer waiting outside the apartment block was just the distraction he needed to entirely dismiss that weird idea he'd had of choosing Hazel to be the mother of the children he was never planning to have.

'He didn't see you,' Hazel assured him.

'Good.' Finn let his breath out in a sigh as he straightened up. 'I'm getting to the point when I'd prefer to get on with making this public so I'm hoping they're going to find Jamie soon. We don't want to scare her off because having her involved will make things a lot more straightforward. We can do whatever needs doing to help her look after her baby but, if that's not going to happen, it would be easier if she was part of an adoption process that would let me do it.'

'You're planning to *adopt* Beanie?' Hazel's swift glance was astonished. 'You'd bring her up yourself?'

'If that's what it takes,' Finn said. 'I need to protect her.' He pulled in a deep breath. 'I'm not going to let her grow up thinking that she wasn't wanted.'

Like he had been…

Maybe like her own mother had felt…?

This was where it would stop. History was not going to repeat itself yet again.

Hazel was looking at him again as she stopped for a red light before turning into the street where the car dealership was located. He could feel that she was watching him. And, even though—for some reason—he didn't want to meet her gaze, he knew it was one of those soft looks. That he'd impressed her in some way. That she liked what she was seeing. It gave him an odd curl of something in his gut. Pride? Maybe. It was something nice, anyway, but he didn't want too much of it.

Because it was an emotional gift from someone else and it was better not to accept them. Because they couldn't be trusted. Sometimes they got taken away again. Sometimes, people just took them and walked out of your life. For ever.

But this was Hazel and, deep down, Finn knew she would never walk out on anybody she cared about. Because she knew what it was like to not be wanted, too. Not that he'd pushed her to talk about how badly she'd been bullied at school but it was easy to see that her confidence came through caring for others and that she shrank back if the spotlight was turned on her. Like the way she'd been flustered when she'd seen something in his face that told her he was thinking something nice about her. About how much fun it was to make love to her…

Oh…that did it. If she was still looking at him when he turned his head, she might have to accept an emotional gift from *him*. But even as the thought formed the light was changing and the van was moving again. And Finn had to admit it was kind of a relief to have their interaction head back to something entirely platonic.

'Red,' Hazel said firmly. 'Like the colour of this van. You can't go wrong with red.'

The luxury European SUV that Finn took delivery of a couple of days later had been awarded 'Car of the Year' honours for good reason but it was the colour that Hazel approved of the most—a shimmering, metallic red. The dealership had thrown in a state-of-the-art baby car seat that Finn was currently carrying by its handle, with Ellie tucked up inside and clearly so comfortable she had fallen deeply asleep.

'I've decided it's time to road test this contraption,' he told Hazel. 'What are you and Ben up to?'

'We're watching Isabella. The farrier came again yesterday to do some more work on her hooves and… look… I think she's about to come out of the stables. But we've been here for fifteen minutes and she's just standing there watching us.'

Finn was watching Ben, who had slithered under the bottom rail of the fence and was now moving slowly towards Isabella.

'He's touching that toe down now.' He nodded. 'That's good.'

'It is.' But Hazel was frowning. 'I'm not sure it's good that he's in the paddock, though. I've heard donkeys don't like dogs much and I don't want him being chased. Hey… Ben…come here.'

Ben stopped, looked back at Hazel, wagged his tail but then lay down instead of coming back.

'Looks like he needs to think about that,' Finn said. 'I'll go and get him if Isabella doesn't like him. I was going to ask if I can borrow him, anyway.'

'What for?'

'To come into work with me and Beanie.'

'You're taking Beanie into work?'

'Sandra had to go and I have to film a *Call the Vet* episode—we're getting behind schedule. Anna and the others are only too happy to babysit while that's happening and Jude's keen on doing an update on Ben, with me giving him a check-up. I can talk about that X-ray you did the other day and pretend it was just done. The team love the footage of that emergency with Ben's accident and us working on him.'

'Oh…'

Hazel sounded as though she'd prefer to forget about her upcoming appearance on the show and that reminded Finn of why she might be reluctant. And then *that* reminded him not only of just how gorgeous he thought her body was but of that strange thought that hadn't been entirely suppressed. The one about wanting to have a future with Hazel? About her being the mother of children that he'd been so sure he'd never wanted to have? Wanting what they had together at the moment to turn into something he could trust to last for ever, even?

Oh, man…

Finn was confident that Hazel had no idea of what had just landed in his head again but maybe he needed to reassure her as well as himself that there was no pressure here. No expectations.

But then again, he really wanted her company.

Especially today. He'd made plans to try and make it happen, in fact.

'I got Sandra to make us a lovely picnic lunch before she left. Ham and egg sammies and some of that amazing caramel slice she makes.'

Hazel glanced down at the sleeping baby Finn was holding. 'But you're going into work now, aren't you? I don't need to be there until the afternoon clinic.'

'I thought I might be able to persuade you to come in a bit earlier,' he said. 'It's such a gorgeous day and we could have a picnic on the beach.' He offered Hazel his best smile. 'Jude says she's also keen to leave in the mention of your friend's refuge in the episode and follow that up soon so it would be good if you could talk to her about that.'

And that had been the reason she'd been brave enough to be on the show again, hadn't it? To help Two Tails. It might be too late because the last time she'd spoken to Kiara she'd said it sounded like her friend was starting to close things down at the refuge but it couldn't hurt to let people know how expensive it was to run places like Two Tails. If donations were raised, they could always be given to another animal refuge.

'Mmm...'

It was Hazel's unconvinced sound. And it made Finn stop trying to reassure either of them that there was no more than friendship involved here.

'I'd... I'd really appreciate your company, to be honest.'

It worked. She caught his gaze with the same kind of concern he'd seen in her eyes the night she'd agreed to help him when he was floundering so badly looking after Ellie. The kind of care he'd seen when she'd wanted to distract him from his awful day by introducing him to Isabella. The same kind of willingness to be as close as he wanted her to be that he'd seen in her eyes the first time he'd made love to her. A look that should be more than enough to make thoughts of a future with her even more compelling.

Hazel was frowning now. 'What's wrong, Finn?'

'The police think it's taking too long for Jamie to make contact. They think some publicity could help. That's the real reason I'm taking Beanie with me, today. I'm going to out myself as a grandparent later this afternoon and make a public appeal for Jamie to come forward.'

'Wow…' Hazel caught her lip between her teeth. 'That's going to be big news.'

'I'm not looking forward to the fallout,' Finn admitted. 'Right now I think I'm completely over being so well known. I'd rather be here with a baby and kittens and a limping dog and…' He shifted his gaze and a corner of his mouth lifted. 'And…that…'

Hazel turned her head swiftly to see what he was looking at. Isabella was walking towards them and she *wasn't* limping but she did pause to dip her head and sniff Ben, who lay very still and slowly wagged his tail.

'They're making friends,' Finn said quietly. 'How cool is that?'

Hazel smiled back at him. 'So cool…'

Oh… It was just as well that Finn was still holding the car seat or he might have swept Hazel into his arms to hold her as tightly as he could. To tell her just how important she was becoming to him.

To tell her that he loved her?

Not as in being in love with her, of course, because he had been burned too deeply to ever be capable of feeling like that again. But caring deeply about someone was love. Friendship was love, wasn't it?

'*We're* friends.' Finn tried to smile but his lips wouldn't quite co-operate.

'Mmm…'

Hazel had an odd expression on her face. One that he couldn't interpret but he managed to find at least a crooked smile. 'Friends do things like have picnics together, don't they?'

She was turning to watch Isabella, who was on the move again, but Finn could see that her lips were tilting into a smile of her own.

'You know what?' Hazel didn't sound as if she was

aware of any undercurrents to his invitation as she held out the carrot to let Isabella bite the end off.

'What?'

'I think a picnic sounds perfect.'

CHAPTER EIGHT

IT WAS, INDEED, a perfect picnic.

Not just because they could avoid getting sand in Sandra's delicious food by using one of the picnic tables on the grassy area beside the beach. Or that they found a space in the shade beneath a tree so they didn't have to worry about either a young baby or an elderly dog getting too warm in the bright sunshine. Or even that they were within walking distance of work so there was more time to enjoy everything. Like the cloudless sky and soft breeze of a gorgeous spring day, the shrieks of happy laughter from children playing on the grass, building sandcastles on the beach or paddling in the wash of gentle waves and the barking of dogs chasing frisbees or balls. Fortunately, Ben was content to lie underneath the picnic table in the hope of some crumbs falling so he wasn't in any danger of damaging his healing fracture. His hope wasn't misplaced, either. Did Finn really think she couldn't see him slipping tiny slivers of ham and cheese under the table?

And it was Finn who unbuckled Ellie from her car seat and lifted her when she finally woke up and started whimpering.

'Look at that, Beanie.' His hands circled the baby under her armpits as he held her up, turning her towards the beach. 'Can you see those big kids making sandcastles and going in the waves? We'll be able to do that soon, won't we?'

Ellie didn't appear to be impressed as her whimpering got louder. Ben crawled out from under the table to find out what was going on and Hazel put her hand on his head to reassure him that there was nothing to worry about.

Finn lifted the baby high above his head. 'Baby aeroplane…?' He swooped her gently from one side to the other.

She liked that more. The whimpering stopped but there was no hint of a smile yet. Still holding her securely between his hands, Finn dropped her to the same level as his face.

'Boo...' he said.

Ellie looked startled, her eyes comically wide. Then she opened her mouth and Hazel thought she was going to start wailing but, instead, her lips curved into the biggest grin ever and she began to make odd, hiccupping noises.

'Oh, my God…' Hazel said. 'I think she's laughing…'

Finn repeated the lift and drop and elicited another huge grin and the sound effects. This time, Ellie waved her arms up and down as well.

'She wants me to do it again,' Finn said. But, as he lifted the baby past his face, he frowned and then leaned closer to sniff her.

'Uh, oh…'

He hesitated for a split second and then he was grinning again as he changed direction and pushed Ellie towards Hazel instead of lifting her above his head.

'Isn't it your turn in the nappy roster?'

Hazel laughed. 'Uh-uh… Grandpa. It's definitely your turn.'

But she automatically reached out to take the baby and, for a moment, as they transferred her safely they were both holding her at the same time. Holding each other's gazes as well and they were both laughing and…

And it felt like one of *those* moments.

Pure love.

Not simply the love that Hazel had for this man. It was love for the adorable Ellie as well. And for Ben, who had put a paw onto her knee to let her know he was close. For baby aeroplanes and first laughter and the whole background of sunshine and good food and other families enjoying themselves.

Other families…

Yes… Because that was what this felt like.

A family of her own. A perfect family.

The final piece of a puzzle that had been coming together piece by piece, day by day as Hazel fell more and more in love with Finn. After what he'd said earlier today about preferring to be in his country property, in this fantasy they'd created of an idyllic home for children and pets, that seed of hope that had been growing—despite Hazel's determination to be realistic—suddenly sprouted leaves.

Not that Finn seemed to be feeling it, mind you. Hadn't he reminded her that they were simply friends, like they had witnessed Isabella and Ben becoming this morning? And, right now, it simply looked as if he was having fun. He was even laughing.

'Just kidding,' he said. 'But, if you could hold her for a sec, I'll go and get the nappy bag. I left it in the car. Or why don't we pack up and head into work now that we've had lunch? We can change her pants, heat up her bottle, hand her over to Anna and then we'll be all set to get on with the rest of the day.' He was already collecting the food containers to pack away leftovers. 'I know you don't need to start the clinic for a while but I'm sure Jude would love to have a chat with you before we get rolling. And, you could be there for Ben's examination, too, perhaps?'

Hazel shook her head. 'No. You can have all the on-camera limelight this time.' She cuddled Ellie closer. 'I'd rather deal with the dirty pants.'

This felt…normal.

Okay…a bit weird, maybe. Finn had just been outdoors in the warmth of the spring sunshine, seeing the sparkle of it on a gloriously blue sea, and here he was inside, with someone dusting powder on his face so that his skin wasn't going to be shiny under the lights as they filmed enough material to cover a couple of episodes of *Call the Vet* to catch up on scheduling deadlines.

Jude the producer was clearly thinking even further ahead, and she'd cornered Hazel as she was checking her list of patients booked in for the upcoming afternoon surgery hours.

'So…obviously we can't use all the footage of the surgery you did on the old stray dog but…wow…we all absolutely adore what you said about your mate's refuge. We'd call the episode "Two Tales" and find an example of a really heart-warming before and after story. Can you give me the contact details for…what was her name?'

'Kiara. Kiara Brail.' Hazel was sounding cautious, however. 'I don't think she's going to be interested in a television appearance for no good reason, though. She'd only let you in if it was going to benefit her refuge in some way and she's under so much financial pressure, she's on the point of closing.'

Jude flapped her hand. 'I'm sure we can rustle up a decent donation upfront.'

'Maybe I should talk to her about it first. She's got a lot on at the moment.'

This time, Jude shrugged. 'Up to her. And it would actually be better to wait so that we could use the dog that had the surgery. And you haven't found a proper, forever home for him yet, have you?'

'No. I'm lucky enough to be fostering him myself until he's recovered from the surgery.'

Finn shook his head to dislodge any loose particles of powder as the makeup technician turned back to her kit. He could see Ben waiting patiently with Anna in the consulting room where the camera crew were setting up and, when he shifted his gaze, he saw that Hazel had been looking in the same direction. Their gazes snagged for a heartbeat.

'And after that? Is he going to get the happy ending that would be exactly what all the fans of *Call the Vet* would want?'

'I don't know,' Hazel said quietly. 'But I certainly hope so.'

How amazing was it that you could read so much into a split second when you had eye contact with someone that you were getting to know really well? Finn knew how much Hazel loved Ben. Even though she'd never said anything, he also knew that it would be a dream come true for her to live somewhere she could keep Ben with her for the rest of his life. The determination to help her was born in that moment. Because, if anyone deserved to have a dream come true, it had to be Hazel.

'We'll keep in touch, then.' Jude was sounding less

enthusiastic now. 'It is just an idea at this stage, of course. We've got lots of other exciting things on the boil for our Dr Finn.'

Yeah... Like sending him out to rescue a platypus or Tasmanian devil? Or making a fool of himself on a celebrity cooking show? Finn shook his head when the makeup technician turned back to him with a mascara wand in her hand.

'No, thanks,' he said firmly.

'Fair enough. Let's give your hair a comb and get a bit of hairspray on, at least. You look like you've been out surfing or something.'

'Nah...' Finn shoved his fingers through his hair. 'I'm going for the natural look today.'

The natural look? The kind of look that went with just hanging out with someone whose company you really enjoyed. On a beach. Or out in the countryside, watching a donkey walk freely, without severe pain, for possibly the first time in years. Knowing that a small black dog was getting pleasure from scraps of a picnic lunch he was thoroughly enjoying himself. When had he last had a picnic, for heaven's sake? Lunch with Shannon had usually been a freebie at some Michelin starred restaurant eager to court the approval of an influencer's hundreds of thousands of followers.

And what about how it felt to listen to a baby laugh for the very first time...?

Yeah...it was more than weird having makeup thrown at you and knowing you'd be under the bright lights with cameras in your face for the next few hours. It felt fake. Irrelevant?

Except it wasn't really irrelevant, was it? Finn wanted the footage of Hazel operating on Ben to be used because he wanted people to see her skills and passion and her kindness, which were all things he loved about her. And he wanted the follow up episode to show Hazel and Ben living happily together—not in a basement flat—and so this bit that would be filmed today and used to link those 'two tales' was important, too.

'Ben came in as an emergency a bit over a week ago after being hit by a car and suffering a fracture of the tibia, which is the shin bone.' Finn had Ben on the table, a short time later, and he was stroking the dog's silky head. 'My amazing colleague, Dr Hazel Davidson, used specialised implants of a bone plate and screws to stabilise the broken bones. You can see them clearly on this X-ray that was taken recently.'

Finn picked Ben up and held him under his arm as he moved to the illuminated screen on the wall, knowing that the cameraman would be zooming in on the image.

'This smudgy bit here is the callus forming over the fracture line. A callus is a type of soft bone that replaces a blood clot where the bone is broken. It can hold bone together but isn't strong enough for the leg to be used but...' He smiled as he looked down at Ben, who very obligingly looked up and licked his neck. 'Ben's doing very well. In another couple of weeks, that fracture line will have disappeared completely and a month or so after that, we'll expect him to be running around just as good as new, chasing a ball, maybe.'

At least that point in Ben's recovery was far enough in the future to not have to think about it being the end of Hazel having a reason to live in his house.

With him...?

It was still weeks away, Finn reminded himself, as they finished filming with Ben and set up a new case for Dr Finn to diagnose and treat. And he had far more important things to sort out before he let himself wonder how much he might be going to miss Hazel's company. Or whether Hazel might miss being with him? It wouldn't be a problem to sidestep thinking about it at all, actually, given how much practice he'd had doing exactly that. The easy way was to take emotion out of the equation by focusing on something practical. Like finding a place for Hazel to live with Ben. Maybe not too far away from where he was living, so that they wouldn't lose the special friendship they'd discovered?

The simplest solution would be to help her find and buy a suitable property of her own but, if Hazel had that kind of money available, she would probably have done that for herself already and even Finn's healthy bank accounts would be noticeably dented by the kind of prices Sydney properties were going for these days. His Coogee Beach penthouse apartment, for example, would sell for millions. Did he really need to live between two properties? Imagine what he could do with that kind of money at his disposal?

It was precisely the kind of practical problem that Finn knew he could solve without his involvement threatening to become too emotional. And he would solve it. Later. There were other things that were a lot higher on his current list of priorities and the most important one was Beanie. They'd been in limbo, trying not to scare the baby's mother further into hiding, doing what they could to track her down discreetly while giving her the opportunity to make contact herself, but they had to accelerate the process somehow. Jamie had taken herself to a very isolated town in outback Australia to give birth. If she was already on the run again, the more time she had, the harder it would be to find her.

* * *

Fifteen-minute appointments were never quite enough but, today, the pressure was almost welcome because it kept Hazel's mind firmly on her job and not thinking about Finn being in front of the cameras in the adjoining consultation room. But, even that level of focus and the need to keep to time as much as possible wasn't quite enough to dispel that…what was it, exactly? A hollow sensation was the best way she could describe it. A bit like embryonic fear, perhaps.

Hazel knew it had been the picnic that had left this hollow sensation in its wake because she'd recognised the core of what family felt like, had felt an almost desperate longing to be able to make it the centre of her own life but was also aware that this particular combination might not last much longer. Because Finn hadn't noticed that feeling of family. Or maybe he had and it simply wasn't something he wanted in his life. And maybe the clock had started ticking in a countdown for his return to his normal life. He was not only filming a new episode of *Call the Vet*, he would be making another television appearance later to try and speed up the conclusion of the current disruption in his life that the arrival of his granddaughter had created.

One patient after another got called in from the waiting room for Hazel and it was a struggle to keep appointments anywhere near on time. She had to sedate a young beagle in order to extract a grass seed from his ear and the elderly, overweight Labrador was clearly showing the signs of diabetes and needed more than simply a blood test.

'Take this flat container,' Hazel told the owner, 'and take Penny over the road to that nice grassy area by the beach.'

Where she and Finn had had that gorgeous picnic that was already beginning to feel like a memory filed away in an album to be opened in years to come. Would she still remember the longing? And the hollow aftermath? Would it be a lovely memory because the dream had come true and they'd ended up being that family, or would it create heartache because the dream had evaporated?

Hazel shook the thought away. 'If she's urinating as frequently as you've told me, it shouldn't take too long to get a sample. Walk a little bit behind her and slide the container underneath when she squats. Just slowly—you don't want to give her a fright.'

'What do I do with it then?'

'We'll give you a jar, as well. You can tip the sample into that and bring it back. With both the urine and the blood sample we'll be able to make some decisions about how we start treating Penny.'

'It's bad, isn't it?' The dog's owner had tears in her eyes. 'If she does have diabetes? Can't it make you go blind?'

'Let's take it one step at a time. We're going to take good care of her and there's no point crossing bridges before we even know they're there.'

It was advice Hazel needed to take herself, she decided, as she led the way to the waiting area. One step at a time was all she could take because she had no idea what the next turn in her life might be or when it might happen. What she did know was that today's step belonged to Finn as he went public to try and make contact with his daughter and he needed her support. The timing of walking with Penny and her owner to the front door was spot on and she managed to catch Finn's gaze and offer an encouraging smile before joining other staff members who were standing to one side to watch.

He wasn't smiling as she watched him facing not one, but two sets of television cameras on the steps outside Coogee Beach Animal Hospital. Jude and her team were filming the news crew and the young reporter about to interview Finn. Because this was about the star of *Call the Vet* and they might want to include the footage in a later show?

Hazel's heart was sinking as she let her gaze settle on Finn's face. Was it the natural lighting that was making him look so much older and more serious or simply that he wasn't exuding the light-hearted, roguish charm that had made him such a celebrity? That the blanket-wrapped bundle in his arms wasn't a domestic pet of some kind was making a contribution to the atmosphere being so sombre, but what made it dramatic enough to have paused any normal services at this veterinary hospital was the fact that Finn was flanked by a uniformed police officer on one side and a motherly looking woman that had to be Margaret from Social Services on the other.

The young reporter was facing the cameras to one side of the trio to start with, a hand raised to gesture towards the big red letters above the hospital's entranceway.

'We're here today on the set of one of Australia's most popular television shows, *Call the Vet*, but it's not because of one of the animals that the star of the show is caring for.' The reporter turned towards Finn. 'It's about a small baby who's been in the care of Dr Finn because…?' He held the microphone out, his words trailing off in an invitation for Finn to explain for himself.

Hazel found herself holding her breath as she

watched Finn take a deep breath. He was gathering his courage and she had to stop herself walking towards him to stand by his side and offer him some of her own. He didn't look at the cameras as he spoke but he looked down, at the face of the baby sleeping in his arms.

'As unbelievable as it seems and, trust me… I was as surprised as anyone to find out—this beautiful little girl is my granddaughter.'

'Sorry…did you mean daughter?'

'No. She's my granddaughter.'

Hazel could see the way Finn took a deep breath and she could hear the pride in his voice. Wow…he'd come a long way from the moment he'd been so alarmed by what the title of grandfather might do to ruin his image and lifestyle. She was so proud of him. That seed of hope sent up another shoot as well. He *did* feel the bond of family. And he had wanted her here with him today.

'She was left in your waiting area over a week ago, yes?' the reporter stated. 'Abandoned.'

'She wasn't abandoned.' It was Margaret who spoke. 'She was left, for whatever reason, in the care of someone known to be a family member.'

The reporter nodded but instantly turned back to Finn. 'How can you be so sure that you're related to her?'

'There was a note with her that indicated a connection.' Finn looked up as he spoke. 'It was enough for me to take on the responsibility of caring for this baby—with the permission and support of both the police and Social Services—and to have DNA testing done. And that's why I can be very sure that I'm related to her. The test results were very clear. This little girl's mother is a daughter I never knew I had.'

There was a moment's silence then, as if everyone

knew how shocking this news was going to be to a lot of people.

The reporter targeted the senior police officer next. 'What did the note say?'

'This is an ongoing investigation. We're not going to reveal information that might jeopardise that.'

Finn turned to look directly at the camera. He looked in control now, Hazel thought. As comfortable as he was when he was filming his own show.

'You're not in any trouble, Jamie,' he said quietly. 'But we need to make sure you're okay. That we can provide any help you might need.' He paused and took another breath. 'Please come forward,' he added.

He was smiling at the camera now. A slow, totally genuine kind of smile. The kind that, even in these extraordinary circumstances, was enough to give Hazel that melting sensation deep inside. So were the soft words he finished with.

'I'd really like to meet you.'

Thanks to social media, nobody had to wait for an evening news bulletin to find out about breaking headlines and, while the startling news that Australia's most eligible bachelor was actually a grandfather wasn't exactly of international interest, it was certainly making a big splash locally.

As they made the journey back out to the Blue Mountains, Finn's phone was running hot with requests for appearances and interviews. By the time they got back to the house, clips of his interview were being shared and shared again.

'You did really well,' Hazel told him. 'I'm sure somebody's going to come forward.'

'Hmm…' Finn was shaking his head, looking at the

screen of his phone as he waited while Hazel held the front door as Ben slowly climbed the steps to the veranda. 'Good grief…there are pictures here of me at university. How on earth has someone got hold of them so fast?'

'Have you any idea how many articles have been published about you in the past few years?' Hazel closed the door after Ben came inside. 'You'd only have to do an internet search to find hundreds of pictures.'

Finn led the way towards the kitchen. He put Ellie's car seat on the table and began to undo the safety harness buckles but he was looking at Hazel as he smiled wryly to acknowledge her point.

'Don't know about you,' he said, 'but I could use a glass of wine.'

'Sounds good,' Hazel agreed. 'It's been quite a day, hasn't it?'

'There's white in the fridge. Red in the wine rack in the pantry. Champagne in the cellar.'

Hazel opened the fridge. 'Good to know. We'll find it when it's time to celebrate.'

Finn lifted Ellie from the car seat. 'Yeah…that's not yet, is it? Who knows who's going to come forward? What if it's not Jamie? What if it's Beanie's father and *his* family and they want to take her away?'

Hazel handed him a glass of wine. 'One step at a time,' she told him. 'That's not a bridge that's even on the map at the moment. Why don't we go and sit on the veranda for a few minutes and enjoy this wine and the sunset?'

Finn smiled. 'You're full of good ideas.'

'Here's another one. Leave your phone in here.'

'Okay…' But the ping of a new alert made him glance at the screen as he put it down. 'Oh, no…'

Hazel's heart skipped a beat. 'What?' She stepped close enough to see what he was looking at. 'Oh, my God…who took that? That was hours before the news broke.'

It was a picture of Finn. Holding Ellie up in the air to play 'baby aeroplane'. It was also a picture of Hazel, smiling up at him and even Ben was included, with his paw on Hazel's knee. It was a picture that perfectly captured that family moment that was going to stay with her for ever. And that made it so intimate that it seemed a violation to have it out there for the whole world to stare at.

'I'm so sorry,' Finn said quietly. 'I never meant for you to get splashed all over social media. I've got used to ignoring trolls but…' He put his phone face down on the table. 'Just don't look at anything for a few days, okay?'

Hazel was still reeling from the exposure that image represented when they went out to the veranda. Surely it was obvious by the way she was looking at Finn in that photograph that she was in love with him? If he couldn't see it, no doubt there'd be plenty of others happy to comment on it.

'This is just the start, isn't it?' she asked quietly. 'It's going to get worse.'

'Not tonight,' he said. 'Tonight it's just us.' He offered a gentle smile as he settled Ellie into the crook of his arm and then raised his glass. 'And, hey…it's a lovely photo. A real family picnic…'

Oh…that look in Finn's eyes. As if he really thought of them as a family. As if he wanted it to be real as much as Hazel did. It was a moment of teetering and it felt like Finn was about to say something that could make that happen. Except he didn't say anything because the sound of tyres crunching on gravel made them both turn their heads.

A police car was coming down the long driveway towards the house. Ben barked as it stopped by the front door. Ellie began crying as two people got out of the back seat. The police officer that Hazel recognised from the interview this afternoon stayed in the car, along with a uniformed driver. One of the people that got out was Margaret. The other was a young girl with long dark hair, wearing a hoodie and ripped jeans.

Finn had gone very pale as he stood up. They both knew who this had to be but Margaret told them anyway.

'This is Jamie,' she said to Finn. 'Your daughter. Elena's mother.'

Again, Finn looked as though he was about to say something. Again, he didn't get the chance, because Jamie spoke first.

'I've come to get my baby back,' she said.

CHAPTER NINE

IT WAS A kick in the guts like no other.

Finn could only stand there and stare, the protective cover blown off that part of his heart where overwhelming emotions had been shut away. He took in the girl's tall, slender body, high cheekbones and the long hair that matched dark, dark eyes. That the look he was getting from those eyes was frankly hostile didn't make any difference and the words that finally emerged from his throat were as raw as the wound that had just been reopened.

'You look just like your mother...'

So like her that Finn could actually feel the memory of the piercing intensity of that first love in his life. The *only* love.

'How would you know?' Jamie's tone was a sneer. 'It's eighteen years since you even wanted to see her.'

'Let's go inside,' Margaret suggested. She was looking past Finn. 'Maybe we could make some tea?'

She was talking to Hazel, of course, but the reminder that he wasn't alone made Finn turn his head. Ellie was still there in his mind, along with that memory, so it was impossible not to make a comparison and they were so, so different. The difference between a warm glow rather than a shower of fireworks. A softness rather than endlessly fascinating curves and angles.

A friend, not a lover.

But it was a friend that Finn badly needed right now. An anchor that he knew he could trust as soon as his gaze met hers. And it wasn't just that he'd always been able to rely on her support. Hazel had become an integral part of the huge change that was happening in his life—a change that had been settling into a new normal in the last few days but was suddenly being upended again. Maybe even Beanie was sensing a new disruption and that was why she was crying so much more loudly than usual.

'Let me take her.' Hazel was close enough to touch his arm. 'I can make her a bottle at the same time as the tea. Unless…' She looked at Jamie, who glared back at her, her lip curling, as she watched Hazel gather Ellie into her arms.

'That's a great idea.' Margaret spoke calmly but gave her head a tiny shake, as if to warn them not to expect Jamie to want to take responsibility for her baby too soon. 'We all need to have a chat, I think.'

'I just want my baby back,' Jamie muttered. She was still watching Hazel, Finn noticed. Sideways glances as she cuddled Beanie, her soft words to the baby still drowned by the unhappy cries.

'That's exactly what we need to have a chat about.' Margaret's tone was kind, but firm. 'You've been living on the streets, Jamie. We'll have to find a better place than that if you're going to look after little Elena, won't we?'

It seemed that Jamie wasn't ready to chat about anything, anytime soon. Ten minutes later, they were sitting at the kitchen table with mugs of tea in front of them but it was Margaret who was doing the talking.

'So Jamie saw you on television in a shop,' she explained to Finn. 'And she went into a nearby police station. That was where I was taken to meet her and we had a talk while I got her something to eat. She only agreed to come and see you if you weren't told she was coming.'

'But how did she know who I was in the first place?' Finn asked. 'Who even suggested that I was her father?'

'We talked about that, too.' Margaret nodded. She tilted her head, looking at Jamie, who was sitting with her hood up and head down, making her face invisible. 'Do you want to tell Finn about that, Jamie?'

There was no response but Finn saw a movement that suggested Jamie was still keeping a close eye on Hazel, who was sitting at the table with them, giving Ellie her bottle of milk. She did care about her baby, he thought. That gave them something in common, at least. Somewhere to start?

Margaret ignored the lack of response from the teenager. 'Jamie knew she had the opportunity to go to the Department of Child Protection to search for her biological family when she turned eighteen and, because she was pregnant with her own child, she decided she would do that. She…um…was ready to ask for support.'

'Money.' The word was a snap from Jamie. 'That's all I want from you. Lucky you're rich, eh?'

'I'll give you whatever support you need,' Finn said quietly.

'Yeah, right…' Jamie's snort was dismissive. 'Like you did for my mum when *she* got pregnant.'

'I didn't know about that. I had no idea you existed, Jamie…and…and I can't tell you how sorry I am. I'm prepared to do whatever I can to try and make up for that but…'

'But you didn't bother when it really mattered.' Jamie was on her feet. 'You didn't try and find my mum, did you? And she never stopped telling me how wonderful *you* were. How much she loved you…'

Oh…that hurt. Finn caught the flash of sympathy from Hazel. She knew it was true. She'd said that Ellie must have loved him to have called her daughter after him. That their love had been precious…

'Her father told me she'd got a job up north. That she'd had enough of school. Had enough of me…' Finn had to swallow past the lump in his throat. 'Why didn't she *tell* me?'

'Maybe because she didn't want to ruin your life—the way her father told her she'd ruined hers. She was supposed to go away and have an abortion. He told her to never come back if she didn't.'

Finn closed his eyes as he remembered the pain of assumed rejection. The way he'd chosen to stop believing in love at that point and to protect himself from it ever happening again. He'd made the biggest mistake of his life, hadn't he? And being barely more than a child himself wasn't enough of an excuse.

'But I don't understand,' he said slowly. 'Why didn't she make contact later? Why wasn't I told when she died and you went into care? Somebody must have known the truth…'

Jamie folded her arms and turned her back on Finn. She walked towards where Ben was in his basket near the pantry door and the little dog stood up and wagged his tail.

'Ellie's mother.' It was Margaret who supplied the information Finn wanted. 'She was approached to take

Jamie in when her mum died and she said it was impossible because of her family circumstances. She said Jamie would be much better off with a different family. What she did do, a few years later, was to write a letter which was to be kept with Jamie's records and given to her if she ever chose to try and find out about her background. That's how she knows about why her mum had to leave home. And about how you ended up being the famous TV vet.'

Finn was watching Jamie as she crouched beside Ben to stroke him. 'It must have been hard for you to leave your baby in the waiting room like that,' he said quietly. 'I'm so glad you trusted that I would take care of her.'

Jamie shrugged. 'I didn't think you'd want her,' she said. 'Any more than you wanted me so there was no point asking you. I had to make sure you'd take notice.'

'I want her in my life more than anything,' Finn told her.

'Depends on how much it's worth to you.' Jamie sounded offhand. 'If it's not enough, I'll take her away and give her to someone else.'

He had to shift his gaze to look at Beanie, as if to reassure himself that she was still here. Hazel seemed to sense that that wasn't quite enough. The bottle was empty now and she handed the baby to Finn, who held her against his shoulder. He was rubbing her back as he turned to try and talk to Jamie again.

'I want you in my life as well, Jamie,' he said. 'To be Beanie's mum and for me to be your dad. Or try to be. I know I don't know anything much about being a dad. Or a grandpa, for that matter, but I'm willing to learn. Stay here with me. Let's get to know each other before any big decisions are made.'

Jamie said nothing. She was sitting beside Ben in his

basket now, her hood pulled over her forehead. Ben put his nose on her lap.

'It sounds like a good way to start,' Margaret said. 'Or, I can find some emergency accommodation for you, Jamie. For you and Elena. In a motel in the city, probably, but I can help you get settled. We'll all work towards doing what's best for both of you. You *and* your baby.'

'We've got everything you could need, here.' It was the first time Hazel had spoken to Jamie and she was walking towards her as she spoke. She crouched down when she reached the basket. 'You'll be safe, I promise. How 'bout staying just for tonight and then we'll talk about it some more tomorrow? We only ever need to take one step at a time.' She was smiling as she leaned down to pat Ben's head, her hand touching Jamie's. 'He really likes you,' she said softly.

Jamie stopped patting Ben. 'He's got something wrong with his leg. It's gross.'

'It got broken,' Finn told her. 'He was hit by a car.'

Jamie stood up, flicking a glance back at Hazel. 'So she's your girlfriend now? When I looked you up on the Internet it said your girlfriend was that model chick who goes around in bikinis all the time.'

'Hazel's my friend,' Finn said, ignoring the reference to Shannon because his love life was none of Jamie's business. None of anyone else's business, come to that. The difficulty in keeping personal things private was a real downside of being a celebrity. The anonymity of this time of hiding out in the country had been surprisingly enjoyable in more ways than he'd realised.

'Hazel's a vet, too,' he added, to take the conversation in a less personal direction. 'We work together. She was the one who did the surgery on Ben to fix his leg and she's staying here to help look after him. And to help me look after Beanie.'

He didn't look at Hazel as he spoke because it felt wrong, labelling her as simply a 'friend'. She was a lot more than that, wasn't she? But right now wasn't about Hazel. It wasn't about himself. It certainly wasn't about whatever new level he and Hazel had found in their relationship with each other or any possibilities the future might or might not hold. This was about a lost teenager who was a mirror image of a girl he'd loved so much, so long ago. And it was about a tiny baby who was ultimately vulnerable. A baby he had bonded with. A tiny person that he was not only responsible for—he had fallen in love with her.

Jamie looked up at him, her eyes narrowing. 'Her name's Elena, same as my mum. Why are you calling her a stupid name like "Beanie"?'

Everything had changed.

That moment, on the veranda, when Hazel had actually thought that Finn was about to say something that would somehow magically weld them into a family and give them a future, felt like a lifetime ago. A dream that she had been rudely awakened from by the stormy arrival of an unhappy teenaged mother.

The daughter Finn had never known existed but who apparently looked exactly like her mother—the love of his life. No wonder he was devoting all his time to try and connect with Jamie. Or that there was never a moment that it was just him and Hazel and Ellie in the kitchen or on the veranda. Having a glass of wine or supper in the evening or breakfast in the early morning and watching kangaroos on the far side of the paddocks near the trees that the sulphur-crested cockatoos loved to visit.

Hazel was doing her best to be encouraging and supportive but it was getting hard not to start feeling a bit superfluous. Sandra had been here more often to help with meals and housework and baby care, which was great because Jamie certainly wasn't showing any interest in anything other than sleeping, eating and shopping. Finn had taken her into the city on more than one occasion to buy clothes and toiletries and the kind of electronic accessories that all teenagers apparently couldn't live without, like the latest phone.

Margaret was a frequent visitor and Hazel knew that all options were being explored for Jamie and Ellie's futures, including formal adoption of them both by Finn. She'd heard snatches of conversations in the house.

'You could go back to school. Go to university if you wanted...'

'Why would I want to do that? You're rich enough. I don't need a job.'

'We could all live here. It would be a wonderful place for Beanie to grow up.'

'Out in the middle of nowhere? Are you freaking kidding?'

Jamie was hostile and Hazel could understand that. She'd been deprived of a father all her life. Deprived of a real family by the sound of it, as well, and she'd lost the freedom of a normal early adulthood by becoming a mother at such a young age. She could also understand why the focus had to be on Jamie but it was hard to maintain the sympathy as one day trickled into the next and the girl was still refusing to help care for her baby. She didn't want to feed her or bathe her or even pick her up for a cuddle and it seemed like Ellie was aware of the rejection because she was unsettled. She hadn't smiled, let alone laughed, since the day of their picnic.

While Finn was spending all his time at home, Hazel was spending more and more of her time at work. It was no problem to take Ben with her, Sandra was more than happy to take responsibility for Mittens and her kittens and it was a relief to be away from the tension in Finn's house. Even better to be kept so busy doing what she did best, with busy clinics and long theatre sessions. It was high time she spent a few hours at Two Tails, too, either helping in Kiara's veterinary clinic or in the refuge. She wanted to see for herself how well Bunji the dog was doing with her treatment and, well…she could do with a friend to talk through how this new twist in Finn's life crisis was affecting her.

She couldn't plan the visit until she'd got through the rest of the appointments for this afternoon's clinic, though. Penny the Labrador was next for a consultation to see how her owner was coping with having to administer insulin injections at home and whether the old dog's blood glucose levels were back within an acceptable range.

She opened the door and walked into the waiting area, looking forward to seeing Penny again, but she found her view of people sitting around the edges of the space was blocked by a man who was interrupting Kylie the receptionist as she began greeting a woman who was next in line at the counter.

'How can I help you?' Kylie asked.

'So that's the spot, then?' The man was loud. 'Where the kid was dumped?' He was pointing towards the display of dog toys. He raised a camera and there was a whirr of sound as he took multiple shots.

Hazel almost groaned aloud. She'd been deliberately

staying away from the fallout on social media to Finn's news, but she knew there was a lot of gossip going on, with him getting slammed for abandoning a pregnant girlfriend and ignoring parental responsibilities for decades, rumours that his days as a celebrity were over and unkind memes about skipping the demands of fatherhood to go straight for membership of the rocking chair and slippers brigade.

Hazel signalled Penny's owner but turned to Kylie before she led the way back to her consulting room.

'Do you need any help?'

'Nah… I was just about to tell him to leave.'

The man stared at Hazel. 'Hey… I know you. You're the one who was with Dr Finn down on the beach the other day, aren't you? His girlfriend?'

'Hardly.' Hazel even managed a huff of laughter.

It was easy enough to sound as if the suggestion was ridiculous. Finn had said so himself the night Jamie had arrived, hadn't he? She was his friend. End of.

'You need to leave,' she told the stranger. 'Or we'll be calling the police.'

'No worries.' The man sounded almost amused. He was moving to the front doors, but Hazel could hear his camera whirring again as she bent to pat Penny.

'Come on, sweetheart,' she said to the dog. 'Let's get on with the important stuff, shall we?'

'Wait…' It was the woman still waiting to speak to Kylie who called out. 'I think it might be you I need to talk to.'

'Oh?' Hazel waved at the open door to the consulting room. 'Take Penny through,' she instructed the dog's owner. 'I'll be with you in just a minute.'

'I saw you in the paper, too,' the woman said. 'With the dog.'

Hazel felt a shiver of something she didn't like. She could guess what was coming.

'Is he yours?' the woman asked.

'I'm looking after him,' Hazel said. 'He got hit by a car a couple of weeks ago and needed some fairly major surgery on a broken leg. We were told he was a stray.'

The woman nodded. 'That would fit. He looks a lot like my dad's old dog, Max, who went missing about four weeks ago, after Dad had a fall and had to go into hospital. One of the neighbours tried to hold onto him when the ambulance was driving away but he slipped his collar and ran off. Dad's terribly upset about it all.'

'Of course…' Hazel had to fight the wash of something a lot deeper than merely disappointment. She knew that returning him to a loving family would be the best possible outcome for Ben. It wasn't as if she even had a suitable place to keep him after she left Finn's property. This woman's father had probably raised the old spaniel since he was a pup and loved him even more than Hazel did.

'Come with me,' she said. 'He's in a crate out back in our animal room. You can check to see if it is… um… Max.'

Isabella the donkey was on the far side of her paddock when Hazel drove in late that afternoon, but she spotted the vintage red van and had learned that treats were not far away. By the time Hazel parked in front of the house and lifted Ben down from the back of the van, Isabella was heading in her direction—at a trot.

Hazel was standing there with her mouth open when Finn came around the corner of the veranda with baby Ellie in a front pack. He immediately saw why she was so blown away.

'Wow…look at Isabella go. Doesn't look like her feet are bothering her much at all now.' He was smiling at Hazel. 'Feels good, doesn't it?'

'So good.' She smiled back. Baby Ellie, who was facing outwards in the front pack, didn't join in the smiling but she waved her arms up and down and kicked her feet in what looked like shared approval and, for a heartbeat, it felt like it had before Jamie had arrived.

'Ben looks just as happy as we are.'

The small dog was right beside the fence, his paws on a rail as he lifted his nose. Isabella was leaning over the top rail, reaching down to touch that little black nose with her lip. The gentle greeting between the animals should have made Hazel's smile widen but, instead, it was fading rapidly. Nothing was quite like it had been before Jamie's arrival and things were still changing.

'His name's Max,' she told Finn.

'What?' Finn looked startled. 'But…'

But she'd named this dog after her childhood companion. The animal who'd provided his solid warmth and unconditional love in moments that had felt like despair and, while they hadn't really talked about it yet, Hazel knew that Finn would understand exactly what that had been like for her. She could hear the echo of his voice as he'd told her something she was quite sure he'd never told anyone else.

'I was the kid no one had ever wanted, or not for very long, anyway...'

She swallowed hard. 'His owner turned up at work today. Or rather, the owner's daughter. Her dad, Frank, had a fall and broke his hip a few weeks ago—over near Bondi Beach. The ambulance got called and the police turned up to break into the house for them and it was all pretty chaotic and Ben… I mean Max, got upset.

A neighbour tried to catch him and tie him up but he slipped his collar and ran away.'

Hazel couldn't meet Finn's eyes. Maybe she didn't want to see the sympathy she knew she'd find because it would just confirm how much everything was changing. And yeah...she'd known that this was a bit of a fantasy living here like a perfect little family, but...she'd also wanted it to last a bit longer, because she'd always known it was going to hurt when it ended.

'So what's going to happen?' Finn asked quietly. 'Does Frank have someone in his family who'll be able to look after Ben? Or will he be able to himself when he recovers?'

Was it deliberate, not using his real name? Did Finn want to keep in touch with that fantasy as much as Hazel did?

'I'm not sure. His daughter can't take him because her husband has asthma and is allergic to dogs and her father can't look after him because he's going to have to go into a rest home. I said I'd go and talk to him in the next few days. I'll take... Max to visit...' Hazel's voice trailed into silence. She didn't want to say it out loud, that she'd always known that her time with Ben wasn't going to last that long. That her time with Finn was going to be just as temporary...

Finn was silent as well. Which was why it was so startling to hear the peal of laughter coming from the direction of the house.

Hazel raised her eyebrows. 'Jamie sounds happier.'

Finn shook his head. 'She's been lying around all afternoon, glued to that phone. I wish I hadn't bought it for her. She still won't talk to me. She still won't have anything to do with Beanie, either. She says what's the point when she's going to have a new mother soon?'

There was another burst of laughter as Hazel headed inside to go and find a carrot for Isabella and this time, she could see where it was coming from. Jamie was lying on one of the cane couches on the veranda, holding her phone above her face. It was the words that followed the laughter that made Hazel stop in her tracks, however. So fast that Finn and Ellie almost bumped into her. A singsong collection of words that Hazel had heard before.

'Who ate all the pies?'

The taunt that never got old, as long as you had a fat kid to throw it at. There was a part of Hazel that suddenly felt about ten years old again. A part that just wanted to run away and hide.

She heard Finn suck in his breath. 'What's that supposed to mean?' he demanded, his voice dangerously soft as he stepped towards where Jamie was lounging on her back, holding her phone close to her face.

'You're all over the Internet,' his daughter told him. 'And it's kind of funny. Look…' She held up her phone where the headline was clearly visible even to Hazel, who hadn't moved any closer.

One Girlfriend at a Time, Please, Dr Finn!

The picture beneath the headline had been taken today. One of that volley of shots Hazel had heard as she'd bent down to pat Penny the Labrador so it was her backside that filled most of the photo. Her huge bum in those baggy scrubs. And, in case that part of her anatomy wasn't instantly recognisable, whoever put the article together had unearthed a screenshot from the first time she'd appeared on *Call the Vet*, with Finn beside her. Hazel had time, before Finn grabbed the phone and switched it off, to see that a third photo was also there—one of Finn at some social event, looking gorgeously formal in black tie attire with the stunningly beautiful, unnaturally skinny Shannon clinging to his arm.

The ten-year-old part of Hazel had long since fled and a far more current version was spinning out. She could just imagine the thousands of comments that would be racking up below articles like this. The comparisons being made. The vicious bullying that keyboard warriors felt so entitled to unleash. At least she wasn't some vulnerable teenager. Hazel had heard it all before and she knew how to protect herself.

She'd broken the rules though, hadn't she? She'd let herself fall in love. Worse…she'd let herself start hoping.

Another thought surfaced, triggered by remembering that huff of laughter she'd produced when that man in the veterinary clinic this afternoon had recognised her as Finn's 'girlfriend'.

Hazel hadn't been surprised that the physical intimacy between herself and Finn had stopped after Jamie's arrival in the house because she understood that Finn's attention needed to be completely on trying to find a connection with Jamie and encouraging her to reconnect with her baby. But what if there was more to it, than that?

What if having someone else in the house had made him realise that a friendship with Hazel that was close enough to include sex would be acutely embarrassing if it became public? Had the sex only been a distraction from the boredom of being locked out of his normal, racy, celebrity lifestyle? Away from his gorgeous girlfriend, who might have dumped him but their separations never lasted that long, did they?

Everything wasn't just changing. It was falling apart. Imploding.

And, whatever direction Hazel's mind darted towards, she could only see it getting worse. The more she was seen with Finn, the more comparisons would be made. The more people would be laughing, as Jamie had been, at the very idea of her being his girlfriend. And, even if Finn didn't think that, he'd be influenced by it, wouldn't he? He'd admitted how angry he'd been when he thought he'd been rejected by Jamie's mother. How determined he'd been to become rich and famous so that he could be safe from that ever happening again.

Being mocked on social media would have been his worst nightmare not long ago and yes…Hazel could see he was angry now. His face was set in grim lines and Ellie must have picked up on the tension because her little face was crumpling and the whimpers were starting.

'I'm keeping this phone,' he snapped at Jamie. 'And you can apologise to Hazel.'

'What for?' Jamie sat up but avoided making eye contact with Hazel. 'It's not me calling her fat, is it? And you said she wasn't even your girlfriend.' Then she shrugged. 'But, hey…if I'm in the way of you two hooking up or something, I can always go somewhere else. And take my kid.'

Finn stepped closer to Jamie and it was obvious he was struggling to keep control of what he was about to say to his daughter. Ellie started crying. Loudly. Ben was slinking into the house, his tail between his legs, and Hazel realised that, actually, what was going on here had nothing to do with her. She was just muddying the waters of something far more important that needed to be sorted out and her heart was sinking like a stone.

Maybe Jamie was jealous of the easy friendship that

she and Finn had. Or perhaps she suspected there'd been something more going on. Whatever… Hazel could well be unintentionally blocking the attention that Jamie was actually desperate to receive from her father. And if Finn confronted Jamie over finding hurtful comments about her amusing, any hope of a positive relationship developing between them might be pushed even further away.

Hazel had to try and do something to defuse this situation. Fast—before anything more damaging was said. It was possibly the last thing she *could* do to help Finn get through this life crisis and, while her heart was breaking, she still wanted to do whatever she could to support him.

'I didn't tell you,' she said into the simmering silence, her voice artificially bright. 'But my friend Kiara up at the Two Tails refuge is desperate for me to go and look after things for a week or so while she's away. I can take Ben with me. I know Sandra will be happy to look after Mittens because she's offered to adopt her if no relatives or friends of the owner come forward. And Isabella will be fine here by herself for now.' She turned to follow the little dog. She should just bite the bullet and start calling him Max, she thought, as she surrendered to the fragments of any fantasy evaporating. 'I just came home to pick up the things I'll need.'

Finn followed her inside.

'Please don't go, Hazel,' he said. 'I need you.'

It was far from the first time he'd said that to her. It was precisely what had pulled her in and started what had become such an irresistible fantasy. Had started the hope that she might mean something to him one day. Something that was strong enough to make her believe the impossible. And she had…briefly. Before the outside world had reminded her of why she'd never let herself truly believe.

'No, Finn,' she told him gently. 'You don't need me. You need to believe that you can get through to Jamie. That you can make this work. That's your *family* out there...'

He was shaking his head, rocking the still crying baby in his arms. 'She hates me. She doesn't believe that I didn't just abandon her.'

'I think she's pushing you away just because she's afraid of being rejected herself. Talk to her. Properly. Tell her what you told me about what it was like for you. She'll know how much you loved her mum. I knew...'

She knew that Ellie had been the love of his life.

How on earth had Hazel started to believe that Finn might love *her* that much as well? Even now, as she let herself sink into the way he was looking at her, she could still believe...

'Trust me,' she whispered. 'It will be better for everybody if I'm not here.'

Including herself?

Hazel paused only to dial Kiara's number before she drove away a short time later. Her friend must be busy out in the pens, she decided, as the call went to voicemail, but maybe she'd get the message before Hazel actually arrived at Two Tails.

'I'm heading your way,' she said. 'I'll fill you in when I get there but it's best if I get away from here and I need to go somewhere I can take Ben. I don't know if that job opportunity's still there—the one with that guy who needs you to live in and get a rehome settled?' Hazel started the engine of her van. 'But, if it is, this might be the ideal time to take advantage of it. I'm more than happy to take care of Two Tails for a week or so.'

She couldn't look back as she drove away because, if she saw Finn standing on the veranda, she might not hold onto the strength to do what she knew she had to do. Removing herself from this situation *was* going to be better for everyone.

Especially herself…

CHAPTER TEN

THERE WERE TEARS.

Of course there were. The staff at Frank's rest home were only too happy to welcome Hazel and Ben when she went to visit and there were very few dry eyes when the little black spaniel's entire body was wriggling with the joy of being reunited with his person, Frank, who was in a big, squashy reclining chair in the rest home's conservatory as Ben climbed up to snuggle in beside him.

The tears were too close to the surface anyway, for Hazel—they had been ever since she'd left Finn's house, so it was almost a relief to have a perfectly acceptable excuse to let some of them escape. She was quite well aware that the many tears that had been shed in the last days, due to heartbreak because a fantasy bubble had burst, were a kind of self-indulgence, really. After all, she'd always known that living her dream was only going to be temporary.

Maybe it hadn't been the best idea to take a week's leave from work to look after Two Tails because it had shut her off from the rest of the world and given her rather too much thinking time. She had a couple of hours in the afternoons of keeping surgery hours in Kiara's small vet clinic and Maureen, who'd been a friend of Kiara's grandmother, helped out in the mornings but, apart from that, Hazel was entirely alone with Ben and the handful of dogs left in the refuge now that it was being wound down.

In other ways, however, it helped quite a lot that Hazel had shut herself away. She only switched on her phone to make an occasional call and check messages, which kept her well away from the danger of tapping into whatever unpleasantness was still happening on social media. She would have loved to find out how things were going between Finn and Jamie but, instinctively, she knew that completely disappearing from Finn's life might convince Jamie that there were no barriers between her and her father.

In order to distract herself, Hazel was keeping herself as busy as possible. The pens for the dogs were probably being scrubbed twice as often as necessary, she had reorganised all the storage cupboards in the clinic and the dogs were all being very well exercised, apart from Ben, who still needed care even though he was almost walking without any limp at all now. In the evenings, with Ben asleep in his basket, Hazel still kept herself busy. Kiara's grandmother had been an avid collector of all sorts of things like lamps and ornaments and china and Hazel still had some work to do to meet the challenge of making sure they were all free from dust before Kiara came home.

Taking Ben to visit his owner in the rest home was another distraction and, although it happened days later than Hazel had promised Frank's daughter, it was the first foray away from what had provided a refuge for herself as much as the remaining residents.

So that made the tears feel excusable. It was probably also the reason that it had been so welcome to have someone to really talk to, after she and Frank and Ben had been left alone in the conservatory.

'Sorry… I've got to stop calling him Ben,' Hazel said, nearly an hour later. 'He's Max. And I think he's the happiest dog in the world right now.' She blinked hard, to prevent new tears trying to collect at the back of her eyes. She could feel the joy in the connection between this elderly man and his old dog and the glow of that love reminded her of those special moments she'd had with Finn and Ellie—like when the baby had smiled for the first time. When they'd heard her laugh. When Finn had said that he really wanted to make love to her…

Oh, man… Missing someone was a kind of grief that could be astonishingly painful.

'You called him Ben for the best of reasons,' Frank said. 'I'm so glad you told me about your old dog. And about Two Tails and your friend Kiara. And Isabella the donkey.' He was smiling. 'And let's not forget the baby that arrived in your life on the same day that Max did.'

They'd been talking non-stop since staff members and other residents had left the three of them to enjoy the sunny corner of the conservatory uninterrupted. Or, rather, Hazel had been talking non-stop.

'Oh, help… I've been talking far too much. I've probably tired you out completely. Look, Max is so bored he's sound asleep.'

'Quite the opposite. I feel better than I have ever since the accident,' Frank said. 'Like I'm part of the adventure you're having. I hope you'll come back soon and give me an update.'

Oh… Hazel desperately wanted an update herself. But the longing to know how things were going between Finn and his daughter, whether Jamie had taken any step closer to bonding with *her* daughter or even how the kittens were doing was strong enough to be a warning that she was too involved already. It wasn't simply that she had cleared the way for Finn and Jamie to connect. Keeping up her own connection with them would only prolong the painful journey of getting back to her own real life.

'It's certainly been a roller coaster,' she admitted. 'And I've been short of people to talk to about what's going on in my life. No one that talks back to me, anyway.' She leaned over to stroke Ben. 'This little guy's a great listener, though.'

The dog didn't open his eyes but his tail thumped against Frank's legs as he felt Hazel's touch.

'He loves you,' Frank said quietly. 'And, you know what? I reckon you should keep calling him Ben because he doesn't care what he's called. He just wants to be loved by you.' He touched her hand. 'And I can see why he does. You're a very special person, Hazel Davidson. I hope you know that.'

Okay…blinking wasn't quite going to do the job with those tears. Hazel had to swipe away one that escaped. The words were a balm to a self-esteem that had been far too easily knocked back all over again, after reading what was being said about her, thanks to all those years of being bullied.

Finn had thought she was special, too, hadn't he? Hazel only had to remember the way he'd looked at her sometimes and, dear Lord, the way he'd touched her, to know that she hadn't been wrong to believe that was genuine. What she shouldn't have started believing in was that it could be her future.

He'd said it himself. That he'd been so devastated when the girl he'd loved had vanished from his life that he was never going to let anybody hurt him that much again and it was easy to translate that into him never letting himself fall in love again. Or trust in a future with someone. That was the real obstacle between Finn and his daughter connecting, wasn't it? They both needed to lower their barriers. To make themselves vulnerable. They both knew how much it hurt to lose someone they loved but…even the way Hazel was feeling right now, she knew it was worth it.

'Did you really mean what you said about adopting Ben?' Frank had kindly busied himself scratching the dog's silky ears as Hazel found a tissue and got rid of those tears. 'Because, if you did, I would love you to do that. I can't think of a better home he could possibly have. Or a better name when it belonged to another dog you loved so much.'

'Of course I meant it.' Hazel nodded. 'Not that I actually have a suitable home just yet. I'll have to find somewhere new to live.'

'I was thinking in terms of "home" being more about people than places,' Frank said softly.

Hazel didn't want to let his words sink in. How sad would it be if she'd left more than simply Finn's property? If she'd walked away from the only 'home' she might ever find? No, she couldn't afford to think that.

'I've started looking already,' she assured Frank. 'I've got the rest of this week at the refuge—probably longer if I need it.'

'There's my house in Bondi,' Frank said. 'It'll have to get sold eventually, I expect, but you'd be welcome to live there in the meantime if it helps. That way, you'd be close enough to come and visit sometimes.'

'I'll do that anyway. *We'll* do that…won't we, Ben?' Hazel smiled as she got to her feet. 'Look at how much he's loving being here. It makes me think he might like to do visiting like this on a regular basis—for other people, as well, perhaps.'

'He's always loved people. And who wouldn't want cuddles like this? You know, that could be a way to get people interested in helping the refuge. It might even help solve those financial problems.'

'Something to think about, that's for sure.' Hazel got to her feet. 'Come on, Ben. We'd better get back to Two Tails and get to work. Those pens won't clean themselves and there's exercise and training that needs to happen.'

'Thank you so much for coming to me.' It was Frank's turn to dab at his eyes. 'I can't tell you how happy it's made me.'

'It's been such a pleasure,' Hazel said. 'And I should be the one thanking you. That kind of happy is contagious and it was exactly what I needed today.'

As always, the drive back to the Blue Mountains was another form of therapy for Hazel and, for the first time since she'd walked away from Finn, she was feeling hopeful again, which was probably due to Frank's pleasure in her visit—and the nice things he'd said about her. He'd inspired her to not give up on the future of Two Tails and Kiara's vet clinic, either, and that positivity was growing to include what might be ahead for Finn's relationship with his daughter and his granddaughter. About a future that was grounded in family and was *real*—with all the highs and lows that real life delivered.

Their friendship was also real, she knew that. And friends didn't abandon each other when times were tough. Okay, she might be right in keeping out of the way for the moment, but that didn't mean she couldn't let Finn know that she was thinking about him, did it? That she cared…?

She turned her phone on as soon as she arrived back at Two Tails and texted.

Thinking of you. Hope it's all going well. xx

Finn hadn't realised he'd been holding his breath until the bleep of an incoming text message made him release it in an enormous sigh.

He'd come outside, after Beanie had finally exhausted herself enough by crying to fall asleep, because he had to try and ease the sheer frustration that was building to breaking point. In what was becoming an automatic habit, he'd picked up a carrot for Isabella on his way outside. He'd been waiting for the little donkey to trot over to the gate, his phone bleeped and when he looked at the screen to discover that it was Hazel messaging him he felt that tightness in his chest being released with that huge sigh.

To his surprise, it felt like something else was also being let go. Self-control, perhaps? The ability to convince himself that it was better for both of them that Hazel had left? Better for all of them, because if Jamie had gone any further down the track of enjoying the comments of those vicious online trolls that thought Hazel was fair game, he might have given up on ever connecting with this young woman who was his daughter and simply told her to get out of his life?

Surely that prickle behind his eyes and the new lump in his throat wasn't the threat of tears?

No…of course it wasn't.

It was just that things weren't going well at all, really, and knowing that Hazel was thinking about him was like…like feeling her touch.

He was just *missing* her, dammit…

'Nothing's been the same since our Hazel left, has it, Isabella?' Finn hung onto the end of the carrot as the donkey gently took the pointy end between her teeth and then tilted her head sideways to break it off. 'No… that's not true, is it? Nothing's been the same since Jamie turned up.'

Maybe that should be since Beanie turned up. His life had been tipped upside down in an instant at that point. It had been Hazel who'd suggested the appalling possibility that the baby might be his granddaughter and what had his first thought been? That it would destroy his image. His television career. Possibly his entire lifestyle.

And what had Hazel said? That it could be the best thing that had ever happened to him. He'd started to believe that, too. How good had it felt that morning in the kitchen when Ellie had smiled at him for the first time? And when they'd both heard her first laughter on that picnic. And, if it hadn't been for Ellie—and Ben—it might never have occurred to him to spend so much time with Hazel and, quite apart from now having an infant in his life who'd totally captured his heart, getting so close to Hazel was competing for the status of being the very best thing that had ever happened to him.

'You miss her too, don't you, Bella?' Finn gave the donkey the rest of the carrot and scratched her neck just behind her ear as she ate it.

Finn had such a clear image in his head of Hazel sitting on the veranda that first morning. In her PJs with all that gorgeous softness undisguised. He found himself smiling as he remembered the look of delight in her eyes when she'd spotted the kangaroos but then his smile faded as he remembered the look in her eyes when she'd told him that making love with him was the only thing she wanted…

That was what he was missing most of all. Not just the sex—although he had to admit his bed had never felt quite this lonely—but that closeness that came when he could sleep with her in his arms. A closeness that was there by just breathing the same air, actually. Hazel Davidson was the first person who had seen right through the image he'd created with his celebrity lifestyle and all the flashy tokens of his wealth and deemed them shallow. She'd recognised the unhappy, unwanted kid he'd been and she knew that so much of him now had been carefully crafted and…yeah…*fake*, but she still thought he was worth loving. Just by being there, Hazel could make this huge house feel like a home. She'd created a glue that had made them feel like…a family.

And, despite having told Hazel that he didn't do dependants on a long-term basis, he desperately wanted that feeling back again.

But she'd gone—because she'd wanted to—and that feeling had gone, too. Over the last week, things had gone from bad to worse. Finn had tried to talk to Jamie, on several occasions, as Hazel had advised him to do. He wanted to succeed. To fix things. Not only to make up for not having been there for his daughter or even to stop history repeating itself with Ellie, but to honour the memory of Jamie's mother and her importance in his own story and…and he wanted Hazel to truly believe that there was nothing fake about him any longer. Maybe he even wanted her to be proud of him?

He knew Hazel had been right in thinking that being here alone with Jamie was his best, possibly only, chance to establish a relationship with the daughter he'd never known he had and he'd done his best to get her to believe that things would have been very different if he'd known about her existence but Jamie was still refusing to listen. She simply put her ear plugs in and watched videos on her phone or walked off and shut herself away in her bedroom.

It was getting harder to resist the urge to contact Hazel and ask for more advice but he'd already asked enough of her. Too much, perhaps. Was that part of the reason why she'd left? Did she need some space? If he had some good news to tell her, it would be a great excuse to make contact, but day after day was passing without any kind of breakthrough and now Finn was in need of some space himself. It was tempting to rely more and more on Sandra's help so that he could escape by spending more time at work in the city but his loyal housekeeper had finally lost patience earlier today, when Jamie had gone off to slam doors after Finn suggested she gave Ellie her lunchtime bottle.

'She needs her mum,' Finn had pleaded with Jamie. 'Please…just try?'

'I'm not going to *be* her mum. Who are you to try and make me, anyway? You didn't even *try* to be my dad. *You* never fed me, did you?'

The door slamming had made Ellie howl so much that Finn couldn't get her to settle, let alone drink her milk, and he was quite sure that she'd never been this grizzly or miserable when Hazel had been here to help. She was still crying and hungry when he'd rung work to let them know he couldn't come in this afternoon, after all. Sandra had apparently just remembered an appointment she couldn't break.

'Jamie needs boundaries,' Sandra had told Finn as

she left. 'I know she's had a lot to deal with in her life but you've been tiptoeing around her and she's still behaving like a spoilt brat. My two cents' worth is that she needs you to be a parent and provide boundaries. You can't trust something if you don't have any idea what shape it is. What picture it's making.'

So here he was—outside, soaking in a moment of peace with a small donkey. The shape of a donkey's ear was an amazing thing, Finn thought, as he ran it through his hand. Isabella pushed her nose forward to lean her chin on his shoulder as he stroked her ear again and it made Finn smile. It also gave him a new thought. Maybe the good news to share with Hazel didn't have to be about his relationship with Jamie?

How happy would she be to know that this little donkey she'd rescued was enjoying being here this much? How much would she love to see it for herself? Was she busy at the moment? Two Tails refuge wasn't that far away, if she wanted to pop over for a cup of coffee or something. He wouldn't put any pressure on her to come back. Why would she want to, when Jamie had been so rude to her?

Finn picked up his phone again, to respond to her text message and invite her to come and visit, but he couldn't find the words he needed because there were others trying to come out.

I need you...

I miss you...

I miss that feeling of family we made together. You and me and Beanie and Ben.

There was something else that he needed to say even more urgently but he had no idea what it was with so many other words competing for his head space and then that effort was interrupted as the handset clipped to his belt crackled into life with the sound of a baby waking up and beginning to whimper. He stayed where he was for a long moment, however, trying to recapture the threads of what he'd been searching for, but the cries were getting rapidly more demanding and, to be honest, it was kind of a relief to be able to push it all to one side. Finn slipped his phone into his pocket without having responded to Hazel's message at all and turned to go back to the house.

Then he heard another sound on the monitor. Jamie's voice.

'Fine… I guess I'll *have* to do something with you, then, if nobody else is going to.'

Finn could hear the sound of footsteps and the change in Beanie's cry as she was picked up. He increased his pace, as the sound of the baby crying got fainter with her being carried away from the baby monitor. Where was Jamie taking her? And what was she planning to do with her baby? Fear was competing with what felt like a certainty that Jamie would never harm Beanie but the need to protect his granddaughter was strong enough to override anything.

He paused in the wide hallway of the house when he was able to hear Beanie crying again. The sound was coming from the kitchen and it covered the sound of his footsteps on the polished wooden floorboards as he headed towards that part of the house. He slowed and then stopped just outside the door, to take a breath and not rush in looking like he thought he had to rescue the baby from a mother who couldn't be trusted, and that was when he heard the beep of the microwave as it finished heating something and the baby's cry changed to a hungry squeak. He stayed where he was for a moment longer.

'I told you I'd come back,' he heard Jamie whisper. A chair scraped on the floorboards. 'I told you that we'd be okay...'

She couldn't see Finn as he moved just enough to see past the open door. Jamie was sitting at the table, holding Ellie, whose face was bright red from her distressed crying. She slipped the teat of the bottle into the baby's mouth in what looked like a well-practised move and then sat very still, looking down at her baby.

Finn eased back before he was spotted. Beanie was clearly perfectly safe and the worst thing he could do right now might be to interrupt this moment of bonding that was finally happening again between a young mother and her baby. He could go back outside and talk to Isabella again but the temptation to return and try and build on Jamie's change of heart—to see if *he* could also find a connection between himself and his daughter—was getting stronger by the second.

When his gaze caught the spot under the tree where he'd parked his new SUV, he had a much better idea. He could take himself right away. Just long enough for that bond between Jamie and Ellie to take shape again. Thirty minutes should do it, he thought. And that was more than long enough to drive over to Two Tails, which might solve the dilemma of what to say in a text message to Hazel.

If he could see her, surely he'd know what it was he wanted to say to her—whatever it was that he couldn't put in a text message.

He needed be close enough to touch her because missing her was a physical ache and nothing felt like it was in its right place. His life had been tipped upside down and shaken and there were pieces all over the place and there was only one way to deal with any kind of jigsaw. You had to pick up the first piece and make a start.

The easiest way to do that was to find the edge pieces, wasn't it? To make boundaries, as Sandra had suggested were needed. There was, hopefully, the shape of a new picture forming between Jamie and Ellie right now. Finn needed one that might make sense of what was happening to his life. And he needed a shape for what he and Hazel had found with each other because it didn't seem to have any edges at all and that was confusing. Because it couldn't be trusted?

Finn was ready to put his foot down as soon as he got to the road at the end of his long driveway. He knew where Birralong was and it wouldn't be hard to find the only animal refuge nearby. He waited impatiently for the automatic gates to slide open but he didn't put his foot down on the accelerator, after all. His car wasn't about to go anywhere. Because he could see another vehicle coming down the road. A vintage, red van that could only belong to one person.

Hazel turned in through the gates and stopped the old van alongside his shiny new SUV. Her driver's side window was only inches away from his. She was winding a handle to lower her window. Finn just needed to press a button.

'I thought I'd pop in,' Hazel said. 'You…you didn't answer my text.'

'I couldn't,' Finn said quietly. 'There were too many things I wanted to say so… I thought I'd come and see you.'

Hazel was holding his gaze. Because she wanted to, or because he had no intention of letting hers go? Maybe it didn't matter when he was looking at a reflection of what had to be showing in his own eyes. The sheer *re-*

lief of being close again. The feeling that he'd not only found the first piece of that puzzle, it was the most important piece of all.

He wanted to reach out and touch her. No…what Finn actually wanted to do was to get out of his car. To reach in through Hazel's open window to hold her face gently between his hands and then lean in to kiss her absolutely senseless. Even the thought of doing that was tilting his lips towards a smile. And perhaps Hazel could read his mind because she was touching her bottom lip with the tip of her tongue.

That did it. Finn went to open his door but the vehicles were too close. And something else was creating static in the spell that had been cast the moment his gaze had captured Hazel's. She was aware of it as well and a frown was creasing her forehead.

'Is that Ellie crying?'

Finn killed the engine of his car. He hadn't realised that he still had the handset of the baby monitor clipped to his belt. Or that the range of the device extended this far. Jamie must have taken Beanie back to her bassinette after feeding her because she was obviously close to the monitor. He was frowning now, too. He'd never heard Beanie cry with this odd, high-pitched note in her voice.

And then the crying stopped abruptly and they could hear Jamie's voice.

'Oh, my God…what are you doing? What's happening…?'

There was the sound of rapid footsteps and then a piercing shriek, but it wasn't coming from a baby.

'*Finn*…where are you? Something's wrong with Ellie. Something *bad*.'

Again, Finn could see exactly how he was feeling himself reflected in Hazel's eyes. He could see pure fear. He restarted the engine and began backing up so that he could turn the vehicle in front of the little red van.

'Follow me,' he called to Hazel. It was a plea rather than an instruction.

This time he did put his foot down but it still didn't seem fast enough. The voice he could hear was fainter now. Was that because of the engine noise or was Jamie getting further away from the monitor as she searched for him.

'*Finn…* Where are you?'

He could hear a choked sob.

'*Dad…*please… I really *need* you…'

CHAPTER ELEVEN

HAZEL HAD SEEN Finn shocked, as he had been when she'd suggested he could be the grandfather of the baby left in Coogee Beach Animal Hospital's waiting area. She'd been so disappointed at that point in time, not only because it made Finn seem so shallow but she'd been disappointed in herself at the same time. Because, even then, she knew she was in love with this man and how could her instincts have been so misplaced?

She'd seen him overwhelmed—lost, even—as he had been when she'd arrived that first evening in response to his plea for assistance in looking after that baby and when she'd seen the glimmer of potential tears in his eyes, she'd known that her instincts hadn't been so wrong, after all.

And when he'd spoken… *'I'm hopeless at this...'*

Oh, my…looking back, that was quite possibly the moment the love she'd had for Finn hidden in a secret place in her heart had broken out of any restraints. She had felt it like something melting. Trickling through her whole body.

And Hazel had seen him still devastated enough by what had happened so long ago to really shed tears and that had been the night she had given herself to him—body and soul—for as long as it could last.

But, right now, she was seeing something that took her love for this man to the next level. He was showing a determination to protect and care for someone he loved that was second to none. And, while this was directed towards his tiny, vulnerable granddaughter, that seed of hope that he could feel the same way about her had not been buried. Or, if it had, it was pushing its way clear with astonishing power. The way Finn had been looking at her just a minute or two ago, when they'd met at the end of the driveway. He'd been coming to see her. He had things he wanted to tell her and Hazel thought she might know what those things were because she had a few of her own things to say but, oddly, it felt as though they'd already *been* said. Just not aloud.

And, saying them aloud didn't matter. Even thinking about them was no more than a background to what was going on in Hazel's mind as she watched Finn take charge of this emergency. Her thoughts were not even that coherent. She was aware of total confidence in his ability. Pride. A need to be by his side so that she could offer total support in whatever way she could.

'She's burning up,' Finn said, his hand gently covering Ellie's head. 'We need to bring her temperature down and then get her to hospital asap.'

'But what's wrong with her?' Jamie had both arms wrapped tightly around her own body but she was still shaking. 'What did I do wrong?'

'This isn't your fault,' Finn told her. 'It's quite likely that she's picked up some kind of infection. A high temperature can make a baby have a seizure, which is what was happening when you saw her body jerking.' He was peeling off the cardigan and booties that Ellie was wearing over her stretchy onesie. 'I should have realised she was off colour. She's been a bit grizzly all day.'

The baby was still grizzling now. An unbearably miserable sound.

'It's my fault,' Jamie insisted. Then she burst into tears. 'I miss my *mum*...'

Oh...there was so much more than merely acknowledging the absence of someone beloved in that cry. There was the echo of so much grief and lost opportunities and possibly the aftermath of feeling totally abandoned? It melted Hazel's heart instantly and it wiped the slate clean of any unpleasant behaviour or words that had come from Jamie up till now because she could understand exactly where it had come from. Hazel put her arm around Finn's daughter's shoulders.

'Of course you do, love. But you've got Finn here and...and that's a good thing, believe me.'

'He's just a vet,' Jamie sobbed. 'Ellie's not an animal.'

'He's your dad,' Hazel said quietly. 'And he's Ellie's grandad and he's going to take care of you both. He knows what he's doing.' She tried to give Jamie a gentle, reassuring squeeze. 'I'd trust him to look after me more than anyone else on earth.'

Baby Ellie was wearing only her nappy now. 'I need tepid water,' Finn said. 'And a sponge or a cloth. Could you get that, please, Jamie? In a bowl from the kitchen?'

'What's tepid?'

'Lukewarm. Body temperature.'

Jamie nodded, pulling away from Hazel's arm to run from the room. It was only then that Finn caught her gaze and she could see the fear was still there.

'It's not impossible but I think Beanie's a bit young to have had a febrile seizure.'

'What else could it be?'

'If she didn't have an obvious fever, I'd be worried about a birth injury or a brain abscess or head injury.'

'And with the fever?'

Finn picked Ellie up and held her. She squirmed in his arms, still crying. 'The most worrying thing it could be is meningitis.'

'Do you want me to call an ambulance?'

Finn shook his head. 'The seizure's stopped and there's no sign of a rash. We'll take a few minutes to cool her down and then we'll drive her to the closest hospital ourselves. We'll be there before an ambulance could even get here.'

Jamie was back with a bowl of water and a kitchen sponge.

'Good girl.' Finn smiled at his daughter. 'Come over here. We'll put Beanie on her change table and you can sponge her down.' He turned to Hazel. 'Can you see if there was any liquid paracetamol in that box of pharmacy supplies? It might help to bring her temperature down.'

'Do you know where the box is?'

'I think Sandra tucked it away in the pantry. It got delivered in the first day or two after we brought Beanie home, remember?'

As if Hazel was ever going to forget. Especially that first morning when she'd woken up to find herself smack bang in the middle of a fairy tale. Living a fantasy that she'd given up on ever finding in real life. This didn't feel like a fairy tale any longer, though. She could see the way Jamie was watching her father lay Ellie down on the change table. She could feel their fear. This might be a moment that would bond a father and his unexpected daughter for ever, but it wasn't the way either of them would have chosen to bridge that gap. This was far too real to be a part of any fairy tale.

'Call Sandra if you can't find it.' Finn squeezed water

from the sponge and handed it to Jamie. 'She'll know where it is.'

Hazel was pulling her phone from her pocket as she left the room. She might not need to call Sandra but she definitely needed to call Maureen and let her know she wouldn't be getting back to Two Tails any time soon. Kiara might need to come back a little earlier than she'd planned? There was no way Hazel could go back to the refuge yet. Even increasing the distance between herself and Finn this much was hard. Hazel could feel the pull to get back to be by Finn's side as if it were an irresistible force.

The receptionist in the emergency department took one look at Finn's face as he carried the baby into the hospital, flanked by Jamie on one side and Hazel on the other, and sent them straight through to a resuscitation room to be assessed by the medical staff. He couldn't fault the response of the doctors in the department either, especially how seriously they took their examination of a sick baby.

But, as accustomed as he was to medical scenarios and procedures, this experience was overwhelming. Because he was so emotionally involved? It felt like his heart was completely exposed. Raw, even, and there was nothing he could do to protect it. Nothing that he was going to take the time to think of, anyway. He was too focused on what was going on in front of him, watching his precious Beanie get examined and listening to what the doctors were saying to each other and the questions they were asking Jamie.

'Did you have any problems with your pregnancy? Or the birth?'

'No… I didn't tell anyone for a long time, though… I…didn't have anybody.'

One of those raw bits in Finn's heart bled a little. How hard had that been for Jamie? If only he'd known…

'Temperature's thirty-nine,' a nurse reported. 'Heart rate one-eighty.'

'Respiratory rate?'

'Over fifty. Hard to count.'

'Kernig's sign?' a doctor asked.

'Negative.' Another doctor was bending the baby's legs and then she lifted her head. 'Brudzinski's sign also negative. And there's no sign of a rash.'

'Good. I'd like to get some bloods off. I'll just have a look at her ears.' The first doctor glanced up at Jamie. 'Is she up to date with her vaccinations?'

'They said she didn't need them until she was two months old.'

'Has she been unwell in the last few days? Not sleeping or feeding well?'

'I…um…'

'She's been a bit grizzly,' Finn told them. They didn't need to know that Jamie had been avoiding looking after her baby, did they? He needed to protect his daughter as well as *her* baby. Hazel had been right.

This was his family.

And…he'd been wrong in thinking he had no way of protecting his heart, because he only had to glance sideways and catch Hazel's gaze to know that he already had all the protection he needed right here beside him.

'Temperature's climbing. Thirty-nine point five. Heart rate's going up as well. One-ninety now.'

The doctors exchanged glances and one of them nodded. 'We need to rule out meningitis,' they told Jamie. 'And that means we need to do a lumbar puncture to be absolutely sure. You might want to wait somewhere else while we do that?'

It was Finn's gaze that Jamie sought. She looked terrified, even though she probably had no idea what was involved in collecting cerebral spinal fluid. She wanted his reassurance. Or maybe she just wanted to be told what she should do.

Or perhaps his daughter just needed to have him witness her taking a huge step into a new maturity.

'I'll stay with Ellie,' she said. 'I'm her mum.' But she was still holding Finn's gaze.

'I'll stay too,' he said. 'I'm Ellie's grandfather.' He'd stopped himself saying he was Jamie's father because that wasn't a relationship she wanted to claim. Or was it?

'And he's my dad,' Jamie said, tears rolling down her face as she stepped closer. 'I need him here.'

Finn held out his hand and Jamie took hold of it. Tightly.

The team were setting up rapidly to do the invasive procedure of a spinal puncture. One doctor was scrubbing his hands at a sink. A nurse was unrolling sterile packs onto the top of a trolley. There were needles there. Syringes. Small containers to collect fluid. Vials of local anaesthetic.

'I'll go and wait outside,' Hazel said.

'No...' Finn turned his head. It was Hazel's gaze he needed to catch this time. And he held out his other hand, in case she couldn't see what he was trying to communicate. 'Please don't go,' he added quietly. 'I need *you* here.'

Until the results came back and cleared baby Ellie of a serious infection that could potentially be transmissible, she was in a private room off the PICU's main corridor. On her way back from making a quick phone call to Sandra to ask her to go and check on Ben, who had been left alone at home, Hazel found Finn standing in that corridor, looking through the internal window of Ellie's room.

The expression on his face—as if he was very close to tears—made her catch her breath and Finn must have heard that small gasp because he turned his head to watch her walk towards him. When she was just a few steps away, he held out his hand and took hold of hers.

'The results are back,' he told her. 'From the lumbar puncture and the first blood tests.'

Hazel bit her lip. She was hanging onto Finn's gaze as if her life depended on what he was about to say.

'It's nothing more serious than an ear infection,' he said quietly. 'Come in with me and let's give Jamie the good news together.'

The relief was overwhelming.

Right up there with the relief of what she'd seen in Finn's eyes earlier today, when their paths had crossed because they had both set out to find each other. Only hours ago but it felt so much longer. Too long. This was the first moment they'd actually had alone together since the moment their vehicles had been parked side by side in the driveway. Maybe that was why Hazel could feel her eyes filling with tears. Why she felt the need to hide her face for a moment in the safest place she could think of—in that hollow below Finn's collarbone—just above his heart.

And maybe that was why he let go of her hand so that he could wrap both his arms around her, so tightly it was hard to breathe, but Hazel couldn't have cared less. She needed this more than breathing. This feeling of safety. This warmth with the solid beat of Finn's heart against her cheek and the rumble of his voice so close to her ear he only needed to whisper.

'I thought I had too many things I wanted to say to you,' he said. 'But I've just figured out there's only one thing I really need to say.'

Hazel tilted her head so that she could see his face. Was it the same thing she was so desperate to tell him?

I love you...

'You're my heart, Hazel.' Finn dipped his head to brush his lips against her forehead. A soft touch that reminded her instantly of their first ever kiss. 'I love you so much that it's in every single cell in my body so it feels like that's what my heart is made of.'

Oh... That was so much better than a simple *I love you.*

It felt like the world had stopped turning.

Time had stopped ticking.

Hazel's heart was so full right now it felt like it might actually burst, even though she knew perfectly well that that was a physical impossibility. It was mostly full of the love she had for Finn but that was also laced with joy. Because not only did she no longer have to hide how she felt but there were no barriers to letting it grow. And, along with that joy was an enormous amount of hope. For the future. For the happiness she knew they were going to find together. And hope was such a powerful emotion—right up there with love. And trust...

'I love you, too,' Hazel whispered, because she couldn't think of anything more poetic to say, other than that simple truth. 'I always have. I always will.'

'I think I knew that,' Finn whispered back. 'But it was too hard to trust. It was easier to pretend I couldn't see it. Or remind myself that I could never love anybody that much again. But I can. And I do… And…'

And something made him turn his head back to the window. Hazel followed the line of his gaze and saw Jamie, sitting beside Ellie's bassinet. It was obvious they were both crying. Hazel's hand found Finn's again and they were both holding on tightly as they went into the room together.

'It's okay, Jamie,' Finn said. 'Ellie's going to be fine.'

'She doesn't look fine.'

It was true that baby Ellie's face still looked red and she was making distressed snuffling sounds as she tried to cry.

'Kids are good at looking really sick,' Finn told her. 'And then they bounce back really quickly. But we know now that it's only an ear infection and not something worse. The antibiotics will kick in very soon. They're just keeping her here under observation for a bit longer to be on the safe side. I expect we'll be able to go home before too long.'

'I don't have a home,' Jamie sobbed. She reached into the bassinet to pick Ellie up. 'Neither of us do.'

'Of course you do,' Finn told her. 'You're my family and I love you. You and Beanie. And… Hazel.'

Jamie's gaze swerved to Hazel and then back to her father. 'You said you loved my mum.' There was an accusation in her tone. 'That you would never be able to love anybody else like you loved her.'

'I did say that.' Finn nodded. 'And it's still true.'

Hazel's breath caught in her throat. Hadn't he also just said that *she* was his heart?

'It was a first love with your mum,' he told Jamie softly. 'And it was the best thing that had ever happened in my life and I was completely devastated when she disappeared.' He paused to swallow hard.

'It's true,' Hazel put in. 'When he told me about your mum I knew he'd been so hurt that it made it impossible for him to trust anybody enough to love them that much. I knew how much I loved your dad but I never thought he'd be able to feel the same way.'

But he did. It was written all over his face as he watched her speaking. Hazel's heart got even more full. Maybe that was what was pushing tears up to fill her eyes yet again. The joy was overflowing.

'But…' Jamie was looking bewildered.

'Me and your mum—we were just kids,' Finn told her. 'And we *were* in love but it was an escape from the real world that we both needed. Me and Hazel? This is a grown-up kind of love. The kind that's not an escape—more like a rock that's a part of the real world. Something that's solid enough to get you through anything in life.'

Jamie was looking down at the baby she was rocking back to sleep, so they couldn't see her face but it sounded like she was still crying. 'So you get to live happily ever after, then. Like in all the fairy tales. You're lucky…'

'Real life is never a fairy tale,' Hazel said quietly. 'There's really no such thing as a happy ending because life doesn't stop. It goes on and tough things happen. But your dad's right. Love is a rock you can hang onto. So is hope.'

She looked up as she felt Finn squeeze her hand even more tightly as if he wanted to let her know he agreed and she could see that love in his eyes. She could see the same hope that she had for their future. She could also see how much he wanted to kiss her but that was going to have to wait for a more private moment than they'd managed to find in the corridor outside.

She squeezed back on Finn's hand as he turned back to his daughter.

'You're part of our lives now, Jamie. You and Beanie.'

'Am I?' Jamie finally looked up. 'But I've been horrible. Why would you want me to hang around?'

'You're family,' Finn said. 'I'm just sorry I wasn't there while you were growing up.'

'I'm sorry, too,' Jamie muttered. 'For everything.' She caught Hazel's gaze and the way she was biting her lip was an unspoken apology to her as well. 'It'll be different from now on.'

'Before and after.' Finn smiled. 'Like the two tales of Two Tails.' His smile widened. 'I've just had the best idea.'

'What?' The smile was contagious. Hazel could feel her own lips curling. Even Jamie looked like she was about to smile through the remnants of her tears although she probably had no idea what Finn was talking about.

'You know how Jude was asking if Ben was going to get his happy ending—the kind that fans of *Call the Vet* would want to see?'

'I remember…'

'What if we told his story properly? What if we told a whole bunch of stories like his? A whole series of Two Tales. A before and after. Of lives that get transformed, not just for the dogs but for the people as well?'

'I know where you could find any number of stories.' Hazel loved the idea. 'It's what Two Tails refuge is all about. And it would be wonderful because it would give people hope that, if things aren't great, they can get better. Two tales for people. Before and after. Like us.

Before and after we were lucky enough to find a baby in the waiting room.' She had to kiss Finn now, despite not being alone. Just a quick kiss. A soft one. A promise of what was to come later.

'You're my after,' she whispered trying to be quiet enough to not be overheard.

'You're my for ever,' he whispered back.

'I'm here, you know,' Jamie said, with exaggerated patience. 'And I can hear you. You need to get a room, you two.' But she was definitely smiling now.

They were all smiling again a short while later, when the new set of observations on Ellie suggested that the antibiotics were already having a positive effect. Her temperature had dropped and her heart rate and breathing were back to normal. And when she woke up she wasn't grizzling at all and Jamie was able to feed a much hungrier baby.

'We're happy for you to take her home,' the doctor said.

Finn and Hazel stood up at exactly the same time. They reached for each other's hands at exactly the same time. They looked at each other and then they looked at Jamie, who had Ellie in her arms again, and Hazel could see, and feel, the one emotion that was bigger than any other in this moment.

Hope.

There was a tiny pause in the room, as if the world were holding its breath. Or maybe there was a bit of magic in the room because the pause ended with them all saying the same thing at the same time.

'Let's go home...'

EPILOGUE

Eighteen months later...

'COME ON, ELLIE...come inside, now. Grandpa's going to be on telly.'

'*No*... Soon...' The little girl with the astonishing thatch of dark curly hair was standing by the post and rail fence in front of the house, holding up single blades of grass that Isabella the donkey was taking delicately between her lips and, each time she did so, Ellie laughed.

'But Bella might be on telly, too. And Ben...'

'Ben?' Ellie turned and held up her arms to her mother. 'Where?'

'He's with Hazel.' Jamie scooped up her daughter. 'They were having a wee sleep.'

Ellie nodded solemnly. 'Hazel tired,' she said kindly. 'Bubba.'

'That's right.' Jamie carried Ellie up the steps and into the house. 'Bubba's going to arrive any day now and that makes mummas tired.'

Hazel was still lying on the huge sofa in the living room but she was propped up within the circle of her husband's arm, a very contented smile on her face. The old dog with the snowy white muzzle was curled up on her other side, leaning on *her* arm. Finn pointed the remote control at the television and turned it on as Jamie sat cross-legged on the floor in front of him, tucking Ellie in for a cuddle.

'All good?' Finn glanced sideways at his daughter. 'Did you get that assignment done for uni?'

'Not quite. I'll finish it later. I'm not going to miss the very first episode of *Two Tales* going live.'

'Hmmm…' Finn sounded uncharacteristically nervous. 'I'm still thinking it's going to come across as being a bit… I don't know…corny?'

They watched as the opening of the new series showed Dr Finn walking up the steps of a lovely, old cottage with a small black dog at his heels. A sign could be seen in the background—*Two Tails. Please Ring and Wait.*

Finn sat down on the top step. The smile he had for the camera had all the charm and sincerity that had made him such a star in the past. The little black spaniel that sat beside him and gazed adoringly upwards was clearly about to become a new star.

Finn fondled the dog's ears gently as he spoke. 'I've learned a lot of things in the past year or so,' he said. 'And one of them is that there are pivotal moments in life where everything can change. Points at which a story takes a breath…where a new chapter starts. And every life has its own story, doesn't it? Things change. That's another thing I've learned. It's always possible to start again.' His smile was poignant now. 'To find happiness. To find love…'

'Aww...' Hazel had to wipe her eyes.

'I know,' Finn groaned. 'I told you it was going to be corny.'

'Shh,' Jamie ordered. 'I'm listening to this.'

'I love it,' Hazel whispered. She snuggled in closer

and Finn's arm tightened its hold as he dipped his head to kiss her hair.

'The stories in this series are mostly about dogs,' Dr Finn continued. 'But their stories are only part of the picture. They can only start a new chapter of their lives because of the people they meet and the lives of those people change as well. This could be seen as a series about happy endings. And it is.' He tilted his head. 'Or perhaps it isn't. It could be seen as a series about happy beginnings, instead. Anyway…' He had his hand on his companion's head now. 'This is Ben. And this is his story…'

He got up and walked down the steps, with Ben following. They walked towards pens that had other dogs in them. There was a woman working in the distance, with a girl beside her and a black and white collie nearby.

'There's Kiara,' Jamie said. 'And Bunji.' She looked up at her father. 'Bunji's getting her own story, isn't she?'

'Next episode.' Finn's face crinkled into a special smile because Ellie was also looking up at him. She held up her arms so he lifted her into his lap as the picture on the screen was blurring and then morphing into a very different scene.

A beach, a busy road, a sign that advertised the Coogee Beach Animal Hospital and then automatic doors that slid open to reveal a waiting area with a stand of dog treats and toys available for sale. Right in front of the stand was a solid, plastic pet carrier but nobody was taking any notice of it because someone was rushing through the doors. A sobbing woman.

'Please...can someone help? It just ran out in front of me...'

* * * * *

A RESCUE DOG TO HEAL THEM

MARION LENNOX

MILLS & BOON

This duo marks Alison Roberts' one hundredth book.

I've loved Alison's beautifully researched,
exciting, passionate, emotional reads
since I picked up her first, and for many years now
I've been privileged to call her my friend.

Congratulations, Alison. Here's to friendship,
and to many, many more wonderful romances.

CHAPTER ONE

'MY BROTHER'S AN autocratic, over-indulged idiot. Yes, he's a skilled surgeon, but his people skills leave a lot to be desired. Now he's injured, from a stupid act of bravado caused by his failure to wait for the proper emergency services. He's accepted the care of his niece—*our niece*—but in his condition he's the last person fit for the task.'

That statement had been made two days ago. The woman had arrived at Dr Kiara Brail's veterinary-clinic-cum-animal-refuge unannounced. She'd introduced herself as Lady Beatrice Stonehouse, striding imperiously in without an appointment, almost a caricature of English aristocracy: a stocky, strident woman, ridiculously dressed for the Australian springtime in a tweed suit and stout shoes. Her clipped British accent had obviously been accustomed to delivering decrees, not asking for advice.

'I need to return to England,' she'd announced. 'I only came over to take care of the child until my brother was released from hospital. I won't trust my husband with my horses and dogs any longer, but I can't leave this pair without something to hold onto. In my opinion, a dog or a horse are the only solutions—aren't they the answer to everything? With that stupid designer house my brother insists on living in, horses are out of the question, so it needs to be a dog. I've done my research. Your establishment has the best reputation for matching dogs with difficult owners, and my brother's certainly difficult. Both of them are. I can't get a word out of the child. But if you can find the right dog for them and get it settled, I'm prepared to be more than generous.'

And she'd named a figure that had taken Kiara's breath away. And made her think.

Kiara had far too many clients for the dogs she had available. She didn't need to find another home for one of her dogs, but the builder's advice she'd received the day before had been terrifying. Termites. Foundations no longer fit for purpose.

Money she didn't have.

Which explained why Kiara was now standing outside the gates of what looked to be almost a mansion. She was in Clovelly, one of the most beautiful coastal suburbs of Sydney. It was also one of the most expensive. The gates she was standing in front of managed to be both discreet and imposing. No massive lions guarded this entrance, there was just exquisite ironwork set back from the boundary, with a gorgeous garden in front. The owner was obviously prepared to sacrifice a few metres of land to give the public a gorgeous vista to walk past, and make his entrance more…

Daunting was the word that came to mind.

She could see glimpses of the house through the wrought iron. The house was set low, built of pale stone, seemingly almost part of the cliffs. She could see a wide parking area, paved with the same soft stone. Enough parking for half a dozen cars? She bet there was garaging as well. She could see the glimmer of a swimming pool behind the trees. And the garden…

She thought of her own tangle of garden back at Birralong in the Blue Mountains. That was a glorious muddle, a mixture of English cottage planted by her grandmother, mixed with the ever-encroaching bushland.

She wouldn't part from her rambling, dilapidated home and her beloved Two Tails animal refuge for the world, but for a moment she indulged in just a tad of envy. What could she do if she had a tenth of the money this house was worth?

Get rid of termites?

And that was why she was here, she told herself sharply. All she had to do was to find a home for one of her needy dogs, and to part Bryn Dalton—whoever he was—with some of his hard earned.

Or hard inherited. Lady Stonehouse had been blunt. 'My half-brother is very wealthy. We all are. Our parents were unsatisfactory to say the least, but they've left us all…' She'd corrected herself then. 'They've left us *both* well provided for.'

Well, I'm not here to be intimidated by wealth, Kiara told herself firmly, and took a deep breath and pressed the central button on the very intimidating intercom.

And waited.

The silence seemed to go on for ever. Kiara had taken the train from her home in the Blue Mountains—much more sensible than trying to drive in city traffic—and had walked along the cliff path to this house. The street was silent, apart from the squawk of lorikeets in the flowering gums, and the wattle birds in the frangipani trees forming an avenue for the wealthy homes.

'He'll be home,' Lady Stonehouse had told her. 'He's injured his leg—badly. A crushed knee—he needed a complete replacement. He's now doing rehab at home.

He'd like me to stay longer to help with the child, but I can't help any more than I have. If he thinks I'm hanging over his shoulder he's even less likely to agree to this proposal. Stupid man.'

If I had Lady Stonehouse hanging over my shoulder I might be tempted to disagree, too, Kiara thought. It sounded as if this man was being coerced to see her. This visit might well be a waste of time.

She had to try. She pushed the intercom again, and almost jumped when a gruff voice finally answered.

'Are you the vet?'

'I'm Dr Kiara Brail,' she confirmed. 'Yes.'

There was another silence. Kiara glanced up and then quickly glanced down again. An overhead camera was angled so that, inside, Dr Bryn Dalton would be gazing straight at her.

He'd see a woman in her early thirties, dressed sensibly. Her clothes weren't as ridiculously sensible as Lady Stonehouse's tweeds, but she was wearing her best jeans and a soft white blouse. Her dusky skin, the shade she'd inherited from her indigenous grandmother, didn't take easily to make-up, so she wore little. She was short, thin and if she didn't tie back her mass of deep black curls they ran riot. Her father had described her to his friends as scrappy. *'She's built for work rather than decoration,'* he'd said, *'and at least she knows how to keep out of the way.'*

Right now she wanted to be six feet tall and imposing. For some reason she felt very, very small.

And she also felt like telling this family to stick their offer. She was way out of her comfort zone.

She stared at her toes as she avoided giving whoever was behind that camera the satisfaction of seeing her face, and she reminded herself of why she was here.

She had a refuge full of dogs who needed care. She had buildings that needed maintenance.

She was desperate for money.

Needs must when the devil drives. Why had that saying popped into her head right now? Was it the sensation of being overwatched by someone even his sister had described as being an autocratic, over-indulged idiot?

He can't be a complete idiot, she told herself. She'd checked him out on the Internet before she came—well, why wouldn't she? Apparently Bryn Dalton was a neurosurgeon. The articles she'd read had declared him to be top of his field, the go-to surgeon for the type of tricky brain surgery others wouldn't risk. His résumé was impressive, to say the least. So he wasn't an idiot—at least, not an idiot career-wise. In her thirty-two years Kiara had discovered there were many ways of being an idiot.

Like her being here, being checked out, while the man doing the checking took his own sweet time figuring whether he'd admit her or not.

Enough. 'I'm billing your sister for this call,' she said, brusquely. 'I've been standing here for almost ten minutes and I work on billable hours. Billable minutes rounded up. You want to waste more of your sister's money by not letting me in?'

There was another pause. Oh, for heaven's sake. She turned on her heel and took two steps away.

The gate clicked open behind her.

She stopped. Took a deep breath. She was pretty angry now. No, make that very angry. These people in their huge houses, their privileged positions… They thought they held all the power.

'I'm sorry,' the voice said, and his voice did hold a note of apology. 'Please come in.'

Deep breath. Calm down, she told herself. She did have a temper, but she was good at supressing it, and now certainly wasn't the time to let it out.

There was serious money in this establishment. If she had to grovel a little to get some of it for her dogs, then so be it.

But she did vent a little by stomping up the beautifully paved driveway, then along the landscaped artistry of the perfect garden path to finally arrive at the front door.

She almost expected to have to knock again, but it opened seamlessly in front of her. No one was behind it. She stepped through and stood, solitary, in a version of interior decorator heaven.

The entrance hall was the size of her kitchen. She saw gleaming marble floors, vaulted ceilings, exquisite designer furniture—a hall table that had to be antique and French, and two perfectly useless chairs that no one would be stupid enough to sit on. There was a flower arrangement that if, as she guessed, it had been delivered by one of Sydney's top florists, must be worth more than a week's feed for her dogs.

Which was why she was here, she reminded herself, trying desperately not to be intimidated. Dog food.

But wow, she felt small. Like Oliver in *Charles Dickens*…cap in hand, please, sir, can I have—?

'Don't just stand there, come through.' The voice barked through the intercom above the door, and she almost jumped. Okay, she did jump. If ever there was a set-up designed to put the peasants in their place…

Deep breath. The door to the left of the hall was the only one open. The others were firmly closed.

Another deep breath and she walked through.

A study. Really? She thought of her own cubbyhole

of a study and almost snorted. A library, then? A vast room lined with impressive books. Leather furniture. An enormous mahogany desk set into a bay window at the end of the room.

A man in a wheelchair, spinning from his desk to face her.

Her first impression was dark, both the room and its occupant. The room was all books, dark polished floor, deep brown leather, a mahogany desk. The window he'd been sitting at was surrounded by ferns outside, which made the room look designer perfect, but it didn't light the room more than absolutely necessary. He'd obviously been using a desk lamp, but it didn't show his face.

So all she could see was a dark figure, lean, bearded? Maybe just unshaved. His leg was on some sort of support in front of the wheelchair.

He wheeled from the desk to face her but made no move to come closer. Nor did she make any move to come further into the room. There was a moment's silence while he seemed to assess her, his shadowed eyes raking her from the toes up.

Oh, for heaven's sake…

'I'm Kiara Brail, and I'm pleased to meet you, Dr Dalton,' she said, trying very hard to sound brisk and professional. 'Your sister tells me you'd like a dog.'

'She's my half-sister and I personally want no such thing,' he snapped. 'This is Beatrice's half-cocked idea. A dog…' He took a deep breath, as if summoning patience. 'However… I agree, the child needs something, and I'm prepared to try. But I want nothing to do with the thing. As soon as I can get back to work, I'll barely be home. Beatrice has told me she's paying. It'll make her feel better and she can finally leave us, which is what we all want. So bring the dog, but the deal is that you stay here for a week to make sure the thing's settled, house-trained, not likely to disrupt my routine. If at the end of the week my niece wants it to stay and it's no fuss, then it's sorted. Otherwise, the dog goes, but you'll be paid regardless.'

Whoa.

In the middle of that extraordinary statement two words stood out.

'The thing.'

Two Tails wasn't a standard refuge. It was geared for finding the perfect companion for people whose need was great.

If a family wanted a perky puppy, if a tradesman wanted a boisterous mate, if someone wanted a dog for companionship and fun, then there were a myriad breeders and rescue organisations that provided any number of dogs. Two Tails, however, was a specific refuge for specific needs. Its role was to find the right dogs for the right people, with Kiara taking all the trouble in the world to make that match work.

Two Tails' specialty was taking in elderly animals where the owner was no longer able to care for them, often pets that would face euthanasia at most refuges, because how many people wanted to adopt an elderly pet with a very limited life span? And how many refuges were prepared to rehouse animals with elderly or disabled owners?

Two Tails was named for two reasons—one, for the saying 'happy as a dog with two tails', because that was Kiara's aim for all her charges, and two, because there was the truth that Kiara's dogs were mostly facing two tales: a before and after.

The local vets knew Kiara and knew her work.

If someone's pet died and they thought they were

too old or too worried about the future to get another, vets would often refer them to Two Tails. Conversely, if someone came tearfully in and said they were moving into a retirement village and couldn't take their beloved dog, and maybe it should be put down, Kiara would be called to assess the dog. If it fitted the criteria, she'd take it in and work with it, including retraining if necessary. No matter that it be a greying, aged retriever with maybe only a limited time left, if it was the right dog, she'd find it a new home.

It was a niche service. A great service. It worked because Kiara personally vetted each animal and each potential owner.

'So you don't want a dog,' she said now, trying to keep her instinctive revulsion to herself.

'I have enough on my plate.' There was a moment's silence, and she sensed he was trying to suppress anger. 'As you see, I've been injured. I need to concentrate on rehab, plus I'm up to my neck with work that's been put aside because of my injury. However, I've agreed to take on the care of my niece, and my sister says she needs a dog. Thus—'

'Why are you caring for your niece?'

That brought another silence. By this time she was expecting to be told to mind her own business, but instead he stared at her some more and then told it like it was.

'I have… I *had* two sisters,' he said, and suddenly he sounded weary. 'Half-sisters. We have three different mothers. Our father was indifferent to all of us, so we've had practically nothing to do with each other. Beatrice's the oldest—she lives in the UK. I'm the youngest and, as you can see, my home is here. Skye…well, until three months ago Skye lived in California where she, probably encouraged by her mother, seems to have made some very bad life choices. One of them was having a daughter. Alice is ten years old and until three months ago I'd never met her. Then out of the blue, Skye arrived here, insisting she and her daughter needed to stay. I let her—I'm barely home and there seemed no harm. I should have…'

He caught himself then, his face twisting as if in pain, and then forced himself to continue. 'No matter. There was nothing anyone could do. It seems Skye had come here with a plan. Dump Alice and…' He shook his head as if trying to shake off a nightmare. 'We don't need to go there, but two weeks after she arrived, Skye took her own life.'

And there was a stomach lurch.

Two minutes ago, Kiara's instinct had been to get out of this house, fast. Now…

Ten years old. A child brought to stay with a half-uncle she didn't know and was 'barely home'.

Her mother's death.

'I can't leave this pair without something to hold onto.'

Lady Beatrice's words echoed hollowly in her head. She stared at the man before her, and he stared back. As if he'd thrown her a challenge.

'Your leg?' she said, and it was a question. Once more she half expected to be told to butt out, but his face seemed to close even more. Her eyes were starting to adjust to the dim light now. She'd thought he was bearded but he wasn't, just shadowed from maybe two or three days without shaving. With his dark hair, ruffled and unruly, and his deep-set eyes, he looked…

Haunted? It was a crazy adjective, but it was the one that came to mind.

And when he spoke again, his voice was clipped, distant, and she decided haunted was maybe appropriate. For she heard pain.

'My sister chose to throw herself off the cliffs down from the house. You've seen the cliffs around here? They don't leave any room for doubt. Unfortunately, she left a note, and Alice found it too soon. She followed her mother, saw her fall and tried to climb down. By the time I reached them Skye was gone but Alice was trapped far down, just below the high-tide mark. I rang emergency services but climbed down after her—there seemed no choice. Stupid—I fell as well, smashing my leg. But at least I ended up on the same ledge as Alice. The rescue chopper took us off an hour later.'

'Oh, no.'

'As you say,' he said, and he had his formal voice working again. 'So now there's no one for her. Beatrice says the child should go to boarding school, but she's silent and withdrawn and she's terrified of the prospect. So I'm letting her be until school starts again next term. But now Beatrice is demanding that she have a dog.'

To say her heart was twisted was an understatement. A ten-year-old kid…

But one thing Kiara had grown accustomed to in the world she lived in was her heart being twisted. People coming to her, asking for her to care for a beloved pet, tears streaming down their faces as they left. People coming to her in need—*I just need a pet to love…*

Pets of all sorts, neglected, abandoned, bereft. Somehow she had to sort them, make hard decisions. Which ones could she help?

And here was another ask. Could she help?

Here, however, there was a bottom line. 'But you don't want a dog?'

'All I want is my life back.' It was a savage snap. And then he seemed to catch himself, regroup. She could almost see him brace, finding the professional, business-like side of himself.

'I'm a neurosurgeon,' he told her. 'A busy one. I practise surgery at Sydney Central. I'm also a professor at our local university, so I teach. I'm on any number of medical and hospital boards. I've had to put everything on hold because of this...'

'Because of Alice?' She couldn't help herself.

'The thing. Because of this...'

'Because of my leg,' he said, smoothly again though, explaining professional needs. 'I smashed my kneecap and broke both tibia and fibula. Compound fractures. I've had to have a complete reconstruction. It'll be another month before I'm fit to stand for long periods, so I've accepted the role of carer until then. After that, Alice will have to go to boarding school.'

He must have seen the look on her face because his tone changed a little, became defensive.

'You know, I understand Alice. Oh, not the trauma, that's not something I've been burdened with, but she was brought up a loner and that's the way she likes it. Our family has money, so Skye was always able to pay for decent childcare. That's how Alice seems to have been raised—by paid staff. So she understands how to cope by herself. Of course, she's now being treated by psychologists—the best—I organised that. But she hardly saw Skye, so she can't have been all that attached. Give her a little more time to get over this trauma and I agree with Beatrice—she'll be better off at a good school.'

'And then?' Focus on what you're here for, Kiara told herself, trying hard to keep hold of her temper. Focus on her own area of expertise. Finding a home for her animals. 'What happens to the dog then?' she asked.

'It can stay here if it's no trouble,' he said, offhandedly. 'The staff will see to it, and I assume Alice will come back here during school breaks. She has nowhere else. So if she wants the dog then she can keep it, but Beatrice tells me you're willing to take it back if we no longer need it.' He paused, looked at her face and seemed to see what she was thinking. Which was dismay. Almost hurriedly he added: 'However, I'll bow to your judgement. I've never kept an animal. If you think it's more satisfactory, I'm prepared to pay whatever you need to board it when it's not required. Maybe you could keep it for us, bringing it back every holiday.'

There was so much in that it almost took her breath away. She struggled with herself, fighting the urge to turn and walk straight out.

'So the dog is to be a tool for your niece's recovery?' She could scarcely make herself say it.

'Beatrice says your organisation is strapped for money, dependent on donations. I'd imagine you'd be grateful.'

'I'm not the least bit grateful. My dogs aren't things.'

And that caused a long silence.

Kiara was accustomed to the low light by now, and she could see him clearly. He must have been fit before his fall, she thought. He looked long and lean and muscled. He was wearing a faded T-shirt with a sports-type emblem discreetly on the chest—an expensive brand. His jeans had one leg cut off to accommodate a brace. He was looking straight at her—his hooded eyes direct and challenging—but all of a sudden she saw a wash of what looked like almost overpowering weariness.

For some reason she was hit by a vision of the many

injured creatures she'd treated in her career as a veterinarian. Dogs and cats, hissing or snarling, but underneath just plain terrified.

But she wasn't here to treat an injured man and his orphaned niece—or even to care for such. She was here to find a home for one of her needy pets. She thought—with some regret—of the donation Beatrice had mentioned, but this was no home for a creature that had already undergone trauma.

'I'll let myself out,' she said, and he stared up at her in surprise.

'You won't help us?'

'I can't see that giving you a dog would help you at all,' she told him, gently now. She'd had a moment to pull herself together, and this was the voice she used when letting prospective clients down.

No, she couldn't let ninety-year-old Mavis have the active young Doberman she'd set her heart on. Could she maybe introduce Mavis to an elderly pug?

She'd been hit by a walking stick when she'd suggested it, she remembered, and the memory almost made her smile. They'd compromised. Mavis had gone away with a whippet with a limp, and the pair had shared four happy years.

She couldn't see a solution here that was even remotely happy.

'I wish you all the best,' she said. 'But maybe...' This was way out of her area of expertise but she could sense pain underneath the brusqueness, and it wasn't just pain from an injured leg. All her professional life had been devoted to alleviating pain, emotional as well as physical, and she couldn't help herself. 'You say you've organised psychological help for your niece. I'm thinking...maybe it could help you as well?'

Another silence. A long one. Then those shadowed, hawk-like eyes met hers for the last time.

'Get out,' he said.

'I'm leaving,' she retorted, and did.

The kid needed a dog. That was what Beatrice had decreed.

What the kid really needed was parents. Parents who cared.

Left to the silence, Bryn returned to his desk. His work was waiting. He'd kept his teaching role. He had queries from a couple of students he needed to answer.

Instead he put his head on his hands and, just for a moment, gave into despair. He'd almost yelled at the woman who'd just left. Bryn's mantra in life was control, and Dr Kiara Brail had shaken it. For a couple of horrible moments she'd made him feel as if his world was slipping away.

And right now, he felt as if it was.

A half-sister he hadn't even met had decided he'd be a suitable parent—no, make that guardian, he reminded himself—for her daughter. Even the word guardian was laughable. He knew nothing about parenting. He knew nothing about families.

Bryn's life was his work. Emotion, commitment, took time and effort, and it left you totally exposed. Hadn't he learned that almost before he could walk? His father had moved on to the next woman before he was out of nappies. His mother…well, the least said about his mother the better. He was raised by money, by staff. People who moved on.

He'd learned early that you never got close to anyone. His bachelor life suited him down to the ground. He put everything he knew into being the best neurosurgeon he could be—and he *was* a good one. He helped people with his work, but he didn't get close, but here he was, suddenly the only available family of a child he hadn't even known existed until this had happened. Beatrice wouldn't take her. There was no one else.

He'd accepted responsibility. He'd faced that in the weeks he'd had to spend in hospital, and by that time he'd already learned of the personal barriers the child had drawn up to protect herself. Beatrice might be right. A dog might help get her over these first hard months, but from his own experience he knew that to face boarding school, to face life, those barriers would need to be reinforced.

And there was no choice. They both had to move on. He had his work, his life. He'd support Alice as much as he could, but the bottom line was that she'd already learned to be alone.

He thought back to that gut-wrenching night when Skye had taken her own life. He remembered standing at the top of the cliff, looking down. Seeing his niece huddled on a ledge almost to the water line. Thinking for a moment that she looked dead.

Shining his flashlight and seeing her face turn up to him. Desperate.

He'd gone down. Or tried to go down. He'd rung the emergency services first—he'd had that much sense—and then he'd tried to do the impossible. How Alice had got down there he could never afterwards work out—she surely wouldn't tell him—but some massive internal emotion had set him inching down a crumbling cliff face to reach her.

He'd fallen—of course he'd fallen—and then there were two to be winched to safety, not one.

What use had he been? No earthly use at all. He

should have used sense, not emotion. Surely Alice would have survived alone.

And there was life's most important lesson, instilled in each member of his dysfunctional family. Alone was the only way *to* survive.

It was okay, he told himself, trying to shake off the way the woman had made him feel. Things would sort themselves out. Alice would recover from the shock of her mother's death and go on to a life of independence. He'd support her as much as he could—with a good school, carers during the holidays, even a dog.

Or not a dog. What he'd heard from the woman who'd just left was scorn—*'My dogs aren't things'*—and also...pity?

He didn't need pity. His leg was healing. He'd get his life back.

But the pity hadn't been for his leg. Those last words... *'You've organised psychological help for your niece. Maybe it could help you as well?'*

Stupid. He almost had his life under control again. Who was this woman to suggest otherwise? She knew nothing about him and had no right to suggest such a thing.

His flash of anger had been stupid. He had things under control. All he needed was his leg fixed, his niece sorted...and to put out of his mind the flash of pity he'd seen in one impertinent vet's dark eyes.

She'd intended to stomp right out of there. What a waste. She'd come all the way into Sydney on a fool's errand. Not only had she wasted a morning, she'd also been caught emotionally, and she knew she wouldn't be able to forget this for weeks.

She felt guilty.

Which was nonsense, she told herself. There were psychologists looking after the child's needs. She had an aunt and an uncle. Kiara's job was looking out for the needs of the animals in her care, and just because her heart had been wrung…

By both of them, she thought tangentially. By the story of an orphaned child, but also by her uncle. Bryn Dalton might have come across as overbearing—autocratic, his sister had called him—but Kiara spent her career dealing with people relinquishing loved pets, or people desperate for something else to love. She knew emotional stress when she saw it.

But there was no way she could help. Her responsibility was to her refuge, to Two Tails and to the animals in her care. She had to haul herself together and get out of here.

She walked out of the front door—and there was a child, sitting cross-legged on the path leading to the gate. Blocking her way.

Kiara stopped and the child raised a pale, too-thin face to hers.

'My uncle says you're getting me a dog,' she said, and it was a flat, defiant challenge. 'I don't want one.'

The kid was small for ten, a bit too thin. Her fine blonde hair was wisping to her shoulders and she was dressed in shabby shorts and T-shirt. Kiara recognised the logo on her T-shirt as an absurdly expensive children's brand, but nothing else about her looked expensive. She looked a string bean of a kid. She had pale blue eyes, shadowed, and her hair was badly in need of a brush.

Was her face…tear-streaked?

Oh, heck. Kiara recognised a wounded creature

when she saw one and leaving this kid and walking away was more than she could bear.

'You don't have to have one.' It was said automatically, an instinctive response to the situation that had been made clear to her.

This was nothing to do with her. She should just walk on past.

But Kiara would have had to step on the manicured garden to get past the child.

And besides…there was something in the way she was sitting.

Her statement hadn't been an aside, something to be tossed at her as she left. It was an invitation to discuss.

And somehow, Kiara sensed all the pain in the world behind that belligerent statement. *'I don't want one.'*

For some reason she was suddenly thinking of her own childhood, of her at about the same age this child was now. Of her father. Of a litter of pups from one of the farm dogs, watching buyers come and taking them away. Of her holding the smallest, pleading, *'Please can I keep him? Please can he be mine?'*

'Don't be stupid,' her father had barked. *'Dogs are for work. These are pedigree cattle dogs—we sell them for cash. Put the pup down.'*

Why was she thinking that now? Why was her heart lurching?

Don't get involved, she told herself harshly. Your responsibility is to your dogs.

But her heart was still twisting. Surely it wouldn't hurt to talk to the kid for a minute.

'You're Alice,' she said, and the child nodded. She was staring up at Kiara, almost as if challenging her. To do what?

'Why don't you want a dog?' she said and sat down

in the middle of the path with her. Cross-legged. Face to face.

The kid looked a bit taken aback. She edged back a little, but not far.

'I'm Kiara,' Kiara said, gently, lightly. 'Why don't you want a dog?' she said again.

'I'm not staying here. My mother says…said… I have to, but I don't.'

'You'll be going to school.'

'No.'

'So where else will you go?'

'I don't know.' And it was a wail of distress, a cry so deep and painful that Kiara flinched.

'You'll stay here.' It was a low growl and it made Kiara jump. Unnoticed, Bryn had silently wheeled along the path behind her. Maybe Alice had seen him come, maybe she hadn't, but she didn't react. She certainly didn't look at him.

'You'll stay here, for as long as you need to,' Bryn said, still gruffly. He was ignoring Kiara, concentrating solely on his niece. 'I've promised you that, Alice.'

'You don't want me. You never wanted me to come.'

'We're family. I'm your uncle.'

Wrong answer, Kiara thought tangentially. She thought, what would she have done given the same set of circumstances?

Who knew? She had no solid family herself, no well of life experience to draw on.

Except for the animals she loved—the bereft creatures that ended up in her charge.

She thought of one of the few cats she'd rehoused. Two Tails was geared to rehome dogs, but Mops had been an exception. She'd glimpsed him out in the bushland behind the refuge, trying to fend for himself. He was scrawny, his grey and white hair matted. He was also scarred, probably from encounters with the native possums.

Even if her emotions hadn't been caught, cats decimated the wildlife, so Kiara had set a trap for him. She'd caught him on the third night. He'd been wild, terrified, spitting his fury and his fear.

She'd fed him, talked to him, and gently, gently encouraged him to trust.

He was now living with an elderly man who'd lost his wife. The last time she'd seen him—on the home visit she made to all her rehoused animals—Mops had been sitting on his new owner's knee, purring so loudly it almost interfered with the television. Whenever the old man's hand stopped stroking, Mops shifted and nudged until the stroking continued. Both of them had been deeply content with the new arrangement.

And that's what this kid needs, she thought. Nights of holding, telling her she's loved.

Not an assurance such as *'You'll stay here, for as long as you need to.'* That was an implied ending. Alice was expected to leave.

'I don't want the dog.' Alice jutted her jaw and met her uncle's look full on.

'You don't have to have a dog. Your aunt thought—'

'My aunt doesn't care.'

'She thought a dog might help. You might enjoy it. If Kiara—'

'It's Dr Brail,' Kiara said abruptly. She was here on a professional visit, she reminded herself, and it wouldn't hurt to remind them all of that. She might be sitting cross-legged on the path with a bereft child but, for her sake as well as anything else, she needed to keep this businesslike. 'I'm a doctor of veterinary science. I did my doctorate with a study of rehoming animals in need. But it seems I'm not needed here.'

'There's an open invitation,' Bryn said, still watching Alice. 'If you think it could help, then bring us a dog. Beatrice has offered to pay you to stay for a week and see what happens. You must see that Alice needs… something.'

'I want to go home,' Alice said.

'I'm sorry but you can't,' Bryn said, and once again, Kiara thought wrong answer. The answer should be *This is your home now.*

But she had things to do. Animals to care for. She'd been away from Two Tails for more than half a day and Maureen, the part-time assistant she could scarcely afford, would be aching to leave. Maureen was an old friend of her grandmother's, a woman who'd been there for her for ever, but she had her own family needs. She could ask no more of her.

This was a mess—an emotional nightmare—but it wasn't her nightmare. She rose, carefully closing her heart.

'Good luck to both of you,' she said softly. And then, even more softly, 'I'm so, so sorry that I can't help.'

And before her heart could be tugged a moment longer, she turned and fled.

The gate slid silently closed, leaving Bryn staring down at his little niece. Alice didn't move, just sat on the path with her arms crossed. As if shielding herself from pain?

He needed to contact the psychologists again. He knew she was hurting, but what could he do?

'I don't want a dog.' It was a muttered whisper, barely audible.

'You don't have to have one.'

'I want to go home.'

'You have an appointment with Dr Schembury tomorrow. You can talk about that then.'

Silence. Hell, he was so far out of his depth.

The words of the woman who'd just left was still replaying in his head. *'Psychological help... maybe it could help you as well?'*

It wouldn't help at all. What good could talking do? For Alice, yes, but for him… He didn't open up about emotions. Why should he?

Alice rose and slipped away. Who knew where? To another part of the garden? Back to her own room where she could be solitary? Safe?

Solitude helped, he thought. It worked for him.

But for some reason he was left staring at the closed gate, seeing a slip of a woman with pity in her eyes.

He didn't need pity. His leg would heal. The psychs would sort Alice and she'd learn to be strong. He didn't need Dr Kiara Brail and her dogs.

But Alice?

She didn't want a dog either. She didn't want…him.

He thought of the night he'd found her, huddled on the cliff ledge, desperate. Of holding her, trying to keep her safe. Of her despairing whisper. *'I want Mom.'*

She didn't want him, but he was all she had.

He thought of the psychologists in their hospital consulting rooms, empathising, asking all the right questions, treating Alice by the book.

And he thought again of Kiara, sitting cross-legged on the path, acting almost like a kid herself. Who was she to succeed where the psychologists couldn't?

No one, he thought. And anyway, she'd refused to help.

Because she didn't like his terms?

Maybe…

'You're clutching at straws,' he told himself bleakly. 'She's knocked back Beatrice's offer and what would Beatrice know anyway?'

What would Dr Kiara Brail know?

'Nothing,' he said out loud and that was that.

But why, as he turned and wheeled back to the house, did the look in her eyes stay with him? A look that said she understood the pain Alice was feeling. A look that said, given half a chance, she might just be a friend to his damaged niece.

A friend to him?

'Ridiculous,' he said. He—and Alice—had enough to worry them without including a slip of a vet who also had judgement in that same gaze. She was judging him and finding him wanting?

So what?

'Forget her,' he told himself and wheeled inside and allowed the big front doors to close silently behind him. Closing out the thought of that judgement?

It didn't quite happen.

CHAPTER TWO

SHE DIDN'T HAVE the right pet anyway.

All the way home on the train, Kiara told herself over and over: 'They don't need a dog. They need help far above anything the addition of a dog can cure.'

They needed help far above anything *she* could cure.

She'd brought her laptop with her. She had plenty of work she should be getting on with as she travelled, but instead she found herself staring out of the window. But she wasn't looking at the scenery, which grew more and more breathtaking as she neared her Blue Mountains home. Instead she saw a wisp of a kid declaring she didn't want a dog. A kid who, in some intangible way, reminded her of the lonely child she'd once been.

Alice has it much, much worse than I ever did, she told herself, and that made her feel even more bleak.

As did the thought of… A man who looked gutted?

He's nothing to do with me, she told herself. He's rich, arrogant and insensitive. He doesn't want a dog. He just wants to get rid of responsibilities.

But when she got back to Two Tails she couldn't help herself. She leafed through the files of the dogs she had in care, and then went out to check the pens, greeting the dogs in question, asking herself…could this one help?

And of course there wasn't one.

Two Tails was a refuge with specific aims. It was Kiara's dream refuge, a vision she'd had since she was… well, as long as she could remember.

The animals on her father's farm had been just that, animals. A means to an income. Her father had never treated his livestock badly—that'd hurt his income. But he'd never looked at an animal with anything other than consideration of how useful it could be.

The same went for how he saw his daughter. Kiara's mother had walked out when she was six, and in fairness Kiara couldn't blame her. She'd married a cold, hard man. The only thing Kiara blamed her mother for was not taking her with her, and hearing of her mother's death a couple of years later had only cemented that feeling of abandonment.

So Kiara had been left with her father, who treated her as a nuisance when she was small and free labour as she grew. But she'd also been left with her father's animals. He never knew that she had a name for every one of them, that she cried her eyes out every market day.

So Two Tails was her answer. Early on she'd set her heart on being a vet, but the aim of veterinary science, for Kiara, was to give as many animals as possible as good a life as she could manage. She ran a normal clinic at the rear of Two Tails—she had to do something to earn a living and the tiny town of Birralong appreciated having a resident vet—but the rest of the time she spent matching relinquished pets with those who most needed them.

And that didn't include Bryn Dalton, she told herself as she walked from pen to pen. But still she found herself thinking…

The little Peke whose owner had died unexpectedly

two weeks ago? The relatives had taken the dog to a vet on the other side of Sydney. 'Can you put it down, please? There's no one to look after it.'

Pamela the Peke was ten years old and spent her life trying to find a lap for a cuddle. She also yapped, but that was a small price to pay for a friend. Kiara had a score of clients waiting; she just had to decide the best match.

But a yappy Peke for Bryn? No, she corrected herself. She'd meant to think, a yappy Peke for Alice? Either way the answer was no.

Who else? The wolfhound in the next pen? Ralph was gorgeous but aging, and wolfhounds had such a limited life expectancy. The last thing Alice needed was another heartbreak, and she had two alternative clients wanting Ralph already.

A whippet? Maybe, but the whippet in question was a bit stand-offish. Kiara's career was matching people with pets, and she just knew they wouldn't suit.

It was the same for all the dogs in her charge, she decided, and then she thought that it was just as well because if there'd been such an animal she would have been torn.

And she couldn't have helped, even if she was torn.

'Kiara?' The voice came from the front yard, hauling her out of her thoughts of the two people she'd met that morning.

Hazel.

Hazel Davidson was pretty much Kiara's best friend. They'd met at university, had bonded over their love for animals, and Hazel had helped Kiara set up Two Tails.

Two Tails was established on the property that Kiara's grandmother had left her, but establishing the refuge had cost money neither of them had. They'd worked side by side at a vet clinic in Coogee until they'd saved enough to set the refuge up. But the refuge and tiny clinic didn't provide an income to support them both, so Kiara worked here full-time, and Hazel came when she could.

Kiara wasn't surprised at her arrival. What she was surprised at, though, was the urgency she heard in her friend's voice.

'Kiara, where are you?'

'In the pens. Hang on, I'm coming…' she called out and headed out to see what the matter was.

Kiara's grandma had been an indigenous Australian. She'd married an Irishman who'd died soon after the birth of their only child—Kiara's mother—and she'd lived at Birralong ever since. Her passion had been the native bushland and the garden within the house yard, and she'd eked a living by propagating and selling plants. When she'd died, the garden had been overgrown but gorgeous. It was gorgeous still. Kiara walked into the front yard now and saw Hazel stooped over something lying under the shade of a native frangipani. The soft yellow blooms were wafting down on Hazel's head and the perfume was everywhere.

But this was no time for taking in the beauty of the place. What was the urgency? She headed down the path—and stopped short.

A dog. A collie? Hard to say from here.

Hazel was bent over it. What…?

'I found her on the side of the road near the bus stop in Birralong,' Hazel told her. 'She's… Oh, Kiara, this is just awful…'

There was a stomach lurch. This had happened before. The bus stop was at the corner, right by the sign to her clinic. What was it about the sign 'Veterinary

Clinic' that made people feel they had a licence to dump animals nearby? Kiara crouched by her friend, seeing what Hazel was seeing.

A border collie. Small for its breed. Black and white.

But this was no healthy dog suffering simply from road trauma. Kiara had seen neglected dogs in the past but this…

Hazel sat back, tears in her eyes, as Kiara moved in to check. The dog was lying on its side—*her* side—on the grass. Her bones stood out with horrific clarity. Kiara could see grazes along her side and her legs, from the bitumen on the road? What fur she had left was filthy and matted. But there was worse.

There were deep sores around her neck—a gouge where, at first guess, she thought a rope must have fastened so tight it had dug in. There were still traces of rope left in the wounds. Her hindquarters were a mass of pressure sores. She looked as if she'd spent her life sitting at the end of some appalling roped existence, with no choice but to sit, and sit, and sit. Or lie.

There were similar sores along her ribs, and her thigh… It was swollen, oozing. A massive infection?

Kiara put her hand gently on the dog's head. She expected nothing. The dog looked too far gone to flinch, to snarl, to react.

The little collie did none of these things, but instead of passive stillness, as Kiara's hand moved under her head to cradle and lift, the collie's eyes widened. Big, dark eyes met hers.

She saw calmness.

Trust?

And as she shifted her hand to see the damage, the dog raised one filthy, matted paw to rest on her arm. Like a plea for help?

If ever there was a heart twist, this was it. A dog, appallingly mistreated, looking up at her as if humans were to be trusted. As if Kiara was to be trusted.

'Can we even do anything to help her?' Hazel's voice was a wretched whisper. 'It might be kinder to… On top of everything else that's happened today, I don't think I can bear it.'

What was happening with Hazel? Kiara cast her a concerned glance, but her attention had to be solely on the dog. She could hardly tear her gaze from that of the dog. These wounds were indeed horrific but…

'She's only young,' she whispered. 'Maybe…'

'Oh, Kiara, look at her. She's been so abused that, even if we did manage to save her life, how scarred is she going to be? Physically and emotionally? Then there's the cost. Who's going to pay? We both know that sometimes the kindest thing to do is…is to let them go. We can make sure she's not in any pain.'

The dog's head was still in Kiara's hands, and she was still looking into those trusting dark eyes. But Hazel was right, she thought grimly. What lay ahead if she decided to treat were X-rays, blood tests, and who knew what else? Then coping with infections, refeeding programmes, months of treatment. And after this amount of mistreatment the dog might end up a snarling, terrified neurotic. Who could blame her?

But those eyes… That paw, still resting on her arm…

She took a deep breath. 'We're going to do more than that,' she said. 'Let's get her into the surgery. I know it doesn't make sense, and we can't afford to take on a case like this but, dammit, Hazel, we set up Two Tails for a reason. If I'm going to end up bankrupt, then I'll go down doing what I do to the end.'

* * *

They carried the dog into their clinic at the side of the house. They X-rayed and, thanks be, found no breaks. No sign of major internal blood loss from injuries like a ruptured spleen or liver.

They set up an IV to rehydrate. They organised anaesthetic—no easy feat in a dog so near death—and then they worked together to painstakingly get rid of the matted fur so they could clean and debride the myriad foul sores.

The thigh was the major problem. The wound had ulcerated and the infection was deep. And the smell…

Clostridial myositis? That was a heart sink, but the look of the wound, the smell… Years ago she'd seen a similar wound in a horse that had been left unchecked for too long. The owner had elected to have the animal put down.

Sensible? Yes, it was, but now…those eyes…that paw…

'I'm suspecting clostridium myositis,' she said grimly, and Hazel looked at her in astonishment. She'd settled now, emotion taking a back seat to allow veterinary competence to hold sway. They were two vets, two friends, working their hardest to save a dog that would cost Kiara a mint.

'How can you tell?'

'I'll need blood tests to be sure, but I've seen it before.'

'Oh, Kiara…'

And she knew what Hazel was thinking. Kiara's focus was on her role, coping with the ulceration of the thigh, but some part of her was still conscious of Hazel's reminder of money—or the lack of it. The astronomical quote to repair termite damage had been hanging over her since she'd first seen it, growing more and more impossible, and in the silence as they worked it seemed to grow even bigger.

'We can fix this.'

'Yeah, but the cost.'

'Let's just do it.'

What followed were hours of meticulous work, to clean and debride what seemed an endless number of lesions. And because Hazel was her friend, because they were used to working together and knew exactly what they were doing, they were able to distract themselves a little by talking about other things. Even if they were also unpleasant.

'Have you any idea how you might cover costs?' Hazel asked as they worked.

'Why bother?' She shook her head, the dreariness of her situation closing in. 'What's another debt among so many? Two Tails is doomed to close anyway.'

'What?' Hazel had known they were strapped for cash, but not about this latest disaster. 'No!'

'I got a quote to repair the termite damage and it's… well, it's impossible. Even if I mortgaged the property to find the money, I wouldn't be able to meet the repayments.'

'You can't close!' It was an exclamation of horror. 'What if you charged more?'

'How? By taking in more dogs and selling them to the highest bidder? That's not how we do things.'

'Publicity, then?' Hazel asked slowly.

She thought about it. Hazel's boss, Finn, was a celebrity vet, hosting a TV show called *Call the Vet*. Finn would know all about publicity—but her shy friend? Not so much.

'I took part in an episode of *Call the Vet* that was being filmed today and I talked about Two Tails,' Hazel told her, sounding a bit self-conscious. 'The show's producer is interested in coming out here and doing an episode, and with a bit of luck it could lead to donations.'

'Wait a minute.' Kiara's interest was caught. 'I thought you swore over your dead body that you'd never appear in that programme again.'

'I did. But there was a hit and run outside the clinic.' Hazel shrugged. 'I guess it comes with the territory but this one got to me. A gorgeous old black spaniel who's apparently a stray. He needed surgery to plate a tibial fracture. Finn thought he must be about fourteen or fifteen years old. He also needed a name, so I called him Ben.'

So that was what had made it so awful. Two abandoned dogs in one day.

But… Ben?

'Ben? Wasn't that your first ever dog?'

'Yeah.'

'So we're both suckers for dogs.'

'I guess we are.'

They worked on for a bit, but there was something about Hazel. Something she wasn't saying.

'Well, then,' Kiara prodded. 'Was that what made it a bad day for you? Having to work with Finn? Or did Ben not make it?'

'Ben's doing well, as far as I know,' she said diffidently. 'I'll go and check on him when I'm done here.' There was a self-conscious pause and then, 'It's Finn who's not doing so well. A baby got left in the waiting room with a note that said it was his.'

'No! Tell me!'

So she did. It seemed as if Hazel's boss had been landed with a baby. A baby he swore he didn't know.

As they carried on chatting about Finn's predicament more and more of the dog's matted hair fell away. She could now see clearly what she was dealing with, and as the dog's breathing stayed steady, Kiara was starting to feel positive again. There was nothing like a bit of gossip to make a girl forget her troubles.

So…why not share?

'I had my own share of drama today, too,' she told Hazel, and as she worked she told her about Beatrice's visit, and her own trip to meet Bryn and his little niece.

'The amount she offered me was ridiculous,' she told her. 'And I don't even have a dog suitable for a child.'

'How about this one?' Hazel asked, and Kiara stopped what she was doing and stared. Then she stared down at the ragged, skeletal dog they were working on.

'Are you out of your mind?'

'Maybe.' Hazel paused as well and stood back, looking at the dog they were treating. Surely no one would want this dog, at least not for months, and even then, not if her temperament proved impossible. 'But it sounds as if there are two wounded souls that need help. Why not make it three?'

'Hazel, that's ridiculous.'

'You'll need to find a home for her, even if you are bankrupt,' she said, reasonably. 'Especially if you're bankrupt. You know, I've sort of fallen for her, too. Why not give her to someone who can pay?'

And for a crazy moment Kiara let herself think it might be possible. She let her thoughts drift forward…

'Maybe I could call her Bunji,' she murmured, thinking back to her grandmother, who often slipped into her First Nation language. 'It means a mate. A friend.' She smiled ruefully then, hauling herself back to reality. 'Who am I kidding? How could I give such a dog to a ten-year-old?'

'Give her to the uncle. He sounds like he needs a friend, as much if not more than his niece. And hey, if he falls for Bunji he might even be prepared to backpay for her treatment. How's that for a thought?'

Okay. For a moment Kiara let herself seriously consider.

She thought of the pair of them, of their underlying desperation.

She thought of Bryn.

For some reason Hazel's words resonated. *'He sounds like he needs a friend, as much if not more than his niece.'* She thought of his shadowed face. Of the pain she saw, a pain that wasn't just physical.

That's not my problem, she told herself fiercely. She had enough problems of her own to deal with.

'They really don't want a dog.' She tried to say it with authority, tried to believe it was true. 'Besides, I'd have to stay there. A week at least, he stipulated, and who's going to take care of this place? I can't ask you to take more time off.' Hazel had used her last holidays helping her build new pens, and there had to be limits to how much she could ask. 'I can't afford to pay anyone. The whole thing's impossible.'

She looked down again at… Bunji. How had that name stuck so fast? She looked like something out of an anatomical diagram, Kiara thought grimly. Almost skeletal.

And yet part of Kiara was still caught by the look in the dog's eyes as she'd carried her inside, as she'd organised the anaesthetic. There'd been such trust…

And then Hazel's phone beeped and beeped again. Whoever was trying wanted her urgently.

They'd done almost as much as they could do tonight. Hazel cast her an apologetic glance, stripped off her gloves and went to check. She read and her face changed.

'I need to go,' she said.

'Ben?'

'I…no. I'm sure he's okay but I would like to see for myself. And you'll want the results on those blood samples as soon as possible.'

Kiara nodded. 'No worries. We've done all we can for the moment. I'll finish up and get her settled. Thanks so much for your help.'

'Think about what I said before,' Hazel said as she gathered her gear. 'About giving Bunji to that uncle. Maybe it's true that people—and dogs—come into our lives for a reason.'

'Maybe,' she said, as the door closed behind Hazel. Then she sighed. 'Or maybe not. Oh, Bunji. Mate. What are we going to do?'

CHAPTER THREE

WHAT FOLLOWED WAS a dire couple of weeks, taking care of her dogs, trying to salvage the wreck that was Bunji, trying to figure a way she could keep Two Tails running—and finally there was a frank discussion with her bank manager. Who put it to her straight.

'Your best bet is to put the place on the market right now,' he'd told her. 'It'll never sell as an animal refuge. We suggest you pull the pens down and present it as a possible luxury home. A renovator's delight if you will, and there are plenty of cashed-up couples who'll buy it as such. What you get should leave you a little to go on with—enough to rent a place in town and give you enough time to search for work.'

The thought broke her heart, but she was starting to accept it. She was already starting to wind down, figuring how long it would take to rehome the pets she had, how long it would take to walk away.

But not from Bunji.

The little collie was doing brilliantly, though only a vet might say so. To an untrained observer she still looked like a train wreck. The diagnosis of clostridial myositis had been confirmed, and the wound on her thigh was finally starting to heal. Her fur was starting to grow back but she still looked half shaved.

She slept now in a crate by Kiara's bed. Not because she needed the warmth of the house—the spring weather was warm enough for her to be safe in one of the pens—but because those eyes followed Kiara, almost as an act of desperation. She never whined; she never made any demands. She just looked as though being close was all she asked in life.

It would take months before she could be made presentable enough—trusting enough—to rehouse with Kiara's usual needy clients. So wherever she went, Bunji would have to come with her, Kiara thought, but the impossibility of finding a rental that'd take her—and the unfairness of leaving such a dog while she was forced to take a full-time job…

The future was filling all her thoughts and she almost missed the blinking on her phone that told her she'd missed a call. It was from Hazel; she'd left a voicemail.

'I'm heading your way. I'll fill you in when I get there, but it's best if I get away from here and I need to go somewhere I can take Ben. I don't know if that job opportunity's still there—the one with that guy who needs you to live in and get a rehome settled?—but if it is this might be the ideal time to take advantage of it. I'm more than happy to take care of Two Tails for a week or so.'

She rang her back. Her friend was already driving. She pulled over to take the call, and sounded abrupt. 'Could you still take that job at…what was the guy's name? The guy with the niece who wanted Bunji?'

'He didn't want Bunji.'

'But he needed Bunji. And he'll pay. Kiara, I have… I have a week or so off. I can care for Two Tails if you still want to go.'

What the…? 'Have you been sacked?'

There was a loaded silence. 'No,' Hazel said at last. 'But…it's complicated. If this guy is still offering that sort of money…'

'It was his sister who was offering.'

'But it's huge, right? Maybe enough to keep Two Tails going for a while longer?'

'He doesn't want a dog.' How many times had she said that, mostly in her own head, over the last two weeks?

'So take the week to find out. What's the alternative?'

'Hazel…'

'Just do it,' Hazel told her.

So she did.

CHAPTER FOUR

THE VET WAS HERE. Bryn had agreed, and now he was regretting it.

What Alice surely needed was someone skilled in treating neglected, traumatised kids, but by now Alice had been under the care of the best children's psychologists he could find. Bryn's medical network was wide. The people he'd found were skilled, but they'd made no difference at all.

Alice was aloof to the point of clinical detachment. She was outwardly a biddable, obedient child. She slept, woke, dressed, ate—though not enough. She answered politely when questioned. When the psychologists worked with her, Bryn got the impression she was expecting every question, had heard it all before.

What sort of life had she led until now? After a lot of research, he'd managed to locate the last of the many temporary nannies and housekeepers Skye had employed back in the States. The woman had been blunt.

'I only worked with them for a month, and that was all I could stand. I was sorry for Alice but there was no way I could help. The mother threw money around like water, but she was screwed up. To her the kid was just a nuisance—or a servant when everyone else quit, which was often. She used to scream at us to get out of the house and I can't tell you the hours I spent at the park, with Alice staring into middle distance, engaging in nothing at all. I couldn't get through to her. So her mom's died? I'm sorry to hear it, but part of me thinks it's the only hope the kid has. Good luck with her.'

So he'd spent the weeks while his own leg healed, waiting for Alice to heal. But her mental wounds seemed so much worse than his physical injuries. She sat in her bedroom or out in the garden and she stared at nothing. Waited for…nothing?

And now, weeks after that initial approach, the vet with the dog had finally agreed to take up his sister's offer. She'd agreed to bring a suitable dog here, she'd stay for a week or so, and she'd see if it could make a difference. Nothing else was working and Beatrice was on his case, so why not accept?

He'd researched Two Tails by now, a do-good organisation run on a shoestring. A little digging had him discovering its founder, Dr Kiara Brail, was in dire financial difficulties. For all the contempt she'd shown him at their first meeting, he knew she'd have accepted this job for money. She'd offload one of her dogs, she'd get some much-needed cash and be out of here. She'd said she had a dog she thought might be suitable, but he'd cut her off. He wanted no details. He was pretty much certain Alice would take one look at any fluffy bit of yappery and…

No. She wouldn't even look, he thought. Every single thing he'd produced for her, every suggestion, every attempt to get close, had been met with a blank stare, a polite response and then indifference.

But he couldn't get away from the fact that Alice was deeply unhappy. Her remoteness was a shell he couldn't pierce, but for a ten-year-old to have no joy at all… The longer it lasted, the more desperate he felt.

The return call from Dr Brail had come at a time when he was feeling at his wits' end. The sensations he'd felt when he'd first met her were still with him. He didn't need her pity—or her judgement—but for Alice… Okay, he'd try anything he could, even if it did mean infringing even more on his precious isolation.

So he'd agreed to her coming, but when the doorbell went he made his way out to greet her thinking this would be another week wasted. Luckily this house was big enough to keep them all separate.

He opened the door and here she was, the woman he remembered. Little, dark, fiery.

Fiery? That had been the adjective that had come to mind when he remembered her. He'd been pretty much out of it when he'd interviewed her last, seeing her as someone his sister had foisted onto him. Businesslike, determined, she'd hardly dented his radar—until she'd fired up. *'My dogs aren't things.'* He'd got it, he'd even admired her for it.

It didn't help his opinion of her now, though, when he knew she'd accepted Beatrice's offer because she needed cash.

But she was here, and he might as well make the most of it. She stood on his doorstep wearing jeans and a plain shirt—pretty much the same as he'd seen her the last time.

Her dark curls were tugged back tight.

She was wearing a battered backpack, and at her side was probably the most appalling dog he'd ever seen.

It was a black and white border collie—or at least what fur it had was black and white. It looked a mass of healing sores. Its thigh was shaved and dressed with a thick white wad. One of its ears looked torn—its good ear pricked up as if interested, the other flopped uselessly down, as if a muscle had been torn. Its eyes were too big for a face that looked almost cadaverous. It was wearing a harness and lead, but it stood pressed against her leg, as if it needed her support.

It looked…appalling.

'What the hell is this?'

He spoke instinctively and he spoke too loud. Both the dog and the woman flinched. But Kiara didn't back away. She stooped and lifted the dog into her arms and held her close.

'This is Bunji,' she told him, defiance front and centre as she met his gaze head-on. 'Bunji's had almost as hard a time in life as Alice. I thought they might help each other.'

'I don't need another…'

'Another what?' Her chin tilted. Her eyes held anger, pure and simple.

Another what? Another hopeless creature? Her words held condemnation and he deserved it. But he was floundering.

'You can't foist another…'

'I'm not foisting anything on anyone. You want me to leave, I will.'

He stared at them both, woman and dog. Her eyes didn't leave his. She was cradling the dog—surely too big for her to carry—against her breast, and the dog was huddling against her. While he watched, it suddenly raised its head and licked her, throat to jaw. A measure of trust.

And suddenly he felt ashamed. He'd read of the work this woman did. Two Tails Animal Refuge… Yes, she was here because she needed money, but she needed money because of the work she did.

But this dog?

'My niece doesn't need this dog,' he said, sure of his ground on this one. 'She's wounded herself. For heaven's sake, we need something to cheer her up.'

'What's foist?'

The voice came from behind him. Alice had simply appeared, a silent wraith, watching on the sidelines of life. Even getting two words from Alice was unusual.

He turned. The little girl, dressed as always in the shabby shorts and shirt she seemed to live in—she loathed it when his housekeeper insisted they had to be washed—was hard at his heels, staring out at the dog in Kiara's arms.

What had he said? *'You can't foist another...'*

'A gift,' Kiara said promptly. 'Foist means give a gift. Your uncle was saying I can't give another gift to him. I guess that meant you were the first gift. Bunji is the second. If you both want her, that is.' And she set the dog gently down again by her side.

There was a deathly silence while Alice stared at Bunji, and Bryn felt a surge of gratitude so great it threatened to overwhelm him. This kid had been through so much. The last thing she needed was to think her uncle didn't want her.

The fact that he didn't…

No. It was no longer true, he accepted. When he'd woken in hospital to realise what Skye had done, he'd felt overwhelmed. Injured, battered, shocked, all he'd wanted in that moment was to get his old life back. But in these past weeks, as his pain levels had decreased, as he'd done the research on his niece's background, as he'd had the space in his head to see Alice's needs, he'd come to realise that even if he could wish Alice away, he wouldn't. If some magical relative appeared from the States ready to transport his niece back overseas to a happy ever after, he'd at least follow. He'd at least make sure the kid was safe.

He'd want to stay involved.

But try as he might to find one, there was no such relative, and now, as he watched Alice watch the dog, as he thought of Kiara's words—*a gift*—he thought just maybe…

'It's hurt?' Alice said it tentatively, but the words themselves were important. She spoke so rarely. *Please…thank you…yes…no.*

Mostly no.

'This is Bunji and she's very hurt,' Kiara said, gently now, speaking only to Alice. 'She's just one year old—she's little more than a baby—but she's had a very bad time. The people who had her didn't look after her. They bought her as a cute puppy and then they seemed to forget about her. They hardly fed her, they never let her play and when they decided they didn't want her any more they threw her away. She's been lonely and hungry and afraid all her life. My friend Hazel found her on the side of the road, all by herself. She brought her to me because I care for dogs like Bunji. I've treated her sores, I've fed her and cared for her, but what she needs now, most in the world, is someone who wants to be a friend. Someone who cares for her. Bunji's an Australian word for friend, and for some reason I thought that friend might be you. If you think you might be able to help. And if your uncle agrees, of course.'

'She looks far too damaged to be out of care.' Bryn's words were too harsh. He caught himself, backtracked, tried to soften. 'I mean… Dr Brail, surely this dog needs more treatment than we can give? Even if Alice wanted her…'

'That's why I need to come and stay for a while,' Kiara said calmly, still looking at Alice. 'To teach you both how to care. Alice, do you remember me? I came here a couple of weeks ago. My name's Kiara. Your aunty Beatrice asked me to stay with you for a week, for you to get to know Bunji. To see if you'd like Bunji as a friend.'

The little girl was still staring at the dog. 'Would she only be here for a week?' It was a flat response, but at least it was a response. In answer Kiara fondled the dog's ears and looked at Bryn. Her gaze said the next answer was up to him. The response was something she had no business giving. This was between him and his niece.

He stared down at the dog. A more miserable, wounded, neglected creature he'd never seen.

Alice was looking at the dog as well. Saying nothing. Standing back. Waiting.

Would she only be here for a week?

He looked at Kiara, who looked blandly back at him. This was his call. Dammit, why couldn't she have brought something cute? Something a kid could really love?

Love? He thought suddenly, tangentially, of the women he'd dated before Skye's suicide had propelled him so viciously into uncharted waters. He'd been a serial dater. With his money, his looks, his professional connections, the world had pretty much been his oyster. He'd dated some gorgeous women in his time.

But…*love*? Why was the word suddenly wobbling, as if it had some kind of meaning he hadn't figured?

And maybe Alice got it before he did. She took a

couple of tentative steps forward. Kiara was cradling the dog's head, holding it steady. Was she holding the dog's head to prevent snapping? If it was vicious…

'She's a bit scared,' Kiara said gently to Alice. 'She hasn't met many people who are kind to her.'

'People hurt her?' It was a whisper.

'They did. They didn't love her, and they threw her away when they didn't want her any more.'

She didn't say more, and he had the sense to stay silent himself. They stood in the early morning sunshine, while girl and dog seemed to take stock of each other.

Most young dogs would have sniffed forward, Bryn thought. Investigated. Or pulled back if they were afraid, maybe cowered behind legs. This one—Bunji—did neither. She simply stood, totally passive. But she looked at Alice. Just looked.

And Alice looked back. Moments passed. Nothing was said. And then he realised Alice's question had gone unanswered. *Would she only be here for a week?*

Up to him.

'She's here for as long as you want her to be here,' he said, a bit gruffly because for some reason the words were hard to say.

'But you said… Aunt Beatrice said… I'll have to go away.'

'If you like…if you end up caring for her then she can stay with you.' Why had he said that? Didn't he have plans to send this kid to boarding school? But the words had been said now, and they couldn't be unsaid. And he glanced at Kiara and caught a look of approval.

Wow.

What was it in that look?

Up until now her approach seemed to have been pure belligerence—even judgement. Well, so what? He had enough on his plate without worrying about what this slip of a vet thought of him. She was here at Beatrice's bidding. She was nothing to do with him, and what she thought of him was totally immaterial. But now…that one glance, quickly hidden, sent something fast and warm, something he had no hope of understanding. But as he turned back to focus on Alice and the dog, the look stayed with him.

'I don't know how to care for her,' Alice was whispering. To his amazement she'd dropped to her knees so she could look at the dog face to face. Kiara's hand was still on the dog's head, but he had the feeling it was more to reassure the dog than to protect Alice.

'That's why I'm here,' Kiara said, briskly now, and she squatted down as well. 'Your aunt Beatrice and uncle Bryn have paid me to come for a week, to help you learn to look after her. She'll take a lot of caring for, though, Alice. It's weeks since we found her and she's starting to recover, but she'll still take a long time to heal. And that's just her body. She's never been taught that she can trust. It'd be up to you to teach her that she can trust you as her friend.'

'But you'll go away.'

Dammit, he felt like an outsider. They were crouched, Kiara and Alice, with the dog between them. He stood above them and he felt…yes, outside.

Well, he couldn't crouch if he wanted to, he thought harshly. This damned knee… He'd smashed it completely. What he had now was a mechanical replacement, and the rest of his body was taking its own sweet time coming to terms with it. He was no longer in a wheelchair, but he needed his sticks and if he crouched…he'd have to ask Kiara to help him back up.

She'd do it. That was her obvious forte, helping

wounded creatures. He was dammed if he'd be included in the list.

'I will go away.' Kiara was answering softly. 'Alice, I'm a vet. I run an animal refuge called Two Tails, and my job is to help animals like Bunji.'

'My uncle and aunt are paying you to stay here?'

Spot on, Bryn thought. This kid was accustomed to hired help. It wouldn't help if she got to think of Kiara as anything else.

'My animal refuge is in trouble,' Kiara told her. 'Our buildings are starting to fall down. Your aunt and uncle have offered to help me fix things, which is how I got to meet you. So yes, I will be leaving after a week. I have to go back to Two Tails, but if you decide to keep Bunji then I'll keep checking and checking. And every time you need to talk about her then you can phone me straight away.'

And there it was, a direct, uncomplicated offer of friendship.

What was it in that offer that made him draw in his breath?

It also made Alice stare at Kiara for a long, long moment, almost as if she didn't believe, and she was searching in Kiara's face for the truth.

Kiara held her gaze, and for some reason to Bryn it felt as if the world were holding its breath.

And in the end it was Bunji who ended the impasse. She'd been standing unmoving between woman and child. Like a dog who'd been waiting for a very long time and was expecting to do more of the same. But for whatever reason, she suddenly decided on action.

She took a tentative step forward, just the one, but it was enough to put her almost nose to nose with Alice.

Then, cautiously, as if she was expecting a rebuff, she lifted a paw.

Alice looked down at it. Almost as tentatively she put her own hand out and the dog's paw rested on it.

'She's very hurt?' she whispered, so softly Bryn could hardly hear.

'She is. She's healing though, and now she needs a friend, very badly.' Kiara's response was almost as soft.

'And you'll tell me what to do?'

'That part's easy,' Kiara told her. 'But what Bunji needs more than anything else is the promise that people won't let her down.'

'I won't let her down.'

'You'll be her friend?'

'I'll… I'll try.'

'Then that's a start,' Kiara said and grinned. She rose then, and smiled up at him, seriousness put aside for the moment. Her smile seemed wide and happy, and it leaped out and seemed to grab him in some way he couldn't explain. She was smiling straight at him, and that smile…

He'd thought she was plain. Suddenly she seemed anything but.

'This is indeed an excellent start,' she said, and put her hands together and raised them, a gesture of triumph. 'What do you say, Dr Dalton?'

'Bryn,' he said faintly.

'Bryn, then,' she agreed happily. 'Right, can you show me to my quarters? Alice, it's time we got on with it. You and Bunji have a whole lot of getting to know each other to do.'

CHAPTER FIVE

He hardly saw them for the rest of the day.

Oh, he stayed around to make sure Alice was safe. His housekeeper, for some reason looking almost rigid with disapproval, showed Kiara to her room—at the other end of the house from his. The dog followed beside her, pressed against her leg, and Alice trailed after, a shadow, ten feet away. Watching from the sidelines.

They ate lunch together. Kiara made small talk, bubbly nothings about his gorgeous house, the swimming pool… Was it heated? Did Alice swim? Did she think they might eventually teach Bunji to swim?

Alice either didn't respond or did so in monosyllables. Yes, no. That was her way. After all those words at the front door, she'd retreated.

Bunji lay under Kiara's chair, pressed against her leg. Not moving more than she had to. Every now and then he saw Kiara's hand slip down to pat the dog's ears.

The housekeeper came and went—a sniff or two to show her displeasure at a dog being inside her pristine house—but, dammit, this was his house.

And then he thought, was it? All the time he'd lived here, it was his succession of agency housekeepers who'd made the decisions on how to treat it. There'd been an architect first, then an interior designer, then gardeners and housekeepers.

He was surrounded by competence and cleanliness. Up until now, no dog would have dared show its face.

'Where will Bunji sleep?'

It was a whisper of a query, made as Alice pushed her half-eaten meal back. He'd expected her standard 'Please may I leave the table?' which was what he always got, almost as soon as she sat down. Surely this had to be an improvement.

'She can sleep by my bed,' Kiara told her. 'Until she wants to sleep by yours. That is, if you want her to. Would you like her to?'

'Dogs sleep outside.' It was a snap, coming from the middle-aged woman who was clearing the plates. She'd been sniffing her disapproval ever since Bunji had entered the house.

'Then I guess I sleep outside, too,' Kiara said, unblinkingly cheerful. 'Do you guys have a tent?'

'A tent?' Alice was clearly taken aback.

'You know, one of those canvas shelters you sleep in outside. It's called camping. It looks like it'll be warm tonight. We could set it up on the front lawn. It'd be fun.'

'The dog sleeps inside,' Bryn growled, and was he imagining it or did Alice's face fall a little?

'I'm allergic.' The housekeeper ceased clearing and crossed her arms in a stance that could only be called belligerent. 'It's already making my eyes run. I'm sorry, but enough. Either the dog stays outside, or I leave.'

There was a challenge.

If there was one thing Dr Bryn Dalton valued above all others it was order. He'd valued it before Skye and her daughter had arrived and thrown his life into chaos, and since then it had been the one thing he'd held to. Routine. Control.

Mrs Hollingwood had been with him now for over twelve months and he valued her. His meals arrived on time. His home was spotless. His possessions were never messed with. She'd seamlessly taken on Alice's care, making sure she was fed and clean, bringing out the useless games he'd purchased at the recommendation of the psychologists, clearing them away when it became clear Alice wasn't interested.

She was probably the best of the housekeepers he'd had, and she was now standing with her chest thrust forward, a line in the sand. The dog or me.

'There's plenty more jobs I can get through the agency,' she told him, and she thought she had him over a barrel. She knew his love of order. Her frustration had matched his the day his wheelchair had crunched over something Alice had left on his Italian mosaic floor and irreparably marked it. Mrs Hollingwood had cleaned it noisily, hmphing her displeasure.

And now…his perfect housekeeper was prepared to walk away because of a dog?

'She won't make a mess,' Alice said in a small voice.

'It'll shed,' the woman said, and jutted her bosom out still further. 'And look at those sores. You can't tell me that's hygienic.'

'Tents don't cost much,' Kiara said, semi-helpfully, from the other end of the table, and he glanced at her and thought—was she laughing? 'I have one back at Two Tails. If it's just for the week I can go home and fetch it, if you like.'

'Can I sleep in the tent, too?' Alice asked.

Oh, for heaven's sake… 'I'm sorry,' he said, definitely. 'But, Mrs Hollingwood, I'm afraid the dog stays, and it stays inside.'

Her face puckered, prune like. 'You won't get another housekeeper at short notice.'

There was a moment's silence. Something had to give, but by the look on Mrs Hollingwood's face, it wasn't going to be her.

The dog or the housekeeper…

'Why do you need a housekeeper?' Kiara said at last, head cocked to one side as if interested in something she didn't understand.

'Don't be ridiculous. I can hardly cook and clean.'

She looked at him for a long moment, glanced at his walking sticks leaning against his chair, and nodded.

'Fair enough, but Alice and I can. That might give you time to find someone else.'

'My niece isn't here to be a drudge.'

'A drudge?' Her brows rose. 'Cleaning and cooking? That's hardly fair on Mrs Hollingwood.'

Uh-oh. Somehow he'd thrown petrol onto the fire and, predictably, it flared.

'I'm not a drudge,' the woman snapped. 'Don't you dare talk to me like that.'

'I'm sorry,' he said, appalled. 'I didn't mean…'

'But I won't work with the dog here. I mean, maybe one of those cute ones that don't shed, but not this one. This dog's disgusting.'

Alice had stood up. Now she moved, almost imperceptibly, to stand by Kiara's chair. 'I can learn to cook,' she said, and it was a frightened quaver, but her chin jutted a little.

'Hey, I can cook eggs,' Kiara said brightly. 'I can do 'em three ways, boiled, fried, poached. Though,' she admitted thoughtfully, 'sometimes my poached don't work too well. I watched a video on putting them in water after you've made the water twirl—you know, like going in circles down the bath plug. All that happened was I got twirly strings of egg. I had to get them out with a strainer. They tasted good on toast though. Hey, Alice, I can make toast, too.'

'Me, too,' Alice said, a bit more firmly.

And then, to his amazement, Kiara put up her hand and grinned. 'Snap. High five! We're home and hosed in the cooking department.'

And what was even more astonishing was that his little niece looked up at her upraised hand and smiled—she actually smiled!—and she high-fived in response.

Was that the first smile he'd ever seen from her? The first chink in her stoic impassivity?

Whatever, he felt like high-fiving himself. He needed a photo to send to Beatrice.

He needed Kiara to stay. Which meant…

'I'm sorry, Mrs Hollingwood, but if you can't stay with Kiara and her dog then we'll have to terminate,' he said gently. 'I'll organise terms with the agency.'

'You'll never get anyone else at this short notice.'

'Then stringy eggs it is, I guess,' he said, not taking his eyes from his niece. Unless it was to look at the chuckling woman who was now grinning at Alice as if she knew what a wonder she'd just achieved.

This woman was used to healing wounded creatures, he thought, and maybe, just maybe, her skills could be used to bring some joy to Alice.

He watched her for a moment longer and the thought flashed stupidly through his mind… Maybe she could bring some joy into his life as well?

Well, there was a stupid thought. Yes, he'd been wounded but only physically. His leg was healing. Soon he'd be back to normal—he'd have his life back to where he wanted it.

He could go back to having a decent housekeeper who kept his ordered world in the state he liked it. He could return to work with colleagues who shared his passion for state-of-the-art medical technology.

He could return to dating the women who understood his world, who didn't mess with his boundaries.

This woman was here for his niece. He might have to put up with stringy eggs for a while—and a shedding dog for a while longer—but she was a paid employee, here to do a job.

And that was it.

He excused himself and returned to his study as soon as lunch was done. Mrs Hollingwood was noisily clearing in the kitchen—'I'll wash up and then I'm done,' she'd snapped, and the noise she was making made the whole house aware of how angry she was.

She did have her reasons, he conceded. Drudge had been an insulting word. He'd tried to apologise but she was having none of it.

'You've said it, you'll pay,' she'd sniffed, and when he rang the agency to try and find a replacement, he found she'd got in before him.

'You've insulted one of our best workers,' he was told. 'And childminding was never on your list of requirements when you engaged her. Our staff is pressed to the limit. With what's happened I'm afraid you'll go well down the list. We'll let you know when we have anyone available.'

He made another couple of calls to alternative places but no luck.

So he had a gammy leg, a kid, a dog and a vet. He had no help.

But in a way he did. He glanced out of his window and saw Kiara and Alice had settled on the lawn, under the shade of a gorgeous flowering jacaranda. The dog was lying stretched out in front of them. Kiara seemed to be talking, but not much. He couldn't see any response from Alice, but while he watched, her hand tentatively came out and stroked the dog's flank. A tiny stroke, almost immediately pulling back.

Kiara didn't seem to notice, was making no comment. She lay back and put her hands under her head, looking up through the dappling leaves. Sunlight was filtering through. While he watched, one of a drift of soft purple flowers disengaged from its branches and wafted down to land on her face.

She lifted it up and put it to her nose, and then smiled. And gently put the flower on the grass about three inches from Bunji's nose.

For some reason he found he was holding his breath.

There was a long pause while the dog didn't move and neither did Alice or Bunji. And then, almost at the same instant, the injured dog stretched forward a little—and right at that moment Alice leant over and put her nose on the bloom.

Noses touched.

They stayed, just like that, noses touching, for a long, long moment. Kiara didn't say a word, she just lay and watched.

This time he was sure it wasn't just him who was holding his breath. Maybe it *was* the whole world?

And then finally Alice lifted her head. Her hand came out and fondled the dog's uninjured ear. Her face turned up to Kiara's and she…

Giggled.

Oh, my…

High fives were never enough. Why did he feel like crying?

He had a student's PhD thesis on his desk. The 'Study of Neurological Problems After Heart Surgery' had some dubious sections—he needed to check references. He also had housekeeper problems.

Instead, he sat by the window and watched a kid watch a dog.

And watched a woman perform miracles?

They ate pizzas. Ordered in. Compared to the healthy food Mrs Hollingwood had been serving up, it left a lot to be desired. It couldn't last—he needed to find a cook or at least discover a healthy order-in source—but, watching Alice eat, he couldn't feel all bad.

Because she did eat. Bunji was stretched out on her dog bed, which Alice had set up beside her own chair. Kiara had said it was fine for Bunji to lie on the floor, but Alice had defiantly gone and fetched a blanket from her own bed. They'd compromised by lugging Bunji's big cocoon bed into the kitchen. 'I guess it can go wherever Bunji goes for a while,' Kiara had said.

'Do you always provide such a bed for your clients?' Bryn asked, trying not to let Alice see him watching her. Was she really eating her third slice?

'Bunji's special,' Kiara said blithely. She was on her third slice, too. He'd ordered big, thinking it could be reheated for lunch tomorrow, but he obviously had another think coming. 'Besides, if you decide to keep her, it goes on your account.'

He blinked. Kiara grinned happily at him and kept on munching.

She really was extraordinary.

'So, I read about you on the Internet,' she said, and he nodded, torn between watching her and watching his niece. 'You're a doctor.'

'I am.' Cautious.

'That's excellent, because for the next few days I could use an assistant. I guess if you have qualifications, you might just do.'

And there was another blink. He might just…do?

'Um…thank you,' he said, cautiously. 'I might just… do what?'

'You can see the dressing on Bunji's thigh?' She motioned down. The dog's wounds were in various stages of healing but there was still a pad over her left hind thigh. Nothing else was covered.

'I wondered,' he said. 'Why isn't she wearing a cone?' He'd seen dogs before, friends' dogs, recovering from surgery and wearing wide plastic cones to stop them ripping at dressings.

'Because she has the sense to leave it alone,' Kiara said. 'Actually, we didn't have a choice. Her neck was so ulcerated we couldn't put anything on it. We sedated her for the first few days, but after that…it seems anything we do to her is okay with Bunji.'

'Her neck was sore?' Alice asked, looking down at the dog with concern.

'Her owners didn't check her collar,' Kiara told her. 'So when she grew, her collar got tighter and tighter.'

There was a silence while Alice thought this through.

Would he have told her that? Bryn wondered. Probably not. This kid had been through so much, she hardly needed more trauma. Alice ceased eating, then she put her hand down and tenderly stroked the dog's neck.

'I'm glad you have me,' she said, softly. 'I won't let you get hurt again.'

And there it was, an almost instant acceptance of ownership. Or responsibility.

Of connection.

Dammit, he was blinking again, and this time it wasn't through astonishment. Real men didn't cry. Like hell they don't, he thought savagely, and closed his eyes for a moment to give him time to pull himself together.

When he opened them, Kiara was watching thoughtfully. And was there a hint of laughter there as well?

'I guess I'll be billing you for the dog basket,' she said, and there it was. Definitely laughter.

This woman was unlike any woman he'd ever met before, plainly dressed, direct, and totally focused on her animals. She was here to get what she wanted—money for her shelter, a home for one of her strays.

What was it in her laughter that made him feel like joining in?

He managed a smile, but only just. He was suddenly feeling on shaky ground.

He wasn't accustomed to emotion. He wasn't accustomed to feeling how this woman made him feel.

No. It was the way the situation made him feel, he told himself harshly. Get a grip.

'Early days yet,' he growled.

'Yep,' she agreed cheerfully. 'You have a whole week to change your mind. Or Alice does.' But the appraising look she gave Alice—who'd returned to her pizza—also had a hint of smug. 'So meanwhile, can I take it that you'll accept the job as my medical assistant? Assuming, of course, that you don't faint at the sight of an open wound.'

'I'm a surgeon,' he said faintly.

'Yes, but my research says you're a professor in neurosurgery. What I know about neurosurgery is that it's pretty much all done with technology. Tiny cameras. Robotic stuff. Plus, you'd have nurses to clean up any mess. How long since you got your hands dirty, Dr Dalton?'

'I do work with trauma patients,' he said stiffly, though he had to admit, by the time he was called in the messy stuff had generally been dealt with.

'Well, that's a relief.'

'So what do you want me to do?'

'Help me change her dressing.'

'You need help with that?'

But he got a look then. A look that said back off.

'Alice, I'd like you to help me with most things for Bunji,' she said, talking to them both. 'If you're willing. But there's this one spot that needs your uncle's help. The sore on Bunji's leg needs cleaning every day, and Bunji wiggles. I need your uncle to hold her still. I do it first thing in the morning and last thing at night.'

'You mean…after I go to bed?' Alice asked.

'I guess,' Kiara told her. 'You probably go to bed earlier than we do. But…' She hesitated. 'It's up to you,' she told her. 'If your uncle says it's okay, then Bunji can be your dog now, and you can make the decisions. Is that okay with you, Dr Dalton?'

'Bryn,' he said, a bit too gruffly. Hell, where were these emotions coming from?

'Can Bunji be my dog?' Alice was all eyes.

So was Kiara. They were both looking at him, hopeful, expectant.

Even the dog was looking at him.

He thought suddenly of his sister, ten years older than

him, bossy, gruff, overbearing. It was going to kill him to ring Beatrice and tell her she'd been right.

'Well?' Kiara said and her voice sounded almost teasing. Her laughter was insidious. He met her eyes, and he couldn't help smiling back.

And that smile… It felt as if something was cracking inside, something he didn't even know existed until now.

This was nonsense. It was emotional garbage, but Alice was waiting for an answer. They were all waiting for an answer.

'Fine,' he said, and he hadn't meant to sound quite as exasperated as he did. But he was feeling out of control, and control was something he valued above almost all else.

'If Dr Brail needs help, then I'll help her,' he told Alice. 'And if at the end of the week you still want her, yes, you can have her. Dr Brail will teach you all you need to know.'

'It's Kiara,' Kiara said gently and that smile softened.

But she was smiling at Alice, not at him. Her focus was all on the child. And the dog.

That was why she was here, he told himself. She needed to find this dog a home and earn money for her shelter. Then she'd be gone.

But why did he need to remind himself of that?

He didn't, he told himself. It didn't matter. *She* didn't matter.

She was a paid professional, here to do a job. She'd move on at the end of the week, leaving with the alacrity his housekeeper had just shown.

Leaving him with Alice.

That was what this was all about, he told himself,

and no one could help him there. He needed to forge a relationship with a kid who needed…family?

If he could pay someone to fix that…

'So is it agreed?' Kiara asked, cutting across his thoughts, and he had to focus on here, on now. Where had this conversation started? Asking for help to change a dog's dressing?

'I can help,' he muttered and there was that flicker of amusement again.

'I *can* do it myself,' she told him. 'But it's so much better to work as a team. I'd imagine you'd find that in your working life, too, Dr Dalton.'

His working life. High-end neurosurgery. A team of brilliant clinicians, doctors, nurses, technicians.

'You know, I'm thinking one vet, one neurosurgeon and one little girl to love her, that's a force that might just make Bunji completely well again,' she told him, still smiling. 'So what do you say, team? Alice, are you in?'

'I'm part of a team?' Alice ventured, unsure.

'A Bunji-loving team,' Kiara said. 'What do you say?'

'I want to,' Alice whispered and then looked at Bryn. 'All of us?'

And what was a man to say to that? 'All of us,' he said weakly—and why did it suddenly feel like falling?

CHAPTER SIX

BEDTIME.

Every night since he'd been home from hospital Bryn had sat on Alice's bed and read her a story. That was what the psychologists had recommended. They'd given him a list of bland, non-threatening tales they said were designed to hold the traumatised Alice's interest just enough for her to drift into sleep, without the nightmares that trauma had burdened her with.

He never knew whether it worked with Alice. He suspected not. Every night she'd lain unmoving, politely waiting for him to finish, and when the last page was done, she'd turned her face against the wall and pulled the covers high. Hunching her shoulders. No hug required.

But tonight, after discussion that had itself amazed him, Kiara had set Bunji's bed beside Alice's. 'Your uncle and I will sneak in late and change her dressing,' Kiara had told her. 'Then I'll get up in the night and take her outside. And even if an accident happens—I guess it might as it's her first night in her new home—I'm your new housekeeper, right? I can cope with puddles.'

'You'd mop up wee?' Alice had asked, sounding awed.

'I'm a vet. I've mopped up a lot worse than that in

my time.' Then Kiara had looked at the book Bryn had ready. 'This? Really? I like a book with a bit of action myself. Alice, how about if I tell you and your uncle about the time me and my friend Hazel rescued a whole bunch of poddy calves from drowning in a flood? With kayaks. Though my friend Hazel ended up swimming. You want to hear?'

Of course Alice did. And of course Bryn did. So he sat and listened and watched Alice's face.

She was entranced, and so was Bryn, and when the story ended and it was Kiara who tugged the covers up—did Alice really not flinch as Kiara gave her a kiss goodnight?—he was aware of a stab of loss that the story had ended.

'Right,' Kiara said briskly, the moment the door closed behind them, leaving child and dog to sleep. 'I have bookwork to do, and I need to ring Two Tails to find out how things are, so how about we convene in the laundry in an hour?'

'We can't do the dressing now?'

'The wound's still looking messy,' Kiara told him. 'It was the worst of her wounds. It's healing now but she's still on antibiotics and I thought it'd be best if Alice didn't see under the pad for a few more days. So I thought it'd be best if we waited until Alice is asleep.'

'Why is it so bad?'

'Clostridial myositis,' she told him. 'I suspect that's the reason she was finally dumped—there's nothing like a smelly wound to make low lifers get rid of a problem the easiest way they know how. In this case dumping her near an animal shelter. You know clostridial myositis? It occurs in horses, pigs, dogs—bears, too, I hear—but it's as rare as hen's teeth. It's pretty much the same as clostridial myonecrosis—you may have heard of that as gas gangrene?—in humans. It was touch and go for the first few days, but I think I have it nailed now. I'd have liked to keep her at the shelter for another week for daily cleaning and dressing, but I only had this one chance to leave. So… See you in an hour, Dr Dalton?'

And without waiting for a response, she headed off, back to her part of the house. Brisk. Businesslike. Getting on with her life.

Which was what he needed to do.

He gazed after her for a moment, and then went back to his study.

But there was no way he could focus on the finer points of checking the thesis he'd moved on to—'Cognitive Disturbances in Systemic Lupus Erythematosus'. Instead he found himself reading everything he didn't know about clostridial myositis.

An animal disease. An infection that left untreated meant certain death. Where treatment involved firstly skill to diagnose, including specific and expensive blood tests and scans. Then surgery. Then weeks of broad-spectrum antibiotics.

No wonder she was broke, he thought, stunned. To do this for a stray…?

Finally the hour was up. He emerged from his study to find Kiara bringing folded towels through the front door. 'What the…?'

'I brought my own,' she said, cheerfully. 'I had 'em in the car. I know, the gorgeous monogrammed pink things you've provided in my private bathroom would be marginally more comfortable for Bunji to lie on, but she's not all that fussy. Neither am I, come to think of it, but hey, I'm enjoying them and I'm not as likely to ooze as Bunji is.'

'Ugh,' he said faintly, and she grinned.

'Second thoughts, Dr Dalton? Do I need to keep smelling salts at hand?'

'Um…no,' he managed. 'But just how bad is it?'

'It's actually no longer likely to ooze,' she admitted. 'But the wound needs checking and it's not pretty. I could do it myself but it's easier with someone to hold her.'

He followed her as she headed for the laundry. Obviously she'd already sussed out her operating theatre—she'd cleared the massive granite bench and now she set the towels on its surface, her bag at the side. She spread a small sheet that had been wrapped in plastic, then set out businesslike tools. Surgeon preparing to operate?

'I wouldn't have brought her to you if I didn't think you'd have a fit, healthy Bunji by the time I left,' she told him, surveying her preparations with satisfaction. 'And I knew you were medical. There's still a chance that edges need debriding, which is why I have the gear. Your job is to hold and reassure. Not a lot of neurological skill involved, Dr Dalton, but maybe you can show off your skills some other time. Hang on while I fetch her.'

'I'll fetch her.'

'Yeah?' Her gaze moved from his face to the sticks he was still forced to use, and her brows raised in mild enquiry. Amusement? 'Will she leave a nice comfy bed to follow you? I don't think so. So you'll carry her?'

'I can.' He couldn't. He knew it but, dammit, he was disgusted with himself. He felt humiliated, and to add insult to injury she had the temerity to pat his shoulder.

'It's okay,' she told him kindly. 'You and Bunji will both be better soon. You can spread out the towels while I carry her.'

'Kiara…'

'Yes?' She gazed up at him and her eyes were twinkling. Teasing? The way she'd said *'You can spread out the towels...'* It was as if she were offering a treat to a three-year-old.

'I am competent,' he growled.

'I'm sure you are.' There was that smile again. 'Or you will be. You and Alice and Bunji… It seems I have a week to fix you all.'

And for some reason that silenced him.

She was just talking of his leg. Of course she was. She had no idea that ever since Skye's death he'd been feeling almost as vulnerable as the little girl who'd been hurled into his care. Which was stupid.

His world was carefully constructed to keep him in control, to block out the need for personal connection. His cold and solitary childhood had left him with a lifelong aversion to any kind of attachment. Now he had great friends, an awesome career, a magnificent home…

It was only the advent into his life of one small child that had tossed him into a sea of uncharted emotions.

The answer of course was for Alice to learn self-reliance. As he had. Then they could both move on.

So…self-reliance. Emotional safety.

Why did the arrival of this bouncy, impertinent vet seem to threaten it?

And then she was back, Bunji cradled in her arms, legs up. The dog's eyes were wide, but she was looking up at Kiara with complete trust.

Which meant a heart lurch—which was stupid.

He did *not* need to get personally involved. Or at least…okay, he did need to stay involved with Alice. Maybe even with this dog. But not with this woman.

His towels were laid out—at least he was that competent. Kiara laid the dog gently down.

'There you go, girl. Dr Dalton's assisting tonight and I've checked his medical credentials. Awesome. I bet he charges a mint, but add it to his account, not mine. Now, Dr Dalton is going to hold you steady and chat to you while I check out your leg.'

'Wouldn't it be better the other way around?' he asked. Kiara was surely the best placed to reassure, while checking a healing wound seemed simple.

But the look she gave him put him right back in his place. 'Hey, I might have checked your credentials online, but I'd need personal references to let you treat.'

'You're doubting…'

'Would you let me operate in your theatre without checking every facet of my qualifications? No? There you go, then. I'm very sure you're supremely qualified at what you do but this isn't something simple like brain surgery.' And she grinned, lifted his hand and placed it on Bunji's head. 'So accept your role, please,' she said. 'Words of reassurance, Dr Dalton. After all, you're Bunji's family from now on. It's time you two got acquainted.'

The man looked stunned. What was it with this guy? Kiara thought as she worked. He was acting almost as if he was afraid. But he did what he was asked. He stroked Bunji gently behind the ears, he spoke softly, and Bunji accepted him as someone who cared.

Did he care? This was such a strange situation—a brilliant surgeon with injuries, with a lonely, traumatised little girl. The two of them seemed as if they needed therapy. What they had was a vet and an already traumatised dog.

But something seemed to be happening. Maybe Beatrice had been right, she thought as she removed the dog's dressing. Alice's reaction to Bunji had seemed almost miraculous. And this guy… He'd been cold, aloof, but the way he was speaking to the dog…

'Tell me her medical history?' he said softly, in the same voice he'd been using to calm Bunji. She was carefully cleaning and checking the edges of the almost healed wound. It still took caution—the last thing Bunji needed was further infection.

'What you see is pretty much what we got,' she said, concentrating on what she was doing. 'You're looking at massive trauma—only that trauma's occurred since puppyhood. She's about a year old now. She's been severely malnourished and mistreated. The worst thing was the clostridium, but in a way it probably saved her life—the smell probably made whoever owned her get rid of her.'

'So…treatment?'

'First we had to figure what the problem was—I suspected, but there were so many other things going on and confirmation took time. The infection was well into deep tissue, and she was severely ill. The surgery on such a malnourished dog was tricky. After that… broad spectrum antibiotics, debridement, debridement, debridement. She may be left with a limp, but we're hopeful she won't. She's young. All she needs to do now is forget how much it hurt when she tried to use it.'

She finished what she was doing and reached for the antiseptic ointment. 'I guess…that's what you hope for Alice as well,' she said cautiously, without looking up. 'All she needs to do is forget past hurts. But how possible is that? Her trauma must be bone deep.'

'As you say,' he said curtly, and she did glance up then.

'And you, too,' she said, much more gently. 'There are hurts worse than physical pain. You lost your sister. I'm so sorry.'

'I hardly knew her.'

'But she was still your sister. I gather Beatrice hardly knows you, either, but she cared enough to leave her horses and her dogs to do what she could. That seemed quite some sacrifice. She must love you.'

'No one in my family loves anyone.'

'Really?'

There was a moment's silence at that, while she focused on what she was doing, and he regrouped. She'd pushed into places she had no right to push.

'So what about you?' he asked at last, and he knew he sounded defensive. Even a bit combative. Well, maybe he had the right.

'My grandma loved me,' she said, and she sounded defiant.

'Not your parents?'

She cast him another quick glance, as if she acknowledged that this was none of his business. Then, almost to his surprise, she responded. She spoke absently while she worked, as if it were a story about someone else.

'My dad's an egoist and a bully,' she said bluntly. 'He runs a big cattle property inland, but he treats cattle like objects, not creatures who need compassion. It seems he treated my mum the same way. She was good-looking and attracted him at a time when he'd decided he needed a wife. But he didn't want a partner. He needed a housekeeper and he needed sex. He also needed a son. I arrived after three miscarriages, and from them on I can only imagine how Mum was treated. She walked out when I was six—or maybe she ran. Heaven knows how broken she was. We don't know where she went but a couple of years later the police told us she'd died. Dad got himself another wife, and then another, but still no sons. However, I was a possession. *His.* Grandma wanted me, but she wasn't allowed to have me. When Dad was away I got to stay with her, though. Grandma's home was my refuge and now it's an animal refuge. Two Tails. I love it.'

'So parents…'

'I decided I didn't need 'em,' she said curtly. 'But I do need someone. Grandma was my someone. As I guess—I hope—you'll be Alice's someone. Maybe she'll be yours.'

'I don't need…someone.'

'Everyone does,' she said simply, and went back to applying a new dressing. 'That's it, then. I reckon a week and this pup will be right as rain, ready to start her new life. A life where someone cares. You will care, won't you, Dr Dalton?'

'Bryn,' he said, sounding goaded. 'And yes, I'll care.'

'For Bunji and for Alice.'

'Butt out,' he growled, and she did, but she ventured one last smile.

'I think it's wonderful,' she said simply. 'Your sister says you're a loner, Dr Dalton. Well, not any more you're not. You have Alice, and now you have Bunji, and I have every hope in the world that you'll end up like Grandma and me. A family.'

A family.

With the dog safely treated and seemingly settled beside Alice's bed again—Alice's bedroom was right next to his and with both the doors open he could hear if there was trouble—he was free to sleep.

He couldn't.

Of course he couldn't. He'd hardly slept since the accident.

His leg ached—no, make that hurt. The surgery had been extensive. It'd hurt for months. He could use drugs—they'd make him sleep as well as ease the pain—but since Beatrice had left, he was the only one in the house with Alice. And she had nightmares.

He had to be there for her.

Family.

Kiara's words kept playing over and over in his head. *'I have every hope in the world that you'll end up...a family.'*

It had already happened, he thought savagely. He had no choice.

When Skye had brought her daughter here, demanding he take care of her, he'd reacted with incredulity. He'd had no intention of being a hands-on uncle, much less a father figure. He wasn't the least sure he had the emotional depth for anyone to depend on him.

But this woman—Kiara—seemed to have emotional depth in spades. She seemed to know how to talk to Alice, how to draw a solitary, damaged child out of her shell. She was warm, kind—loving?

That was who Alice needed, not someone who'd never figured out what loving was.

He could learn?

But it wasn't something learned—he had the intelligence to figure that out. It was something instilled from childhood, the ability to give and receive affection.

Kiara's grandmother must have been quite some woman, he thought. Somehow she'd figured it out.

Could he?

You can't teach an old dog new tricks. For some reason the phrase came into his mind and stuck.

Hell, he was only thirty-seven.

Yeah, but how did you learn to love?

By feeling for Alice? The child's plight had gutted him. He was prepared to do whatever it took to make her happy—even taking on a dog. Even maybe keeping her here in this house, not sending her to boarding school. The plan to send her to boarding school had now been complicated by letting Kiara load her with the dog. Maybe he could send her to the local school, pay other parents to involve her in after-school activities, pay a nanny.

As his parents had done? Yeah, as if that had worked.

But the alternative? One of the shrinks he'd talked to had suggested—tentatively—that he might cut back on work, be a sort of part-time parent.

And do what? Be there at the school gate, walk her home every night?

His work was his life.

This was doing his head in. He had not a single clue what the future held. The only thing he could focus on was getting his leg healed, getting back to work, getting back to some kind of normal.

Which right now meant figuring out how to get to sleep.

Which meant not lying staring at the ceiling thinking of a slip of a kid, a vet, looking at him and saying...

'I have every hope in the world that you'll end up...a family.'

And at the other end of the house—in what the housekeeper had brusquely described as the guest wing—Kiara was also wide awake.

Thinking of a wounded kid. A wounded dog.

A wounded man?

What was it about him that had got under her skin?

The first time she'd met him she'd actively disliked him. Oh, sure, she'd felt sorry for his situation, but he'd been arrogant, wanting to throw money at a problem that any idiot could see money couldn't cure.

But watching him tonight… While she'd related the story of rescuing the poddy calves, while she'd embellished the story to entrance a sleepy child, while she'd tried to make Alice smile…she'd glanced up at him and seen…what could almost be imagined as hunger.

As if he was as desperate for a world he could escape into as Alice was.

Well, she was only going to be telling stories for a week, she told herself briskly. He'd have to figure a way to tell them himself.

Why did that make her feel suddenly desolate?

Stop it, she told herself harshly. She had enough to feel desolate about without adding Dr Bryn Dalton and his niece to her list.

Go to sleep.

But sleep was evasive. Finally she flicked on her bedside light and propped herself on pillows. A bit of Internet drifting, she thought. Puppies. Reruns of silly bits from movies. Something to turn her mind from where it kept heading.

To the man sleeping at the other end of the house.

And almost unconsciously she found herself typing his name into a search engine, looking not for professional qualifications but for media reporting of Skye's death.

And here it was.

Heroic Doctor Saves Child from Local Cliffs!

At three this morning a woman's body was retrieved from the rocks directly under the notorious cliffs near Clovelly. The woman was thought to have fallen from above. A child, believed to be the woman's daughter, appears to have tried to climb down after her, but fell herself. It seems she was trapped on a ledge almost at water level, with bad weather, heavy seas and a rising tide.

This set the scene for what police say was an extraordinary rescue.

A Clovelly resident, reportedly Dr Bryn Dalton, an eminent neurosurgeon at nearby Sydney Central hospital, was first on the scene. With the child in danger of being washed off the ledge, he managed to crawl down the cliffs to reach her.

Police say he had almost made it before the cliff face crumbled. He somehow still reached the child, and managed to cling to her until emergency services were able to retrieve them—a process that took almost an hour while waves constantly washed over the pair.

The child was lifted by rescue services, seemingly unhurt, and has been taken to Sydney Central for observation. Dr Bryn Dalton has been admitted to Sydney Central with serious leg injuries but is expected to make a full recovery.

Early reports say the woman's body was found wedged between rocks under water.

It is not known at this time what relationship, if any, exists between Dr Dalton and the pair he attempted to rescue, but police are recommending he be referred for consideration for Australian's highest award for acts of conspicuous courage, the Cross of Valour.

This broadsheet can only agree.

Me, too, Kiara thought as she read and reread the article. She definitely agreed. The cliffs around here were notorious. To climb down them was impossibly dangerous and, living here, he must know the risks.

But then her attention was drawn back to the screen. The next Internet feed had followed automatically. Instead of a written report, it was a video, obviously filmed by a media channel chasing the rescue chopper.

Kiara never looked at these sorts of scenes. They mostly seemed a voyeuristic intrusion on what must be an appalling enough trauma for those involved, without seeing endless replays in full technicolour.

This time she couldn't look away.

The rescue was filmed in darkness—of course—but the scene was lit by the massive floodlights beaming from the rescue chopper. She could see the maelstrom of breaking waves, flattened a little by the massive whirring of the chopper blades.

It had been pouring with rain, and the wind looked fierce. It must have been dangerous for the chopper, much less for the people on the cliff.

She watched, caught, seeing the initial sweep of the chopper, the storm-tossed seas, the bottom of the cliffs.

A hesitation, a shift of the chopper from its sweep path.

Then figures huddled on a ledge, not even clear of the breaking waves. A man, lying on the ledge, his back to the water. The waves crashing over him.

The chopper rising, obviously to try and get a better view.

A glimpse of the child spooned against the man's chest, his arms fiercely wrapped, holding her, using his body to protect her against the force of the sea.

She watched in sickening fascination as the chopper steadied or tried to steady against the wind. Waited, obviously hoping against hope for the wind to die.

Then a lone figure—another hero, Kiara thought—was being lowered down, a stretcher with him. He was using the stretcher as armour against the cliff face.

She saw Bryn turning, holding the child up. Another wave crashing over them. How did he keep his hold?

She saw the stretcher man waiting, watching the sea. Then a break… Steady, sure hands, fastening Alice. Bryn, his body wedged between rocks to hold him as safe as such a tenuous hold could make him, helping secure his niece.

Alice clinging. And Bryn… At the last minute, there was a fierce hug, then he released his hold on the rocks so that momentarily his hands held her face. Words, unheard and yet obvious, the care was unmistakeable.

The love?

And then the rising of the stretcher and Alice was safe.

What followed was an interminable wait while Alice was pulled into the chopper and the camera abandoned Bryn. Then the return to retrieve him.

She saw the moment stretcher man realised the extent of the damage to Bryn's leg. As he pulled out from his crammed position, even with the grainy image she could see its grotesque break.

There was no time for bracing it, though. With the rising tide there was no time for anything. He was almost roughly hauled onto the stretcher. It's a wonder he didn't pass out from the pain, she thought, but at least he was safe.

At least the little niece he'd saved was safe.

He must love her.

Yeah, but he doesn't know it, she thought. Or maybe he does but he's not admitting it.

She thought back to Beatrice's words at that first meeting. *'A stupid act of bravado caused by his failure to wait for the proper emergency services.'*

She had no doubt what the outcome would have been if Bryn hadn't performed that *'stupid act of bravado'*.

Dear heaven…

She flicked off the light, but the images from the news reports were too vivid, too awful. A little girl, whose mother was lost.

Okay, she couldn't help herself. She'd just check on Bunji, she told herself, and she slipped out of bed, poked her toes into her shabby slippers—she really should have supplied herself with new ones to fit into this fancy house—and padded through the darkened house to Alice's room.

And stopped short at the open door.

Alice was in bed, curled under the blankets, the night light showing a child fast asleep. Her fine blonde hair was splayed around her on the pillow. Her face was still far too pale.

One of her skinny arms was hanging down. Her hand was resting on Bunji's coat.

Bunji was in the cocoon of a dog bed, and beside the cocoon…

Bryn.

He was sitting on the floor, his bad leg stiffly out before him. He, too, had his hand on Bunji's coat, as if to say, okay, girl, I might have woken you, but I mean you no harm.

He was watching both girl and dog.

Kiara stood in the doorway, and suddenly another memory came, unbidden.

She'd been ten years old. Midsummer on her father's farm, she'd been an unsupervised child playing in a field of uncut hay. Then, she'd come across a tiger snake—one of Australia's most venomous. It had taken her twenty minutes to get back to the house, and by the time she did the venom had taken hold.

Her father hadn't wanted the bother of nursing a child, so three days later her grandma had picked her up from hospital. Home she'd gone with Grandma. That night… In the small hours she'd stirred and found her grandmother sitting beside her bed. Just sitting, which seemed astounding all by itself. She could never remember her grandma's knitting needles being still, but that night they had been.

'I'm just watching,' the elderly lady had said as she'd stirred. She'd put her hand on Kiara's face and then leant over and kissed her. 'I'm just watching you breathe, Kiara, my love. You go back to sleep. Your breathing's safe with me.'

And she had. She'd remembered the fear and pain of the snake bite, her father's disgust that she'd been so stupid, and he'd had to lose half a day's work. She remembered the loneliness of hospital where she'd understood little.

But mostly she remembered her grandma's hand and the kiss. *'Your breathing's safe with me.'*

And now, without warning, her eyes started swimming with tears.

She backed away—there was no way she would interrupt such a scene—but she must have made some faint noise because Bryn saw her.

'Don't get up,' she whispered, but he already had, pushing himself to his feet—and that was pretty impressive for someone as injured as he was.

'Just checking,' he muttered. He was dressed in boxers and T-shirt—designer, she'd bet—but then who was looking at pyjamas? He'd caught the sticks beside the bed and limped out to the passage. 'I don't like the idea of the dog being with her. A strange dog…'

Liar, she thought. *There's no way you're worried about Alice's safety with Bunji.*

You were watching them both breathe.

'There's no risk,' she told him. They were outside the door now and could speak. Though he was a bit close.

Actually he was very close. She thought suddenly—she wouldn't mind another layer or two of clothing. She was wearing a skimpy nightgown and worn slippers.

It was crazy to be conscious of it—as if a guy like this would even look twice at someone like her—but even so, she wished she'd brought her nice thick woolly dressing gown.

It'd be crazy in this season, in this climate-controlled house, but she wanted it all the same.

Professional, she reminded herself. She was here in a professional capacity, so she had to act like it.

He was saying he was here because he was worrying about risk?

'I've had Bunji in care for days now,' she told him, still speaking softly, but having—stupidly—to focus on preventing the ridiculous way her voice wobbled. 'In that time she's been stressed, hurt, ill. I've had to give her injection after injection. I've had her on a drip, and I've had to keep sedation to a minimum because she was so weak. In all that time, no matter what I've had to do to her, she's never offered so much as a tiny growl. She's bombproof, Dr Dalton. Do you really think I'd expose Alice to risk?'

'And yet you came to check.'

'I'm here to do a medical check on my patient.' She assumed a tone of virtue. Thankfully she almost had her voice back to normal. 'You're paying for a veterinarian to stay here for a week. Nightly checks are part of my job.'

'So you're playing Florence Nightingale—the lady with the lamp.'

'There's no need for sarcasm.'

'Believe it or not, I didn't mean to sound sarcastic.'

'No? Well, thank you.' She glanced up at him and found he was looking at her strangely. Creature from Mars? Creature in flimsy nightie and shabby, fluffy slippers.

'If all's well here, then I'll go back to bed,' she told him.

'Kiara?'

'Yes?' Unconsciously she lifted her chin. Braced?

'Thank you,' he said.

'I…there's no need,' she managed at last. 'You're paying me, and this is my job.'

'Bunji's not just another dog, though, is she?'

'No,' she admitted. 'She's not.'

'Beatrice says you specialise in finding homes for dogs who are sometimes…less than desirable. Elderly dogs who'll cost heaps as they near the end of their lives. Dogs with problems. But thanks to you, Bunji is recovering to have no problems at all. A dog less than a year old? Bombproof, as you say? In another few weeks you could have sold her…

'Not for as much as you're paying.'

'Is that the only criteria for giving her to us?'

'No,' she admitted. 'I thought… Alice needs her.'

'And me?'

'I'm not going there.' She hesitated. 'But okay, I'll be honest. Bunji's got to me in a way few other dogs have. I've seen maltreated dogs, treated them, seen them successfully rehoused. But something about Bunji…' She took a deep breath.

'She's touched my heart,' she said, feeling self-conscious for saying such a thing, but she could think of no other way to put it. 'And in a way, Alice has done the same thing. And you. Your situation… So I thought… I hoped that you could all heal together. Yes, the money Beatrice is offering will help keep Two Tails going for another few months, but maybe the end of my refuge is inevitable. If Bunji doesn't fit here, if she doesn't get the love she deserves, and give the love she's capable of in return, then I'm taking her right back.'

'And why did you come to the other end of the house in the middle of the night?' he asked, and his voice sounded a bit strange. As if he was in uncharted territory?

'Because I like a happy ending,' she retorted. 'Or the prospect of the same. Because I suspect how much both Alice and Bunji need it and I'm aching for it to happen.'

'Because you care.'

'Is there anything wrong with that?'

'No,' he said, still in that curious voice. He was watching her, his dark eyes expressionless. Giving nothing away of what he was feeling.

Did he think she was stupid?

Well, maybe she was, she thought, and once more she was acutely aware of her faded nightie and her shabby slippers. And her bare legs and the fact that this was the middle of the night, and she was in this man's house and…and…

'I need to go back to bed,' she said, a bit too brusquely, and maybe he got her unease because he stood aside fast. Assuring her he meant no threat?

Which was crazy. No threat had been implied. But there was…something.

Some pull.

A man and a woman in not enough clothing, in the middle of the night? A guy who looked like Bryn Dalton?

Get over it, she told herself, and turned to leave.

'Kiara?'

'Yes?' But there was silence and finally she turned back to face him. 'Is there…is there something else?'

'Just…' The silence hung. Everything hung. She was waiting but she didn't know for what.

And finally he propped one of his sticks against the wall and lifted his hand, tentatively. If she wanted to—if her body was capable of moving—she could have stepped away, but she did no such thing. She simply stood and waited for what was to happen.

Which was little enough. His fingers reached her face. One long finger ran the length of her cheek. Lightly. A feather touch, that was all. And still those eyes remained…expressionless?

Or maybe not. Maybe there was a touch of tenderness…

And why she should suddenly think back to the moment Bunji had raised a paw… A connection?

Ridiculous. As he withdrew his hand and she took a step back, the thought disappeared.

'Goodnight, Kiara,' he said softly, and she managed a brusque nod.

'Goodnight, Dr Dalton.'

And she turned and fled.

Bryn should go to bed, too. Instead, he stood in the darkened passage and wondered what on earth had just happened.

He'd reached out and touched her.

Why? She was an employee, here to do a job. It was the middle of the night. Hell, she could just about have him up on an assault charge for what had just happened.

He hadn't held her.

He hadn't kissed her.

He'd wanted to.

What was it about her?

It was just the situation, he told himself. He was a man, she was a woman, there was chemistry.

She was beautiful.

But not in the way most of the women he knew were.

Not one of those women would be seen dead in what she was wearing tonight. And it wasn't just her night-wear. Her normal clothes were plain, serviceable, well worn. She wore her hair scraped back. No make-up.

The research he'd done on Two Tails had led to its website, where Kiara had included a brief summary of its proprietor's life. She'd been raised on a farm, somewhere in rural New South Wales, and she'd spent many of her holidays at her grandmother's home. She'd lived in central Sydney during her training, but the city wasn't her thing.

That was what she looked like—a woman who

spent as much time as she could outdoors. And by the look of her hands, she spent much of that time working. Hard.

So what was making him stand in the dark and feel as if…he'd just touched something precious? Something quite, quite lovely?

He needed to get a grip, to refocus. He needed to get Alice sorted…

Get Alice and Bunji sorted.

There was an issue. Boarding school had seemed the best option but now… He wouldn't send Alice even if he could, he realised. He was becoming as emotional about this whole issue as Kiara.

And there he was, thinking of Kiara again. What was it about the woman that had him so unsettled?

Was it just that he'd been too alone for too long? He liked his solitude, but since his accident that solitude had been multiplied to the point where he saw Alice, he saw rehab staff and hardly anyone else. And now here was a woman he didn't know, but someone who cared, someone who'd come through a strange, darkened house to check on his niece and her dog.

Someone who had, in some small way, already eased his weight of responsibility.

So that was why he must be feeling like this, he told himself harshly. This was gratitude and relief. Nothing else was appropriate, so he needed to stop thinking about Dr Brail…as he was thinking. She was here for a week. She'd be working with Alice and Bunji and that was a great opportunity for him to get some work done.

Right. Go back to bed.

He went, but as he limped back to his room the thought of a woman stayed with him. A woman in a shabby nightgown, a woman who was nothing to do with his world, a woman who'd be gone in a week.

He'd get over it. He had enough academic work to last him for months. He could use this week to clear the backlog.

He could use this week to gather his independence once more—and in the process he could keep as far from Dr Kiara Brail as he could.

CHAPTER SEVEN

THE NEXT DAY saw Kiara and Alice spending almost all their time together. Alice was still aloof, still wary, but she was desperate to learn everything she could about her new pet and communicating with Kiara was a necessary evil to achieve it. Bunji was still attached to Kiara, where Bunji went, Alice followed, and they quickly became a pack. Kiara, Alice, Bunji.

Bryn wasn't part of it.

He appeared for lunch—the fridge and pantry were magnificently stocked, and Kiara did the basics. She was supposed to be here as a vet, she thought wryly, but for the money she was being paid a bit of basic housework seemed a reasonable inclusion. She hadn't expected to be left completely alone with child and dog, though, and was vaguely disturbed when, as soon as he finished lunch, he pleaded the need to work and headed back to his study.

He did the same at dinner. Kiara had whipped up a basic pasta. He asked Alice if she'd prefer Kiara to read to her that night and Alice said a simple yes. So he disappeared again.

Kiara headed to her bedroom, tried to read and then tried to sleep. She did neither well.

The next day followed the same pattern.

So what? She was being paid, she told herself. Actually she was being overpaid—a lot—and what did it matter if Bryn kept to himself? In a way it even seemed a good idea.

The way he'd touched her had caused a frisson of sexual awareness that stayed with her, and in her bed that night there was a restlessness, as her mind wandered into a fantasy of what-ifs?

There'd been men in Kiara's life—of course there had—but they'd been fleeting. Her only experience of family had left her with no real desire to start one of her own and, besides, where would she find time? Her passion was Two Tails. It took all her energy, all her waking hours, and the thought of a lover…

A lover like Bryn…

Was impossible. Even if he was interested—which he wasn't.

But still there was this frisson of awareness, a heightening of senses that left her disturbed. This man seemed extraordinary. He was so aloof, so like a grown-up version of Alice, but underneath she could sense something more. A lot more. The feel of his fingers on her cheek… That touch… It had woken such feelings…

Which were useless and she had to keep them in check. The best way to keep them at bay was therefore to avoid him, so his distance was a good idea. For her.

But not for Alice.

As the days wore on she realised there were deeper issues at stake. Alice was starting to relax with her, even to chat, maybe even to think of her as a friend—and Alice needed a friend. Or more. Kiara knew from personal experience how vulnerable a lonely child could be, and she knew Alice was aching for someone to love. But that someone couldn't be her.

She was starting to wonder how sensible was it to encourage a solitary child like Alice to get close to her. She was here as a paid employee, but she was a vet, not a nanny, and soon she had to leave. She was no psychologist, but even she could see that if Alice and Bunji were to end up with a happy ever after, Bryn had to be included.

And finally, she called him on it.

Dinner had just ended. 'Will you tell me the story about the kayaks and the cows again tonight?' Alice asked shyly, and Kiara took a deep breath and shook her head.

'You know, I've been talking so much today that my throat's sore,' she told her. 'So tonight's my night off. I'm going to sit by the fire in the sitting room and rest my voice so I can talk to you tomorrow. Your uncle's on story duty tonight.'

'I have...' Bryn started but she flashed him such a look that he rethought. 'I guess I can,' he conceded. 'You choose a book.'

'I like real stories,' Alice whispered.

There was a moment's silence. Real stories. Stories where this man revealed something of himself. Kiara could almost see the armour he had in place. How much easier to read someone else's story?

She found she was holding her breath, waiting for him to refuse. His face was closed. Every instinct was to rush in, suggest, fix things, but she compressed her lips and held her thoughts in.

And finally, he cracked.

'I guess I could tell you about porriwiggles,' he said, almost as if the words were forced out of him.

'Porriwiggles?' Alice stared at him in confusion.

'Most people call them tadpoles,' he explained. 'Or

baby frogs. When I was a boy, my father had a property with a dam in the home paddock. He used to send me and my nanny there when he was…when he wanted the city house to himself. Nanny taught me to catch porriwiggles—that's what she called them. We put them in tanks and watched them grow, and then put them back in the dam when they turned into frogs. But funny things happened to those porriwiggles—and to me, too, as I tried to catch them.' He thought for a moment. 'You know, your mom was older than me, and she'd gone to America by the time I was born, but she would have spent time on our dad's farm as well. I bet she would have caught porriwiggles.'

And he'd caught her. A story that included porriwiggles—and her mother. 'How…how did you catch them?' Alice whispered, and Bryn cast Kiara a goaded glance—an unspoken *What have you got me into?*—but then softened as he answered Alice.

'Let's get you to bed and I'll tell you,' he told her. 'We must give Dr Brail's voice a chance to recover, mustn't we? I've heard her yelling at you and at Bunji—wow, she's such a bossy teacher. You must be really scared of her.'

And Alice got up from the table, looked up at her uncle—and giggled.

Kiara sat by the fire in the sitting room, because she'd told Alice that was where she was going—and also it seemed somehow mean to disappear to her bedroom when she'd pushed him into taking charge. Plus, it was a gorgeous living room. The open fireplace was huge, surrounded by a magnificent marble surround. There were massive, down-filled settees—four of them—and in front of the fire was a vast wool rug, all colours, a rug so rich it looked as if it had just this minute arrived on the plane from Persia.

Alice thought briefly of the squashed, worn and slightly puppy-chewed rug in front of her fire back at Two Tails and almost grinned.

The fire had been set—probably thanks to Mrs Hollingwood. Kiara put a match to the kindling, and watched it grow into a truly wonderful fire, but as she watched her desire to smile faded.

She had a sudden urge to fetch Bunji to share. She couldn't. Bunji was Alice's dog now, but she needed a dog. She needed…someone?

If she lost Two Tails…

She'd never be without a dog, she told herself, or at least, not for long. Once she found herself a decent job and secure place to live, she'd be in the position to have another.

But right now, sitting by the fire, thinking of Bryn telling stories of porriwiggles to Alice, she was aware of a void that had nothing to do with dogs.

Family…

One day…

Really? She was thirty-two and she'd always been far too busy for serious relationships. And besides, she had no idea how they worked. To give your heart to a man…to surrender control as her mother had…the thought had always terrified her. She'd settled with herself that she'd be happy and safe with her cottage and her dogs. It was only now, when she was feeling as if she were being torn by both, that she was having these strange feelings.

The door opened and Bryn limped in. She should jump up, say goodnight, go, but he crossed the room and sank into the closest settee, as if he wanted to talk?

It would have seemed mean to flee. Sensible though, she thought. But mean.

'How did it go?'

'She liked the porriwiggles.'

'I imagine she would. She needs as many stories about her family as she can get.'

He cast her a strange look. 'I guess.'

'So...porriwiggles?' she asked, figuring that had to be a safe bet for conversation.

'I had a menagerie,' he told her. 'The ducks used to eat the frogspawn, so I figured I was saving lives by taking the spawn up to the stables and keeping it safe until they hatched and grew into frogs. I guess I didn't realise all I was doing was making ducks fatter by giving them a much bigger diet of froglets.'

She smiled. 'I hope you didn't tell Alice that.'

'No.' He shrugged. 'I told her the funny bits, how I used an old bath as a boat to get to the island in the middle, how my bath floated away, and nanny had to wade in up to her armpits to rescue me. How I used old petrol cans to cart water from the dam to replace the water in my tanks—I learned the hard way that tap water has chlorine in it. And one day I remember thinking hey, this can is full already, I must have already filled it, so I tipped it in and it was petrol. I realised as soon as I smelled it. I remember flying into the kitchen and yelling at the cook that I needed the strainer, then tipping the whole tank through the sieve and washing and washing the little froglets in dam water. And the amazing thing was that they survived.' He shook his head. 'There's a veterinary miracle for you.'

'Amazing,' she said and grinned. 'I should write it up for *Aus Vet Monthly*.'

'It's copyright,' he told her, and he smiled back down at her.

And that smile…

Uh-oh. She had to get out of here. She rose, and he rose, too, and once again they were too close. How had that happened?

Maybe it just *seemed* too close. Maybe, the way she was feeling, half a room away would seem too close.

'I need to go to bed,' she said, a trifle unsteadily. 'I just stayed here to see how you went.'

'To check on me?' But he was still smiling.

'No!' She flushed. 'Sorry. It's none of my business.'

'But you did force me to read to her.'

She tilted her chin at that. 'It *is* none of my business,' she repeated. 'But I'm leaving soon and you're staying. She needs you to be her friend, not me.'

'I don't know how…'

'Then learn. Tonight was a great start.'

'You're the psychologist?'

'No,' she said, gently now. 'I'm an interested onlooker who has to move on. But you and Alice… I hope you'll be friends for life. You can do it. I know you can.'

And then, there was something about the way he was looking…something about his expression… Fear? Longing? Bewilderment? She couldn't figure it out, but somehow, before she could stop herself, before she even realised what a crazy thing it was to do, she stepped forward and rose on tiptoes. 'You'll be fine,' she said—and she kissed him.

It was a feather kiss, a brushing of lips on his cheek. It was a kiss of friendship, a kiss of warmth, a kiss of some deep recognition that this man was in as much need of human contact as his niece was. It had been entirely instinctive, and as soon as she'd done it she backed away. Horrified. She'd shocked herself. What was she thinking?

And he looked…as if he didn't know either. He put his hand to his cheek and looked at her. Just looked.

They were both in uncharted territory.

The silence stretched on. He raised a hand as if to reach out to her and then he paused and looked down at it—and so did she. They were on the edge of something…

Which was stupid and unprofessional and doomed to lead nowhere, she told herself, panicked. This man was a client, nothing more. She had only to glance around his amazing, over-the-top designer sitting room to see that he was a world away from her world. As her mother's world had been so far from her father's.

And she wasn't stupid. She was a vet, here on a job. She backed away, almost in fear, and her hands came up in an instinctive gesture of defence.

'I… I'm sorry,' she muttered. 'That was totally inappropriate. Goodnight, Bryn.'

And somehow, she managed to get her shocked body to move.

He didn't follow her as she fled. He didn't call after her.

He just stood in silence, for a very long time.

She'd performed a miracle. She and her blessed dog.

Bryn sat in his study, supposedly working. They'd come to an arrangement. He now spent the mornings and the evenings with Alice. The afternoons, though, they'd decided, could be his. Kiara needed to train Bunji with Alice, and he really did need to work.

But increasingly he was finding it harder to concentrate. Right now, instead of focusing on notes on neural pathways, he was looking out over the lawn to where a child and a dog were tumbling down the grassy slope toward the swimming pool. For the last hour Kiara had been trying to teach Bunji—and Alice—to roll, using a pocket full of treats, laughter and pats. Finally she'd done it. Now child and dog were nose to nose, rolling down the slope as one.

Alice was squealing with delight.

Kiara was sitting at the top of the slope, beaming as if she'd been given the world.

He felt as if *he'd* been given the world. Alice was a child again.

What a gift.

But tomorrow Kiara was leaving.

The thought was like a storm cloud heading his way with frightening speed. But they'd be fine, he told himself, as he'd been telling himself for days. The way Alice felt about Kiara—and increasingly, the way he was starting to feel about Kiara—it wasn't practical or sensible to continue. He and Alice would figure out a new normal. Kiara been employed for a fixed time and that time was over. Alice had to learn independence.

They'd manage.

And then his phone rang.

The screen said the call was from Archie Cragg, the hospital's administrator. He and Archie had last talked just before Kiara had arrived. 'I'll be back as soon as Alice starts school,' Bryn had told him, and Archie had agreed.

'Take all the time you need,' he'd assured him, as he'd said all along. 'We want you back healthy, with things sorted at home.'

But now Archie's voice held a note of strain. 'Mate?' And instantly Bryn knew something was wrong.

'Problem?'

'You could say that,' Archie said grimly. 'We've lost Rod and Caroline.'

What the…?

Rod Breehaut was second in charge of Neurology—he'd taken charge while Bryn was off work. Rod was married to Caroline, who was also a neurologist.

Bryn, Rod and Caroline made up Sydney Central's quota of fully trained neurologists.

Not another accident, surely. His heart seemed to hit his boots, but Archie was still talking.

'It's a bit of an affair.' The voice on the end of the line was tight with fury. 'It seems Rod's been having it off with one of our med students. A student! He knows the rules. He's fifty and she's twenty-two—poor kid, it's like she's star-struck. Her assessment's about to come up and he's her supervisor—can you imagine the situation that puts them both in? Anyway, Caroline caught them at it, in the staffroom of all places, and she screeched the place down. I've had to sack him on the spot, and now Caroline's decided to go home to her mother. Who lives in Birmingham! She leaves tomorrow. Bryn, I know I told you to take all the time you need, but you're pretty much recovered, right? Mate, we have patients in real trouble. We need you.'

She looked up and Bryn was limping across the lawn to join them. And her heart seemed to sort of…jolt.

Well, that was dumb, she told herself. Just because the man was too good-looking for his own good… Just because he was so darned sexy…

But it was more than that. Nothing had changed in the sexiness department since she'd first met him, but since the night she'd found him watching over his little niece, the way she'd felt about him had definitely changed. And after the night of…the kiss…she'd watched his interaction with Alice with a kind of wonder.

Until Bunji had broken through, uncle and niece had seemed tightly bound within themselves, shielding themselves from personal connection.

She watched him now and saw his face crease into a smile as wide as the one she'd felt when Bunji and Alice had finally nailed their nose-to-nose roll. And she felt as if she'd been given the world.

To make a wounded man smile?

No. She'd come here for the dog, she reminded herself. And for Alice.

But this week seemed to have changed things for Bryn, her sense of satisfaction was well justified, and she might even feel sad about leaving tomorrow.

Who was she kidding? *Might?* She knew she'd feel desolate. But she had to leave. Hazel had to return to Sydney. Maureen was holding the fort, but she could only work part-time and there was no one to run the clinic. Even if there was a point in her staying…well, why would she?

Bryn had been smiling as he watched kid and dog roll, but as he reached her his smile faded. He was still gazing down at them, but his face was suddenly grim.

'Problem?' she asked, and he took a deep breath and turned to face her.

'Kiara, I need you to stay.' Then, as she opened her mouth to respond, he held up a hand. 'Please. Hear me out. This isn't for me—or for Alice. This is desperation.'

And briefly he outlined what he'd just been told.

'I know you think it's impossible,' he told her. 'But Sydney Central is without its three senior neurologists. There's no one else in the short term. Kiara, if I don't head back, people will die.'

What was he asking? She stared at him in open-mouthed astonishment. 'You're kidding.'

'I don't think I am,' he said bleakly. 'Archie's looked at every option. He's desperate. But I can't leave Alice. Kiara, I've tried to think but I can't get past it. There's no one but you.'

'So ring Beatrice,' she managed, feeling winded. More. She was feeling almost as if a gun were being pointed at her head. She had needs. Her dogs were her life.

'If I don't head back, people will die...'

The medical imperative. Unarguable.

'Do you think Beatrice would come?' he asked.

She stared at him for a long time, playing it out in her head. Thinking of what she knew of the acerbic Beatrice. 'No,' she said at last.

'Neither do I.'

And then they were silent because Alice and Bunji were at the top of the slope again. They watched as kid and dog repeated their roll, as they ended up in a tangle of arms, legs, tail at the bottom. As Bunji was cuddled. As Alice was licked. They were content, Kiara thought, and she thought of the miracle it had taken to get them this far.

'There's a child-minding service at the hospital,' Bryn said at last, talking heavily, as if the weight of the world were on his shoulders. As maybe it was. 'Archie's asked. It's for littlies, but because it's an emergency they'll take Alice until I can find someone else. But I can't bear...'

And neither could she. The thought of Alice being left in a strange setting…without Bunji…

'No,' she said, and Bryn raked his already rumpled hair.

'Kiara, I know I have no right to ask, but is there anyone else to take on Two Tails? I'm prepared to pay as much as Beatrice has already paid you. Per week. Just until Archie can find replacements, or until the new school term starts? You need cash and I need help. Could it work?'

He was serious?

She turned and looked down the slope, at Alice and Bunji, mutually engrossed in blowing dandelion seeds. How had a dandelion dared show its face in this perfectly manicured garden?

Who knew?

What was he asking?

That she step in and take over care of dog and child, so he could go back to his perfectly manicured life?

No. That was unfair. She'd read enough about the work he did to realise that his statement—*'people will die'*—was probably the truth.

'It's three weeks,' he said.

'Until boarding school?'

'I know that's no longer an option. Even I can see how much she needs Bunji. But I've been making enquiries. There's a local school only four blocks from here. It seems to have a good reputation. I've talked to the headmistress. There's only a week before end of term so we've agreed Alice can start in three weeks' time. But, Kiara, I don't have three weeks. I've wasted enough time.'

Whoa…

I've wasted enough time?

All at once she was thinking back to the time after she'd been bitten by the snake. Danger over, both her grandmother and her father were at her hospital bedside, discussing her convalescence.

Her grandmother had been due to leave on a visit to a beloved sister in Perth. She'd laid her plans long since. Her flights had been booked for a year.

But her father had stood there, arms folded, angry, unmoving. 'You'll have to take her,' he'd snapped. 'I've wasted enough time.'

Her grandmother had taken her—of course she had, and it had only been much later that Kiara had realised how much of a sacrifice missing that trip had been. But she'd known enough to accept without question that she had a place in her grandma's heart.

And here was another man, his face set, demanding someone else accept his responsibilities. Knowing that his life was far more important.

'I've wasted enough time.'

She opened her mouth to snap—but then she paused.

He'd closed his eyes and when he opened them again what she saw was a weariness that was almost bone deep. Months of shock, of pain and a responsibility he'd never asked for had left their indelible mark.

'Sorry, that was badly said,' he said at last. 'I haven't wasted my time. Believe it or not, I do care. I'm doing my best, and this has come at me from left field. I know this feels like emotional blackmail but I'm desperate for help. Kiara, I need you.'

'But I can't,' she managed. She was feeling desperate herself. 'My friend Hazel has been looking after Two Tails and she has to leave. I have dogs in care. I have a vet clinic to run. Like your hospital, there's no one else who has the skills and availability. If Hazel agrees to stay on at Two Tails, then she loses her job. If I don't go back to Two Tails, my dogs will starve.' She shook her head, thinking of the impossibility of what he was asking. 'And, Bryn, honestly, it's not fair to Alice to make her more dependent on me. It's you she needs to learn to love, not me. You and your friend Archie need to find a Plan B.'

'There's no Plan B.'

'Well, I'm not Plan A.'

She felt sick, but what choice did she have? The thought of abandoning Two Tails… She couldn't do it. No!

And then, because any further discussion would achieve nothing, she crossed her arms across her chest, and she lay down on the grass.

'No,' she said again and rolled deliberately away down the slope.

Plan B. What the hell was Plan B?

And why, when there were so many convoluted problems filling his head, did he suddenly want to forget them all and roll down after her? Kiara had obviously managed to put away her anger. Woman and child and dog were now in a tangle of licks and laughter below.

Joining them would be more than stupid. He'd end up twisting his mending knee, setting himself back months.

He needed to block out emotion—block out desire?—and think.

Kiara's refusal was understandable. It wasn't fair to demand it of her, but for the life of him he couldn't think of an alternative.

It was three weeks before Alice could start school. The thought of Alice in hospital childcare… He couldn't do it. If he offered more—a lot more—to an employment agency he might well find someone willing to work for him, but employing a stranger, expecting her to care for Alice full-time and hoping Alice didn't retreat again into her shell… Once again, he couldn't do it.

He had two conflicting imperatives, and they *were* imperative. He had to start work, but he was Alice's guardian. He had to do what was best for her.

And it wasn't just that he was her guardian, he thought as he watched the group below him. With Kiara's help he'd grown closer to Alice this week than he'd been since she'd arrived. If he could wave his wand and send her back to the States he wouldn't do it, not unless he was convinced it'd make her happier. Boarding school was out of the question. Like it or not, she was now part of his life, living here with him, for… how long?

For however long she needed.

And that brought back what Kiara said. That Alice needed to learn to love him.

That thought was practically overwhelming, and he shoved it away with force. One day at a time, he told himself, fighting back panic.

And suddenly, through the panic, there was Plan B.

He checked it out, examining it from all angles and finding it…okay.

Three weeks. Trust was already established. It might even be good for all of them.

'Kiara,' he called.

She looked up, wary. He should head down the slope and join them, but rolling was out of the question and his leg was too stiff to try walking. He'd have to use the path, which would look wussy.

Besides, by the time he reached them they might well have climbed back up again.

Not for the first time he cursed his injured leg. Not only had Skye's death blindsided him emotionally, he was accustomed to his body doing what he demanded. Now…these last months had left him feeling as if he were on quicksand. He longed, no, even stronger, he *yearned* to be back at work. Back where emotional and physical injuries were his to treat, not his to endure.

Cutting-edge medicine had always been his retreat from emotion. The hospital needed him and suddenly, more than ever, he longed for it as well. The emotions he was feeling were starting to seem overwhelming.

'Kiara,' he called, louder, and she looked doubtfully up at him, said something to Alice he couldn't hear and then made her way back up the slope. Then she stood, hands behind her back. Dutiful employee waiting for orders?

Employee until tomorrow?

'I've had a thought,' he said.

'That's great.' She nodded encouragingly. 'Thoughts are good.' He glowered, and infuriatingly she tried a smile—trying to make light of an impossible situation? 'As long as it doesn't involve me abandoning my responsibilities, I'm all ears,' she told him. 'Tell me your thought.'

She was teasing?

She was like an annoying buzz fly, he thought. Deserving of swatting.

Honestly?

Honestly, despite the pressure he was under, right at this minute he didn't want to swat her.

Of all the inappropriate thoughts he could have, he actually, stupidly, wanted to kiss her.

He was so far out of his comfort zone here. He needed to pull himself together. He was in a mess enough. A kiss…even if he didn't get slapped, it'd make what he was about to suggest a whole lot more complicated.

So get on with it, he told himself fiercely. Outline Plan B.

'What if you take Alice and Bunji to your place?'

'Pardon?' She looked at him blankly.

'I'd pay you to keep them at this refuge of yours,' he said, quickly, sensing her first instinct would be to reject it out of hand. 'Kiara, Alice likes you a lot. She's old enough to be little trouble, and Bunji would be safe. I could pay you to care for them for the three weeks until Alice starts school.'

'Really?' she said slowly. 'And then what?'

'By then I'll have sorted the mess at work. Sydney Central has a great reputation—we'll find new people. My pressure will ease, and Alice can come home again.'

'Define home.'

He frowned. 'Where she lives, of course.'

'So you agree that she lives here?'

'It doesn't stop her being somewhere else for a while. She can't depend on me for everything.'

And at that he copped it again, a flash of anger from her dark eyes.

'So who can she depend on?'

'I meant—'

'I know exactly what you meant,' she told him. 'Alice can depend on you in an emergency—like when her mother dies, or when you have time and space to allow her to share your life. But as for being there whenever—'

'I can't put my life on hold.'

'For a child. Why not? What bigger reason is there?

I told you. What Alice needs is someone to love her, and that someone can't be me.'

She paused then and took a few deep breaths. She turned away and looked down the slope again, obviously thinking, and when she finally turned back, she had her face under control. The anger was gone, but when she spoke again her voice was flat. Decisive.

'Okay,' she said. 'If it really is life or death that the hospital gets its precious neurosurgeon—and, yes, I believe you—then for Alice's sake I'll let her come with me. But on one condition.'

'What's that?'

'That you come, too.'

'But—'

'No buts. That's my offer and you can take it or leave it. For whatever you think, Alice needs a home in the true sense of the word. She's the same as Bunji. Bunji seems to have found her home with Alice, but Alice's home needs to be you. Not me. You. So, Dr Dalton, it's up to you. You can come and go to work as you please—go save the world—but every night you need to come home to Alice. I'll provide three weeks' board and lodging, care and kindness to Alice and Bunji while you're away, but for these three weeks, Alice's home is still you. As it has to be, now and for ever. So…deal?'

Three weeks…

Now and for ever?

What was she asking?

But he looked down into her face and what he saw there was implacable. Take it or leave it.

Three weeks away from his home.

Home? She was saying it had a whole new definition.

He couldn't process it, but he was up against a brick wall, and he knew it.

Could it hurt to spend three weeks in this refuge he'd only heard about?

'Is it big enough?'

'I have four bedrooms,' she told him. 'Two of them are habitable and I have an attic I think Alice might love.' She glanced around at his swimming pool, his manicured lawns, his stunning house. 'It's not quite up to your standard,' she confessed. 'But if you're prepared to slum it…'

'Slum it…'

'Well, maybe not slum exactly. Two Tails might be wonky but it's clean, and it is a home. So, what do you think, Dr Dalton? Last offer?'

He stared at her, and she gazed back, her look direct and challenging.

Okay, he thought. It'd take longer but he could travel to work from her place. It might even do Alice good.

But then… Three more weeks staying with this woman?

What was there in that that gave him pause?

Pause or not, he had no choice.

'Thank you,' he said weakly.

'You're welcome,' she told him, and she smiled a tight smile, then turned away and proceeded to roll down the slope again.

CHAPTER EIGHT

WHAT HAD HE EXPECTED?

Given the state of Kiara's finances, some sort of dog pens, and a run-down house attached?

It might be run-down, but it was beautiful.

He'd followed Kiara in her battered van as she'd driven back to Two Tails, and when she pulled into the drive, he could only stare.

The house was built at the beginning of a valley, the road in front winding on to the town of Birralong. From here the land was zoned a national park, thick, untouched bushland, fantastical gorges, a landscape as wild as it was beautiful.

The house itself was a cottage, weathered with age but stunningly beautiful. A wilderness of garden was practically taking over. Crimson bougainvillea washed across the corrugated roof and trailed along the wide veranda. Huge eucalypts formed a vast, bird-filled back-drop, and the peaks of the Blue Mountains towered in the distance.

A discreet sign on the front door said *Two Tails. Please Ring and Wait.* Another sign said *Clinic* and pointed to a winding path leading to the left.

'Wow!' Alice had driven with Kiara, and now she and Bunji were out of Kiara's battered van. The little girl was looking as awed as he felt. 'This is where you live?' she asked Kiara.

'It's my home,' Kiara told her, and the way she said it told him how much she loved it.

This was why she'd given them Bunji, he reminded himself. And it was why they were here now. This was a paid service.

The door opened and an elderly woman with a mass of wild, white curls appeared in the doorway. 'Oh, Kiara. Thank heaven you're back. Hazel had to go in a hurry, so I stayed on, but my Jim's got a doctor's appointment. So this is Alice. And you must be Dr Dalton. Pleased to meet you, I'm sure. Kiara, sorry, love, but I need to be off.' And she grabbed a battered purse from inside the hall and bolted.

'That's Maureen,' Kiara told Alice. 'She tries to do way too much, but she's awesome. She was my grandma's best friend. She treats me as if I'm a kid, and she'll treat you just the same. She's bossy but she's great.' She hesitated and then added: 'Sometimes I think without Maureen I might fall apart. But come on in. Alice, Maureen's set up a room I think you'll love. It's in the attic and it's very private, your own personal space. The stairs up are a bit wonky, but it has a great gable window looking out to the mountains. I asked Maureen to put some of my favourite books in there, plus a pile of bedding for Bunji. Would you like to see?'

And Alice cast her a look of wonder and headed upstairs without a backward glance.

She'd turned into a child again, Bryn thought. What had happened to her in the last week?

Kiara had happened.

She was standing beside him, watching kid and dog

bounce up the stairs. 'They have their brave back,' she said, smiling as they disappeared.

'Thanks to you.'

'I know, I'm a matchmaker,' she said smugly. 'Bunji and Alice—a match made in heaven.'

He looked at her curiously. There was so much he didn't understand about this woman. 'So how about you?' He had no business asking but he couldn't help himself. 'Have you made any matches for yourself?'

She cast him an odd look. 'You know, since I'm your employee I'm pretty sure you're not supposed to ask that question.' And then her irrepressible smile peeped out again. 'But no. I have nine dogs here and who has time—or the need—for a love life when there are nine dogs requiring as much love as I can give them? When they've all found their forever homes, there might be time for me.'

'But there'll always be dogs.'

'I guess there will,' she admitted. 'Even if I can no longer run Two Tails.' She spread her hand, encompassing the big living room they'd just entered. 'Maybe I'll just live in poverty here, letting the termites do their worst around me. I'll be a modern Ms Havisham, but with termites and dogs instead of cobwebs. There are surely worse places to be stuck.'

Maybe there were.

But…

The Miss Havisham reference—Dickens' fictional jilted bride, dwindling into old age in her decrepit house—could never be a reasonable comparison, he thought, but there were points of resemblance. He was gazing around with a certain amount of awe. How could one person have all this…stuff?

But it wasn't just 'stuff'. Fascinated, he started to

prowl. How could one room contain so many pictures? Piles of bric-a-brac loaded each side table. The room was crowded with eclectic furniture, crazy lamps. What looked at first glance to be almost a product of hoarding was, on second, third, even fourth inspection, a massive collection of personal wonder.

'Did you gather all this?' he asked, stunned, and she gave a self-conscious laugh.

'Grandma was a bower bird. She loved history, loved the stories of her people, but she and her sister lost most of their family and I think she collected things to make up for it. Once she lost my mother, her collecting seemed to become even more frenetic.'

He lifted a wooden carving, a piece of ironbark magnificently formed into a figure of woman and child. 'This should be on public display.'

'I love it.'

'Of course.' He frowned. 'But all of this? You love it all?'

'You haven't seen the half of it,' she admitted. 'Every room is crammed. And, no, I don't love most of it—dusting it is a nightmare—but I have no idea what to do with it. If…when I leave here it'll have to be sold. Or donated. The local charity shop will be grateful.'

'Don't you dare.'

She flashed him a look of surprise. 'Because?'

'Because it's worth…' Once more he gazed around. One of the women he'd dated, a top of the trees' radiologist, had been a collector of old porcelain. For the few months they'd been together—a long time in the history of his brief relationships—he'd indulged her by spending weekends prowling junk shops and car boot sales. He knew the crazy prices people paid, and what Kiara had here was a goldmine. 'If you really want to get rid of it, it'll bring heaps,' he said at last, feeling the inadequacy of the word. 'I have friends who know the right people to value it, to help you sort it, so you get what it's worth.'

'Really?'

'Really. No pressure but I'm thinking Two Tails is just as deserving of cash as your local charity shop.'

She flushed and smiled, and then shook her head. 'I'm sure most of it's worthless.'

'And some of it isn't. This bowl…' He lifted a crimson and green glass bowl that was filled with potpourri and held it to the light. 'I know someone who'd pay serious money for this. Enough to keep even Bunji in dog food for a month.'

'Really? That much? Wow!' She smiled. For the last week Bunji had suddenly found her appetite, wolfing down each meal and pleading for more. But then she shrugged, moving on. 'It's a possibility,' she conceded. 'But you've helped me enough. I'll show you to your room.'

'Show me more,' he urged. 'Where do you keep your dogs?'

She cast him a doubtful glance and then led the way out to the back of the house. Here the veranda morphed into a line of dog pens, each a small 'cubby' under the extended roofline of the veranda. The enclosures opened at the rear, so each dog had its individual run. The runs were wide and generous, running down to the lawn and ending under the shade of the eucalypts.

The pens seemed to be three quarters empty. 'We're whittling down,' Kiara told him, seeing his enquiring look. 'Bunji was the last dog we took. We have tentative homes for most of these but they're undertaking training before they go. We don't just rehouse, we rehome. See Mickey, the corgi? He's eight years old, a gentle lamb, but his owner died two months ago. He's being retrained for Shirley, who's in her seventies and has rheumatoid arthritis. She lives in a second-floor apartment, so we're training him to use a doggy door through to the fire escape, which leads to a little back-yard. He's had two sessions so far. Hazel says the last time he was brilliant. I thought Alice might like to come with me this week while I take him for one last trial. Then he's set to go.'

She headed over to let Mickey out, stooping to scratch behind his ears. 'You know, Bunji's pretty clever,' she said thoughtfully. 'She might even help.'

'You're a trained vet,' he said, cautiously. 'You spend your time teaching dogs to use fire escapes?'

'Hey, I do lots of vet stuff, too,' she retorted. 'I run a clinic for a couple of hours every afternoon. But re-homing successfully is what I love.'

'And when you leave here?'

Her brightness faded. 'I guess… If I have to leave then I'll just go back to being a normal vet. Patching up and moving on.'

Well, maybe that was no bad fate, he decided, as she led him through the pens and introduced him to her weird mix of clients. That was what *he* did, after all. He patched people up and moved on.

No emotional attachment there.

'So,' she said briskly. 'Let's get you settled and then you can head off to work as you will. As long as you're home at a reasonable hour for Alice, then I'm happy to keep her entertained. All these guys are pretty much certified bombproof. My grounds are dog safe. Apart from the fussy ones who think romping in a paddock is beneath them, Alice can walk as many as she wants.

I have a feeling she'll like that, and so will my dogs.' She hesitated. 'She's a loner—she's had to be. Hopefully you'll break that down, but she'll still need space.'

'I guess.' He thought of the psychology sessions he'd organised for Alice and thought…this woman is helping just as much, if not more.

'I have clinic at three,' she was saying, oblivious to where his thoughts were taking him. 'But I'm still just through that door if Alice needs me, and it shouldn't take long. I've put notices in the local paper saying clients need to start thinking of where they'll go when we close, and we've already noticed a drop off.'

'You'll miss this place.'

'Like a hole in my heart,' she admitted, her voice tightening. 'But as you—and especially Alice—already know, holes just have to be papered over if you're to move on.'

He was back! Gloriously he was back in his rooms at Sydney Central. His receptionist, assigned to other duties while he was away, had returned to her rightful desk. Apart from her concerned question… 'Do I need to space appointments, give you time to adjust?'…she was acting as if he'd simply been overseas to a conference.

He fielded a few concerned queries about his leg from his colleagues. There were brief quips about idiots who didn't leave rescues to those who knew how, but then the ripples caused by his absence simply moved to the horizon and disappeared. The gossip about Rod and Caroline had overtaken almost everything, and their absence caused pressure on the whole department.

Was that why there was no talk of Alice? No one

asked. Or was it that the advent of a child in his life wasn't supposed to affect him at all?

But this was what he'd longed for—demanding, technical work that necessarily blocked out all the emotion of the last few months. Work, where he could be self-contained, fully focused on the highly skilled procedures that saved people's lives. Work, where he didn't need to think about Alice and her needs.

Where he didn't have to think about Kiara?

How had Kiara come into the equation? He had no clue, but both Alice and Kiara stayed in his mind.

He'd always had the ability to focus solely on what was at hand. This subconscious backdrop of Alice—and Kiara—was disturbing.

His first hour or so, of necessity, had to be spent at his desk, catching up on what had to be done, on the mess that had been left by his two colleagues. It was Saturday. There'd hopefully be no urgent surgery today, but Archie and Rebecca had moved some of Rod's urgent consults to this afternoon. He thus had to be totally focused, and he was fast immersed in patient histories, consulting with radiologists over results from MRIs, consideration of medications, alternatives to surgery. Discussion of dangers, for and against. Assessments of possible outcomes of surgery.

He had to be at the top of his game, and part of him welcomed it—this had been what he'd ached for over the last months.

But still, part of him was separate. Part of his mind was back at home with Kiara.

No. Home with Alice, he reminded himself harshly, and then he thought… Home?

Wasn't home back in Clovelly?

But maybe his real home was here, at the beating hub

of a huge teaching hospital. Here, where he'd felt more in control of his world than in any other place, ever.

Except now he didn't. He felt…

As if he needed to give himself a decent shake and get on with it?

He had no choice. A family was ushered in, a kid with epilepsy. He'd made a thorough study of his history before he saw him, previous treatments and prognosis. He was tentatively scheduled to do the surgery Rod had recommended, and now he had to say it as it was.

'With this procedure there's over a fifty per cent chance that your epilepsy will subside to the point where it can be well controlled by medication.' Felix was fifteen years old, a kid whose epilepsy was spiralling out of control. His parents were sitting behind him, having the sense to let their son do the talking. Letting Felix make the calls. Even so, they were clutching each other's hands as if they were drowning.

'I just want to get better,' Felix muttered, and his mother couldn't contain herself any longer.

'But not if it's dangerous.'

This surgery came with risks—he outlined them, and they hung over the little group. There was a fifty per cent chance of massive improvement, maybe a thirty per cent chance of some improvement, but there was still a possibility of no improvement at all. Also…he had to admit that there was a minute risk of death.

He watched the parents blench, but not the kid, and who could blame him? 'I want to be able to kick a footy without everyone making a huge fuss,' he muttered. 'Like I am, they won't let me on the team. And as soon as I'm eighteen I want to drive a car. I want to be normal.'

'What would you do if it was your son?' his mother quavered, and her husband interjected.

'Yeah, Doc. If it was your family…your kid… If it was your wife you'd have to hold up if things go pear-shaped…'

And there they were again, front and centre. Kiara and Alice.

Kiara.

He thought of her perky grin, her spirit. He thought of Kiara with her arms folded, rolling down the slope to join Bunji and Alice.

He thought of her, head bent over Bunji's healing wound, skilfully debriding but speaking to the dog in such soothing tones she hardly needed anaesthetic.

He thought of Kiara, organising Alice her attic room, acknowledging that Alice still needed space to be alone.

He just thought…of Kiara.

'It'd probably be my wife who'd do the holding up,' he said at last, because the group was waiting for an answer. If it could help this group by inferring he had a wife…if it'd help a decision…

For whatever reason, the sudden image of Kiara as his family helped him form his response.

'I guess, whatever happens, you hold each other up,' he said. 'Because that's what families do.'

That was what Kiara would do.

Enough. He needed to stop thinking about Kiara and move on without her in his head. He turned back to Felix. 'But you know what? If you're prepared to go through a few tough weeks after surgery, then there should be no holding up to be done at all. You won't need it.'

As he didn't need holding up?

Of course he didn't. It was only Alice…

'We'll always need it,' Felix's father said soundly. 'Doc, I side-swiped my brand-new car against the garage wall this morning. Inattention. Worrying about this appointment. But you know what? It was Felix who hugged me. Who held me up. We're a family, mate. Whatever the outcome there'll always be holding up to be done, and no matter what Felix decides, we're in this together.'

And there it was, decision made. Bryn sent them back to Rebecca to organise dates, times, pre-admission forms, and he moved on. Still feeling unsettled.

Two more patients and he could head home.

Home. There was that word again.

He worked on, and then, just as he was packing to leave, the call came in from the emergency department.

'Are you up for some tricky surgery, mate?' the head of ER asked him. 'We know you're only just back, but we're coping with a multiple-car pile-up, major trauma. We have a young guy with a skull fracture, a major cerebral bleed. Can you deal?'

There was no choice. For the first time ever, though, there were consequences for him. Kiara's words replayed. *'As long as you're home at a reasonable hour for Alice...'* He phoned Kiara and told her what had happened.

'The kid's seventeen,' he said. 'I need...'

'Of course you need,' she told him, and then spoke to Alice in the background. 'Hey, Alice, a kid's been in a car crash and the hospital wants your uncle to sew him up. Can we cope without him, or should we let our pizza get cold while we pine for him?'

'What's pine?' he heard Alice ask.

'It means sit on the back doorstep and cry because he's late and we miss him so much. What's it to be, Alice? We eat crunchy pizza without your uncle, or we cry into soggy tissues while we wait for him?'

And to his astonishment he heard a giggle. ‘Pizza,’ Alice decreed, and Kiara chuckled as well.

‘Good choice. You heard that, Dr Dalton? You get on with saving lives and we promise we’ll leave at least two slices of pizza in the microwave for you.’

He disconnected and headed for Theatre, but, stupidly, now part of him…part of him ached to be home.

Home.

To microwaved pizza.

To his…family?

CHAPTER NINE

IT WAS AFTER nine before he arrived back at Two Tails. The surgery had been a success. He should be pleased with himself, but instead he was as drained as he'd ever felt.

Three months away from work, a full day moving around, followed by four hours in Theatre had tested his gammy leg to the limits. And driving home…for some reason the emotions he'd felt as he'd talked to Felix came flooding back. Was he going home to family? He had little idea of the concept, but it surely didn't apply to coming home to Two Tails.

Coming home to wife and child and dog? The thought was…unnerving. He was far too tired to think about processing it.

The front door was unlocked. He knocked but when he received no answer he went on in.

Kiara and Alice and Benji were all in the living room. The vast open fire formed a soft glow behind them. Kiara was sitting on a rug before the fire, reading.

Alice was lying beside her, her head on Kiara's knee. A fluffy rug was wrapped around her. Asleep?

Bunji was lying full length beside them both. She opened her eyes as Bryn entered, offered a lazy wag of her tail and then went back to the important job of snoozing.

He stopped dead. It was such a picture. For Alice to be this relaxed, to be sleeping on Kiara's knee… Kiara's hand was on her wispy hair, gently stroking.

She looked up as Bryn entered, laid down her book and put a finger to her lips. 'Shh…'

He came and sat beside them—on the settee because it seemed far too familiar to sit on the rug itself.

'Welcome home,' Kiara whispered, and what was there in that to make his gut twist? 'How did it go?'

'One seventeen-year-old who'll live to do something stupid again, I dare say,' he told her. 'Joyriding. Kids.'

'But you succeeded.'

'Impossible to say for sure until he wakes up but I'm hopeful. We got the pressure off fast.'

'Well done, you,' she said and smiled and there was that gut twist again. 'So, pizza… It won't be great but it's edible. If you're anything like me, you can subsist quite nicely on reheated dinners.'

'Too many wounded dogs in your life?'

'And too many wounded kids in yours,' she said gently. But then Alice stirred a little and she hesitated. 'Actually… Bryn, are you up to helping her up to bed?'

He frowned. 'She didn't want to go herself?'

'She was waiting for you. She was trying to stay awake, but it's been too big a day. It'd be great for her to have you tuck her into bed.'

'Kiara…'

'Mmm?' The look she gave him was of innocent enquiry, but he had her figured by now. Ever since he'd met her, every step of the way, she'd hauled him into Alice's life.

Why did it make him feel he needed to back away?

But still he stooped and lifted Alice—she was such a featherweight that with the help of the bannisters he could even do it with his gammy leg. And when she woke and questioned him, he told her yes, he'd managed to sew the kid from the car accident up, and yes, he'd have a scar but he'd be okay.

'Like Bunji,' Alice murmured as he carried her upstairs, and then added sleepily… 'Like me.'

'Like all of us,' he said, tucking her into bed and then, because it seemed like the right thing to do, even though she'd shied from any sort of affectionate gesture from the time he'd met her, he bent and kissed her on the forehead. And to his amazement her skinny arms clung and hugged.

'I'm glad you're home,' she whispered. 'Is Bunji here?'

Bunji had followed them up the stairs and was indeed now in the bundle of rugs beside the bed.

He took Alice's hand and guided it down to lie on Bunji's soft head, and then he left them to sleep. And as he made his way down the stairs, he was suddenly overcome with a stupid urge to weep.

For heaven's sake…he must be more tired than he thought. He gave himself a moment at the foot of the stairs to recover, and then headed back into the living room.

Kiara had cleared the muddle on the coffee table to make room for a plate of pizza and a glass of wine. She was on the rug again. She was wearing shabby jeans and a faded windcheater. Her dusky curls were loose and tousled, her shabby windcheater was way too big for her…and he thought he'd never seen anyone as beautiful.

He needed to pull himself together.

'Dinner,' she said, and he sank down onto the armchair and looked at what was before him. And looked again.

Yes, it was pizza, but this was like no pizza he'd ever had delivered. A thick, buttery crust. Tiny baked tomatoes. Fresh…*everything*. Vegetables that had obviously been grilled beforehand—tiny mushrooms, red peppers, aubergine, zucchini… He could smell herbs…oregano? Thyme? Gorgonzola cheese had been sliced and spread to melt as the pizza cooked, then black pepper sprinkled on and finally a scattering of fresh basil.

'This is leftover pizza?' he said, stunned.

'Pizza's one of my splinter skills,' she said proudly. 'Yours isn't quite up to scratch because of the reheating, but I have a microwave with a pizza function. It's therefore not as soggy as it might have been.'

It looked fine to him. More, it looked great. 'I thought you said you didn't cook.'

'I cook pizza.'

'You made the whole thing?' For heaven's sake, he sounded accusatory.

'I make a heap of dough and freeze individual servings,' she told him. 'So yes, Alice and I made it, but we didn't make it from scratch. Without my store of frozen bases, I'd never have tried them at your place. And,' she added smugly, 'apart from the cheese, the topping's all from my veggie patch. Except for the mushrooms, which are from my little mushroom factory in the back of the hall cupboard. And there's another lack in your fancy house. I checked your hall cupboard and found not a single mushroom.'

He had to smile back. As far as he knew, his hall cupboard contained one winter coat and one squash racket. It was dusted and aired regularly by his housekeepers. No mushroom would dare show its face.

'Did Alice eat hers?'

'Yes, she did.' She still had that smug smile, and,

wow, her smile was infectious. 'Hers might not have looked quite like ours, though,' she confessed. 'She made her own, with tomato sauce, cheese and bacon, and we used a bone-shaped cookie cutter to make her base into mini pizzas. I occasionally make doggy biscuits for my clients. We had to sterilise my cookie cutter to make sure it was an okay for pizzas, but her bone-shape pizzas were excellent.'

He thought of Alice, of how little she'd eaten over the last weeks. Alice, eating bone-shaped pizzas. 'You're a marvel.'

'I know,' she said smugly. 'Now, if you'll excuse me, I'm up to a very exciting part of my book.'

And that was that. She tucked Alice's rug around her knees and disappeared into her story. Leaving him to enjoy his dinner.

Which was, in itself, extraordinary.

He thought briefly back through the long list of women he'd dated over the years. Of nights spent. Not one of them would abandon talking to disappear into a book.

But this wasn't dating.

No. It was more than that. It felt…comfortable. He'd come home stressed and tired, fighting emotions he was struggling to understand. He was aware that he was late, aware that there were responsibilities facing him. And instead of more stress, he'd carried a sleeping child up to her bedroom and been hugged. He'd been handed a truly excellent meal, with wine. He'd been allowed to sink into a saggy armchair by an open fire and just…be.

The sensation was extraordinary.

She was sitting beside him, leaning back on an armchair, knees tucked up, rug tucked over her. She was frowning with intent at something she was reading.

There was a wisp of a curl dangling down over her forehead. Close to blocking her sight. It needed to be brushed back.

She was too intent on her story.

Dammit, he couldn't help himself. He leaned forward and wove his finger through the curl, tucking it behind her ear.

She looked up at him, surprised, but not alarmed. It had been an intensely personal gesture, but she didn't seem to have noticed.

'Thanks,' she said and smiled up at him—and went straight back into her book.

He was left with his pizza and his wine.

He was left feeling…winded.

And that was how their days went. One following another.

He left every morning for Sydney Central, Alice and Kiara waving him off as if this were part of a lifetime routine.

He couldn't believe how quickly Alice had settled. She was practically blooming. Bunji was hardly limping now, her fur was growing almost to the point where she looked respectable, and she followed Alice with slave-like devotion. Kid and dog were happy.

Kiara was busy. Maureen usually arrived before Bryn left for work and settled into whatever needed doing. She and Alice seemed to become immediate friends, but she could usually only fit in two or three hours. Kiara therefore had little help. Each of the dogs had a training routine, she had clinic to run, but somehow, she seamlessly wove Alice and Bunji into her day. By the time he left for work they were out in the paddock, teaching dogs to heel, to recall, not to jump up when excited.

And every morning when he left, he was aware of a pang of loss. He wouldn't mind being out there with them.

Which was stupid. His career was medicine. His *life* was medicine. Kiara was simply taking over part of his responsibility for Alice, while he returned to where he belonged. At the end of the term break, Alice would start at her new school. They'd be back at Clovelly. They'd be back at their new normal.

With Rebecca's help he'd hired a housekeeper from another agency—a woman he interviewed in a brief break from work, a week after they'd been at Two Tails. Mrs Connor seemed pleasant, happy with the prospect of taking on the care of Alice and Bunji. 'I have dogs of my own and I'm a grandma,' she told him. 'My husband's retired and my sister lives with us, so I won't need to rush if you get stuck at work.'

She seemed excellent. His future was therefore starting to feel in control again.

Except…where was Kiara in this picture?

Nowhere, and nor should she be. She'd been employed to do a job. She was doing it handsomely and she'd be paid. Then they'd move on.

With a bit of luck, she might agree to keeping in touch with Alice, he thought, and he told himself that was all there was to it. But as the days passed, the more he thought that wasn't enough. The relationship between woman and child…it was like gold.

And then there was…the way he felt.

If he got back to Two Tails early enough, he'd usually find them in the kitchen. 'I don't usually cook when there's just me,' Kiara told him when he queried it. 'But

Alice and I are pulling out Grandma's recipe books and having fun.'

If he came home later, he'd find them curled up before the fire with books that Kiara had found from her childhood. Alice would be entranced, while Bunji snoozed beside them. He'd carry Alice to bed and be hugged goodnight and then return to the fireside.

To Kiara.

More and more the word family was messing with his thoughts.

'How do you know how to make Alice so happy?' Alice was now in bed, he was on his second glass of wine, his leg had miraculously stopped aching and he felt…okay.

'I guess… Grandma,' she said simply. 'Grandma never treated me as a kid—or if she did it was only when she was acting like a kid herself. Anything I know about happiness I learned from Grandma.'

They were in their customary positions, he in his favourite squashy chair, she on the rug, her book ready to be sunk back into. She loved thrillers, she'd told him. The darker the better, and he'd started watching her face as she read, watching her eyes grow rounder as the story got gorier.

He loved watching her.

That errant curl had dropped again. He badly wanted to tuck it back again.

He didn't dare. If he let himself touch her…

'So how about you?' she asked as he fought back the urge to move closer. 'I've told you about me, so tit for tat. Three siblings who don't seem to know each other. What's the story there?'

'Money.'

'Money?' She appeared to think about it. 'I guess,'

she said at last. 'I hear it does weird things to families. I wouldn't mind getting involved in some sort of social research myself. If someone were to offer me, say, a million dollars, to see how much it messes with my life, maybe I'd even take the risk.' She ventured a cautious smile. 'But go on. Don't mind me. Tell me the appalling things that money did.'

And he had to smile back. She was irrepressible.

She was gorgeous.

She was waiting for his story—which wasn't nearly as gorgeous.

Nor was it as bad as hers.

'Just…socialite stuff,' he told her. 'My father married three times. He probably would have added to the tally, but he died of a heart attack when I was eighteen. Before that, he was the heir to serious money, and he was pretty much a serial womaniser. Beatrice was the result of his first marriage. Thea, his first wife, was related to royalty and stood no nonsense. She caught Dad having an affair with an American actress when Beatrice was two, and she took Beatrice straight back to England. Beatrice has been knee-deep in dogs and horses ever since. Dad then married his actress and they had Skye. I believe both of them had affairs, but that marriage ended for good when Skye was five, probably because Dad was having a very public affair with my mother. Mum had money and social connections and the affair hit the media. Thus his next marriage, and me, but that was also a disaster. Mum…just enjoyed the limelight. Domesticity wasn't her thing, and even now I scarcely know her. She walked out and married someone with even more money when I was three, but she didn't take me with her. So I was the only one left with Dad.'

'Ouch.'

'Not really ouch. I was well treated, big houses, servants, nannies to cater for my every whim…' He tried to say it lightly, but it didn't come off.

'So no Grandma.'

'I do have a grandma somewhere,' he told her. 'On my mother's side. She's never shown the slightest interest in meeting me, and vice versa. I don't need family.'

'Everyone needs family.'

'You've managed okay.'

'I had Grandma until four years ago, and I have substitutes. My best friend Hazel—she's the one who found Bunji—she's always here for me. And Maureen… You only see her as a part-time worker, but she was my grandma's best friend and she'd lose an arm for me. Then there's this community…'

'Which you'll leave if you sell.'

Her face clouded. 'Yes,' she said shortly. 'But Two Tails was a dream, and maybe it's time to move on from dreams. Maybe I'll set up another such shelter in the future, when I've saved up again. Find another community somewhere a bit…'

'Cheaper?'

'I guess termite-ridden heritage cottages don't exactly fit my budget.' She gazed around the room, her eyes suddenly thoughtful. 'But not yet. What you're paying me will keep me afloat for a while and this Saturday…well, this is your idea, but Maureen and I have organised a yard sale.'

'A yard sale…'

'Yep.' She motioned to boxes he hadn't noticed at the side of the room. 'I'm not being dumb,' she told him. 'I rehoused an ancient Peke a while back with a gorgeous old lady—Maire. Her son, Howard, is incredibly grateful—and he runs a chain of antique shops. I asked him to come out and go through this place. If you look, he's now put stickers under everything he thinks would sell better at auction—or in one of his shops—and the rest will go in the yard sale. Donna, the local newsagent—she owns one of my greyhounds—has organised posters, plus social media stuff. Some of my clients are coming to help—they're adding cake stalls, fancy goods, you name it. There'll be balloons on the gate at seven a.m. Maureen and Alice and I are beyond excited.'

'You're selling a lot?' he said faintly, and here came that smile again.

'I am. Thanks to you. I don't know how it is but after Grandma died…well, the place was just…how it is. When you showed interest, I thought why am I keeping it? Grandma would love if it keeps Two Tails going a bit longer.'

'Kiara, let me help,' he said, suddenly sure. 'Financially. You know money's not an issue with me. I hate to think of you selling your belongings to keep it going. Maybe I could even become a silent partner. Whatever you need.'

What followed was a long silence. He could see her running the idea through her head as she considered it from all angles.

'Wow, that's a great offer,' she said at last, and she sounded a bit confused. Cautious. 'And part of me says yay. But there's another part… Bryn, that's hugely generous but I don't… I don't think I can do it.'

'Can I ask why not?'

'Because I'm stupid?'

'I'm very sure that's not the case.' He was watching an inward struggle, not sure where it was going.

'I guess…' She frowned. 'Look, it doesn't make

sense, and maybe I should take time to consider, but my gut reaction… Bryn, it's that I don't want to be bought.'

'I'm not buying you.'

'No, but it's my life. I can't even explain. Only that Two Tails has been my dream, mine and Hazel's, and it's all done on our terms.'

'I wouldn't interfere.'

'No,' she said, doubtfully. 'But…' She hesitated again. 'Let me give you an example. Bunji. She came to me a mess, she's cost me a fortune and she was a huge risk. There was a strong probability that she'd either die or be unable to be rehomed. But the risk was mine.'

'I'd never interfere…'

'You wouldn't have to. You'd just be…there.' Once again, that hesitation, and he could see her struggle to find words. 'Bryn, it's Dad. He comes into play here. Whatever I wanted in life, he had control. When I finally got free, the feeling was amazing, and I never want to go back.'

'I'd never control.'

'You wouldn't have to. You'd just be there.'

'You wouldn't trust me?'

'You can't just turn on trust,' she said sadly. 'Look, I know it doesn't make sense, but I need to do this my way. I've accepted your salary and Beatrice's contribution with gratitude—it really will make a difference. I've run with your idea of selling some of Grandma's possessions and that'll make a difference, too. But, Bryn, I'm independent and you have no idea how important that is to me.'

'More important than keeping Two Tails running?' He heard a current of anger in his voice and had to bite it back.

Why was he angry? That she wouldn't allow him to help?

That she wouldn't allow him to be a part of her life going forward?

And maybe that was what she was afraid of. He thought it and accepted it, and the anger died. If it was his independence that was being threatened, then maybe he'd feel the same way.

He *would* feel the same way.

So, he understood—or he thought he did. And he also understood the slight constraint as she picked up her book, rose and said goodnight.

'It's an incredible offer,' she said. 'I'm a fool not to accept and I know it. I don't even fully understand myself why I can't, but all I know is that it's the way things are for me.'

He rose, too. For a long moment she just looked at him, questioning? He wasn't sure why, but he had a strange feeling she was seeing something that maybe he didn't even understand himself. For suddenly she took a step forward, stood on tiptoes and kissed him. It was the same gesture she'd used before. Their lips brushed, for the most fleeting of moments, and it was done.

'I suspect we're two of a kind,' she said, and there was sadness in her voice now. 'Tarred with the same brush? So, I'm rejecting your offer for no reason at all, other than I don't know any other way to live. Thank you, Bryn, and goodnight.'

She'd just rejected an offer to keep Two Tails running. To keep her dream alive.

Why?

Because...of the way Bryn made her feel?

It was crazy and she couldn't explain it. But as she lay in the dark, searching for elusive sleep, she knew her explanation to Bryn wasn't the best she could do.

There was another underlying reason that was scaring her witless. The way she was starting to feel.

Of being out of control?

There was that word again. When she'd managed to escape her father's iron discipline, she'd vowed never to let herself be controlled again, but what Bryn was offering... Surely there was some way they could set things up...a financial partnership where she could still do as she willed... No control on his part at all?

He wouldn't interfere with her decisions to save her dogs. She knew him well enough to believe that.

But there was the problem. She knew him well enough, and part of her was starting to ache to know him better. Part of her felt that when he came home at night...no, when he came back to Two Tails, not home... that part of her was...complete. His smile as he walked through the door. His stoop to hug his little niece. His hug that embraced Bunji.

The way he smiled at her—and, oh, that smile...

It was nonsense, this way she was feeling, and it had to stop. It made her feel as if her world were teetering and she didn't know what was on the downside of a fall.

It made her feel as if her precious control of her life was growing more and more fragile and she had to haul it back. To continue seeing him...to have him part of her life, even if it was only financially... It was starting to scare her. She was beginning to feel like a moonstruck teenager, and she had to pull back.

For some reason, letting Bryn Dalton any further into her life was a step that terrified her too much to contemplate.

CHAPTER TEN

SATURDAY. THE DAY of the yard sale.

There'd been an emergency at Sydney Central the night before. An aneurism, a young mum. Bryn had arrived home in the small hours, mentally and physically wiped. He'd expected the house to be in darkness, but Kiara must have heard his car pull into the yard as she'd come into the hall to greet him.

'How?' she'd asked simply, and he'd managed a tired smile. His leg was aching, he was exhausted, but underneath there was a tinge of hopeful triumph.

'We think she'll make it. She'll be in an induced coma for a few days to let the swelling subside, but the worst of the pressure's off. We can hope.'

'Well done, you,' she'd said, and for a moment he'd thought she might walk forward and hug him. And he badly wanted her to.

But neither of them had moved. 'If you want, there's a bowl of pasta ready to be microwaved,' she'd said simply. 'Or toast and tea if you're past it.'

'Thank you.' He'd hesitated. 'I see the stalls are set up outside for the morning. Do you need help?'

'You sleep and let us worry about everything else,' she'd told him. 'Alice and I are into money making tomorrow. You need to recoup so you can keep on saving the world.' And once again there had been that moment of hesitation where he'd thought…hug?

It didn't happen. They were adults who knew where their boundaries lay.

'Goodnight,' she'd said simply, and disappeared back to her bedroom.

And he'd taken her at her word. He'd left his alarm off and slept, and it was almost nine when he woke. There was noise coming from the yard. He flipped back the curtains and saw…people. The yard was packed, and he could see a line of cars stretching back along the road until they were out of sight.

Ten minutes later he was outside, and Alice was racing to greet him, Bunji at her side.

'Bryn, come and see, come and see. Kiara gave me my own stall and it's all sold out. Grandma had shells—you must have seen them, she collected them for ever—and I sold the big ones for two dollars and the little ones for a dollar, and I've made a hundred and thirty-seven dollars! And Maureen made pink cupcakes, but she was feeling tired, so I helped her sell them, too. And the man called Howard is going to auction other stuff, and a whole lot of people have got dogs and they know who Bunji is, and there's even a dog-biscuit stall. Come and see!'

He couldn't believe it. His damaged, introverted niece, towing him around the yard as if she owned it.

It was a miracle. Kiara's miracle.

And here was Kiara, haggling with a gentleman over the sale of a hay-rake. She'd opened the run-down sheds at the back of the property to reveal her grandmother's mass of ancient farm equipment. There were prices on everything.

'It's vintage,' she was saying.

'It's a piece of junk. I could use it as scrap metal.'

'Howard says it's collectible and he also pointed you out as a dealer,' she said stoutly. 'He gave me a bottom price. Take it or leave it.'

And the guy took it, and Kiara pocketed her wad of banknotes and beamed as she saw Bryn and Alice.

'He did not,' she crowed. 'Howard did not tell me a reserve price, or that a falling to bits hay-rake was worth anything, but he did tell me that guy was a dealer. Hooray for Grandma. Hooray for me.'

She'd obviously spent the morning carting out and selling the dusty, rusty shed contents. Her hair must have been caught back to start with, but it had tugged out of its band and curls were wisping everywhere. She was wearing baggy overalls over jeans and T-shirt, and grease and rust were liberally spread. A smudge of grease lay right across her cheek and he wanted…

No. He did not want.

Liar. He wanted so badly. But she was grinning in triumph and high-fiving Alice when Alice told her she'd finished selling all Maureen's cupcakes and…

And she didn't want him.

And then a voice boomed across the crowd, that the auction of some of the more valuable goods was about to start, so Kiara closed her shed and headed over to stand under the jacaranda trees in the front yard to watch.

And Bryn and Alice stood with her and Bryn thought…

Family?

The thought almost blindsided him. What was he thinking?

But he was thinking it.

This was a woman who cared. She cared for her lost

dogs, and she cared for the little girl who stood beside her now.

'Twenty dollars feeds all our dogs for a day,' Alice had told him, and he could practically see the dollars adding up and being divided. An ancient wicker pram, surely too old to be of practical use to anyone, sold for a hundred and twenty dollars, and Alice and Kiara high-fived again.

They were having fun. *He was having fun.*

And the idea in his head was growing stronger.

There was a query about two of the auction items-could they be sold as a pair or not?- and Kiara moved away to confer with Howard. Alice went with her.

And then someone nudged him—Donna—he recognised the town's newsagent. 'Doc?'

He was busy watching Kiara thread her way through the crowd and talk to Howard. He was watching her excitement. Watching her hold Alice's hand, smiling, engaging with the kid as if she were her own. He didn't want to be distracted.

'Doc?'

The voice was more urgent and reluctantly he turned away. 'Yes?'

'Doc, it's Maureen.' Donna's face was creased in concern. 'She said she was feeling queer. I've helped her up to a seat on the veranda. She doesn't want a fuss and she's been saying she just has a headache, but now her speech is a bit funny. I don't like the way she looks.'

He frowned and turned away. As he did Kiara turned to find his face in the crowd, her beam a mile wide. They'd sold the two vases as a pair, and the price was astonishing.

He smiled back, caught in that gorgeous smile, but

Donna had grasped his arm and there was no mistaking her urgency. 'Please… We need you.'

He pulled out of the crowd and limped as fast as he could over to the veranda. As he reached the steps, Kiara was suddenly back beside him.

Without Alice? He glanced back and saw Alice was at the to-be-sold table, handing something up to the auctioneer. Given a job?

What had Kiara read in his face—or Donna's face—to have her delegate so swiftly? To think of a need to delegate?

'What's wrong?' she breathed, but Donna was already hauling him up the steps and he had no time to answer.

Maureen was slumped in one of the ancient wicker chairs on the veranda. A little woman, she was dressed as she always was, in a vast flowery polyester dress that made her look a whole lot more voluminous than she really was. In honour of the occasion, she was also wearing a straw sun hat, liberally decorated with fresh daisies. A capacious apron covered her middle, its white surface showing signs of the cupcakes she'd been selling.

One hand lay limply on her thigh, and she was clutching that hand with the other. She looked…terrified.

The sounds of the crowd, Donna's presence—even Kiara's presence—dropped away as Bryn slipped back into the role he was trained for. He crouched beside her and took her hand. Her pulse was racing. 'Hey, Maureen. Donna says you have a headache.'

She tried to turn her head to see him but failed. Gently he supported her neck, holding her face so he could meet her eyes.

And also search…

'I… I dunno…' Her speech was slurred and came with a massive effort, and Bryn was already making a tentative diagnosis. As she spoke, one side of her face didn't move. The left side of her mouth had drooped.

'Can you lift your arms?' he said gently, and she gave him a look of helplessness. One arm lifted, the other didn't.

A stroke? By the look of it, a big one.

'Let's get you inside,' he told her. Her pulse was dangerously fast. Cardiac failure? 'No, don't move, I'm going to carry you.' He was unbuttoning the top of her dress as he spoke, then pulling free her tight apron ties. Her dress seemed capacious enough—a quick touch of her tummy told him there was no corset restricting things underneath. He needed to lie her down, put her in the recovery position, do a full check, but he couldn't do it here. The veranda was being used to store sold items. It was crowded with junk, and already people were turning to look up in concern.

With one easy movement he lifted her into his arms. Kiara protested—'Bryn, your leg…'—but he was stable enough to hold her. And as he did, he felt the rigidity of her panic, plus that racing heart.

'Maureen, I'm thinking you could be having a minor stroke,' he said as he held her. 'No biggie. We've caught it fast and I know what to do. You haven't had any surgery in the last few months, have you? Any accidents?'

'N… n…' She could hardly get it out.

'Have you taken aspirin for your headache? Or at any time in the last few days?'

Her eyes answered, she couldn't.

Kiara was holding the front door wide. He carried Maureen through, and Kiara was looking almost as terrified as Maureen.

He was thinking back to something Kiara had said to him when she'd introduced Maureen.

'Sometimes I think without Maureen I might fall apart.'

Kiara was a woman who'd been brought up mostly with the same bleak childhood as his, but there had been people who loved her. Her grandmother. Maureen.

Was that what enabled her to love in return? Was that why she'd seamlessly taken the wounded Alice under her wing?

Was that why he felt…?

Enough. There was no time for examination of emotions now.

'How long have you had the headache?' he asked, and Maureen looked up at him wildly. Either she didn't understand or there was no way she could respond.

'She told Alice she had a headache almost an hour ago,' Kiara said, her voice unsteady. 'That's when Alice took over her cupcake stall. I should have…'

'There's no need for should haves,' he said, and managed a reassuring smile. 'I'm sure the last thing Maureen wanted was a fuss, isn't that right, Maureen? And she has help now. Donna, the keys to my car are in my left trouser pocket.' He was laying Maureen down on the settee, carefully supporting her limp arm. Seeing the way her left leg flopped, her foot falling limply to the side.

This was definitely a stroke, but what sort? An ischaemic stroke, caused by a blood clot, meant urgent intervention, an IV injection of a plasminogen activator—alteplase—to dissolve the clot before it could cause major, long-term brain injury. For optimum results that injection had to happen within three hours—and how long since Maureen had started displaying symptoms? An hour, when she'd first confessed to a headache? Or longer?

But he couldn't administer alteplase yet.

The alternative to an ischaemic stroke, something that could be causing similar symptoms, was a haemorrhage. If it was a haemorrhage, clot treatment would turn an emergency into a disaster.

Maureen needed state-of-the-art medical tools for diagnosis, and she needed them now.

'My car's the crimson sports coupé in the driveway.' He was talking to Donna as he thought. 'Can you grab my bag from the trunk? There's a portable defibrillator there, too, clearly marked. I doubt we'll need it but bring it anyway. Kiara, I want you to ring emergency services. Tell them who I am—a neurologist at Sydney Central. Tell them I believe Maureen's having a stroke and we need urgent assistance. Tell them sirens, speed. And I want a MICA unit to meet them—I'll talk to them if necessary.' A MICA vehicle—a mobile intensive care ambulance—would be absolutely essential if Maureen's heart was to fail under pressure.

'S…str… Am…am I…?' Maureen was trying to talk but only one side of her face was working. He was adjusting cushions, supporting her so she was lying on her side with her head slightly raised. While he worked, Kiara crouched in front of her, gripping her hands.

'It's okay, Maureen. You'll be safe. If this *is* a stroke, we have the best doctor in the world right here, isn't that right, Dr Dalton?'

And she smiled at Maureen with such love, with such assurance, that Bryn felt his breath catch. Kiara's smile would make a patient recover all by itself.

'Bryn?' Kiara's voice was reproving, and he hauled himself together. What had she said?

'Best doctor in the world'?

'Yep, I'm good,' he agreed, because there was no choice. Maureen needed reassurance. She needed to believe he knew what he was doing.

He set up a drip. He quietly asked Kiara to have the defibrillator ready. He was swiftly preparing for anything a stroke could throw at him.

He knew his medicine, but anything else? Like the way he was feeling about Kiara?

He knew nothing at all.

The two paramedics who arrived with the ambulance turned out to be young and inexperienced. The only available MICA crew was caught up on another job. Bryn therefore needed to accompany Maureen, and there was room in the ambulance for no one else.

Bryn knew that Kiara wanted—desperately—to follow in her van but she couldn't. Once Alice had realised something was wrong, she'd come running, and one look at Maureen and she'd disintegrated. Alice knew dreadful things happened, and to her this seemed yet another. Staring down at Maureen, who'd bossed her and mothered her over the last few days, she'd turned again into the solitary, white-faced child she'd been only weeks ago.

'Bryn, I'll stay,' Kiara decreed, seeing Alice's fear as soon as he did. 'I'll phone Maureen's family, and then Alice and I will look after things here. Take care of her for me, though, won't you?' Her voice trembled, but as they stretchered Maureen to the ambulance she pulled herself together.

'Right, Alice, that's Maureen, on her way to get better. I have no doubt your uncle will have her home in no time. I'll make a couple of phone calls and then we need to get back to selling stuff. Let's see how much money Maureen's cupcakes made. She'll be wanting to know that the minute her head stops hurting. How are you at counting? I'm terrible, but if we both do it, we should manage.'

The ambulance doors closed—leaving Bryn with a vision of Kiara standing in the driveway, surrounded by a crowd of concerned onlookers. Her community. Her hand was holding Alice's. Bunji was at her side.

Why that should make him feel…

And then Maureen's heart faltered and there was time for nothing but medicine. Which was the way he always wanted it.

Wasn't it?

CHAPTER ELEVEN

It was after midnight before Bryn walked back in the front door, and it had been a tough day. Archie had miraculously organised one locum neurologist to start work, which was supposed to have given Bryn Saturday off, but the locum was young and seemed a bit unsure—and Bryn wasn't trusting Maureen to a colleague he hardly knew.

An initial scan at the nearest hospital had confirmed the stroke was ischaemic—clotting on the brain. He'd injected alteplase—a drug that assisted in dissolving clots. Its early use could have been a lifesaver all on its own, but when they arrived at Sydney Central—a teaching hospital where stroke treatment was state-of-the-art—a further scan showed the clot wasn't dissolving fast enough.

That meant surgery—endovascular clot retrieval—and every one of his skills had to be brought to the fore.

By the time he left Theatre he was wiped.

Why?

The surgery needed hairline precision, with a woman's life at stake, so yes, the surgery was tricky, but he was used to cutting-edge surgery. He wasn't the head of the neurology department of one of Australia's top hospitals for nothing.

Normally he could turn off from the people in his care. He had to. His nerves needed to be rock steady, so during surgery he couldn't afford to think of the people under his care as...people. They could be individuals before surgery when he was assessing, informing, reassuring, and they'd be individuals afterwards when he saw them recovering in the wards. But once under anaesthetic, when every part of him needed to focus on what he was doing, they had to be technical cases, challenges to be conquered.

Today had been different. He hardly knew Maureen, but those shocked white faces—Kiara's and Alice's—had stayed with him. They'd made him see—maybe for the first time—why surgeons stood back when their own family or friends were the patients.

He'd never thought like that. He'd never thought he'd have to, but today, if there'd been someone he was sure was just as competent to call on, he would have stepped back himself.

As it was, he'd held it together. There'd been dicey moments when Maureen's heart had faltered, but his team was good. The intervention had been early enough for him to be able to tell Maureen's anxious family that he held every hope of a full recovery.

Afterwards he'd faced the drive back to Two Tails and his leg had ached—no, all of him had ached. For some stupid reason he wasn't able to stop his hands from trembling on the steering wheel. What the hell was wrong with him?

And then he pulled into the driveway and Kiara was stepping out onto the veranda to meet him. And as he opened the car door, she came down to him in a rush, stopping for a millisecond as she reached him—and then she was folded in his arms. Her face was in his chest, he could feel her trembling—to match the trembling of his own hands—and he thought…

Maureen? Was he was shaking like a leaf over the fate of a woman he'd known for little more than a week?

No. He was shaking because Kiara loved her. Because the outcome of his surgery had never seemed so important.

His trembling had stopped now that she was folded into his arms, now that he held her close, now that his chin was on her curls. Now he was…home?

It was a weird thought, a flash among other thoughts he couldn't process because he was too busy holding her. Hugging her. Feeling that here was…

No. With a huge effort he managed to get his voice to work.

'Hey, Kiara, it's okay. You got my phone call? There's every chance she'll make a good recovery. She has her husband with her, and her daughters. She's surrounded by people who love her, and in the best of places. You can let it go.'

But even as he said it, he knew it was wrong. He felt her stiffen, just slightly. But still she held, still her face was buried in his chest, still she was taking the comfort she so obviously needed.

'Maureen was pretty much my grandma's only friend,' she said, her voice muffled because she wasn't moving from his chest. 'Grandma was a loner, but Maureen just barged in and cared. When I came here as a little girl, Maureen was a constant. She's my friend, like Hazel is my friend.' She took a deep breath and pushed away a little, just enough so she could say what she needed to say. 'She's pretty much all the family I have.'

And what was there in that that made his gut lurch?

That made him want to tug her back tighter against him. That made him want to say…

No. The sensations he was feeling now were almost overwhelming, but he had enough sense to realise he needed to keep his head. He had a sudden memory of a nanny, employed for almost four years from when he'd been three to when he was seven. Of his father telling him that they were moving, and Gloria would be leaving.

'There'll be a new nanny during holidays, and you'll be at boarding school most of the time anyway. Only babies make a fuss.'

Why that memory now? Why the almost instinctive muscle memory to pull himself into himself, to brace…

'C-come in.' Kiara was visibly tugging herself together, pulling away, swiping her eyes. 'Oh, thank God you were here, Bryn, but you must be exhausted. There's a gorgeous rich soup that Maureen made for us…' She choked a little on that but bit her lip and turned back to the house, leaving him to follow. 'She'll give us a hard time if we waste it, so let's get it into you and then get some sleep.'

The house was still a muddle after the sale, packing boxes, furniture shoved aside so things could be moved easily, mess. The kitchen was cluttered, but the smell of the soup was warmly welcoming.

'The mess is for tomorrow,' Kiara said wearily as she poured two bowls. 'I'll eat with you if you don't mind. Alice ate before she went to bed—she loved the soup, and she was so tired and proud of what she did today—but I couldn't eat until I heard from you.'

And then, because it seemed the only obvious place to go, they headed once again for the open fire in the living room. She'd obviously built it up during the long hours of waiting, sitting by the flames, taking comfort from its warmth.

'Bunji should be with you,' he told her, because the thought of her sitting here alone, waiting for news of her friend, was adding to emotions he was struggling to understand.

'Bunji's Alice's dog now,' she said firmly, and managed a tired smile. 'And Alice needed her. She was frightened about Maureen, but we counted our loot—wow, we did well, by the way—then she took Bunji off to a quiet part of the garden and told her all about it. I watched them as everyone left and…it helped. That they're content. That she has Bunji she can talk to.'

He nodded, thinking it through. Hearing the note of strain in her voice. Still remembering the sensation of that hug, of her walking into his arms and holding on.

'So who do you turn to when you need to talk?'

'Same as you, I guess,' she said simply. 'We've learned to be independent.'

'Sometimes independence sucks.'

'Does it?' she asked curiously. 'Don't you need it?'

He didn't answer. He found he couldn't.

The answer should have been obvious. Yes, he valued his independence. It'd been instilled into him since birth, to rely on himself and himself alone, and it was all he knew. But there was something about this night. Something about this woman…

She wasn't waiting for a response. She addressed herself instead to her bowl of soup and left him to silence.

She was letting him be. Respecting his need for space. For his precious independence.

She always would, he thought. All her animals, all her clients—she spent her life figuring who needed what, and then fixing it for them. Alice was healing because of Kiara. Even him… Yeah, he'd been floundering when Kiara had come into his life, but she'd pretty much sorted it. She'd invited them into her home while Alice had bonded with Bunji, she'd allowed him to resume his career without feeling guilty, she'd encouraged his fledgling relationship with his niece. She'd figured a way they could all move forward.

But what about Kiara? He looked around at the stripped living room. She'd obviously gone overboard with her yard sale and the place looked barren. Almost everything had been sold. What he'd paid her, combined with what she'd earned by today's sale, would surely enable her to keep Two Tails running for a good while longer. Even if it didn't, then she must surely agree to let him help even more.

But the thought of her living on here alone…

He'd been shocked when he'd walked back in tonight. He'd expected her to sell things she hadn't needed, but she'd taken it to extremes. No wonder she was pleased with her takings—she'd practically stripped the place bare.

It was still liveable, but without her grandmother's clutter, stripped to the bones of furniture…did it look like a home any longer?

Home?

Why did that word keep surfacing?

It was tied, almost inextricably, with Kiara.

He thought of her as he'd seen her when he'd left with Maureen. She'd been standing in the driveway, holding Alice's hand. With a battered dog at her feet. With a community around her…

Home.

An idea was stirring—or maybe it had stirred already but it was growing stronger by the minute.

A plan?

But overriding his embryonic plan was the sensation that he wanted to be closer to this woman, and he wanted it right now.

She finished her soup and set her bowl aside, then looked queryingly up at him. He'd sunk into one of the two remaining armchairs, but she'd settled on the rug, closer to the fire. 'Finished?' she asked. 'Bed?'

'It sounds good to me,' he said, a trifle unsteadily, and he set his bowl carefully with hers and then reached down and traced her cheekbone with his finger. 'You need to sleep, too.'

'I'm not sure I can.' And she lifted her hand and covered his.

There was a long silence, a silence while the world seemed to hold it breath. Her hand was warm on his, and his fingers cupped her face. The link seemed to be strengthening by the minute. The pull.

The need to be close.

And then he kissed her.

She'd kissed him before—twice. They hadn't been… kisses, though. They'd meant something to him, but he'd told himself they'd just been a part of Kiara's warmth, Kiara's need to comfort.

There was no way this kiss was about comfort. This kiss was about…everything.

The culmination of a hell of a day? The culmination of months of hell?

No. This kiss was so much more. As her mouth met his, as she twisted and knelt so she could sink into the kiss, as the contact melded and burned…

This was about nothing but them. A man and a woman and pure physical desire.

And maybe even more than that.

It was a kiss like he'd never experienced. A kiss that seemed a joining, an affirmation of an aching need to be closer, closer than he'd ever felt with another soul.

She was in his arms now, holding him as he was holding her. He could feel her desire matching his. Oh, this woman… Kiara…

His…love?

The word terrified him—had always terrified him—but right now it seemed the only one available. But he'd think about it later. Right now, there was only Kiara, only this moment, only this kiss.

And when the kiss ended—as even the best kisses must inevitably end—when he finally managed to speak, he hardly recognised his voice. It was deep, husky, aching with want.

The way she was holding him…the warmth of her… the sheer loveliness… He could scarcely make his voice work, but somehow, he said it. 'Kiara, I won't take advantage of you but if you…'

He paused. He had no right to say this, no right to ask.

But she was gazing back up at him, her eyes inches from him, wide, honest, meeting his gaze head on.

'You're asking?' Amazingly her smile emerged again. Half teasing. Half tender.

'It's your house,' he said, feeling helpless because he was way out of his comfort zone. He wouldn't—couldn't—push this woman when he owed her so much.

When he wanted her so much.

'Your house,' he managed again, and his hand was cupping her chin, his eyes locked on hers. 'Your rules.'

'Then hooray for that,' she said, and for heaven's sake, the teasing note was uppermost again. 'Bryn, I've been wanting to jump your body for days now—no, make that weeks. And it's dumb, you're my client and I'm old enough to know that mixing business with pleasure is a disaster, but you're leaving soon and…'

'And?'

'And I think you'd better kiss me again,' she told him, and her hand gripped his even more firmly. Strong and sure. This was a woman who'd made a decision. Who knew what she wanted and had every intention of taking it.

'If you want me,' she said simply, 'I'm sleeping in my grandma's bed and it's a double. There's no pressure, Bryn. No expectations, no claims on a future, but we're both grown up and we've had one hell of a day. So for tonight… It would be my very great pleasure to share.'

Whoops.

That probably wasn't the most romantic thought to wake to, but it was there, front and centre, a great, fat thought bubble the moment she opened her eyes to daylight.

She did, however, wake gloriously. There was no denying that last night had been extraordinary. She'd fallen into Bryn's arms, probably out of exhaustion, or a surfeit of emotion, or relief. But lust had played a big part, too, and sense had taken a back seat. She'd practically invited him into her bed—okay, she *had* invited him into her bed, and maybe it had been worth every moment of whatever the consequences would be.

There shouldn't be any, she told herself. She'd had brief relationships in the past, and surely the guy she'd slept with was experienced? They both knew what they were doing. The sex had been mind-blowingly good. It had been a fabulous night, blasting everything apart from physical need out of both of their minds.

So why had she woken thinking *Whoops*?

Because she'd also woken up feeling as if she wouldn't mind staying exactly where she was for the rest of her life.

And that was crazy. There'd been no commitment on either side, and neither should there be. Soon Bryn would leave. His new housekeeper had been employed. Alice would start at her new school in Clovelly and life would restart for all of them.

With the money she'd earned she could keep Two Tails going a while longer. Maybe there'd be other avenues of fundraising. She'd been running on the smell of an oily rag for years now, and she'd just keep going.

By herself.

No, she told herself firmly, managing to think it through, even though she was spooned into the curve of Bryn's body, even though the warmth, the strength of him were a siren call that was melting something within. She wouldn't be by herself. She'd have her dogs. She'd have Maureen back again. She'd have Hazel's friendship, she'd have her community, she'd…

Not have Bryn.

Which wouldn't matter. There was no need at all for her to lie here and think *Whoops*. The whoops was because of the way he made her feel—as if everything she needed in life was right here, in the curve of his body, in the way he held her, loved her…

He didn't love her. That thought blindsided her and also…the way she felt about him.

What was she doing, falling for a rich, arrogant, self-centred doctor who was nothing to do with her world?

Except she sort of had, and there was little she could do about it except think… *Whoops*.

He stirred and his arms firmed around her. She wriggled around to face him, looping her arms around his neck and kissing him as he woke—because a woman would have to be inhuman to do otherwise. And when he smiled at her, when his eyes were inches from hers, when his gorgeous body responded, and heat and desire flared all over again…

Whoops indeed, but the time to cope with the future… Well, that was for the future.

'Good morning, my love,' he murmured as he gathered her against him and their worlds merged into a glorious moment of pure, animal bliss.

'It's a very good morning,' she whispered back.

Despite the whoops.

The world had to break in, and it broke in soon.

A group of locals arrived to give Kiara a hand clearing up the mess from yesterday's sale, sorting stuff that had been sold, generally turning the day into a working bee. The yard sale itself had generated interest, but Maureen's collapse had tapped into community concern. Kiara was surrounded.

Bryn needed to head back to Sydney Central to check on Maureen. Yes, his new locum was more than capable of doing what was needed, but he needed to clear his head.

He needed to think about the plan that had half formed the night before.

Last night had been life changing. Last night had dispersed any doubts he'd had about his embryonic idea. It was starting to seem brilliant, from every angle he looked at it.

There were problems, he conceded, but they were minor. Two Tails was a fair distance from Sydney Central. Almost an hour's drive was too much when he worked six days a week, with call-backs in emergencies. Could he commute? Would Kiara consider moving her premises somewhere closer? His house at Clovelly wouldn't work, he conceded that, but somewhere else…

They'd work it out together, he thought.

If she agreed.

And the thought came suddenly, the question seeming like a kick in the guts. 'What if she doesn't agree?'

It didn't matter, he told himself. The alternative was surely going on as they'd organised. Plan A had always been to take take Alice back to Clovelly, to depend on his new housekeeper for out-of-school care, to get on with his independent life. The idea of combining his and Kiara's life…yeah, it had advantages, especially for Alice, but surely it was Plan B.

Except it wasn't. He'd woken with Kiara in his arms, and he'd felt…as he'd never felt before. As he'd never expected to feel.

As if he wanted to spend the rest of his life with this woman in his arms.

And that was a dumb thought. His independence was everything. The thought of needing her…

No. This wasn't need—at least, not *his* need. It couldn't be. All the lessons he'd learned throughout his isolated childhood, every time he'd sworn not to get attached…those rules had been rammed home with pain that was bone deep. The thought of opening himself to that level of exposure was unthinkable. He couldn't go there.

But Plan B was practical as well as desirable, he told himself, shoving emotion aside. Alice and Kiara could be gloriously happy together. Kiara would allow him to fund Two Tails into the future and every night when he came home…

Yeah, that was like a siren's song.

But it was still sensible, and he needed to be sensible. So… Where to go from here?

Should he buy a diamond and do the romantic bit?

No. He thought of Kiara's teasing smile, he thought of himself down on one knee and thought she'd probably break into laughter.

He smiled at the vision.

'She's just as sensible as I am,' he said out loud as he drove. 'Just as independent. Just as aware of long-term advantages. If she'd like a diamond, of course she can have one, but this will be on her terms. As my part of the contract will be on my terms.'

It did sound sensible but there was a part of him that wasn't feeling very sensible. The part of him that had woken with Kiara in his arms and had felt as if sensible was…melting.

'Hold it together,' he told himself roughly. 'If you let emotion get in the way of sensible, she'll be the first to back away. We both know the rules.'

And then he was turning into the hospital car park and the world of medicine enclosed him again.

Which was the way he liked it. A world where he could spend his life trying to fix chaos.

A world where he didn't risk exposing his own life to the same.

CHAPTER TWELVE

WHAT FOLLOWED FOR Kiara was a week that was almost dreamlike. Time out of frame. The following Monday Alice would start at her new school, so on the Saturday Bryn would take Alice and Bunji back to Clovelly. The new housekeeper was already installed, and Bryn had taken both Kiara and Alice over to meet her. Alice had been quiet and clinging to Kiara, but she'd come back to Two Tails seemingly resigned.

'I can come back here sometimes,' she'd said wistfully to Kiara, and Kiara had hugged her and told her of course she could.

For as long as Two Tails kept running.

Even then she'd stay in touch, she thought. In the short time she'd known her, she'd been stunned with the connection she felt. Alice's isolation was yet another mirror of her own childhood.

As, it seemed, of Bryn's.

And there, too, was a connection. More than a connection. The way she was starting to feel…

When he'd arrived back from the hospital on the Sunday, after that first night in her shared bed, she'd felt like a woman after her first ever sexual encounter. She'd felt almost absurdly shy, and anxious, and unsure where the relationship could go.

She'd also been frightened, as she'd been waiting to hear how…if… Maureen was recovering.

But on his return, he'd walked back into the kitchen, seen her look of fear and gathered her into his arms.

'She's conscious,' he'd told her. 'We've put her back to sleep now—an induced coma will give her an easier route to complete healing—but we let her stir for a little while I was there. She knew her family. She even managed to murmur her husband's name, and at this stage it's more than promising that there'll be no long-term damage.'

Such a relief! He'd held her while her world seemed to settle, and then Alice had edged close, and she'd somehow been included in the hug. And Bunji had barked, and they'd looked down and the expression on the dog's face—they could have sworn it was jealousy. They'd ended up laughing and Bryn had picked Bunji up and hugged her, too, and Kiara had felt…

Well, she'd felt as she had for a week now. As if things were happening she didn't understand. Yes, Bryn and Alice were due to leave, but every night she lay in Bryn's arms, and as the date to leave grew closer a huge question started to loom.

She didn't dare hope, but the way he held her…

How did a woman stop dreaming?

'How's it going?' Her friend, Hazel, rang halfway through the week. Hazel had been busy since Kiara had last seen her, and when she rang, she seemed almost dazed. The story had escalated. Her boss…the baby… Kiara was scarcely able to take in the events that had overtaken her friend, and then she had to struggle to find words to describe what was going on in her own life.

'I think… I'm not sure…' she started, and Hazel was astute enough to hear behind the words.

'So you and Bryn…'

'Hazel, I don't know,' she said honestly.

'You're sleeping with him?'

'Yes.' There'd never been any way she could lie to Hazel.

'Are you in love with him?'

And how could she lie about something like this? 'I think I am.' Then she corrected herself. 'No. I definitely am. The way he makes me feel… But Hazel…'

'You don't know how *he* feels?'

'He holds me like he means it.'

'But you don't know?'

'It's just…he's been a loner for such a long time. I know he cares. I think…he wants to take care of me.'

'That sounds a bit like a one-way deal.'

'I'd take care of him.'

'Like one of your dogs?' It was meant as a joke. Hazel said it lightly, but Kiara suddenly had a vision of herself, caring for Bunji. And she thought…was that how Bryn saw her? As a woman he could somehow save?

Why did she think that? They were equals, weren't they? A man and a woman who could become friends as well as lovers.

She was growing to depend on him, she thought, with weird self-knowledge. The way she felt when she saw him leave in the mornings… The way she felt as she listened for his car returning every night…

There was a long silence and then Hazel, who knew her so well that maybe she could even read silence, said gently, 'Oh, love, don't let your heart get broken.'

'That's crazy.' She said it strongly but strong wasn't

how she was feeling. 'We're mature adults. Whatever we work out…'

'Working out doesn't sound like happy ever after.'

'Which you've found?'

Somehow she managed to change direction, to get Hazel to talk about her own happiness. The conversation ended. The kennels needed cleaning and dogs needed walking. Alice and Bunji were bouncing beside her, and reservations could be held at bay.

Three more days until Saturday. And then?

Whatever happened would happen, she told herself. She could accept it.

And the way she felt about Bryn?

She could not break her heart.

She would not!

Friday.

Bryn managed to finish work early. He came home to find his girls digging in the veggie garden, preparing a new tomato bed.

His girls… As his idea had progressed, more and more he'd felt the feeling of proprietorship grow. It scared him but he accepted it.

Into the mix of emotions that had been battering his world since the night his sister died had come Kiara. Gorgeous, courageous, caring Kiara.

His girls?

His woman.

It was an emotion that was almost primeval, inappropriate, surely, but the feeling he had for her…

Well, maybe it was primeval. Inevitable.

And the way their bodies responded to each other? Surely she had to agree?

They were digging compost into newly cleared beds,

and they were both filthy. Most of the remaining dogs in the pens had been let out to join them. Bunji was digging as well—at last there were no dressings, no wounds that could reinfect—and she was glorying in being just a pup.

Being cared for. Being loved.

He'd take care of them all, he swore, and he smiled as he saw the trays of tomato seedlings waiting to go in. Three weeks ago, Kiara had been preparing to sell this place. Now she was looking at the future.

'If I'm careful I think I have enough funds to keep me going for a year,' she'd said proudly the night before, and he thought, what he was about to say would extend that indefinitely.

Bunji would have a home. Alice would have someone who cared, someone who made her laugh, someone she could hug. Kiara would be able to care for as many waifs and strays as she wanted.

And him…

He could keep doing the work he loved. He wouldn't lose his independence, but whenever he wanted they'd be here for him.

His girls.

They'd seen him now. Alice waved a loaded shovel and then squealed as the load slid down her front. Then she giggled.

Kiara just straightened and smiled—and that smile was a smile a man could come home to for the rest of his life.

It was strange but the thought was vaguely unsettling. The rest of his life?

'How's Maureen?' It was Alice, and she asked the question every time he came home. In the week they'd spent together the two seemed to have forged a close connection. People come…people go…

What he was proposing was for the rest of his life? The thought was huge. How to get his head around it?

'She's great,' he managed. 'She's still a bit wobbly but she should be home in a couple of weeks.'

'But I won't be here,' Alice whispered, and there was the echo of the scared little girl again. 'Can I go and see her?'

'Maybe in a week or so.'

'Is she very far?'

'She's in my hospital.' He turned and gestured across the massive ravine at the back of the house, over the untamed bushland that was part of Australia's Blue Mountains. 'If there weren't so many trees, we could almost see Maureen from here. Tonight look out your window and you'll see the lights across the valley. Maybe Maureen will be standing at her window, looking at our lights.'

'Oh,' Alice said in a small voice, and Kiara stooped to hug her.

'But you will see her. I promise.'

And once again he was caught by how easily this caring business seemed to come to her. How amazing she was.

She needed to be amazing. This was the woman he hoped to be with…for ever?

And there was that gut-lurch again.

The thought of forever seemed like some sort of chasm, and he had no idea what it held. But in his pocket was a diamond—yeah, he'd had second thoughts because he needed Kiara to see he was serious. For in his head was a serious plan. A sensible plan.

This was no moment for qualms. He was committed to Alice anyway. He was…stuck.

That was hardly an appropriate thought for a man about to propose marriage, he thought wryly, but there were so many compensations. This woman, hugging his niece, smiling at Alice until she smiled back, then smiling up at him. This woman, with dirt on her nose, with dogs at her heels.

She was wonderful.

She was independent. She wouldn't cling.

She was surely perfect.

'I've ordered dinner in,' he said, struggling to move to the practical. He'd thought he ought to take Kiara out, but organising someone to care for Alice would never work. Maureen, maybe, but with Maureen still in hospital his planned romantic dinner had to be at home.

Home. The idea was still unsettling. He knew Kiara loved this place, but it wasn't ideal. Could he talk her into moving? If they found acreage closer, he could talk to the architect who'd designed his place. Something a bit cutting edge. She'd want her dogs, of course—they'd have to be part of the deal—so it'd have to be remote enough not to bother neighbours, but money could solve most problems.

But that was for the future. Kiara's smile was high beam. 'An order-in dinner? It'll cost heaps to get it delivered out here but if you're sure… I could take a long bath instead of cooking. That's only one step below you cooking for us.'

Him cook? He'd never thought… But it hadn't been meant as a jibe. She was still beaming. 'I'd hug you,' she told him, 'but I'd get compost over your suit. That has to be Italian, surely. Did I ever tell you how smooth you look? You fit in here like a pig in a parlour. Just lucky you're heading home tomorrow. Alice, you want first bath or me? Toss you for it, heads or tails…'

'I don't want to go home,' Alice said in a small voice.

'Yeah, well, I have an idea about that,' Kiara said briskly. 'Once you're at school we might organise you a weekend job. How about every Saturday you and Bunji come out here and help with the dogs? I can collect you if your uncle can't bring you. For as long as Two Tails stays open, and even after, you'll still be my friend.'

'I guess. But I'll still miss you.'

'And I'll miss you, but instead of thinking about it, let's have bubble baths.' And they headed to the house hand in hand, heading to serial baths.

Kiara had partially solved Alice's immediate distress, he thought as he watched them go. But his solution was better.

It was better for them all. All Kiara had to do was agree.

He'd gone all out with his dinner order, and it was delicious. Thai food. Crunchy spring rolls filled with garden-fresh sprouts and seasoning. Tiny skewers—meat on sticks—with a chilli dipping sauce. Then dish after dish of gorgeous, fragrant concoctions that had all of them eating more than they thought they could. Even Alice. He watched her agonise over the last skewer and finally decide she had to be able to fit it in. The change to this little girl had been miraculous.

And then Alice yawned and kissed them both goodnight and there was another miracle all by itself. She was still a little teary about the thought of leaving in the morning, but she seemed resigned. Then he and Kiara settled on the rug by the fire, with half a bottle of champagne left between them—and the time was right.

Now or never.

'Kiara…' he began, and thought, How does a guy just come out and say these things? He'd heard of naff proposals in his time—banners flying from aeroplanes, romantic balloon rides and proposals at a thousand feet, declarations of devotion on stage in front of a crowd that would pressure a woman to accept, no matter what her inclination was…

It was surely better this way, he thought. In Kiara's own space.

He felt a sudden shaft of uncertainty. In his pocket was a crimson box with a solitaire diamond. Maybe he had jumped the gun on this. Would it be applying more pressure?

Quit it with the qualms, he told himself and took a slug of champagne—and said it.

'Kiara.' He cleared his throat and tried again. 'I'd like… I think it might work for both of us if you'd marry me.'

There. The thing was said. Not romantic but sensible. Given the way their bodies responded to each other, given their circumstances, surely it was a reasonable proposal? So why did it feel loaded?

The fire crackled behind them, but the silence behind it felt like a ten-ton weight. Or warnings of an avalanche, ready to crash from a height?

They were leaning on cushions wedged against the armchairs. The firelight was playing on their faces. The bottle of champagne was between them.

Maybe he should have chosen somewhere less intimate?

Kiara was looking at Bryn in astonishment. Then, very carefully, she shifted the champagne—and their glasses—out of his reach.

'We've slept together for less than a week and now you're thinking we should get married?' She spoke slowly—as if not wishing to fire up a lunatic? 'You're never serious.'

'I'm serious.'

'You can't be.'

'I believe I am.'

'Why?'

'It's sensible.'

'Sensible?'

'Yes.'

There was a long silence while she seemed to struggle to get her thoughts in order. It took a while.

'Bryn, it's been a great week,' she said at last. 'An awesome few weeks, if I'm honest. I've loved being with you. I love that you've helped me. I love the way you're starting to love Alice, and I love that you're getting your life back on track. I've also enjoyed the sex—truthfully, it's been amazing. But us? Great as this time has been, you don't want to get married.'

'I think I do.' He was feeling faintly absurd. Totally off balance. 'But that's supposed to be your line.'

'I don't.'

'Really?' Her reaction wasn't in the script. Nor was the look of distress he was starting to see.

'Bryn, no.'

'Why not?' This wasn't going well. He had to explain. 'Kiara, hear me out. We're both in trouble. You're financially strapped and you're alone.'

'I'm not. I have friends…'

'You have a community, yes, and you have Hazel and Maureen. But from what you've been telling me Hazel's caught up in her own concerns. Maureen's elderly and she won't be around for ever. You're too busy to get closer to anyone else. You'll be left...'

'A crazy old lady, surrounded by her dogs?' She managed a wobbly smile. 'That sounds like a threat.'

'It's not meant to be. It's just practicality. I know you'll manage alone—as will Alice and I—but couldn't it be better for all of us if we work things out together?'

She looked into his eyes, as if trying to read what was behind his words. 'What you're proposing sounds like a house-share arrangement. You're talking marriage?'

'It *is* sensible.'

'"Sensible" is house-sharing. "Sensible" is a short-term arrangement for convenience. Surely marriage isn't meant to be...*sensible*?'

'Then it should be,' he said. 'For my parents, yours too, for that matter, not being sensible meant disaster. From what I've seen, emotion and impulsiveness remove the ability to make sensible decisions.'

'So you're not saying that you've fallen in love with me?' And her voice wobbled a little as she said it.

And what was it in that tremulous wobble that had him wanting to gather her into his arms, right there and then, as he'd held her for these last wonderful nights? He wanted her face buried in his chest. He wanted to tell her she was loved, and he'd love her. For always. The full romantic bit.

What was holding him back?

But the old fears were there, the certainties battered in from birth. He couldn't lie. He couldn't make a promise he might well not be able to keep.

He surely felt about her as he felt about no other woman, but his life was still out there, his independence, his freedom. If he let himself go one step further, if he let his emotions take him where they willed, then he'd be wide open. Exposed. His previous life was still with him, lessons instilled, reinforced and reinforced again.

'Kiara, we're fond of each other…'

'Fond!'

'More than fond,' he conceded. 'The way I feel about you… I want you.'

'In your bed.'

'Yes.' There was no reason why he shouldn't be honest.

'But not in your life. You'd still work crazy hours. Medicine would be your life.'

'And you'd still run Two Tails.'

'And Alice would fit in the cracks in the middle?'

'There'll be Maureen,' he said, feeling out of his depth. What was she expecting him to say—that he become a part-time parent? He wasn't a parent. 'Plus we'd have a housekeeper. We could also hire a nanny if you think Alice needs it.'

She was looking at him in horror and he didn't get it. What else did she want from him?

That he be a part-time husband? He'd do what he could, but surely other couples fitted their love lives around their careers.

'You don't really want either of us,' she said, and her words were bleak, as if she was stating the inevitable.

'I do want you.'

'But Alice?'

'I have Alice, whether I want her or not.'

'Oh, for heaven's sake… Listen to yourself.' She was angry now, flushed, furious. 'Alice is your niece. You're all she has in the world.'

'Okay.' He was so out of his depth he was no longer sure what he was saying. 'I do want her...'

'But she'll be easier if you have a wife.'

'That's not what I meant.'

'Then what do you mean?'

'Just...that we could make a great family. You and me and Alice and Bunji.' He was floundering and he knew it. 'Maybe even another child if you wanted.'

'If I wanted?' There was no mistaking the anger now. 'I? Not you. Not *us*.'

'It's just that...'

'It wouldn't have very much to do with you, would it? Because your family responsibilities would be taken over by me, by Maureen, by your housekeeper and maybe a nanny. Tell me, Bryn, if you didn't have Alice, would you want me?'

'I wouldn't have met you.'

'That's not what I'm asking. Does sleeping in my bed, in my arms, count for nothing?'

Emotion had never been his forte—indeed, he'd learned to quash it. He could cope when confronted with tearful patients or emotional relatives, but on his own turf? With the woman he'd decided to marry? He was really struggling.

And now her voice was cold. 'I imagine this proposal is because I tick off most boxes for suitability,' she said bleakly. 'Good with children. Tick. Can help train Bunji. Tick. Likes Alice. Double tick. Has a career so won't get in your way too much. Good in bed. How many ticks are we up to?'

'Kiara...'

'I don't get it.' She was now sounding ineffably weary. 'But it *is* like one of your medical forms. I seem to have ticked enough of the boxes, so I win a wedding to the wonderful Bryn Dalton.'

'There's no need to be offensive.'

'Isn't there?' She shook her head, her eyes bleak. 'Sorry, Bryn, no.'

'Is that all you can say?'

'To a very generous offer? Yes, it is. Enough.' She rose and headed for the door but then she turned back. 'You see, Bryn,' she said, in a voice that was now full of pain, 'I have a problem. Somehow over the last weeks I've managed the impossible. I've actually fallen in love.'

'Then…'

'Then nothing.' The pain was almost tangible. 'Because your contract would be totally one-sided. I'd love Bunji, I'd love Alice, and yes, I'd love you. And you… you'd do what you thought was necessary to make us all happy.'

'Couldn't that be enough?'

'There's not one snowball's chance in a bushfire it'd be enough,' she retorted. 'I might be emotionally challenged but I know that much—I'd end up breaking my heart.'

'But why?'

'Because you don't care,' she flashed. 'Not really, not so deeply in your gut that it's a visceral thing. And I know you don't get it, and it's not worth me trying even to explain. So tomorrow you take Alice home and you get on as best you can with the love you're prepared to give.'

'Kiara, I don't know how to love her any more than I already do.'

'Don't you want her?'

'I don't know,' he said, honestly. 'If there was any other way…'

'Well, you'd better make your mind up pretty fast,' she said brutally. 'Your plan to have me take over loving hasn't worked. She's a great kid. I'd keep her myself if there was any way Two Tails could make enough to support more than one of us, but I can't. So it's up to you, and she deserves more.'

'I know it, but I can't…'

'Or won't,' she said bluntly. 'Loving's easy, Bryn. You just have to open your heart and trust.'

'But you won't.'

'It's a two-way deal,' she told him. 'Sorry, Bryn, nice try but I'm going to bed.'

And she walked out and closed the door behind her.

But upstairs…

Alice had settled into bed, but she hadn't slept. The thought of leaving in the morning was too huge. She lay and stared into the dark, and then Bunji had stirred at her feet and started to whine.

And she remembered she'd forgotten her water bowl.

Bunji was supposed to drink downstairs—that was the rule—but her leg was sore and it'd take two minutes to head down to the bathroom on the next level and fill her bowl. And as she did, she heard voices floating up from the open living-room door.

'Don't you want her?' That was Kiara—talking about her?

'I don't know,' Bryn was saying. *'If there was any other way...'*

The words made her freeze.

Somehow, in all the awfulness of the last few months,

she'd never doubted that her uncle wanted her. Hadn't he climbed down the cliff to save her?

Wouldn't he want her to stay with him—wherever he was—for ever?

'Don't you want her?'

'I don't know.'

Something cold felt as if it were squeezing her insides. Something vicious, something searingly painful. Bunji, who'd crept down with her, put her soft head against her knee and snuffled.

She hugged her dog, but all she could feel was pain. If Bryn didn't want her, what would he do with her? Send her to this unknown school he'd told her about? But she'd still have to stay at his place at nights and on weekends. The boarding school, then, the one Aunt Beatrice had insisted on?

Kiara?

The voices floated on from downstairs.

Kiara couldn't afford to keep her.

For a moment she thought she might vomit, but then she hauled herself together. A solitary childhood had left her resourceful.

She was thinking suddenly of one of the last times she'd seen Maureen. They'd been making cupcakes for the yard sale.

'They're brilliant,' Maureen had said of Alice's colourful creations, and she'd hugged her. 'You're so precious. If you were my grandy I'd take you home in a heartbeat.'

'Really?'

'Really. My daughters have left home, and I've always wanted a granddaughter like you.'

Maureen.

The more she thought about it, the more it made

sense. Kiara couldn't keep her. Her uncle didn't want her. Maureen did.

So where was Maureen? She was struggling to remember what Bryn had said.

'She's in my hospital.' He'd gestured across the valley, across the untamed bushland that was part of Australia's Blue Mountains. *'If there weren't so many trees, we could almost see Maureen from here.'*

Maureen was recovering in Sydney Central Hospital. Bryn's hospital.

She crept along the passage until she came to the bathroom. Here, on the second level, balancing on the toilet seat, she could gaze down the valley, over the moonlit mountains, over the tops of the mass of bushland and to the great glow in the distance that was Sydney.

Specifically, Sydney Central.

She knew hospitals—her mother had been in and out of them with drug overdoses many times in Alice's short life. They were easy enough to navigate. You just went to the front desk, told them you wanted to see your mother, and someone would appear and take you to see her. Or explain very nicely why you couldn't. With her mom that'd been because she was being crazy, and Maureen wouldn't be crazy.

Maureen would want her.

So all she had to do was head for the lights, find the hospital—surely everyone would know where Sydney Central was—and then ask to see her… her what? What would she call Maureen?

Grandmother, she decided, and the idea pleased her. She'd love a grandma.

And Maureen would hug her again—she knew she

would—and she'd take her home because Maureen really wanted her.

Someone had to want her.

She sniffed but then swallowed and decided not to cry. She'd done enough of that, and she had a plan.

She'd need to pack a little food—it seemed a long way to the lights. And she'd also take Bunji. Bunji was her friend, and she wouldn't be so alone if she had Bunji. It'd take courage, but with Bunji she thought she could do it. She was brave, and it was a good plan.

And if it worked, she wouldn't need to bother Kiara—or Bryn—ever again.

Why had she bothered to go to bed at all? Kiara lay and stared at the ceiling and tried to figure why she'd knocked back…an offer too good to refuse?

For in the bleakness of the night, without Bryn's body to warm her, that was what it seemed like. A magical offer. A happy-ever-after. Kiara and Bryn and Alice: security for them all, Two Tails for ever. Maybe even a baby. Sometimes in her quiet times she'd found herself aching for a child of her own. So why couldn't her dream include Bryn? A friend, a lover, a husband.

But what Bryn was offering was all on his terms. Financial security. Friendship. But only when he wasn't working or studying or at conferences. She knew full well that the only reason she'd seen so much of him up until now was because he'd hurt his leg.

So what was left? Passion? Probably yes, but even there, love didn't come into the equation.

She knew Bryn well enough now to realise what he felt for her was probably as strong as it was going to get. Even that emotion had surprised him, she decided. He'd proposed with the air of a man doing a business deal.

So…he needed her for practical reasons. He was stuck with Alice, and he was arranging his ducks in a row so he could get his life back into the order he so valued. He might even end up being a decent husband and father. He'd do his best and his best would keep them safe. Maybe even contented? He was talented, he was devoted…

No. He was devoted to his work. To his independence.

Marriage to her would mean he had more independence, not less. The thought left her feeling so bleak she shivered.

Maybe she should go fetch one of her dogs for comfort, she thought, as the night wore on and sleep was nowhere, but teaching dogs to sleep on beds was not in her training scheme. She thought of Bunji, who'd probably be in bed with Alice. That had to be one happy ending.

Alice and Bunji…happy ever after.

Why did that thought make her lonelier still?

CHAPTER THIRTEEN

SHE WAS SCRUBBING the kennels when Bryn came to find her the next morning. Not that they needed scrubbing, but she had to do something. She'd been up since dawn, edgy and unhappy, and here in the kennels, chatting to the last of her resident dogs, she could find a kind of peace.

Today Bryn and Alice would be leaving. With the cheque she'd receive for services rendered she could reopen the empty pens. She could hire someone to help her until Maureen was fit enough to come back. She could move on.

She'd done a great job these last weeks, uniting one sad dog with one bereft child. She should be over the moon.

Instead she was scrubbing and swearing—and occasionally pausing to swipe a sleeve across her eyes.

And then the pen door swung open. Bryn's beautiful brogues were suddenly at foot level. Uh oh. She sniffed and swiped her face a couple more times before she hauled herself up to face him.

'It's the disinfectant,' she said, and for the life of her she couldn't stop herself sounding defensive. 'It makes my eyes water.'

He handed her a handkerchief—oh, for heaven's

sake, it was linen. She repaid his generosity by blowing her nose and pocketing it.

'I'll post it back washed,' she told him.

'Keep it.'

'Then deduct it from my pay.'

'Kiara…'

'Let's get this over with,' she said roughly. 'Are you packed? Where's Alice?'

'I assumed she was out here with you.'

'I haven't seen her.' She frowned. For the last few days, the little girl had been bouncing out of bed at the first sound of anyone stirring. This morning she'd assumed she was in the house with Bryn. 'Maybe she's just savouring her last morning in the attic.'

But she saw unease on Bryn's face at the same time she felt it herself, and wordlessly they made their way back to the house. Up to the attic.

With Bryn still limping—he should still be using his cane—Kiara beat him to the top of the stairs. She knocked. 'Alice?'

Nothing.

Her heart did a stupid lurch. Maybe she was out in the garden, she told herself. Feeding the chooks one last time? But surely, she would have seen…

She knocked again and entered.

No Alice. No Bunji. Just a bed, carefully made, and a note lying on the coverlet.

Dear Kiara

I heard you and Bryn talking last night. I know you can't afford to keep me, and Bryn doesn't want me, but Maureen does. She tells me all the time.

She says, 'You're just like my grown-up girls.

My house is so empty now. I'd love it if I could take you home with me.'

Maureen kisses me and hugs me, and I like it. Bryn says she's getting better, so I'm going to find her and ask. If she says no, then I'll have to stay with Bryn, but Bunji and I want to try.

Bryn says it's just over the mountains. I saw the glow last night. We're leaving now, really early, so I can still see the glow and know the way.

I made Bunji and me two jam sandwiches. I took an apple, and I borrowed your yellow torch. I hope you don't mind. We might be gone all day but don't worry.

Alice

Bryn was now in the doorway. She handed him the note and then went to the high gable window that looked out over the mountains toward Sydney.

Alice could surely have seen Sydney last night. It was such a vast city that its glow could be seen for miles. Many, many miles.

And between here and that glow was a mountain range so vast, so overwhelming that it had taken years before the first settlers had found courage and endurance enough to cross it. The Great Dividing Range. The Blue Mountains. Most of it was impenetrable bushland, peaks, chasms, ravines, land so wild it had never been—could never be—built on.

If Alice had left before dawn… Dear God, she'd been gone for at least three hours. Maybe more. How long before dawn had she left? She'd have been walking in the dark.

She turned and saw Bryn staring at the note. His face was as ashen as hers felt.

'She'll have gone out the back,' she managed, but her voice was a thready croak. 'If she's following the glow… She can't possibly be trying to go by road—from here the road looks like it's going in the wrong direction.'

Then he was at the window beside her, staring out across the wilderness. A few hundred metres from the house the land fell away to a massive ravine. They could see the rock walls of the other side.

'She'll have tried to go around,' Kiara whispered. 'She'll never have tried to go straight across.'

'She doesn't know…' It was a groan. 'Hell. She heard what I said. Kiara, she heard. She thinks I don't want her.'

There was a moment's silence while last night's conversation replayed in both their heads, and if Bryn's face was ashen before then it was worse now.

'We'll find her.' She put her hand on his shoulder and then, because it seemed the only thing to do and she needed it as well, she tugged him tight and held. There was no time, but for these few seconds she took what she needed from that hug. And maybe he did as well, because when they parted his face was set.

'I'll go. There looks a path leading from the back…'

'There is,' she told him. 'But it peters out when the ground drops sharply at the edge of the ravine. There's a viewing platform Grandma built.'

'Then that's where I'll start. She might even have had the sense to stop there.'

'If she did then she'd be back now.'

'Then I'll go on. I have my phone. If I find her, I'll ring, but can you contact emergency services? Surely they'll come.' He was already heading for the door.

'Bryn. Stop!' She made her voice as firm as she

could make it, and it came out almost as a yell. 'No. You can't make bad worse.'

He paused, looked back, looking ill. 'I have to go.'

'Do you know these mountains?'

'No, but…'

'And is your leg strong enough to climb? To move fast?'

There was a dreadful silence. His leg was healing. Every day it grew stronger, but he still walked with a perceptible limp.

'Kiara, I have to.' It came out a groan and she moved again to hug, a strong, all-encompassing hold where she held as much of him as she could.

'It'll be hard,' she managed, forcing back fear that made her own legs tremble. A little girl, out there alone… It felt appalling but she had to be sensible, and she had to make Bryn see sense as well. 'Bryn, you put your life on the line once before for Alice, but this isn't such a life and death situation. Sure, it's thick bush, but it's daylight now and she has Bunji. If she was on her own, she might try and climb down unsafe places to take a shortcut, but Bunji's limping, too, and she loves her.'

'So I'll find her…'

'You won't.' She put all the authority she could muster into her voice. 'Bryn, we'll have help in minutes. The first responders will be the team from the local fire brigade. They know this country like the back of their hands—they spend half their time fighting fires, and the rest of their time looking for lost hikers. I'll go with them because this area around here is my domain. Grandma taught me all about her country. I know every animal trail, every track within five kilometres. There's a sort of track leading down into the first ravine. If we can't find her within an hour, we'll send for back up. Because it's a child, we'll have rescue teams, helicopters, the works. But, Bryn, you need to stay here.'

'I can't.

'You must. There's every possibility she'll change her mind when it gets hard, and she'll come back. You need to be here.'

'I can't bear…'

'You have to bear,' she told him. 'We'll find her.'

He stared at her wildly, raked his hair and then swore and swore again. 'I do love her,' he said helplessly.

And at that, she drew his head down to hers and she kissed him. Hard, long, fiercely.

'I think you do,' she said simply when she finally pulled away. 'I've watched you with her. I think… maybe you love more than you believe you possibly can?'

What followed was a nightmare.

Waiting, waiting, waiting.

As Kiara promised, the fire brigade arrived in minutes. Serious men and women, dressed in bright yellow clothing and sturdy boots, with two-way radios, backpacks with ropes, medical supplies, compasses, maps.

It was obvious that Kiara was right—they did spend half their time searching for lost hikers. Their captain spoke seriously to Kiara and to Bryn, and a search was organised in minutes. The captain saw Bryn's limp at a glance, and she handed him a receiver.

'If I can leave this with you then I won't have to leave one of my team behind,' she told him, and he wondered if she said that to any relative desperate about a lost one. As if giving him a job could take his mind off worry. Ha!

'If we don't find her in an hour, we'll bring in further emergency services and choppers,' he was told. 'We have heat-seeking choppers if we need them—kangaroos mess with thermal imaging but our people are pretty good at discerning what's 'roo and what's kid. And you said she has a dog with her? That's a double image and it should help. We'll report back to you, and you'll hear everything that's going on. Don't worry, mate, we'll have her back to you in no time.'

They didn't.

Three hours later there was a lot more than one fire brigade team searching. Police were tracing every sighting of a kid and dog between here and the hospital—just in case Alice had changed her mind about the route. There were now ten official trucks lined up on the road outside. Emergency services had split into teams and were heading in from here. Others, Bryn gathered, were heading in from the other side of the ravine. As soon as word went out, local bushwalking groups, plus concerned locals, had abandoned their plans for the day and were splitting into more teams, heading down the ravine from a myriad entry points. There were two choppers overhead.

How hard could it be to find one kid and one dog?

There were more people in the kitchen now—they'd set it up as a field base for all services. He was still allowed to be on radio duty, but the set was taken over when orders had to be relayed.

He was going mad, and as the day wore on it grew worse. He tried to phone Kiara, but her phone seemed dead. 'There's no reception at the bottom of the ravines,' one of the emergency services people told him.

'She'll be with a team, and if she needs to contact you, she can use their radio.'

She didn't.

The day wore on. He couldn't eat. He couldn't think. As dusk fell and one of the local ladies—Donna had organised a food tent out at the front—put a hamburger in front of him he thought he might be ill.

Finally, someone handed him a radio. 'It's Miss Brail, sir. Wanting to talk.'

'Kiara.'

'Bryn.' Her voice was unsteady, and she tried again. 'Bryn.'

'No…'

'No news. But I'm at the bottom of the second ravine. The experts have done an assessment and they think, given the time frame, she may well have made it to here. The guys have camping gear. They dropped in supplies so we're staying put for the night. We figure…' Her voice cracked a little, but he heard a ragged breath and then she continued, more calmly. 'The thought is that she and Bunji are probably hunkered down behind a log, or somewhere that takes the edge from the wind. It's breezy down here and…and she'll be cold. Thank God it isn't raining. But we're searching again from dawn. Teams are searching across the top ridges and working their way down. We'll find her.'

'But tonight…'

'She has Bunji and she's a sensible kid. We'll find her.'

'Kiara…'

'See if you can get some sleep, Bryn.'

'As if I could.'

'I know. Bryn…'

'Kiara…'

'I know it won't work,' she whispered softly. 'But for what it's worth… know that I love you.'

And she disconnected.

How was a man to sleep after that? He didn't bother to get undressed, just lay in the dark and stared at the ceiling.

Somewhere out there was a little girl lost. A kid who needed him, who depended on him.

Somewhere out there was Kiara.

A woman who loved him.

He could do nothing.

And at some time in the small hours, when the lorikeets in the gums outside were starting their pre-dawn squawking, when the kookaburras' raucous laughter was once again starting to echo across the valley, he was hit by self-knowledge that almost blindsided him.

He'd been thinking, *Why not me who could be there searching?*

He'd been thinking, *Why not me who could be lost?*

He'd swap with each of them in a heartbeat, and with the first rays of dawn there it was. The sickening realisation that if he lost either of them, he'd lose part of himself.

They were part of him. How could he exist if he lost either? He'd do anything—*anything*—to keep them safe, happy…home.

Was that what was meant by love?

And as the sun slowly rose over the mountains, he knew that it was.

They found them at midday.

There was a crackle on the main receiver set. Bryn was sitting on the veranda steps, staring bleakly at nothing, and he heard someone answer. With so many search teams on the ground and in the air, the job of manning the main receiver had been handed to someone who was not…so emotionally involved? A cop. Sergeant Someone. There were so many people now, so many teams using this as a base.

But as the receiver cracked into life, everyone stilled as they always did. Straining to hear.

'Is that right?' And with that…was there exultation in the exclamation? He couldn't hear what was being said at the other end, but he could hear the cop. And unbelievingly he heard: 'Yeah? Both safe? And the dog? Well, I'll be… Geezers, mate, you've made our day. Give us a minute while I go tell the dad.'

The dad. With strangers coming and going, introductions had been brief and relationships had been blurred. Maybe it had just been assumed that he was family?

But then the cop was out on the veranda, kneeling beside him, hand on his shoulder.

'They're safe, mate. All of them. Your missus was in the team that found them. They've been huddled in some sort of cave, scared to go on. It seems the kid had the sense to stay put when she realised she was lost. She's a bit scratched, hungry and thirsty and cold, but the guys said to tell you your missus is sitting on the ground with them, bawling her eyes out, hugging kid and dog like she'll never let go. We'll winch them all out as soon as we can but, mate, they're gonna be okay.'

There was a cheer around them, small at first as only those within earshot had heard, but then the ladies in the food tent outside heard, the teams changing shifts heard, the nosy parkers who'd edged into the front yard heard. The car horns went, the town heard, the roar of celebration rang out seemingly over the whole mountain range.

They were safe.

His family was safe. His little girl. His floppy-eared dog.

His Kiara. His love.

His life.

Two hours later Kiara was sitting in a chopper, going home. Alice, bundled in blankets, was huddled close. Bunji was wedged somewhere between them.

I'll take them, she thought as the chopper rose from the ravine where Alice and Bunji had spent an appalling thirty-six hours. If Bryn really doesn't want them then they'll stay with me. Whatever it takes… Sure, I'll be broke but if I give up Two Tails, get a job as a normal vet, I might be able to afford…

She was too tired to get past that thought. The chopper was sky-high now, clearing the massive eucalypts, heading home.

And then they were descending, to land on Birralong's football field. She could see clusters of people beneath them. A crowd to welcome them home.

There was a cloud of dust as the chopper settled and then a wait until the blades stopped rotating.

'We're not going to go to all this trouble to see you swiped with blades,' one of the crew told her, and his grin matched the relief in her own heart.

So many people who cared.

Maybe she *could* stay at Two Tails. Maybe the community might help. Maybe…

And then the rotors stilled, and silence fell. The doors were hauled back and people in green camouflage suits—army?—were helping them down.

She hardly saw them, because coming towards them…

Bryn.

Maybe someone had been holding him back because he emerged from the crowd like a runner released by the starter's gun. His limp simply wasn't there. Ten long strides, five interminable seconds, and he was with her.

She was set down by the chopper. The ground felt good under her feet. Great. Alice was being handed down after, and she went to take her into her arms.

But Bryn was before her. He was gathering Alice up, tight against his chest and then, in one purposeful move, he was gathering her in as well. Alice was sandwich-squeezed between them, and they were hugged as if he'd never let them go.

'Br… Bryn…' Alice quavered, as if the child was scared of a scolding.

'Oh, love,' Bryn said and then there was a silence while he hugged some more and struggled to find words to go on.

But then the words came…

'Maybe you'd better call me Dad,' Bryn told her, and he kissed the top of her head. 'I think… You've never had a dad, have you? Alice, I was so scared. I thought I'd lost you. Alice, what you heard me say was dumb. You and me…we're family. We're a team. And if it's okay with you, I'll never let you go.'

'D-Dad?' Alice said wonderingly and subsided into her blankets and was hugged some more.

Bunji was at their feet now. One of the team had set her down and she'd gone straight to them, part of the sandwich hug.

Part of family?

'Love?' Now Bryn was talking to her. To Kiara. She pulled back a little so she could see his face, and what she saw there… She went straight back into the hug. Back into where she most wanted to be in the world.

'You know what I said about marriage?' Bryn's voice was still unsteady.

'Mmff?' It was all she could say. Her face was muffled against his chest. People were milling around them now, people cheering, guys with cameras, journalists with notebooks ready. The noise was deafening but she heard only Bryn.

'I'd like to restart that conversation.'

'Mmm… Mmmff?'

And when he started talking it was as if they were completely alone, in their own world, a world where suddenly, magically, things were as right as they could possibly be.

'I got it wrong,' he told her, and his hold tightened even further. 'Kiara, you know all those dumb banners that people put up when they propose, saying *Love you for ever. Will you marry me?*—that sort of thing?'

'Um…yes?' Sort of. She was so confused but she managed to get the word out.

'I should have organised banners,' he told her. 'In fact, I still will. A million banners, my love, or at least as many banners as the sky can hold. If they're not real to the world, then they'll be real to us.'

'B…?'

'Banners,' he said, definitely and surely. And the banners will say only one thing. *Kiara, you have my heart.*'

They honeymooned in Queensland. If Bryn had ever thought of honeymoons he might have thought of the Bahamas, Hawaii, the Maldives, somewhere exotic and sensational. But when he and Kiara thought about it there seemed no option but to make their honeymoon a family affair. Which meant staying in Australia because…well, dog.

'Because this is what we are,' Bryn had said. 'From this day forth, we're a family, so let's start as we mean to go on. All in.'

Which meant Alice—of course. And then Bunji—naturally.

And then, when Kiara suggested they might like a little—just a little—time alone, Bryn had thought about Maureen, now almost recovered, back home with her beloved Jim, aching to be with Kiara and Alice but still a little shaky and frail. He'd tossed the idea to Kiara and she'd beamed. Thus they'd suggested Maureen and Jim might like to join them. A little Bunji and Alice dog-and-kid-minding might suit everyone.

Then they chose as their destination one of the magnificent islands bordering the Great Barrier Reef—one of the few where turtles didn't breed because…well… still dog. There was no way Bunji could be left behind.

They rented two beachfront villas, but then Kiara's friend Hazel said there was no way her best friend was being married without her. That meant hiring yet another villa, because Hazel would be travelling with her brand-new husband, Finn, and the pair intended to bring their precious, ready-made family as well.

And finally, on a stunning morning on a pristine, sun-soaked, tide-washed beach, Kiara Brail and Bryn Dalton were ready to be married.

Bryn stood on the sand before the celebrant, under the slightly wobbly arch of frangipani that Alice and Maureen and Jim had constructed with care and with love and with laughter. Behind him was Maureen, already sniffing and clutching her Jim, then Hazel's beloved Finn, Finn's daughter, Finn's granddaughter, and then a dog called Bunji and a dog called Ben.

Both rescue dogs.

But who had been rescued? Bryn thought, as he faced the celebrant, a wizened old surfer with a smile almost as broad as his face. It felt as if he had. And suddenly he was thinking of 'Two Tails.'

Two Tails had been named because of the phrase happy as a pup with two tails.

It had also been named for the combination of words: two tales—the story of before and after.

That pretty much summed up his life, he thought. This was his second tale—his happy ever after. His life felt as if it was starting right now.

He'd already made some huge changes. He'd keep his medicine because that was what he did, but it needed to be a part of his life, not the whole. He'd resigned from his teaching role, and he'd quit as head of department at Sydney Central. Amazingly his resignations had left him almost giddy with relief. There was no way they'd move Two Tails—it was perfect where it was, and he wanted to be part of it. With his money, with Hazel and Finn's support, it could be the best refuge ever.

The best home ever.

Where they could always be…well, happy as a pup with two tails.

Coming down the sandhills now were Alice and Hazel, bridesmaids in matching flowing sarongs, beaming like two conniving archangels whose plans had finally come to fruition. And here was Kiara. His bride.

She was simply dressed in soft white broderie anglaise—Alice had whispered to him that that was what the lacy confection was. It was sleeveless, clinging to her breasts, moulded to her waist and then flowing in soft folds to her bare feet and ankles. It was all white, bar for the tiny rainbow ribbons threaded through the lace. Her dusky curls were threaded with the same ribbon, and Alice had tucked frangipani into her hair.

'She's going to look bee-*yoo*-tiful,' she'd told Bryn and as the music swelled, as he turned to watch his bride approach, Bryn could only agree.

Mind, she would have looked beautiful in dungarees, he thought. She was his Kiara. His love. His life.

The music faded from the sound system the celebrant had set up, and the old surfer beamed at the pair of them. 'Are you ready to start?'

Was he ready? Kiara looked up at him, her eyes misty, and he thought his heart might well burst.

Two tales—before and after.

Happy as a dog with two tails.

Perfect.

He couldn't resist. He kissed the bride, right there and then, and then he nodded to the celebrant.

'We're ready,' he said, and Kiara smiled and smiled.

'Yes, we are,' she whispered, and kissed him back. 'We're ready for the rest of our lives.'

* * * * *

COMING SOON!

We really hope you enjoyed reading this book. If you're looking for more romance, be sure to head to the shops when new books are available on

Thursday 31st March

To see which titles are coming soon, please visit

millsandboon.co.uk/nextmonth

MILLS & BOON®

Coming next month

FORBIDDEN FLING WITH DR RIGHT
JC Harroway

At Darcy's front door, she fumbled with her key in the lock, her heart pitter-pattering in anticipation and fear of them being alone in her empty house.

Darcy breathed through the panic of her ill-judged invitation. Already she had a head full of erotic visions involving Joe, except now that they'd worked as a team to save Holly, that he'd needed her in moment of alarm… that meant something more to her than the physical attraction there since that first day they'd met.

Did he see her as an equal…?

In the kitchen Darcy dropped her bag, flicked on the lights and then the kettle. She reached overhead for two mugs with jittery fingers, the hair at the nape of her neck rising with awareness of Joe in her kitchen, filling her personal space with his magnetic aura. When she turned to face him, prepared to fake a bright smile and make small talk or resurrect the personal conversation they'd begun in the car, he'd stepped closer.

Face to face, a mere pace apart.

Darcy fell into the depths of Joe's stare and all thoughts of conversation dispersed.

Heartbeats pulsed through her like lightning strikes, marking the seconds they stood in tense silence.

He raised his arm, slow and steady to brush back that stubborn lock of her hair determined to reside on her cheek.

As if conditioned to his touch, Darcy turned her face into his palm, part of her craving more, craving it all. 'Joe…' His name passed her lips all breathy and pleading. For what? She wanted him physically, of course, but they had complication written all over them, the space between them an emotional and professional minefield.

He was still grieving the death of his daughter and perhaps even the demise of his marriage, and before meeting him, she'd sworn to focus on her career, a career she stood to jeopardise if they started something personal. Even sex would be a far from straightforward exchange between two people who shared insatiable chemistry, for good or bad. Come Monday morning she'd have to face him, he'd still be her boss. She needed his reference for her consultant position applications.

Could she risk clouding their work dynamic just for sex?

'I want you,' he said, his expression starkly open and honest.

Overwhelming need built inside Darcy, its pressure centred between her legs.

'I've tried to resist,' he said, his voice full of gravel, 'but I'm failing badly.'

Darcy wavered. Joe's eyes brimmed with repressed emotion. He was clearly experiencing the same conflict tugging Darcy in two different directions.